Look
G000055372

Looking for Doris will ta~~~ ~~~ ~~ ~~~~~~ ~~ ~~~~~ ~~~ ~~~~~
way that Somerset Maugham's The Razor's Edge did, but the
author in this case leads a journey that does not require covering
large geographical swathes in faraway places and instead traverses
the exotic regions of the heart. — *Catherine Ingram*

Catherine Ingram, author of **In the Footsteps of Gandhi**,
Passionate Presence, *and* **A Crack in Everything**

This is a very sensitive novel about the conflict between the inner
and outer life. Anyone who has been in this position will recognize
the dilemma and its possible resolutions. — *Z'ev Ben Shimon Halevi*

*Z'ev Ben Shimon Halevi, international teacher of
Kabbalah and author of many books*

BARBARA BROWN

Barbara Brown was born in South Africa and in 1965
moved to London where she has lived ever since.
She has two sons and two grand-children.
Barbara created bodytao, a system of working with people
individually and in groups that combines western and eastern
techniques of therapy, Qi Gong and meditation.

Dedicated to George Hardy

PREVIOUS PUBLICATION

Qi Gong: The Chinese Art of Working with Energy
(co-author Gunter Knoferl).
Published by Harpercollins 2001.

ACKNOWLEDGEMENTS

My deepest thanks to all those who helped me through
various stages of this book.

Jane Adams, Patricia Bardi, Simon Beard, Belinda Budge,
Graeme Chaves, Adele Nieto Chaves, Elizabeth Drapkin,
Tricia Gillman, David Hampson, Nina Heim, Catherine
Ingram, Martin Kemp, Marilyn Kernoff, Lucy Liddell,
Celia Macnab, Will Parfitt, Melanie Reinhart, Vida Russell,
Katherine Tetlow, Carole Tonkinson, Evlynn Sharp, Paul
Taylor, Jenny Walden

Particular gratitude to Anne Geraghty and Martin Gerrish
of The Tenth Bull.

And love and appreciation to my original teacher of the
Kabbalah, Warren Kenton;
to all the teachers of T'ai Chi and Qi Gong I have worked
with for the last 25 years,
and to the teaching and the community of
the Diamond Heart School.

Published by The Tenth Bull,
31 James Street, Whitehaven, Cumbria CA28 7HZ
www.thetenthbull.co.uk

First published 2008

ISBN 978-0-9554954-1-0

Cover design by Jane Adams

Printed and bound in Great Britain by
Biddles Ltd, King's Lynn

LOOKING FOR DORIS

BARBARA BROWN

Foreword

The mingling of both
well-being and distress in us
is so astonishing that we
can hardly tell what
state we are in.
But the fact is, that is a
part of being whole.
We stand in this mingling
all our life.

Julian of Norwich
16th Century Mystic

"... if she was feeling something... then she was not
alone... No, if she experienced and was asking
questions, then others like her were experiencing,
others looked for her as she looked for them."

From "The Four-Gated City" by Doris Lessing

PART 1

From the Brocade Purse of the Ivory Empress

The Spirit of the Tao

PREPARATION & CULTIVATION

Before starting the Journey
Prepare and Cultivate the Vehicle.

Stand quietly, Calm down.
Settle into the Deep Intelligence of the Belly.

You are Passive
Images come to you
Sounds come to you
Memories come to you

Before starting on the Journey
Stay quietly in Reflection and Observation
And the Discomfort of Not-Knowing

Do not move into Wilful Action
Allow the Ebb and Flow of Disparate Experience
Until Intention forms of Itself

When you are Full,
When you are Empty,
Ritual will Unfold
And the Threshold will Open

PREPARATION & CULTIVATION COMPLETE

CHAPTER 1

I am in a new place, and, seeking anchorage, sit very still, letting impressions settle. The quieter I become, the more I sink into myself, and, in this deeper inner location I am aware of breath moving in and out of my body. Momentarily, this is all there is. This moment, when breath is all there is and it is enough, carries an extraordinary sufficiency.

The completeness splits open, as it must, and now impressions begin to insist on their own life and my awareness stretches and breath becomes background to sight and sound and reaction.

Sight narrows its telescope through the sea before me, and focuses onto a body rising and falling. I watch my lover as he floats on his back, held by the soft, indolent Andaman sea. From here he looks like a young man.

Mingling with breath, waves of hunger and desire, like strands of seaweed, begin to curl and uncurl within my body. Hunger of the eye, as it catches his shapely form and wet dark hair; remembering from the night before his tongue between my lips. And then, sharply arriving, a wave of dislike, bearing shards of torn shell and marine detritus to complicate the seaweed, and my arms and hands want to rattle the confidence from this sleek animal who will come out of the sea, dripping salt water from his limbs. Something dangerous is playing itself out between us, and it's not easy to tell who will be predator and who will be prey.

I know too that when he emerges and walks towards me I will see, in that slim body, a man no longer young. More evident the nearer he comes. And what I see in him, he will surely see in me: lines on the face, the belly softer, arms and legs not quite so taut.

I'm sitting on a beach in Thailand, pale, newly arrived, watching Guido swimming in the sea.

Thailand starts out stressful as holidays can be in a very different, distant country. The joy of arriving into sun and colour turns into shame as my pale winter English body exposes itself on the long, hot beach. Sea smashing against rock, breaking into foam; the joy of the sea's colour changing with the mood of sky and weather; the joy of a thousand crickets suddenly orchestrated into high-pitched noise and then subsiding. The discomfort of heat, sand, young beautiful bodies heedlessly baking into smooth brown texture, mosquito bites, itchy dogs scratching non-stop, their bony shanks extended to their ears. The ironic despair of surveying a body revealed without mercy in the bright sun, consumed by time, the flesh of the forearm not neat and tight as it used to be, a sag of the flesh, no longer elastic.

And then, I know a sudden movement in the heart: surrender, acquiescence to nature's power, a moment of being present in everything just as it is, no argument, no bargaining, no resistance to slack skin, to a mosquito bite, to the ugly yellow of a dog's eye. No resistance to the ceaseless movement and interaction around me, no resistance to my contradictory feelings about Guido.

'I give in...' I murmur into the ethers, attuning into the abiding, subtle light, softer than the burning rays of the sun.

I sit on the yellow and white striped material of the deckchair in a bikini – its absurd fabric triangle covering my fur – a woman with her lips moving, a woman with a prayer. The saints, the hermits, would flagellate their flesh, fearful of nature, of desire, avoiding provocative invitation from forbidden chambers in the forests or the inviting mattress of leaves beneath a tall tree. It is different for contemporary pilgrims, seeking the forest paths that peel away from urban highways. Deeper to go, exploring rock, matter, libido, resistance, shit; into the coiling innards of the earth – deeper to go, lovingly curious, but without straining to know, without hope for an answer or redemption. No bargaining with God, no holy pact.

And in-between desire and the cessation of desire, in the silence and the breath between movement and counter-movement, sometimes revealed, is the possibility of rest in quiet hidden glades, within unknown architectures; territories mapping themselves within our spines and under the skin of our back, the unchartered structures of each delicate vertebra.

This is the dangerous territory I am moving into: hunger for the edge of the known, hunger for a journey beyond that edge, through the fire and into peace. Invisible beings, without flesh and yet animate, call forth deeper desire than that felt for the flesh and blood man sitting by me on the sand.

Guido responds to mention of this territory with a dismissing smile. It is as if I have produced a masculine rival who could not possibly offer me anything as charming or satisfying as himself. Guido is a confident, elemental man – interested in food, the idiocy of the human race, amusing films or books, elegant appearances, conviviality, very dry red wine, and sex. He is also pragmatic, and has a way of expressing his reality with clarity, sincerity and logic, so that I – somewhere in myself, when I am tired, or drummed away from my beating heart by the pulses of earthly life – surrender my own anchorage and linger, for a while, warmly tethered in his. I know I do this, but sometimes I give up negotiation, separation and the harnessing of my own deepest will. The substance, weight and pressure of sex, food, other people, the way of the world, pull me into disorientation, away from the quiet calling of inner melodies which have sung to me ever since childhood.

As the days go by and I walk the beaches with Guido, morning and evening, I am mindful of the DH Lawrence story, *'The woman who rode away'*. The woman had ridden off to be cosseted and spoiled and fed by a tribe that eventually eats her – feeding off the milk-white flesh they have so lovingly cultivated.

Together in Thailand day after day rather than meeting and parting in the short visits we commonly make between London and Rome, I heedlessly merge with Guido for the first week of our allotted two. Who would have known it? On the surface we laugh and argue and play, we say yes, we say no. Below, in our mutual watery chamber, is a subtle undertow, as if his thin dark form coils and wraps itself around me like a feeding octopus, and my skin chooses to close its eyes so as not to see the wilful snaking of tentacles. In this corner of the waters, I am prey, rather than predator. Something in me gives in to being eaten, wants to be eaten, I know. I have made languid, lazy agreement; I am being swallowed in the darkness.

The relentless heat of the past few days has dropped. Although he knows I don't like motorbikes, he organises one, in unacknowledged rebellion, and shows me, at the breakfast table, over the mango and papaya, the weak coffee and pale yellow omelette, a map and a direction and tells me we will walk to the bike station and pick up the red Yamaha. I am suddenly separate from him, like a stone, hard and sullen and unmoving. A passive rebellion in answer to his active one.

'I'm not coming.'

'What?'

I feel resistance, my form pulling away from his.

'You go – I'd like a day on my own.' He gives me a look that carries many messages – triumph, disappointment, hatred and attraction – and leaves.

I lie on our bed, dull at first, an inert female form robbed of excitement, and then, slowly, separately, find my own wishes and wants.

I end up in the large circular bay with not another soul in sight. I sit for a long time, drifting into the sky as it clouds and clears, into the waves, dirty green under the cloud, bright blue under the sun.

While I sit in my solitary deckchair, alone in the curved yellow bowl, surrounded by blue and green and white, I think about Chinese chequers. It is a simple enough game. Each player has a triangle of colour, regular holes in the board, and small counters which move or hop to the same colour triangle opposite. You can hop over your opponent's pieces. Move by move you create leapfrog spaces, lines to jump and leap, hole by hole, until landed opposite. The last satisfying click of your final Chinese bauble also sends a triumphant grin at the other whose pieces are still spread, wandering and homeless. We have brought a travelling board with us. Guido wins most of the games. I feel frustrated and thwarted.

I watch crabs foraging in the sand, gliding sideways, propelling their circular legs, two front pincers investigating and feeling their way through potential crab fodder. I enjoy tapping my foot on the damp, firm sand and then seeing the crabs speed, like liquid, into their holes. I watch a crab enter a hole already occupied. A large brute emerges and seems to puff out his bony body until the visitor rushes away – pausing at some peripheral point to take stock.

Watching the bully crab, I get a glimpse of something. Visualising the board, I imagine Guido's firm movements, see the way his lean brown hand-claw hovers over the board. I see myself moving my pieces away from his – skirting around an empty corner. I see him leaping over the lines I've made, and see also that I – in my avoidance – have not built possibilities for myself. I'm complicit, allowing myself to be conquered. And yet – I feel my skin suddenly suffused with energy as understanding roots itself in my body – I know what I want. I want the magnetism of my own colour and will to pull me directly home. As I stand up, power and intention spiral from the hot sand into the soles of my feet. I am drenched with heat, external and internal.

Later, I am in the room and pleased when I hear the roar of Guido coming back. The time on my own, re-orientation into my own direction, the heat moving into my body, have released my passive agreement with the octopus tentacles, and so I am free to enjoy desire. I like the rough look of the man I see from the window as he gets off the motorbike. I hear him speak to the rental guy, and then there's a silence that I take to mean the exchange of money. I know the sound of the door to the flight of stairs up to our room. I hear it open and close and then – in my turning belly – feel the familiar tread of Guido's sandals on the stone, feel his movement towards me, wonder what kind of man is arriving. My heart shifts as the footsteps come nearer to the door. What does he bring with him from his ride on the dusty roads towards the humid jungle? He comes in looking sweaty – there are patches of damp on his shirt. We don't discuss our mutiny. He stands in one corner of the room and takes off the shirt. I stand in another and take off mine. He leaves his trousers on and asks me – tells me – to undress completely. I ask him – tell him – to undress me. He looks at me for a moment before coming to my corner of the room. When he removes my soft white trousers, pants and bra, he does it with a quality of devotion that is wonderfully at odds with the hostility that still sits on his skin like steam coming off a hot road after rain. My body feels quiet and new; it is waiting. I close my eyes. I feel the texture of his trousers against me. Then the eroticism of being the unclothed woman with the half-clothed man strips my mind of thought and renders me shameless. I push my hands into the pockets of his trousers and feel for skin through the material. He stands quietly, moving only his hands to cup my behind. The blinds on the window are partially open and warm air mixed with streams of cooler air pushes its way into the room and onto our bodies. Aggression passes from me to Guido. He is active; I am passive. Before we fall onto the bed and before he too is naked, I feel as if he is preparing me. He is spreading the subtle peacock wing of his masculinity. He remains without movement and yet there is a wave of energy and heat entering me. My body creates a liquid intensity that takes its own shape. Within my belly is a sea flower, expanding and contracting. . When we fall onto the bed and I take Guido's weight, he enters that flowering. The peacock wing fully opens; and dies.

When we eat later, rice and fish, we are exhausted, our eyes shadowed. We drink Thai beer, and play a game of Chinese chequers. I turn my hand into a crab-claw, and move my round green pieces immediately into Guido's red enemy territory. I mount his pieces and arrive home. Then I – the victor – stick my hand into the waistband of Guido's trousers, and let it snake around his smooth dark skin. He puts his hand into my hair and pulls me towards him. We leave unfinished bottles of beer and he leans on me as we go to the room. It looks dishevelled in the dim light. We pull the cover into some kind of shape, discard our clothes without sexual intent and fall asleep without speech.

In the crucial split second before sleep, I hover above my satiated human form, and see myself from the eye that observes without hunger.

Infinite I, guardian and witness, it watches from a dimension of curiosity, spaciousness and compassion as we human creatures, flying and falling, play out our game of desires requited and unrequited.

It observes silvery trails of liquid now dried on the bodies of the sleeping pair. It watches tears as they spill from the wound of separation.

CHAPTER 2

This night, on the sand under the trees, we see from our makeshift table, the words Thai Seafood Restaurant written in childish letters on a piece of board slung between the diagonal-stemmed palm-trees, just like in the travelogue. A young waiter strains to understand us, his hand working to cover a mutilation on his lip. The possibility of a lifetime of these shy, awkward very personal gestures and adjustments of the hand over the mouth wraps against my heart, knocks at me. Just as it is, a young boy under the dry palm-leaf roof of the hut, lamps swinging in the breeze, electricity generated from a buzzing apparatus behind the open-air cooking quarters. The struggle of a young boy who can't simply let his mouth be and smile at the girls and joke with the tourists.

When I encounter something like this, when the seeing hurts, when some frailty comes my way – just passing, as this boy – I send a prayer for it. The habit started when I was a child and has remained. I have inside me a wailing wall, my own Jerusalem, and I constantly insert messages, tufts of white paper covered with the dust of stones.

I smile at Guido who looks bronze and polished in the swinging light. It's a false smile, I don't feel it in my heart. My heart is sore. The joy and creativity of our sexuality doesn't seem to enable other intimacy. We're compatible when we do practical or physical things – where shall we eat, what walk to take, where to put the towels on the beach … But when we move towards each other from our archetypal differences, we fumble to take hold, and miss each other, hands helpless, unable to grasp. This leaves a hole and a disappointment for me. It seems to leave anger and frustration for him. Sex sweetens the loss for both of us. And then the effect wears off. And there's hunger again, hunger for the mirror of our own nature in the eye and the response of the other. We have tried at different times to stretch towards each other, to compromise. It doesn't work. Under the cultivation of agreement and accommodation, rough truthful promontories stir and shake. Under pleasant smiles, we show our teeth. We make effort not to blame each other, but sometimes a primitive hatred comes to the surface, the rocks growl and the primal being wants to punish that which doesn't satisfy.

My skin feels silky from sea, sun and sand and from the nightly ritual of the shower, the application of body-cream. I stroke it as I look out over the sea. I see lights from long-tailed fishing boats; they look like old-fashioned egg-beaters.

We are sitting under a palm tree, some distance from the restaurant. Guido is smoking. We are both a little cold. My heartache continues but I am momentarily quiet with him in the dark, under the shadows of tropical foliage. He puts his arm around me. I feel sorrow for us. I know that we will not go the full mile together. We are not heading towards the horizon, the sunset. How much longer will we walk together before we part company? The leaves of the palm tree are splintering now as moonlight moves through the wavering branches.

Guido has a family of five brothers and a sister. His mother is round and dark and has been a widow for many years. She lives with her daughter and is visited frequently by her flock of sons, requiring – and getting – devotion from all of them. Guido, the second youngest, is the only member of the family who has neither married nor had children. This gives his mother pain; my arrival on the scene does not alleviate her anxiety, except that at least he brought a woman home. She is convinced he is gay. Guido nearly married twice, he told me. And each time something happened to bring the whole thing to a halt. He thinks he had enough of living in close proximity to members of a family. He has indeed a quality of fastidiousness and with-drawal that makes it further difficult when we are together for a length of time.

We have five more days, and then we will travel together from Bangkok to London. We move south to Phuket and I miss the peace of our uncultivated beach as we move amongst many travellers and tourists, eating rice and fish in noisy places, and watching the marauding games played by tourists and locals. The bars and cafes vibrate with intense, sexual pandemonium, and some of this seems to drive a further wedge between Guido and me. When we are in bed, the light that comes into our room from surrounding bars has a hard quality. It falls without kindness onto our skin. We quarrel about small things and think of returning to our original beach, but this idea is impractical as we have little time left. We stay where we are.

CHAPTER 3

'I want someone who is with me, not sometimes disappeared,' says Guido angrily, his mouth tight and his eyes narrow. We are back in London, embattled, tense and vicious. 'I don't mean in one place or another, I mean when you are with me sometimes you are disappeared. I don't know where you go…'

'Guido, I don't know how to tell you what's happening… I can't find the right words.'

'What are you talking about, you foolish old chicken! You simply tell me. Yes or no. What's the problem?' Guido walks up and down. Frustrated as I am with him, I always enjoy his way with the English language. He chooses words with assurance, and pronounces them in his rough Roman accent, and even in mortal combat – as now – they have charm.

We stir about with words and gestures, as the gap widens between us; we send out rope ladders, but can't catch hold. My rope ladder anyway is unravelling. Something happened on the plane home.

In the plane, leaving Bangkok, I fear dying. No, not death in a plane falling out of the sky. Fear of death within life. As soon as we lift from the ground, I experience a terrible confinement within my skin. Guido's leg is jammed against mine and our arms touch. Here I am in this body, and if this is all it is, I am confined to its laws, needs, requirements and mortality. If Guido can't satisfy me, I am bereft; if he turns towards me and there is a moment of union, in that moment I forget the perishable identity within this singular skin. Consolation is outside; inside, a tangle of hungry viscera, tissue and bone.

Confined in my body, hurtling above the earth in a metal tube, I restrain agitation by focussing down to the book I am holding: 'The Four-gated City.'

You are the author, Doris Lessing. When I read your work, I am somehow in a place where I can't betray myself. I experience my own integrity and I experience yours Doris, and I am in relationship with you. This is why I can't address you in the third person. I am I and you are you. Not you as a personality in the world, but you as the felt sense of your language, intelligence and honesty. You wake me up to the quieter and more honest spaces within me. I love you for that.

Doris, you talk about the substance of ordinary life being 'drenched or bombarded by a particularly vivid type of atom.' When I read that sentence, my body irritation recedes, the painful light in the aeroplane cabin becomes more luminous. Guido sits in his narrow seat; here am I in mine. The touch of his leg is no longer oppressive. My flesh no longer screams at the thought of joining with his or separating from it.

Who am I? I ask myself, sitting more quietly now in the artificial light and re-cycled air. What do I take myself to be? I have sat with gurus, I have worked with spiritual teachers of inspiring and less inspiring quality, I have read books – including yours, Doris – and been illuminated, as in this moment, drenched and bombarded by the consciousness of another; transmission from being to being.

I feel a different hunger opening up. If I don't begin to live these questions in my body, rather than in my mind or through hitching a ride on another's story, I shall never know myself, slowly die of suffocation and fear. There's something I want to see. To know, to witness. I imagine it is possible to enter this place of inquiry in mutuality. But this is not where our mutuality lies. Guido and I walk different paths. At a crossroads – I have to choose. I feel so sad.

'I want to retreat…'

'What you mean? I don't know what you're talking about. You're not religious, what century are you living in?' The statement sounds inadequate to my ears too. And yet, beneath our communication knotted by language, I know without words what I mean.

Feeling alienated and mistrustful within the current culture of celebrity, wealth, glamour, reification of body through youth and beauty, ruthless almost pornographic self-disclosure, this wordless, invisible movement away from betrayal and into the unknown is more potent to me than sexual attraction, more ravishing than caresses and the promises of a happy life. I am being wooed by a lover unseen who hovers near to me within its discreet realm. I am the apprentice, being called.

And here is my incarnate lover, justly furious, and here is also an aspect of myself aghast at what I am doing. We are both old chickens, he and I – well, oldish. Past our youth, though lively and libidinous still. There aren't a lot of other chickens on the beach – or so my mother would have said. Hang on to the broiler you've got. No, that's not Guido.

He's a lean, mean cockerel. And he's going angrily to bed now, and I am following him.

When we lie together, an inch the size of a canyon is the gap between us. The stones fallen to the bottom are the colour of blood; there is blood on the stones.

'Cara...' says Guido softly, unexpectedly, his guard suddenly loosening as sleep begins to take him.

I put my hand out and stroke his lovely face, the thin dark Roman profile. I want to fling myself onto him, but something holds me back. We lie like this for a while, my hand gently moving, and then I hear his breathing change. It becomes heavier and more rhythmic.

Guido is asleep. I am exhausted and unable to sleep.

To calm myself I think about my house. To calm myself further I imagine telling you about it, Doris. You have a capacity for description that renders every brick, every stone visible. And yet the detail is never tedious. It is your way of looking, calmly, steadfastly, until the nature of what you observe reveals itself.

This house is large and red-bricked. I know not of its history and have never felt prompted to find out. The house is not especially distinctive, though it has a solemnity to it, a weight and a symmetry that makes it pleasing enough. In the front there is a large chestnut tree, which bursts into glory late spring and summer. Sometimes the Council comes and lops off its heavier branches. A straight concrete path invites entrance from the defunct garden gate, then it's up three steps to the solid door and into an entrance hall. On each of the three floors are two flats. Six labels attach to six buzzers to the left of the front door. At the back there is a small garden that belongs to the ground floor owners.

I am the chief gardener. Marte, the other ground floor occupant, never showed any interest even when she was stronger and mobile, and I have kept the garden minimally cultivated. There is a shrubbery of well-established plants, a small ragged lawn and a dominating oak tree that keeps its shadow over most of the area. I have never planted vegetables. Gerry did, when he was here. They ran to seed after he left, odd-looking cabbages and a stringy confusion of marrow vines, fibrous and hairy. It was satisfying when he brought in produce from the garden, but I never wanted to bother with snails or greenfly. Nor did I want a neat garden that I would have to maintain. The oak tree has been my ally in this. It dominates and all the rest organises itself around the stately presence.

I am not especially house-proud or garden-proud. I want a base that

works well, is simple, clean and comfortable. Gerry, who lived here with
me for many years, had more possessions than I did: ornaments, that is,
trophies from travel or chosen for aesthetic pleasure. The booty I brought
back from India was a departure for me. The carved figure and the bowls
I use for ritual are the few possessions I have which I love and have an
attachment to. They are old and beautifully made and have a quality
to them of having been handled many times. My most beloved objects
can be put into a small suitcase. Somehow, this is important. The rest is
functional. I like wood, and cotton. I like white walls and nothing on the
window ledges. I can't bear small tables and little lamps. I like single-
colour clothes, never wear patterns. I suppose an analyst would uncover,
as a contrast, the decorative and personal habits of my family: my mother
placed an object wherever she could put one, and often they rested on
embroidered cloths. My sister, in her sequence of homes in the USA has
a taste for vivid splashes of colour, swathes of rich materials, succulent, fat
cushions laced with gold thread, exotic wall hangings and lamps from the
Arabian nights. My mother hated to throw things away, found a nook or a
corner for all her possessions. When we cleared the house after her death,
it seemed to take forever to pick up each small thing and decide what to
do with it. My father had his own cluster of beloved objects – often worn
out – and he refused to be parted from any of them. We bought him
a new typewriter once. He refused to accept it, saying that his existing
machine, even with three keys missing, was perfectly adequate. We had
to return the gift. No more was said. Some of the furniture, crockery and
cutlery in their house came from Lithuania, was shipped to South Africa,
and then to England. When my sister and I shared the household effects,
she took more than I did. I didn't want anything but the embroidered
linen cloth, in white and blue cross-stitch, which my mother's mother had
worked on. The back was nearly as perfect as the front. You couldn't tell
where she had tucked in snipped-off thread. I hadn't known my maternal
grandmother, but I'd seen photographs of her and had imagined her
hands holding the yards of linen, and moving over the pattern, digging
the needle in and out, changing from white thread to blue. Most of the
stuff we gave away. It was unpleasant doing this. Leonie and I had wept
in an unusual moment of closeness when the cheerful man from Oxfam
came to collect all the boxes.

Leonie and I have minimal contact these days. It just doesn't work
between us. She's a little bit like Joss, my most enduring friend. No, she's
not really like Joss, but the faint resemblance further endears Joss to
me. Maybe one day we'll be able to reach each other. Leonie finds me

impossibly out of touch with the world; I find her world – of corporate business and material success – exhausting. When she occasionally comes to London on business, we meet. We eat together at an expensive restaurant. She spends a lot of time scouring the faces at the other tables with a keen and shrewd look and I wonder why I am there. We exchange superficial news, reminisce a little, and I come away sad and empty. I don't know how she comes away. She always looks vivid and elegant and I want to take time and let my eye explore the skill of the arrangement of scarf and jewellery and the swagger of her coat and the pointed polish of her nails. I feel like an unpolished object in her company. Gerry used to say 'You could be like that if you really wanted to – ' Then he'd look at me and we'd both smile. Leonie occasionally has a man with her. I never know much about her partners. They change quite often. Most of them look a fair bit older than she, and tend to give up on me after the first handshake and look of appraisal. Even if I set off feeling good and well-dressed and okay, a meeting with Leonie acts upon me like the kind of lighting which bleaches colour from your complexion. Like being in a shop's change-cubicle with merciless mirrors and searchlights that reveal every unsightly dimple and pucker of the flesh. She doesn't like staying with me when she comes to London, stays instead at an expensive small hotel in Kensington. I feel sorry thinking about her and me. She has no children; I have no children. End of that particular line with us. She's never met Guido. I look at his sleeping form. I am still wakeful, longing to sleep. It's three in the morning. I am shaking with distress and half wanting to wake Guido. I resist the longing, and think about Marte.

Marte lives next to me, on the other side of the landing. Her flat, to the left of the entrance where mine is to the right, is full of possessions, some beautiful, and it smells of urine and age and medication.

Upstairs, above me, is David, a secretive man, quiet and orderly. He is the one who organises tenants' meetings (about once a year to talk about the roof and the gutter and the dustbins and the post). We all appreciate David for this. He is at home a lot, teaches English to foreign students on a one-to-one basis. He told me once, in an unusual moment of intimacy, that he used to work at a language school, but loathed the staff room and decided to break out as free-lance. Students go up and down the stairs fairly regularly. Fewer these days and they seem more like businessmen than younger students. There is so little sound coming from David's flat that I am sometimes unnerved. In all these years, I have only stood in David's entrance hall once (trying not to look as if I was peering into the interior) His flat is similar in size to mine but looks and feels quite different. He does go out occasionally, but apparently has no friends. I have invited him round but he never comes though he is always courteous when we meet in the hall. Sometimes I feel faintly amiable towards him; sometimes I can't bear him or the painful silence and privacy of his life. What have I just thought? Am I not planning to become a recluse myself?

Next to David, on the first floor, in great contrast, is a family of four, squeezed into a flat above Marte. The mother, small, hectic, always busy, dives up and down stairs with shopping, children, friends and the children's bicycles because the hall is too small to leave them downstairs and David warned of fire hazards. They've lived in Flat D now for four years. The husband is lanky, volatile and affectionate. Their two boys are swept up into his long arms, and just as quickly put down again. He too has a hectic quality, and conversations and shopping lists and quarrels and jokes trail along the garden path, up the stairs and end suddenly when the door closes. Their lives fly in and out of the small flat, up and down the stairs and up and down the path. Marte used to bang on the ceiling with a broomstick but now doesn't seem to notice the noise. Or perhaps Marte is going deaf. They're a friendly family on the move – Greg and Jinny, little Greg and James Harper. There are visitors, adults and children, and endless Harper relatives to be attended to. Then the battered white car is loaded to the roof with sleeping bags and baskets and blankets. Once little Greg accidentally cut his arm, and I stayed with James while Jinny raced off to Casualty. The flat is covered with family paraphernalia, games and books and videos and clothes and packets of cereal and calendars from years before and cards pinned on the kitchen notice-board. James and I decided to watch a video. He seemed quite unperturbed by the family drama. Jinny and little Greg returned quite soon, Greg with a bandage and a look of importance on his face. I left the warm, cheerful, cluttered chaotic flat with mixed feelings. I could have been Jinny, with the mess and the exhaustion, but also with the cuddles and the companionship. I am able to be friendly with children, but I don't have a special children way with me as some people do. I have the same voice with children as I have with adults.

Above David is a short-tenancy flat. Two Australian girls, Sara and Merry, have just moved in. They have a daytime life when they go off to schools as supply teachers, and a night-time life when they set off at midnight in tight tops which reveal their navels, skirts which suggest their apricot-round and small backsides, and pointed shoes and bags with straps and buckles and zips. We smile at each other but haven't spoken much. I feel as if they would speak a completely different language from me. I've moved away from that exclusive club of Party. The careless, elastic days of my youth are over. What is the norm now? What music, what movement? What spoken and unspoken behaviour? Under the shadow of Aids, the historic promiscuity of my youth seems almost innocent. The girls could almost be my daughters. When there are tenants' discussions, the owner of the flat, a Greek, Aristides, arrives in an old and carefully preserved Rover and votes always to keep the costs of repairs and changes very low. He is courteous and evasive. Keeping him reasonably responsible for his part of the building unites the rest of us. He seems to want to duck and dive out of responsibility. He has an ancient mother whom he supports, and I don't think he makes much money from his small travel company in Willesden.

Above the Harpers, next to the girls, are Edie Trammler, a spry and genteel woman of about 70, and her son Max, who lives with her most of the time, and every now and then leaves, either for a girl or a holiday – and then comes back to the order and non-interference of his mother. I've been invited to tea a few times – and they have come to me. We keep these occasions short, and don't repeat them too often. Edie, neat and restrained and small-boned, bears little resemblance to her son who is big-bellied and stocky, with a gruff and hard air about him, a deep voice and the outward appearance of a tough man about town. Max runs a small van rental company and must be in his late forties. Gerry and I once saw him in Islington, helping a raucous, plump, pretty young woman out of one of his vans, and disappearing with her into a first floor flat. Edie and Max have an unchanging quality to them, even through changes. Edie always looks the same, and talks the same, though her skin becomes slightly more cracked and powdery with the years. Max has a set number of expressions, verbally and facially. I find the proximity and predictability of Edie and Max somehow pleasant.

Less pleasant though have been certain thoughts which have been in my awareness, unvoiced, for several weeks and this uneasiness concerns Marte. Maybe this also accounts for my sleeplessness. Who is the one person who is responsible for her? Of course it's Justine, she is next of kin. But she is not here and although a friend of hers, Jo, visits and then presumably sends reports, and although the doctor is in touch with Justine – the line between mother and daughter is a minimal, dutiful one. An awkward line. The family doesn't seem to have been a large one, and if there are any left, they are not in contact. It could also be that Marte severed many connections after Harry, her husband, died, ruled a line under that part of her life. I could imagine her doing this. Marte has two ancient friends from Golders Green, and they totter in occasionally. Marte talks to them on the phone. Edie and Jinny look in from time to time, but I'm not sure how regularly they visit. I try to find out from Marte once and she snaps at me that this is none of my business. I know what lies under that terse statement: don't you dare pity me; don't you dare try to get people to visit me who don't want to come. I drop the subject, fast. Doctor Marcus, busy and yet clearly concerned and attentive with Marte is not far away; Marte is picked up very occasionally by special bus to visit the local Breathe Easy clinic (and hates it); she has a paid carer who puts her to bed and gets her up in the morning, and gives out her medication. Meals on wheels arrives at midday, and these meals are hardly eaten and yet the arrival of the driver is probably an event during the day. Anyway, Marte can no longer cook for herself. Lulu, the carer, makes a light supper in the evening, and prepares her breakfast. Once I tentatively open up the possibility of Marte having to move one day to sheltered accommodation.

'Never. I die here, and that's that. You won't catch me in one of those deadly homes... When it's unbearable, that doctor will help. He understands. Up till now, it's all manageable.' I know that Justine will come if there are problems, or if the present situation becomes unworkable. She indicates as much to me last time she visits.

'I'm not dumping on you, Ellie. If ever you feel overloaded, here's my number. After all, she's my mother not yours.' This is said in a business-like, unemotional way. When I look at their relationship, I see that both are strong women, controlling and independent. They ruffle each other, they pull each others' feathers the wrong way. Justine rings twice a week, and I get out of the kitchen when I know it's her, and Marte will usually have, afterwards, an unattractive bitterness around her mouth, as if she's just sucked a lemon.

CHAPTER 4

In the morning, Guido and I move painfully and coolly around each other. He seems then to reach a decision within himself, reaches out and holds my arm in a hurtful way; dislike comes from him to me. I look at the flickers of white in his dark hair, at the strong lines drawn from his nose to the corners of his mouth.

'I'll be in town, seeing Carlo. I thought I would ask you to lunch – but no. Definitely not. I will see you later. Maybe you will have had enough of this emptiness business by the time I get back.' I say nothing. I want to hit him. I feel violent. We don't kiss. The violence freezes into pain, I descend the front door steps with him and then can't move. As I watch his slim figure walking fast down the road, my arm gestures towards him, but the rest of me doesn't. After a few minutes I wrap my body in a coat and walk fast too, coming soon into the green magnetic pull of Hampstead Heath. My skin, craving its dose of green nourishment, opens pores like trumpets on the way to the great parade of trunk and bark and leaf and wild grasses. Different in impact from the wild foliage of Thailand. I move through well-trodden paths and come to the café.

As I approach the steps, I see in the fire of my longing and imagination, a small figure, wavy grey hair pulled into a loose bun. Doris, I imagine you are here, at the cafe. This is a re-play of your actual appearance some weeks before I left for Thailand. You were talking to a male companion at a table by the wall. I settle into a corner seat, remembering the difficult communication between Guido and me, and hurting.

Under the mild warmth of an autumn sun, disparate hedonists drink tea and sociability, beneath baskets spilling flowers and leaves. This is our balcony; this is my seat. Plates sticky with leftover spaghetti or scone and small tubs of jam, rest on the round tables.

When I leave the balcony I pass the table where you, Doris Lessing, sat all those weeks ago, and I move through the remembered shock-waves of your presence and I can imagine how you might describe this instant – your sentences spearing the loud voices and the mouths covered in lipstick, the leftover food and the abundant hanging baskets.

If you had witnessed Guido and me this morning emerging from my house, walking down the uneven steps, Doris, what would you have seen and understood?

The man and woman emerging from the house and walking carefully down the uneven steps would seem, at first glance, to be well-suited. At second glance – and one would allow a second glance – there is something to be seen which is quietly compelling, and this is that they are not as compatible as first glance would suggest. There is a nervousness brushing between them, though there is also the electricity of desire. The nervousness and the desire rub off, one against the other, and – looking again – this effect, invisible but palpable, invites one, instantly, to see them, to imagine them in close embrace which would be a hard clasping, body to body. No rest with each other; no respite. They are about the same age – late forties perhaps. She is slim, wearing plain white cotton trousers and shirt; her hair is short, curly, light brown with streaks of grey. She has long eyes – this is the best way to describe it – almond shaped, a small, straight, thin nose and well-shaped, firm mouth. One would not say she was pretty, but there is something attractive about her, in her demeanour, posture and clear facial expression. However, there is also perceptible, a shadow, a haunted look about her. Something is disturbing what could otherwise be an impression of equanimity. The man is handsome, elegant, olive-skinned. He has dark, thick hair with distinctive threads of silver. His lips are thin, but perhaps they are pursed in disagreement, for, clearly, there is disagreement and trouble between them. There is something wilful about him, and this adds to his sexuality, to the lithe and somewhat self-seeking movement of his hips, and the casual way he wears his jacket. Only an Italian could wear a jacket in that way, slung loosely on the shoulders without a hint that it might ungracefully fall off. To make up a story briefly, I imagine they are an adulterous couple, the excitement is wearing off, and he is beginning to suggest that he should – for propriety's sake, and for the sake of his children – head back to the matrimonial home. She'll be relieved, but also sorry. It's a tussle for both of them. One cannot detect warmer currents of love between them – the current between them is febrile, akin to a sharp taste, spicy, drawing salt from the blood.

Through irregular leaf-strewn passages, lit with tokens of sunlight, I take with me, Doris, this fantasy version of Guido and me. I meander without intention. Doris this is Ellie; Ellie this is Doris. No, I don't want to meet you. There is distance and privacy for both of us in the way that I meet you as inner mentor. To talk would be to ask questions. I don't want to ask any questions. What would I ask? It is enough, the juxtaposition of creator and created, the intimacy of reading your work without having to know you. Reading your creations is a way of knowing you. Not because they are autobiographical, but because they are insight. They are your way of probing and penetrating experience and compressing thought and perspective and emotions into paragraphs and structures. The world has gone into your consciousness and come out in a singular way.

The way you are significant to me is not to do with meeting. It is your fierce love of truth that bites me. This sharpens my own teeth.

My singular preoccupation with you Doris is this: the almost visceral joy of reading words that have been rolled and pressed like dough, mercilessly pressed to find essence; the effect of energy and elbow-grease and fingerprints, mixing with yeast, put away to rise, then baked and eaten.

And here I find kinship with you, Doris. I am making something – or something is making itself. It's as if my molecules are being rolled and pressed. Like an arrowhead, it is pointing; it has intention.

I continue into the Hill Gardens, along the raised walkway, a monastic, contemplative ambulatory delight, the wisteria so old that its trunk feels like stone; rich red roses, the last roses of late summer, still offering their sensual perfume. In the wooded area, treading carefully on muddy and slippery ground, I notice several men, alone, walking slowly and distinctively, cruising like taut ships, watching out of the sides of their eyes for other men. I pass the pond, and spot the injured, limping moorhen that I saw the week before, being chased through the undergrowth by a rat. There it is, hobbling on the edge. It slides into the water, its disfigurement hidden and moving gracefully now.

From grass to earth, tarmac to concrete, so many surfaces for the foot to negotiate. Finchley Road station, the solid communal entrance to the house, now my private door. In the entrance hall, I pass the half a dozen large empty boxes that I ordered yesterday. I could have waited until Guido left. This act feels like deliberate provocation. I feel ashamed. Into the living room, long and narrow, with a high ceiling. Cards on the mantelpiece. Happy 50th birthday. I was away in Thailand for my birthday.

There in the mirror, small face, pointed nose, curly hair, slender body, the no longer young, junior sister of a temperamental beauty, knowing myself as the one without that kind of noticeable, visible-in-the-world currency. When the inner flame is lit, I am bright. And then comes the heat of interest that follows my movements and then I attract people. At other times, I am camouflaged, invisible. Invisible then as far as the world is concerned, yes. But not in the inner realms where I live with familiar shapes crouched around a fire, observing in the flames, the creation of the arrowhead.

All my love, Ellie, from Gerry; his large writing on a flowery card. What does he mean ALL my love? What is all anyone's love? Gerry and I, together for a long time; Gerry and I separating without really knowing this is happening, he heading to a small house near Brighton. We could go there for weekends and eventually move to the sea! He goes more and more; I less and less. Not a dramatic parting – a sore that takes time to heal, gets a scab and then leaves a permanent small mark on the skin. No, to friends, enquiring, there isn't anyone else. But yes – to myself – not some one, but some thing. A line of questioning, a persistent life forever inside me and increasingly demanding; a passion needing to be fed, an inner force pressing against the inside of my skin staying with me day after day.

There is a message from Guido on the answer machine. He will be back late and by the way I didn't notice this morning that he tripped over the fucking boxes and my place looks like a disaster zone. Ciao signora Emptiness.

Implicated in all of this is the child I was, growing up in this area, father leaving each morning for his surgery ten minutes' walk away from our house. I worry the family, disappearing as often as I can into Hampstead Cemetery, behind our house. 'It's so morbid!' scolds my mother, small, busy, her anxiety quite transparent through shopping lists, plans, diaries, arrangements. And, unexpectedly, secretly, a life as a poet. I discover a little book amongst her effects after death. Hidden, presumably not shown to anyone (or might there have been an unknown someone – or my father – who had shared the small packet of words?) maybe 40 to 50 poems, written over perhaps 25 years – they were not all dated. Behind the organisation, behind the anxiety, lived a wistful soul, tentatively expressing longing for something so elusive it was barely described. Finding the book, I am shocked, an intruder, angry. Why had mother not shared this? We could have had a different time together. Then I am sorrowful – and tears spring hot and bereft.

In the cemetery is a bronze statue in memory of a woman called Marthe. The body of this statuesque carved being is facing square to the wall of her crypt but her face is quarter turned away from the wall, towards those who walk by, her hand up, a runnel of dirt weeping beneath the eye. She is the significant one I always come to see though there are many other carved witnesses to death, angels with tough-looking wings, great bundles of stone feathers that could lift them up and away. I read the epitaphs of all sorts of people who are now lying there broken up and finished, worm-ridden and dusty, composted and down to the bone. Some of the stones are tossed up and broken, thrust at angles upwards as if the hidden body with one last effort, had tried to elbow the confinement away. I see flowers – real and artificial – and grass and stones and the words carved upon them. And at the same time – as if there were a parallel view in my head – I see spent forms, harmless, finished, left. And – in quality like the incandescent filament of a light-bulb – I perceive a flash of some other stuff winging away, leaving the discarded body, moving through an energetic continuum, released, discharged... and then – at this point – I experience a feeling of collision, penetration, and I am back with the physical view. And always with a feeling of time having passed and not passed, and being bigger and lighter, and more myself and less myself.

'But what does she do there?' cries my mother, appealing to the gorgeous and sullen Leonie, my older sister, four years older. Ten at this time when I am six.

'Just looking,' I mumble, searching about for words and phrases that would suit mother. 'I like the stories on the stones.'

'So read a book!' she says sharply. And then – repentant – 'We could go to the British Museum. You are simply too young and small to go alone there. Anything could happen. You are not to go off by yourself anymore.'

I loathe family visits to Places of Interest, but know that somehow I have to placate mother because the nervousness between us at times becomes insupportable. I invent an obedient and mild look which I offer to her, and which she takes. It doesn't really help, I know, but it helps coat the anxiety a little. I never say what really happens at the cemetery. I don't have the words for it and some sense tells me anyway to shut up about these moments of acute happiness, where many lines and planes seemed to bisect and connect at a point inside me.

Staring in the mirror, through the birthday cards, as this memory comes and leaves, I shiver, as the long-ago child stirs in me.

CHAPTER 5

I am waiting for Guido. I want him to stand behind me with his arms very tightly around my body. I will talk to you Doris. After Persia, as it was then, you went to Rhodesia, as it was then. Each significant place of your childhood has been re-named. South Africa is still South Africa. We visit when I am eleven, to see the birthplace of my parents. We travel to the Cape, and then to Johannesburg where they lived for ten years before leaving in the early fifties, unhappy with the political circumstances, feeling unable to make valuable contribution.

'I haven't the courage,' my father had said, packing his belongings into crates and cases for the ship. This refrain repeats itself in many forms

– some disguised – as he lives his life in London. The variations come
in phrases like 'not for me really...' or 'perhaps I'll stand back from that
one,' or 'we'll see.' A not-unsatisfactory life, but – for anyone who can
really observe – faintly haunted, his weak eyes sometimes absent – or
– more accurately – as if what they see is pulled back or retracted into
his head; images and memories which don't quite leave him, threads of
a life lived elsewhere. He is a good doctor, quiet, unspectacular, cares for
his patients, cares for his family.

I am always hungry for stories of his boyhood on a farm in the Orange
Free State. He is not a good story-teller, but sometimes forgets that he
isn't and – as his memory hitches up with an excitement – his eyes come
forward and lose their sadness, and he pulls out words like veld and
gogga and mieliepap, and remembers relatives like aunt Bessie who
had a moustache and recipes for cakes famous in the neighbourhood,
dripping with flavour and poppyseeds. Bessie was married to Ernie, a
no-good, smoking away her hard-earned cash from the family business,
a small shop which sold everything from wireless sets to pickles, soaps,
earrings, vinegar and horrible sweets. Bessie, was famous too for a vast
backside, revolving in several trembling circles all at the same time. 'Tell
me about Bessie's bum, dad' I beg and father reprimands. 'Now young
lady don't you talk about my family so disrespectfully.' I adore him when
he tells stories, when he sits late on a Sunday evening smoking a small
cigar and drinking whiskey. Other times I am furious with his mildness
and want a dad with a commanding, important voice and muscles and
a sexy jacket instead of rather limp tweed. Once – I am four or five – I
come quietly into the living room and see him stretched out on the sofa
listening to some music – a sweet and unusually full and contented look
on his face. I am struck by his expression and the mood of the music and
I run away, frantic, crying inconsolably. No one knows what the matter
is. Nor do I. Later – much later – I hear this music again in a cafe, and
learn that it is the Harry Lime theme.

My father tells me about God when I ask him. We walk together,
on Hampstead Heath. I have grown up with Hampstead Heath. Like
so many others, I know it is mine, really. And I magnanimously share
it, like the habitués of the Golders Hill Park café share their watering
ground.

'All this,' my father says, gesturing with his walking stick on a
day probably 40 years ago, 'all this is God. Well, anything we don't
understand is God. We don't know where things begin or end, or when
it all started. There isn't a start. That's God.' We walk further. 'Take the

synagogue,' he says. 'You don't have to go to church or synagogue. In fact – when I first saw St. Peter's in Rome I wanted to take a golf-club and smash a ball through it.' My father doesn't play golf. I can't imagine him with a golf club.

Mother and father, Ben and Geta, fussy, friendly couple. Misunderstand each other in a fussy, friendly way, irritate each other, support each other within their circle of friends, many South African, most of them Jewish.

My parents and their friends, subdued and frightened after the Second World War. Floating, nomadic Jews, whose ancestors, fled from Russia and Germany to South Africa, stay together, interconnected in displacement, mutual curiosity and protection. Ah yes, this habit of 'Where do you come from?' 'Who do you know?' 'Are you married?' If you have no country, if there is no ground under your feet, you make a lateral ground, a matrix which circles round people, a social ground, a web of personal bound connection. Knowing who you are and if you're married and what you do makes a carpet all can stand on – a weaving of reeds and threads and colour which keeps anyone from falling into an endless hole.

Doris, I pull out of memory into present time. My irritated earthy Roman is somewhere up town and I am waiting for him and I know that we are heading for separation. I stare into two separate roads. Guido looks intently at me from one; the other is empty of human form, and yet it also vibrates with beauty as an unseen, paradoxical energy seeks earth. I try visually to merge the two roads, joining Guido with the empty road. It doesn't work, keeps pulling apart.

A useless tumble of fearful thoughts, plans for action, efforts to create order and safety rattle around in me, create a vibration of random disorder; I am losing myself in an invisible merry-go-round of wild-eyed riderless horses, colours fading and grimy. I hear the distorted sound of rusty fairground music.

Breathing steadily, keeping focus, I gather myself into the central pole, and meet each frightened fragment, each horse, paint peeling from its wooden body, noting scratchy, yellow-brown bruised colours beneath the desperately bright blues and reds and greens. Gently and steadily, I allow my attention to go in, right in, like heated oil, warming the bruises. I know not to be distracted by the maddened curl of a nostril, the flare of a dilapidated mane. As long as it takes, I agree, as long as it takes. The fairground fades, Wisdom guides me as fathoms deep I go, my out-breath pulling me down into innermost sorrows; so deep, so willing, that I come eventually through form and into space, only the space is not outside of me up there in the blue, but inside; and revealed in this spaciousness, an emptiness interlaced with quietness comes to cradle me.

Caught in this embrace so light, I am held, The knot is looser, the bodily sensation eased. In the back of my mind, the merry-go-round comes to a gentle stop, and the horses' breath evaporates like smoke into a white sky.

After this intimacy, there is sleep; a light, peaceful sleep. Guido wakes me when he comes in. I suspect it is very late. He smells faintly of expensive alcohol. Irrelevantly, I think he always smells expensive. I bury my face in his hair and then seek the darker places of his body, feasting on that which I know I will be losing.

CHAPTER 6

D oris, I awake again beside the form of a sleeping man. I want to stroke his head, his hair, dark black and silver grey. The expensive aroma of alcohol has subsided and instead I smell the mingling of our bodies. I stroke him with my eyes; it is so much easier to love the innocent appearance, the sleeping quality of him rather than the awake, engaged, sarcastic, seductive man I face in the daytime.

I think back to the child searching in the cemetery. I see her moving into later years.

As a young adult, dressed in orange I search in India, and on a honeymoon of spiritual seeking, I move through beggars and shopkeepers and cows and dung and food-stalls and – in truth – feel ashamed and embarrassed at the charade. At the ashram frequented largely by European and American seekers, I devour peoples' faces with my eyes looking for something that I know about when I find it, but can't describe... Particularly I am drawn to Indian saddhus outside the gates. Their lean, leathery, dusty bodies and small bundles and faces daubed with ash fill me with fear and excitement. What do they feel like inside? Are they as free as they look, or is this another charade, and inside are they as anxious about life as anyone else? I sit for hours next to this one and that, trying to sniff from them some distinguishable aura that will inform me and give me what I want to know. I look into eyes that are shrewd, ratty, blind and milky. And then – just here and there – I look into eyes as clear as rivers, light brown water flowing easily...

When I find these rivers I am happy, sometimes child-like, contented and nourished. And then I sit without intention, letting the world go by, restlessness momentarily soothed, bathing in these waters.

Naïve and busy amongst the flock of western seekers, I am engage with a nagging question – how do I know any of this is not madness and illusion? How does anyone know what is true? We're an accident, a mistake whirling around in space. The humanists have it right: get on with what's here, what's the point of trying to work it out. Be the best human you can be. Or, cynically, survive with the minimum. Expect nausea. Be clever and dry about it. Be debauched. Die with your fist around a bottle of whiskey or your fingers clutching a cigarette. Die with a sour and witty comment on your lips.

There is a death, and a ceremony of singing and fire. I've seen dead bodies but am disturbed about this one. I am irritated when others say the dead man has 'left his body'. It is as bad as people saying that someone has passed away. They say it with such knowingness. How the hell do they know, and what do they know? Okay, he obviously isn't in that body anymore, it is lifeless, cold, it doesn't move. The day before, he'd been talking, pretty ill, but quite definitely present. Of those who had been with him, some had talked of seeing the spirit leaving the body, or feeling it as a rush of wind. Did they really? What did they see, what did they feel? I am angry that I hadn't been there, that I hadn't seen or felt the departing spirit. I am on the outside of an illustrious clique. Well, I am just spiritually undeveloped, that's all. My karma, my dharma. I dislike using words like karma; borrowed, not owned. But if that isn't my language, what is? 'God' is my language – but over-burdened with history and meaning and judgement. Especially a certain version of the Hebrews' God, the wrathful deity of that raggle-taggle mob of nomads crossing the Sinai. Maybe they needed one so fierce since they were motley and distraught – maybe they needed the carved commandments, the covenant in stone to contain their desperation... And – what do I need?

I want to keep asking questions and at the same time the landscape and the mess and the beauty and the ease of communication and the constant event of life, the gabbling of vendors, taxis, beggars screws itself insidiously into me. I feel the rich and stinking aroma working into my body, the red dusty ground painting itself into my heels. At times I am loose, free, enchanted, smoking dope under the moonlight with a selection of utterly wise ones who appear less wise the next morning; buying fruit and vegetables in the market, struck with joy by the luscious purple of aubergines and the roaring effervescent silks and satins spilling out of material shops.

Late one night I am flirting with a big-deal honcho of the ashram. He whispers to me that I look beautiful. We are entwined on the balcony of his rented room, the crickets and nearby dogs providing night-time sounds behind his quiet talk, when a little yellow and black tuktuk scooter-taxi draws up and a large and menacing female gets out. This is an even bigger honcho, the big lady boss of the ashram organisation, and the black-bearded sybarite is her property. A bitter altercation takes place, I keeping quiet and feeling cowardly. But I don't know quite what the rules are here – and whether I've broken one. Big lady leaves, sybarite mutters a few words, and departs too on his old bicycle, leaving me to negotiate my route back to my room, some distance away. I walk carefully, trying to look like a shadow; I hear wild and noisy drumming. Several Indian men, next to a massive abandoned pipe big enough perhaps to live in, are dancing and drumming, their bare feet scuffling in the midnight dust. I long to stay and join in but I definitely don't know the rules here, so I keep moving.

I don't know the rules. I am not getting what I want. I have a nice time set up and then it leaves on a bicycle – I feel sorry for myself. Everyone is out having a good time, everyone has seen spirit leaving a dead body, everyone is busy and in their place. Doris, at this point the intrepid seeker thinks only of Gerry, and his kind, rather round face and I start to cry, snivelling as I walk. He hadn't stood in my way at all when I said I was going to India. He hadn't wanted me to go, that was clear, I know his facial expressions well. But Gerry has strength, a staying capacity. He plumbs himself into a place if he has to – he doesn't stray around and beg. He continues his life around that fixed point until the disagreeable situation is over. I'm disappointed that he doesn't argue, doesn't tell me I'm a fool on a foolish quest. For two hours after leaving London, in the middle row of an over-crowded Boeing, I hate him. And myself for my ignorance and curiosity and romantic hopefulness projected out into mother India.

CHAPTER 7

Guido and I face another morning. His flight leaves later in the afternoon. He wants me to make up my mind. Either I am with him, and we make plans to maintain our homes in London and

Rome, or we cut the lines and leave it all alone. 'There are plenty other delicious fish in the Adriatic sea, who the hell do you think you are?' He is too old he says for ambivalence. He is fed-up with my nonsense and distorted sense of what is real and important. My dream world irritates him. He wants a proper, present, flesh and blood woman beside him (at regular intervals), to make love, to have fun, to go on holidays. Keeping independent and in separate locations and yet keeping together; thank God no children required. What more can a woman want? The only way to deal with life is to keep oneself amused, to eat and drink well, to have good sex, to keep one's mind healthy and active and not to follow paths of metaphysical thought which lead only to frustration.

'The balls are in your court, Ellie.'

'Yes Guido.' I am urging myself to move towards him, to say that all is well and we will make plans. Something stops me. I stare at this man, at his foxy face, its thin, elegant design. I see us mirrored together above the birthday cards, still on the mantelpiece. He walks out.

Doris, I am a grieving automaton. I remain still, smarting from Guido's remarks. And, as I stand without moving, I re-locate into another dimension, swift and clean into another wavelength, where space is wider and the air is thick with crystalline knowledge. Quietly pouring into me, is a sense of no return. Guido comes back into the room.

'I'm going to leave now. No point staying here arguing with a misguided woman. I go to town, and then to the airport.' His bags are at his feet. His face is like a pointed black stone. His eyes look at me with pain and dislike. 'We have one life Ellie. You live it the best you can. When it's over you are over. Leave all these unknowns alone... or let the priests have this mystery territory, let them try to manipulate us with promise of heaven and fear of hell. I don't want anything more to do with this stuff – here today, gone tomorrow. Basta with this vague mysticism. You drive yourself crazy and me.' He strokes his cock, his hand gleaming on black trousers. 'And I hope your heavenly father gives you as good a fuck as you had from this. More of a head fuck I would say...' He is pleased with these phrases, I can tell by the half smile on his face. The brown hand moves toward the strap on his small travelling bag. Anger moves through me.

'I don't like you when you talk to me like that Guido. I'm not saying I hold the truth – I just know what I want. You think you hold the truth. Your way is the right way. This pisses me off about you.' His hand stops; clenches.

'I don't care whether you like me or not. I'm losing interest in you. I thought you were a good player – intelligent, fun, free. Shows how wrong you can be.'

Hateful words rise up in me. I want to injure this person. I want him to feel remorse and then have a sweeping change of mind – stretching out that hand to me and telling me he has suddenly realised what I am talking about and perhaps we could… I stop myself. Tears come to my eyes. He looks at me.

'Don't start that stuff now. It's too late.'

'Yes Guido, it's too late.' He moves to the door. I don't move. He opens it. I am motionless. He walks through, taking time. He closes it. A silent scream rises in my belly and inundates my body as I hold breath. As I breathe out, the muscles in my face collapse, and a cry breaks out of silence and enters the world.

Lying on the floor, irrationally listening for the sound of his footsteps up the road and towards the station, I fall through a threshold; deeply, painfully inwards. First I am in a tunnel. It has a magnetic quality. Then I come to a place of fragile peace. It is extremely small; a dot within myself. I rest here for a while.

The Indian trip – my guru-trail fifteen years ago – was a different threshold. I know exactly the place on the shelf where I keep photographs from this time. Well now, here's a beginning, here's a way to occupy body and mind while tears well from my eyes and my body wants to rush to the station and find him and bring him back. To keep or not to keep. There are three albums from India and one or two beautiful pieces of material, a pair of exotic earrings never worn. I stare at these objects; I imagine Guido travelling to the airport.

Calling me, through practical thought and the misery of the loss of Guido, a reed pipe sounds through seven notes and fourteen, calling me up and into the distant chamber of clay far back in the interior of my mind (a location of being, wider and unafraid, like the greater river at its source before it runs, loaded with tangled debris, into the town). In this chamber I see small figures of the saddhus, those who retired into the hills to sit with almost nothing, or to walk the roads with almost nothing, searching for the Holy One in naked intensity. I know this is not the form of my love affair. That's not my culture – it's not my inner direction, not my form of marriage. This time there's no ticket to India. This time, the ashram is within, the guru is my own heart, the dusty roads of India start at my front door.

Sitting amongst the saddhus, is the small child from the cemetery. I am the smile on the face of the green angel. I am those times when the mundane world must ricochet into its further octaves, seeking intimate, solitary union with the tumbling clouds, seeking the Holy mirror and letting the reflection then come all the way down to bathe the dusty earth below. The ache in my heart settles down, I become aware of the dimensions and colour of the passageway I am sitting in. I become aware of the solid structure of the house around me. I think of Marte.

I've visited her only briefly since I've returned from Thailand. A social visit with Guido felt inappropriate. I want to go and see her. I wash my face and rub its grieving muscles back into life. I have a key, knock first and then unlock the door and find my ancient friend struggling to her feet.

'Hang on Marte, I'll help you.'

'No – leave me alone. I think I can do this bit. To see you again. That's nice.' Her wrinkled hand clings onto the doorframe and then the wall as she rises from her chair, lifting its seat to reveal a commode. She pulls down her pants and settles for a thoughtful moment, until a small drizzling sound comes to an end. 'Pull up my pants now,' says Marte, hauling herself up to stand, and putting both hands up against the wall as if she were about to be frisked. I once more see the ancient skin, the wizened buttocks, temporarily decorated by a pink semi-circular impression from the commode rim; this, the old, 87-year old fleshy envelope of my friend, the parchment covering. I appreciate her again. Flesh mortified and exhausted, yet is she uncompromising, rude and full of life. Her old eyes crackle with joy and malice even as her body, sick with emphysema and the loss of her husband, groans and wheezes and staggers.

Doris, this is Marte, wife of Harry, widowed now for 26 years. Initially, we passed each other as we went in and out, and responded as pleasant neighbours but no more than that. Each of us had our own lives, as the saying goes. But now her own life is spent mostly in a chair and I visit regularly one who has become my friend.

'What have you been up to?' asks Marte, once back in her capacious chair, surrounded by hot water bottles and hot pads and a blanket and tissues and half pieces of biscuit and empty envelopes. 'That Italian gone? Not sure he's the right one for you – looks a bit shifty if you ask me.'

'I'm sorting things out, throwing out, or beginning to.' I don't want to tell her about the separation from Guido.

'What's the point?' asks Marte 'Why bother? We just end up covered with things and then we go to our graves and get covered with earth.' She coughs painfully and moves herself a little in the chair as envelopes and crumbs float to the floor. I put a hand on her shoulder and say nothing. 'Oh, this body', says Marte, 'what's it up to now?' No point being sorry for yourself, flabby, as Marte puts it. If you can catch the experience with a pointed phrase, an observation that bores its way through the misery – you throw it in like a dart. You check the score, and then watch another round of existence setting itself up on the board.

Marte has an impatient side to her and can be sharp-tongued. 'That hurts,' I tell her at these times. 'Sorry', she says immediately. When she knows she's over-stepped the mark, she is contrite, seeking to make amends, to put things right.

'Go on now,' says Marte, 'I'm done.'

'Nothing else?'

'No. Pop in later if you feel like it.'

I go back across the landing. Call to my guidance. Into the wilderness, that's where we are going. Such a ripeness I feel, now in this older age. Measurement of years, bodily changes, feel irrelevant. I have never felt so alive and present, and yet, from the outside, from the relentless contemporary tape-measure of what's visible and worthwhile, I am embarking on an act of personal suicide. Guido must be boarding more or less now. I ache for him.

I hear the octave seven and fourteen. I am following the imperative, the arrow, through a timeless, unknown portal, a gate between worlds, private and immeasurable. A small cavity opens in my heart; within it, parallel to the gash of sorrow and loss, sounds begin softly to vibrate.

CHAPTER 8

After the time of the householder, the time of the hermit, the sanyassin. On the road, into the cave, into the wilderness, into the un-chartered river, into the body's secret core, the tender nub of flesh, forever renewed as virgin.

Sister Irene, an Irish nun, lives quite alone in a small caravan, at the foothills of a small mountain. The church doesn't quite know how to define her. She looks after her animals and vegetables, and people sometimes find their way to the door of her home. Otherwise, she keeps a vigil for humanity, praying and being quiet, being a still point. This is her self-declared work in the world – to be quiet, to pray, to encounter whatever comes her way in that quiet and prayerful state. Sister Irene, I see you coming towards me in your white, plain wedding garment, a thin ring on your finger.

Before my own prayerful decision comes to its present focus, and some months before Thailand, I go through an extended period – weeks it seems – where I feel as scratchy and alarmed and toxic as if the very life around me scratches and torments; as if the very air grows scabby fingers to poke at me. Nothing obvious or specific is present as provocation. I am healthy and energetic. I am active and generally interested in work and friends. I am connected to the quietness within me and I cultivate that quietness in meditation on my own and with others. I am happy enough in my home and useful enough in the world. Guido and I come and go and there is excitement and diversion and entertainment in the relationship. And yet – something starts to grow, an energy which picks and pokes and leaves me at times in an agony of discontent, where I long only to tear off my clothes and shred my hair and leave the urban domestic environment and leave sociability and root down in the dust and the mud and cover myself with leaves and grass, and howl and screech and bay at the moon. I want to turn into a wolf, a disreputable creature without norms or boundaries. I walk and walk around dark streets, encountering occasional figures that leer and lurch at me, but this gives opportunity for me to hiss and growl and let the creature in me have a shadowed corner for its territory. I can't bear my face in the mirror, my voice on the phone. Interactions in shops, restaurants and banks turn into dangerous encounters where just a small thread keeps me functioning in the social norm, as creatures jostle and bite each other inside me, scraping at my skin, filling my belly. I talk to mentors and friends but the conversations turn into hair-shirts and I go home angry and dissatisfied. I phone Guido but we don't understand each other and the misunderstanding makes everything worse. I ask myself whether I am going mad, whether I am having a breakdown, but, somehow, a cool awareness is too firmly in place. Something is watching me. So I too watch – and keep on watching – wondering why this is happening to me. And without knowing why it is or what it is, I know it is a signal that I want to go layers deeper, scratch away the limitations which keep me tethered. Some nights I weep so that I can't breathe – I know not why. There is a nameless confinement in me – so frustrating I can only lie at its feet observing the futility of thoughts as they scurry hither and thither – attempting to understand and make better that which is strange and uncomfortable. Let me out of here, a voice howls within me. And yet I am not suicidal. I am also exultant and preparing. And, on the outside, life as a specific identity called Ellie Rose, happens in its predictable way, following its course and I stop trying to communicate the turbulent inner experience, knowing somehow that I am being summonsed. And will answer.

Chapter 9

By now, Guido must be at home. I am still sitting on the floor. Like a distracted child, I pull out other albums. Here is a photo from only last year when he and I go to the Italian Alps together. His slender, muscled arm is around me, his head near mine. I look feminine, more dainty than usual. Heart aches to remember the closeness, the intimacy of that time, but how, throughout, it had also felt unreal, a miasm, two figures playing a scene in the Alpine landscape. I live with him for the longest time we are ever consistently together, two months in Rome the year before, over the summer break, co-habiting in his masculine flat and almost convincing myself that I feel OK about it. I shop for fruit and vegetables in the nearby market, I learn a little Italian, I meet his friends, take interest in his work. We wander all around the city streets and riverside, arm in arm, laughing and close and attracted like bees to honey, enthralled by each others' hunger, gloating over bruises on the throat and thigh.

In Italy, as in Thailand, as in London, connection comes – and goes. The having it and then the losing of it is almost worse than not having it at all. Union with Guido is primarily to do with sexual and sensual pleasure. What a bonus at this time of my life, I argue with myself. It is worth having the companionship, even though exposure and irritation and that terrible sense of deficiency is setting in. I can surely handle the myriad adjustments to another creature in my own creature-habitat. But – more deeply – is this a soul-making or a soul-breaking alliance? Can we negotiate inevitable disappointment and adjustment from a deeper, kinder place? I despair at the way I begin to take him for granted after the first month in Italy, the way I notice habits; I resent the way he begins to react to me, correcting my appearance, my way of responding to certain things. I began to feel the spirit of us folding its wings a little. Come on, come on, I grumble to myself – be realistic. This is what relationships are. It's good to be with someone. People need each other. You are beginning to need Guido and he you. It's rare to find a soul mate. Settle for less and be happy with it.

The ache in our wings presses at us; we become sullen and unpleasant. Then nice things happen, a glorious day, good food, an interesting film, sex, friends, and we perk up. Hither and thither it goes, the need for somebody, the fear of somebody. The joy of my empty space, the necessity for it; the joy of intimacy and companionship.

Holding the photographs, memories stirred, I wonder if it is too much to ask of myself. Can I do it, can I step out of customary habit and activity, giving myself time until I am faced with a less adorned self and then go further, descending hand in hand with the unseen Beloved, into the unknown? Can I bear this much naked surrender, this much quietude?

I hear Guido's voice, his impatience. 'Grow up darling, you know what the world is like. Dog eating dog. I like it that you meditate, it is pleasant. But this other business you make all difficult for yourself. It is the realm of madness.' I smile at the thought of Guido's dogs and chickens. Hither and thither I go, looking at the photograph, an ache in my body, the phone nearby to which my hand could move. Close my eyes, drop my hands into my lap, breathe out steadily, notice the pulsing tempo of my heart is slightly irregular, Time goes by, tears prick my eyes, passing by, a cloud of sorrow. Steadfastly I journey into a damp, watery place, of cloud and sorrow. And then, as if by imperceptible gear-change, I fall further inwards. Lucid self awareness pervades my being – the clear structure of shoulder-blades, the breadth of my back, like an amphitheatre, different in quality and experience from the front. Shoulders like ivory coat-hangers; arms loose, belly opening up like a well. My breath is now regular and pleasurable; I am a living form resting quietly in its coat of skin, its mind momentarily making only small noises as if it were in the room next door on low volume. Joints loosen, heart steadies its beat. How long I sit there I don't know; I know only that I want to make ready, so that it can come in. I am ready, I am open. Slowly, very quietly, a quality comes into me, so minimal that maybe it isn't there after all. It is a no-thing, a non-sensation, and it moves like a colour staining and spreading except that it is no-colour yet at the same time somehow my skin feels radiant. After a time, I open my eyes. Dusk. I look at the phone. My hands are still. In my heart is a quiet, distant and peaceful sense of Guido, his beauty, his dark, wilful energy.

Gently, firmly, there is nothing to do; nowhere to go. The journey has begun. The air thickens behind me and I lean back into it. A sense of relief pervades my being.

CHAPTER 10

There are two photographs of Guido I will keep. One where he looks straight into the camera with a dark, insolent look in his eyes; the other where he is unaware of being photographed. He is absorbed in watching the horizon, and this time his eyes have a melancholy quality to them.

Automatically, I keep working. I fill the black sacks and the empty boxes; the room unburdens itself. I feel happy, panic-stricken and foolish, yet deeply guided. There is sensation of being at a river before crossing, where the waters look dark and impassable, and the grass on this side lovely and green and perfect for a picnic. Lots of people are at the picnic, and there are baskets of food, bottles of wine, and cushions to lie on. Seated on a colourful cloth on the ground, Guido waves a bottle of wine. He looks handsome.

But why are you doing this asks an insistent voice, as I tie up a sack bursting with papers. Why not go more into life? Some of the sages tell you – in life you find Divinity, if this is what you want, in service and experience and participation. Not away from. Have a picnic. Stay with Guido. Take on more possibilities – do some research, travel – this is an illusion, an escape, a romantic dream – what are you hoping to find? To prove?

Answer comes there none. My heart is sick with questioning. A fool, I feel, a misguided, deluded fool. The second sack is ready for tying.

I drag both sacks to the hall and then go next door to see Marte. I want to lay my head on that bony lap and tell her what I'm doing. I want Marte to tell me it's OK, or tell me to stop it at once and unpack the boxes. I knock softly, unlock the door quietly and catch sight of her before she notices me. The fierce bony face is in repose. It reveals to me a mute, carved, sad expression. Her eyes are slightly closed, but Marte is not asleep. This is a little death among so many little deaths. She has died to an active life out there. She has had to give up all that she did, dictated to by an aging and sick body that can hardly move, dictated to by basic survival. The marathon between chair and potty; the Everest between chair and bed. I am debating choice; at this stage, Marte has no choice. She calls me the changeling. She teases me, but with love.

'Marte.'

'Hello.'

I sit beside my friend and put my hand on her shoulder. It feels small and sculptured. Marte is irritated by fuss, so I take care just to leave my hand there, lightly touching. She points to a mess of newspaper on the floor and tells me to check out the book reviews.

As I open up to the correct page, and see at a glance what is on it, I know that the unseen lover has dropped a handkerchief, a token, a signal. In this moment I cross the river. I no longer hear conversation, the release of corks from wine bottles, the rustle of paper serviettes from the picnic ground.

Rising from the mysterious water of the crossing, comes a photograph of Martha, my beloved stone woman from the Hampstead cemetery, a single tear scored on her cheek. A book has been published about the history of the cemetery.

On the adjacent page, a review of your latest book, Doris.

Looking for Doris. And there you are. Laid out on the printer's block, side by side with Martha.

Marte normally responds to events about books, or politics, or money. This time, she simply says 'I know she's your favourite…' and forestalls any other conversation with a wave of her hand. Her white skin looks like tissue spread tight over her cheekbones. Lines score and criss-cross like the trails left by the crabs in Thailand as they traversed the firm sand. A personal alphabet, some lines cut in deeply, others very faint. I feel momentarily shy and intrusive, studying my friend so closely. And then feel – as I often do with Marte – that there is something quite willingly naked about her presence. Unmitigated by explanation or decoration she simply is there in her condition, in her situation. Her nakedness is just there, on a plate. I am learning from her as she prepares to cross over from the known to the unknown, mirroring my own private quest, but in a quite different way. There is something respectful about this transaction and something utterly disrespectful. Those of us still in life looking upon the dying with fascination. What is it like? Can you tell me? Can you show me?

'Can I do anything for you?'

'No. She is coming soon. The nice Lulu, not the bitch that came when she was on holiday. You're not supposed to say bitch, are you? You're supposed to say everyone's nice. Makes me puke, that. She's a bitch that other one and I've said it to her too.' Marte sinks back onto her chin, but there is momentary life about her. I kiss her.

'See you tomorrow.'

CHAPTER 11

With one hand Joss rings on the doorbell, with the other she switches off her mobile phone. This is my best friend, disarming in her combination of sharpness and vulnerability. Many nights have we succoured each other when one of us doesn't have enough skin to face the world. Many nights have I held her thin body with its crown of black curls as she weeps; she has done the same for me. Many nights have we held our bellies in pain as we have laughed, ribald and dirty, telling stories and exaggerating them in the telling.

Her long legs are shapely, a very plain dress just covers her body. She is wearing green, delicate jewellery.

'I must talk to you and it's about that bloody man – guess who? – I just don't understand where he's coming from… I know you're just back from Thailand with that Italian dish and I want to know everything, but me first, I'm in dire need.'

'Hello Ellie, welcome home, nice to see you.'

'Fair enough' says Joss unperturbed, ' – welcome back.'

Joss nearly falls over the boxes in the hall but makes no comment. She wants to tell her own story. After Marte, I feel another kind of greed coming up – the voluptuous crunchy taste of Joss and Jack. This will distract me from Guido. And I am not ready to talk to Joss about my impending journey, the prompting of the angel. She too is a seeking soul but a doubting voice might arise to echo my own.

So now I will have the taste of Joss and Jack. I want to feel it in my mouth, move it around my tongue. I see Joss' tongue, rich and pink, rolling inside her mouth the words that are going to come out; I see the separate expressions in her eyes – one is angry and hurting; the other is in retreat and sad.

'I'm a vampire,' I say, 'I'm going to eat you up while you're talking.'

'Don't care – just listen.' We sit side by side. I feel a sense of impending gratification. I feel a surge of love for my friend; I feel distaste, for me and for Joss.

'Go on then.'

And there it goes again. In colour. Joss and me pulling and drawing at each other. She is red, sexy and angry. She is yellow and frightened. Long tendrils come from me, listening and sensing the story within the story within the story of Joss' experience.

'He came in and he just couldn't wait to get at me – and I couldn't wait – well you know how we are together. And I just knew he'd been with someone else and this had turned him on and I was partly furious and partly curious and turned on myself...'

I listen, my curiosity is fed. At the same time, dispassionately, I see from a quieter place. Sometimes I can't bear this seeing, this lighthouse, with its calm and mellow, neutral beam, switched on day and night, winter, summer, autumn and spring. It illuminates the entire landscape and there are very few dark corners to get lost in. It stops me embedding myself in fantasy with Guido or becoming transfixed in a dark corner with Joss and her story. Joss has her own lighthouse, but currently the relationship with Jack has velocity and charge and darkness and she wants to be in it. I want to be caught too in sensuality and revenge and stories and drama. I truly want to believe that Guido and I could live happily ever after. I want an ongoing saga with him like Joss has with Jack, excitement and passion and horror. At this moment, I'm fed-up with my potentially celibate cell and its clear light. As she talks I recall that period in my life – before I met Gerry – when I was in a riotous promiscuous chapter. I see colours and shapes – flurries of jealous passion, moments of ecstasy when two of us curled together and lost ourselves in each other. We come and go and promise and we break promises and keep promises and as I see myself I see Joss and her face is like a child's and grief sits behind the woman-face with is wide red lips and strong words. I see needs satisfied and unsatisfied. I see the daily round, the excellence, the intimacy, loyalty, tedium. Joss' mouth is enormous.

'So what do you think?' she asks.

I want to yawn, I want my own mouth as huge as hers. I want to kiss her elegant hands. I don't know what I think.

'I think –' The doorbell rings. I open the door and Jack walks in, his face angry, his raincoat like a shadow behind him as he moves towards us.

'I've been waiting for you like I said, your damn phone's switched off, but I knew you would be here…' He flings his coat onto a chair. Joss uncurls her legs and her mouth starts working itself into a complicated shape that I know will spit out venom. I sit on the chair in the corner and watch the scene. They have both forgotten me, it seems. Or else, I am the audience they don't acknowledge, but need. And do I need them? I don't know if I need them – but I have them. In front of me, and now I can eat Jack too. He has a sexy body, and chooses perfectly fitting clothes to show it off. I watch myself watching him as he watches himself posing so that his body is always eloquent. His shirt, collarless and slightly full in the sleeve, is of a sage-green colour, pale sage – and his black hair falls over his forehead. I sense that he doesn't really mean any of this but that it is fuel, combustion, excitement that will rocket him and Joss homewards later. Joss' dress is electric with excitement and Jack's eyes start eating her long thighs and slim calves. Her delicate green jewellery, the small variegated stones, shine on her neck as she advances on him with her upper body even as she remains seated.

'I hate you.'

'Doesn't look like it to me,' he says grinning coldly as he moves towards her.

'Don't you come near me!'

'Well then stop inviting me.'

'Take your filthy eyes off me – and anyway where were you last night before you came home?'

'Working hard – to support you…'

They are sexy, energised. I am beginning to feel a little sick of them. I remember you, Doris. My throat feels tight. I no longer want to witness their sexy corner.

'I've had enough now, Joss,' I say loudly. 'Go home guys.'

'Ellie, sweetheart', Says Jack, blinking as if a light has just gone on, and coming towards me. 'I'm such a rude bastard, didn't even greet you. You know what it's like when you're in the middle of a thing.' He wraps sensual, lizard-arms around me and gives me the slightest nudge from his hips.

'Jack, move your ass and go home.'

'OK, sorry we've been a bit over the top…'

Joss winds her arms around us both. 'We're going. Sorry to be so selfish – but that's how it is today. I know that you know.'

Jack shoots me a sombre look before they close the front door and I remember a time when he came, obviously quite drunk, to talk to me, and slithered closer and closer until his hand was on my thigh and his eyes, radiant with sincere dishonesty, were on my face. When I'd said I wasn't going to fuck around with my friend's man, he'd said I was boring. This never happened again. I think he felt bad, but we didn't speak about it. I don't think he had any intention of anything happening. He was playing.

I sit in the room. It is dark. Desultory light comes through the window from the street. The air in the room feels ruffled as if a helicopter has been hovering in it and cutting with its blades. Dozens of words, chopped up, fall onto the floor; streaks of vibrating energy swirl around without focus. I feel a lonely part of me, a sexually provoked part of me. My thoughts pull onto Guido again. Our words from the previous days mingle with Joss' and Jack's. Come and save me from loneliness and sexual desire, Guido. I feel myself getting small and needy. I want to be looked after, I want to be safe, I want to be loved. Take me in your arms. The need in me is silently shouting, like the frightened child hiding momentarily behind Joss' wise adult face. I feel I am heading towards aloneness. I will be boring. Nothing will happen in my life. Everything will happen in everyone else's life. Self-pity and fear arise. Now, here, in the dark, the greedy mouth of Rahu, the mouth without a body, is waiting to feed on me. It is also my own big mouth, and it will never be enough, the appetite will never be appeased. I catch myself just in time. Wake up Ellie – look at what is really happening. You have begun your sojourn in the desert, in the cave. These are visitors, actors in their own temporary play, come to provoke you with your own endless fears and appetites. You know what to do. I take a deep breath and murmur to myself: make yourself big enough to hold this, just hold it. I feel my body calming, opening up a little. The soreness is there, just below the heart. I light a candle and put on quiet music, no melody, no rhythm. Just a support to my breathing, as if the breathing were amplified gently on the outside. I remember a line from the Upanishads: *'May you safely cross the waters of darkness and reach the farther shore of light.'* The dark air of the room, the broken air, mutilated and sharp, begins to right itself again. My breathing reaches the four walls and I weave for myself a vessel of safety. I see my solitary form trustingly sitting in the slender coracle I have made. Unseen gentle winds slowly blow us across the water.

CHAPTER 12

I burn with raw sorrow for Guido and entertain a mad idea that I will phone him and that he will take the pain away. Pushing hard onto my heart with both hands, left over right, I disturb myself out of a tantalising version of Guido rushing to cover me with cooling kisses and tears.

Hands pressed to my body, I disorganise the image of the weeping, consoling lover. Painfully, I reflect on the way the relationship affected my life in London. There were times when friends didn't know whether I was in London or Rome, or whether we were travelling together in some other country. Joss managed to remain attached to me without change throughout the whole Guido relationship, whereas others somehow receded in implicit agreement that a foreign Someone was now in my life and this was being given precedence.

I am not going to tell anyone that we have separated so when I am less visible, people will assume I am in Italy or travelling with Guido. I will negotiate unpaid leave for a year from the Institution. They too might think I am travelling. That's okay.

It has been difficult not to tell. It's unusual that I don't communicate, and retreat from social contact. I value keeping in touch. It keeps me in a web of warmth and connection. Friends keep an eye on each other. I am getting into the habit of silence though. I know very well that if I speak of it, the venture will come to an end. It will have lost its integrity. The times of not speaking have left me feeling lonely and fearful, and yet also clear and quiet.

I am preparing for a ritual that will happen tonight. First I see Marte and she is frail and full of grumbles. I bring her soup and a jelly with fruit. She tells me to put the jelly in the fridge, that she doesn't want it. As I leave she falls asleep, her chin falling towards her chest, her white chrysanthemum head drooping, hair flattened at the back into two halves of the flower, a pink line of the skin in the middle. The love I feel for her brings another raw sensation to my chest.

In this that I am doing, this anonymous procedure, I am a nun without a convent, a disciple without a master. I am both devotee and the locus of devotion. Sometimes I have walked through my life as if sauntering through a bazaar; oftentimes I have cavorted on the stage. Through each changing scenario, I always carry with me under my shopping outfit or theatrical robes, the rough wooden structure of a home-made altar. This altar I now establish in a clear and empty room.

Right now, as I consider the ritual, my mind is murmuring like a swarm of bees: you're embarrassing, you're inventing something which doesn't exist, you're deluding yourself, new-age phoney, you just can't cope with the real world out there. Come back into the measurable world, measure up, make yourself fit.

To balance this humming intrusion, I need mentors, guests for the ceremony: poets like Rumi, those who write of the journey on the sacred path; the divination of the I Ching, the arts of subtle energy-practice, certain pieces of music, Doris, meditation.

I take the buzzing message – you just can't cope with the real world out there – I say it to myself loud, slowly. I listen to each word. I measure it. This and THAT comes the response. This and THAT.

This is a form in space and time called Ellie. I was born and I will die. I am mineral, vegetable, animal and human. I learn and manage many complex tasks and relationships, name the world and differentiate what I see – I learn about good and bad, male and female... I have a garment of skin to differentiate inside from outside, a bony structure to hold me upright. I learn about blue and green, tomatoes and walnuts, sea and land, stagnant water and fresh water, headaches and menstruation. Everyone is a completely different this; everyone is quite the same.

I feel my this as an activation mostly in the front part of the body; a pulsing, reacting, diverse life-engine. Shards of love for Guido pierce my heart, tender fragments of the image of Marte's bowed head remain softly in place; elements of self-ridicule twist my belly.

If my this was now in a place of war or catastrophe, it would be fighting for its very life, primed and programmed to struggle and keep breathing, to maintain its place, its possessions, its safety, its pecking order. If my this had just fallen in love, it would be happy and beautiful in the eyes of another, blessed in the world and making another of beauty in return.

Implicit, prime mover, constant and subtle, invisibly and mysteriously present, is THAT. In the realm of THAT I am propelled and guided. I am breathed. Yes, I say to this one. Be still, be calm. It is all right.

It is dark outside. Allowing the thought and feeling disturbances, but moving slowly within them, I light candles, and burn sweet oil. I bathe in water scattering into it drops of rose-essence. I wear simple, cotton, light-coloured clothes and play a tape of gentle, repetitive music.

This is gradually a baby lulled to rest. The clamour of bees and the feelings in the front of my body settle down. The horror of Guido's silence and my own corresponding silence is soothed.

I create a single point of focus in the room, a low chest on which there is a carved figure, of Japanese rosewood – a figure with slender bowed face and body, long, slim fingers; a simple vase with one lilac rose in it, just shortly before full bloom. Next to the vase, stones from the Sinai desert and from Ramana Maharshi's beloved hill, Arunachala. Next to that, a small Tibetan singing bowl, and its wooden stick.

In front of the chest, I have placed sheets of fine-quality paper, and a fountain pen with dark ink. Also pencils, and water-colour pencils. I have written on one page, extracts from Psalm 139:

> *Whither shall I go from thy spirit?*
> *Or whither shall I flee from thy presence?*
> *… if I ascend up into heaven, thou art there:*
> *… if I make my bed in hell, behold thou art there.*
> *Search me, O God, and know my heart: try me,*
> *And know my thoughts.*

I sit on the floor, facing the chest and take several breaths, noticing particularly the out-breath. I read the verse aloud, once, twice, three times, reading more slowly each time. I have no idea what I am going to do. I am letting it proceed. I like the echo of my voice, and the words, so I read them again, the fourth time and then the fifth. I stop and stay quiet. The candle lights flicker and dance in front of my eyes. Then they burn straight and smooth.

'I promise this,' I hear myself saying, 'to the best of my capacity. I promise to witness quietness in the midst of all action. I am the hermit in the midst of the city. I am utterly vulnerable and fallible. I walk naked towards You. I walk naked towards my Self. I know fear and sadness and anger. I know loneliness and neediness. I am guided by the joy and surrender of those who have gone before. I feel great love and a sense of peace. I feel beauty, strength and ease.

My body is alight with love. I await the arising from within of the Holy visitor.'

Some of the dense darkness beyond the candle-light seems to settle over me like a garment, a raven-black velvet coat of feathers, draping itself initially over my right side, cloaking me in a wondrous, heavy softness. Then I realise that the cloak doesn't cover me all around my body. I close my eyes and an image comes: behind my left arm, there is a gap, and spilling out of this gap, a trailing dusty tail of grey. I know that this is a remnant of dread, sadness and fear, from deep within; it drags at my energy, it interrupts the completion of the cloak. I feel the sharpness of disappointment. A sigh seems to emit from the greyness. I want to be whole and moving imperturbably forward in my magnificent cloak. The grey tail-trail won't let me. Push. Pull. Forward and backwards. I hear the groaning and wailing of my female ancestors. Hard times. Searching for stability and safety and finding none. Putting on a veneer of sophistication and management, but underneath trembling like a child when robbers gallop nearby, coming close to the front door, and then at the last minute veering off and going further away. Dark-skinned girl-children hiding under beds, worried by the rough underside of the mattress as it pokes through wooden slats, smelling the unmistakeable odour of a hidden chamber pot, hearing the desperate whispering of the old women. Life is not all right, not at all, not at all, but above all pretend that it is, put on a good front, be brave, get as much as you can, get a good man to protect you … And then, later, either growing a flamboyant and noisy protective cover because the ground is so unsafe, anything to distract from the holes underfoot; or a sharp toxic armoury to keep the world from poking its finger into the gaping hole in the heart, the terror which will not go away, the dread which is a constant grey companion, an icy fox slinking around the heels, day and night, day after night.

The music has come to an end. Quite some time ago it ended. I am sitting in my own silence, wearing something of a cloak and watching a dirty-grey fox in the back of my head. Now what are you going to do? It's all gone wrong.

I don't understand, at this moment, the word 'wrong'. I am going to continue. But for a while I need to wait.

I pick up the Upanishads.

'The Self cannot be realised by studying the Scriptures.
Nor through the use of reason,
Nor from the words of others
no matter what they say,
By the grace of the Self is the Self known,
The Self reveals Itself.'

I gather the darkness around me; the fox settles at my feet. I stroke its dirty, pointed head. I cradle my mother and my mother's mother and her mother. We sit, all of us, within the incomplete cloak and alongside the fox, an awkward bundle in the darkened room. The candles continue to burn.

I begin to draw us, with my left-hand. The drawing emerges, apt and alive, naïve and uncultivated. I then colour it, and, with a thin brush, turn the pencil-colour into paint. Archaic language moves from my mouth as I draw and paint:

'My words travel like celestial arrows to all corners; they are shaped in the holy ashram that sent me here. Music follows my feet. I tread the holy path. This dancing being is blessed in all she does, coming to this time from ancient places and people. I abide in the teachings of the Christ, Buddha and the Tao and the Blessed Companions of the Holy Tree and the Light. I abide in the teachings of my own heart. There is no more impediment to my sharing the mighty gifts that have been restored to this consciousness. Holy One be blessed; Holy One, be thanked. Blessed be I in thy sight. From the ten thousand things to the One; from the One to the ten thousand, I rejoice in this life and its possibilities for redemption. That which was spoiled is made good; that which is made good is becoming radiant. My words speed like doves to the four corners. There is an echo in the transmission that reaches back through all the other times of life and learning. There is an echo in the transmission that reaches forward into other dimensions and times. I bow my head in humility and receive. I thank the Holy One for all that is given to me. I treasure these gifts and the generosity with which they were given. I surrender to the Holy Order and play my part to the best of my capacity. Shanti, shanti, shanti.'

I feel exultant as these words stream without conscious thought from my mouth; I stand and extend my arms softly, moving them around my body this way and that, head lightly held, spine straight, knees loose, feet firm on the ground.

The commitment with which I am entering this enclosure, of which I am the invisible building and the inhabitants, is now clear. The hermitage is at the same time, a bridal bed, furnished with softest linen, white and fresh. I alone build and maintain the structure and its community. Daily, to calm and nourish the body, Tai Chi; each day a walk. Meditation to focus the mind and cultivate clarity and quietness. Daily I will emerge in nakedness – a nakedness of watching. I want to see how the fear and structures, desires and distractions – the vulnerable and touching baggage of humanity – weaves into, and is held by, the clear light, the Light that also holds the Lover.

I will continue to take care of Marte and keep in touch with Joss – and ride with events that come unbidden into my life. I will be respectful of Guido. This thought carries sorrow. I pause… Otherwise, each day is as it is. I want to witness that which arises without trying to change anything.

The time I have allotted has the shape of a year, but could take longer or end sooner. I seem to be taking myself away from life but I have a certainty that by stepping into the hermitage, I create the possibility of returning tenfold blessed to the glories of habitation within a human form.

A voice whispers in my ear that I am deranged and deluded. This point of view disappears as quickly as it arrives, like grey yesterday-snow melting before the sun. There is simply no argument.

PART 2

THE FORM

The Presence of the Sage
Is Rooted within the Ten Thousand Things

Fullness into Emptiness;
Emptiness into Fullness

Following the Water-course Way
Twinned Fish forever penetrate Each Other

Flexible as a Willow to receive Changes
Gentle as an Embryo's Heartbeat.
The Pilgrim walks the Mountain Path
Guided by Octaves of Invisible Music

CHAPTER 13

'Mel's arriving,' says Marte as I come in early as usual to see how she is. She is coughing at the end of her nebuliser so at first I don't hear her properly. 'Mel, you know,' she repeats, 'the old friend who became a taxi driver in Tel Aviv – used to drive Harry and me around when we were there. Looked after us. He's coming to see me. He phoned – and found out I'm on my last legs so he's coming.'

'From Israel?'

'Yes,' says Marte impatiently, 'he's not coming from Timbuktu is he, what would he be doing there – he's coming from where he's from and he's from Tel Aviv. But now he's already in London - came in yesterday – and so he'll be by this afternoon. And he said he'll stay for a while. He's taken time off from his business.'

Mel? A memory comes forward. Mel at school in London with Justine. They grow up together. His parents divorce and he makes himself at home with Justine, Marte and Harry. He moves to Israel when he is in his thirties, gets married and drives taxis.

'He has lovely hair, Mel, reddish-brown curls.'

'Oh has he?' I say shortly. I don't feel at all interested in Mel's curls. (Memory: 'This is my daughter Leonie.' 'Oh what gorgeous curly hair.' 'And this is my daughter Ellie.' 'Hello'.) 'Shall I buy anything? Cook anything?'

'No, no, no – he'll bring.' I incorporate this unexpected news. Mel could be a godsend; he could be a pain in the neck with smart-boy Israeli taxi-talk. My imagination creates his face and personality and I see a tough, or pretend-tough loud man, a joke-teller with lively energy.

'Actually there is something you could do,' says Marte thoughtfully. 'Make up the bed in the spare room, with clean sheets. And see if the cupboard is empty enough and if there are hangers. Oh damn…' she pauses uncomfortably. 'Not enough breath. I'm talking too much…give me that thing…' I pass her back the nebuliser. It starts pumping as I go to the spare room. I take some of Marte's elegant, elderly sheets, find a towel, and try to make the cluttered room look empty.

I spend the midday walking on hard November streets, up and down, in and out, not specially looking where I am going. I sit in a café with eyes closed, and the whole world boils and bubbles around me. I open my eyes and take in the sharp rims of the tables, the hiss of the coffee machine, the dreamy look of the girl sitting at the table next to me. My eyelids feel heavy and fall closed again. I feel myself in the company of a thousand, a million, a billion other souls. In Italy there is a soul housed in a body called Guido. Maybe tonight I will write to him. Perhaps there will be a letter from him.

I call on Marte when I get back. A stocky, clear-faced, shaven-headed man probably in his forties is sitting comfortably in the rocking chair. He doesn't get up until Marte has introduced us. His movement is unhurried, his handshake neutral.

'Ellie…'

'You must be Mel.' He has clear, steady green eyes, and clear features, sunburnt skin and a strong nose. I thought he'd have more of an Israeli accent, but his voice, deep and pleasant, places him as a Londoner.

'Yes, I've come to see my old friend here –'

'Little less of the old!' snaps Marte. Her eyes, looking upon him, are alight with affection.

'You didn't tell me you were in trouble,' says Mel.

'I'm not in trouble,' says Marte, less aggressively than I would have expected.

'You two have known each other some time?' I look across at Mel.

'You know the story,' says Marte. 'Couldn't stay away from our house, could he? It was my charm, wasn't it darling?'

'Wouldn't call it that,' Mel yawns 'Oh, excuse me girls – flying is no longer the delight it used to be. And flying El Al…'

'I'll go back home now,' I say. 'Have you got enough food? Has she provided for you Mel? I'm just across the way – knock if you want anything. You know this woman, she'll starve you, or offer you what she didn't have from meals on wheels.'

'It's a pity about his hair,' says Marte 'he's cut it all off, like a brute. He used to have these lovely red curls.'

My eyes meet Mel's. His are neutral, but smiling a little. 'I brought a bag of stuff, thanks Ellie. Didn't know what to expect, so I've brought goodies enough.'

As I cross the landing, I think again about Marte's support system. I'm a daily friend, practical in some ways, but mostly company of a different sort. And I don't stay long. I have an overview of what happens in her life, but it is not detailed. I know nothing about her medication, for example. Lulu and the doctor know about all that, and they communicate with Justine.

And now, into all of this steps Mel, bringing with him an air of familiarity and confidence. I think about the other possibility I have thought of recently but not suggested to either Marte or Justine. Should we talk about someone coming to live in? She has a spare room – in chaos at present, the one Mel will stay in – but this could be re-organised. I realise I've got used to Marte simply being Marte, sick and weak and yet strong and surviving in her particular way which gives the illusion of strength – no, it's not just illusion, it is strength. The cobbled-together system of care seems to work, but can it contain emergency or greater need and dependency? I sit quietly on my bed, thinking about Mel. I have an odd feeling that things have changed. One of those light feelings that also carries weight. He has brought in a quality of response to Marte, which is going to change things.

What are the wheels and cogs and turnings and windings that have brought Mel to our house? How does it all mesh in with my unspoken commitment and the currency of change and loss? Somehow, I know that he is going to stay. Mel is moving into place, to take his essential part in a certain kind of unfolding. A fleet thought towards Guido. I feel as if I have lost a limb.

CHAPTER 14

Joss has a way of talking about the gods. 'Oh yes – the gods arranged that,' or 'picture them up there won't you, pulling this bloody string and that... and us poor fools...' I haven't seen Joss since the drama in my living room. I want to tell her everything and tell her about Guido, and the arrival of Mel. I imagine her saying in her droll and cool way 'Oh yes – the gods have taken one away and sent you another. Can't you imagine them looking down on you from their heaven, as you settle into your hermitage? Let's distract her – let's bring in something new...' Joss' gods can be cynical and indiscriminate.

My lack of communication with Joss feels uncomfortable although I know she trusts me and is extraordinarily accepting; it is also a powerful experience that I can be still and germinating without speech – a potent seed of presence: Not my will, but Thy Will. this within That. Be still, Ellie, and wait.

Memory of wandering around the southwest corner of Crete with Gerry. In the late afternoon after a long day's walking, I sit transfixed as a small flock of sheep settles and becomes still and waits at the end of the day under the wide arms of a tree. We are staying for a few days in Loutro, inaccessible but by boat or foot over the cliffs and meadows, a single curve of tavernas and pensions lining a protective bay. No building is more than four stories high and each is painted white with blue shutters, as are some of the flower-pots and wheelbarrows. One house alone has been painted cream, and looks like a cheap false tooth in the midst of dazzling white perfection. The only patisserie has yellow and blue stripes on its awning and yellow and blue flowers on the tables. Each morning, around the curve, the breakfast circus arises; each night, the sharpening of knives, and roasting of pork and fish, and restauranteurs vying for the attention and the cash of the visitors. Loutro, in its bay, is vivid and sleepy, almost-too-pretty, sexy and claustrophobic. Behind it is a steep, vegetated rocky hill, the remains of a Venetian fort on the top, a path zig-zagging its way out of the houses up the cliff and onto the meadow behind, drowsy with beauty, almost biblical in its intensity of olive trees, rosemary, thyme and sage plants, large and small terracotta rocks, small purple, blue, yellow and white flowers, crimson poppies, purple Aaron's rod with its voluptuous tumescent flower and zebra-striped stalk; and ubiquitous deposits of raisin-round droppings, for this is home to aristocratic tribes of brown, white and black silky-haired goats with arrogant Greek foreheads and noses and supercilious jaws, and sheep with similar profiles but showing a meeker disposition and carrying their woolly bodies on spindly legs and nimble hooves.

Coming back to Loutro at the end of our second day, after a long walk from a distant beach, we hear a loud and persistent jangling of bells. A small flock – about thirty sheep – aged to young, is moving in a line without any apparent presence of shepherd or sheepdog, and collecting in a measured way under an umbrella-shaped tree with a spreading and shining green crown, and exposed long roots. They gather, initially standing, and then, here and there, one by one, first scratching speculatively upon the dusty ground, they kneel down and settle, folding their legs under quiet bundles of dusty wool. As each one settles, the neck-bell rings with less vigour, rings with a quieter, more muted sound, somewhat in rhythm with still-moving jaws as the creatures ruminate and chew the few bits of greenery under the tree. Gerry and I sit nearby, as the day softens. We are drawn into the scene by the quality of surrender and restfulness that grows around this company of animals. It is rare, after an animal has settled, for it to get up again. In the end, maybe half a dozen, nearest the tree trunk, remain standing. Chewing, farting noises mingle with the sound of the muted bells, each sheep distinctive, with its stiff, rounded profile above a rotating under-jaw. I feel caught in an ancient, indifferent lullaby, and I recognise it in my body. It is as if each settling animal releases a tension in me. As creature after creature scrabbles the earth and then kneels to rest, I too sink lower and sweeter into the earth until I am almost pinned to the stone I am sitting on, quite unwilling to exert effort and move on.

Maybe half an hour later the shepherd arrives, trim, youngish, surprisingly sophisticated looking. He has a pair of binoculars in his hand. He whistles once, softly, his dog moves upon the path, and the sheep rise to their skinny legs and trot off in a line, fast but unhurried down to the path and round the corner.

The next evening we are back at the tree a little earlier. The sheep are grazing higher up, and under a smaller tree. We walk towards them and later they begin to move in ones and twos to the lower circle-spread umbrella tree of yesterday. I fasten myself to the rock again and go through the same experience. I watch again, notice the black sheep, the smallest lamb and wait for chewing, breathing, jangling-jingling soft noises. Peace descends. This time – after perhaps half an hour – two or three of the animals break away and start moving. The circle opens up as others here and there follow suit. This time, no shepherd, whistle or dog. They round the corner and disappear.

My doorbell rings.

'Got a minute?' asks Mel with ease, leaning against the door-frame. I nod.

'Want tea?' I ask

'Or coffee with a dash of brandy – I see you've got a dusty bottle down there.'

I decide to have the same. We sit side by side with our cups of coffee and brandy. Joss' gods are right, Mel is a new and wonderful piece of meat for my unoccupied mind to chew on. My body is still preoccupied with Guido, cleaving to his side even though he isn't present. I don't register Mel in my body, but I feel the hunger of my mind, the need for entertainment, event, inter-action. What shall I present to him? I feel a surge of mischief at the thought. If I present a face of serenity and piety, pretending to be a nun, a rotten silky petticoat would soon reveal itself. Hello Mel. Here is a bundle of perceptions called Ellie, and here also is all of heaven and hell. I feel as wide as the house, I enjoy the stranger at the table. The dust on the brandy bottle turns to diamonds.

There's a male smell and a cigarette smell around him.

'How long are you here for?' I ask, 'or is that a rude question?'

'Don't know. Could be a while. But I want to be clear before I say anything to Marte. Don't want to lead her up the garden path.'

'When did you last see her?'

'Oh,' he says, stretching out his legs and smoothing a sunburnt hand across his mouth 'not since she was in Tel Aviv. Harry was still alive. How long ago was that?' He doesn't answer the question and seems not to expect an answer from me. We are both silent for a while. 'I always knew she had trouble with her lungs – smoked them to pieces just like I am doing.' He is silent again. 'She looks very thin and washed out. But she's tough. I'm also noticing how immobilised she is.' A soft look comes over his face. Another pause. 'She was like a mother to me.' There's no sentiment in this statement. I notice the similarity between him and Marte in that way. I'm intrigued, too, with the lazy travelling that his hand is doing around his face, stroking, scratching, or simply resting, cupping his chin or resting on his cheekbone. He seems to read my thought for the hand drops, but not as if he's been caught out. The action simply stops.

'You're a teacher?' he asks, looking directly at me with a candid but not flirting gaze.

'No.'

'Oh – Marte said…'

I smile. 'She never quite gets it. I'm in education – but I'm not working at the moment. Taking a bit of time out.' I could tell him! I could tell him right now about Sister Irene and the caravan and the wise ones and… but I have no wish to tell him. I can imagine those clear and straightforward green eyes looking at me after my disclosure.

'I'm taking time off too,' he says

'Yes…'

'Burnt out. Hours a day driving. Driving myself mad too. Trying to rake in the shekels. For the boy, you know, David.' Again that soft look. This time something deeper behind it that I don't want to peer into. I look into my cup. It's nearly empty. 'Do you have kids?' he asks.

'No.'

'Are you sorry?'

'Hard to say.' I want to go on that I don't think I'm very maternal but I decide not to.

'If you don't mind me saying so,' he says reflectively, 'you don't look the maternal type.'

'What's that supposed to mean?'

'Hey – no insult – some of those maternal types could suffocate you – have some more coffee, how are you feeling, do you want a cake...'

'Do you want more coffee?' I ask. He laughs. So do I. We have more coffee and brandy. My edges are starting to feel slightly fuzzy.

'Who's David?' I ask

'My son.' Silence.

'You said,' I say obliquely 'you said Marte was a mother to you.'

'Oh yeah – but can you imagine Marte being a mother? Well, a bossy mother yes, a demanding one in a certain way – I know Justine can be a bitch – but...'

'How old is David?' I ask him.

'Seven.' Again that look. A darkening of the eyes. He shakes himself slightly. 'Hey, do you know the club scene here?'

'Not really – no.'

I feel like methuselah. I don't say anything. Then I tell him that I like all kinds of music. Then I tell him that I have been wild in my time but that time seems to have passed. I don't know why I have said this. There has never been a wilder territory than the one I am in now.

'Oh, come on lady,' he says, but not unkindly 'there's all the rest of life to live. You ain't dead yet. You want to be a bit mad, you want a bit of chutzpah. Cheek you know. Outrageousness.'

I can feel that part of me which wants to join his space, to be comradely and cool and chic, to have the language, the posture, the angle which will fit his so that we can be joined, even in this small introductory moment. I can feel the part of me which wants him to think I'm interesting and okay and wonderful. I can feel an insistent prod in me to produce the stories, the animated face, the complicity, the language of symbiosis. It would be so easy and so warm. I could confide exotic, anarchic, tantalising experiences, and I could lean forward and let my eyes go moist. I could encourage him to tell me similar stories. I sit, looking at my cup.

'Well,' he says, 'I'll check back next door again.' He gets up. 'Thanks for the coffee. If I make a habit of this I'll buy you another bottle of brandy. A better one.'

'Is that so?' I'm laughing.

'Well you know us Israelis. We're a rude bunch.'

'You seem much more English than Israeli to be honest. Or put it this way – you've got an Israeli nuance, but there's English underneath.'

'Mmmm – nuance hey – first time anyone's told me I have a nuance.' I hear him in the hallway, murmuring to himself, and then he opens the door to Marte's flat and disappears, closing the door behind him.

CHAPTER 15

The man-smell fades, the air turns, and, as if despatched by the imperious click of a finger, the clear, knowing hermit disappears into a hidden cave. I am left with a furious, uncomfortable, chaotic woman. Where's the peace that passeth all understanding? What have I given up my life for?

Darkness comes over me. The interior of the cave is black and dangerous. I can't see. I know what's happening. No time even to fasten the seatbelt. Dangerously unprotected, I fall into the pit.

Skinny arms clutch at me, I brush against thorny foliage. Voices curdle my eardrums… It's like this you see – it's a trick. Having given up – to a degree – the action out there, you know there is no silence inside. It is always a hive of bees, a sandy wind from Libya, a screaming lunatic in an asylum. The hermit in the Himalayas watches the erosion of soil, the death of a rat, the drying up of the river. And it all passes. So what. Marte is a diversion; Mel is a diversion, your intention is a diversion. Guido is a salvation. Underneath, there is nothing. You must create something to make it bearable. You can't bear nothing, it's killing you, and you can't bear something either. Your face in the mirror, your voice, the waking up and the going to bed.

The bell again. Oh go away Mel, now what? You with your something and your taxi and your parties. Just go away. I open the door. It's Joss. Black trousers, striped black and white tee-shirt, white jacket. The black and white glares at me.

'What's up?'

'Oh fuck off, I don't want any speeches.'

'What's the matter with you Ellie? What's up with you? It's getting on my nerves. You were much nicer when you were really busy – you always had time for people. Even when you were away with Don Giovanni.

Now you're doing nothing no one sees you. I'm tired of explaining you to people.'

'Who says you have to?'

'If you're going to be horrible, I'll go…' I burst into tears. She comes in and drags me rapidly to the sofa where she wraps her arms around me and breathes into my ears. It's like being held by a right-angled triangle, but it's nice too. I snivel into her white jacket (which she surreptitiously edges away from my nose) and she strokes my hair.

'There's been a man in here, I can tell. I know! You're having a secret love affair - that's what's going on, you're cheating on Don Giovanni, and this new one's just upset you the bastard, tell me who he is and what's happening, and we'll sort it out.'

'Joss, I think it's hormones.'

'HRT Ellie - don't hesitate - who cares - imagine being dry and having no libido - god what a hell. You must go and see my gynaecologist, she's very sympathetic. Was there a man here and he wanted to have sex and you couldn't?'

I fall away from the prying, dramatic persona she steps into sometimes when she thinks I need to be lifted from dangerous subsidence, and start to laugh. She joins in and presently we are laughing, clutching our bellies, tears running from our eyes. There's another ring at the door and it's Mel.

'A good joke?' he asks easily

'Boy if you knew,' says Joss 'I'm Joss - is it you who's been upsetting my friend?'

'Listen girls,' he says, again not flirting, but with an ease which is almost like intimacy 'I need some help next door - she needs the potty and won't let me…' Mel and Joss face each other in a curious and friendly way as I head off across the landing.

Marte's skin feels more like parchment than usual today. I pull up her three layers - knickers, tights, baggy linen trousers. I tidy her up like you see mothers sometimes tucking their children into shirts and pulling up the elastic waists of their shorts. She sits down slowly, gasping for breath, her chest sounding bubbly and unpleasant. Her oxygen supply comes through two small outlets resting just within the nostrils; the tubes trail away around her cheeks, leaving reddish marks under the cheekbones. The tubes clutter the ground, they're always being trampled on. A black oxygen container sits on duty in the corner of her bedroom. Marte, as usual is sitting in her leather chair, covered with personal detritus.

In her small bedroom, she has to sleep upright. She can never lie down. She sits up in the day and she sits up in the night. On the table next to her kitchen chair is a mound of paper – letters unsorted, old envelopes. I once offered to sort through them but it ended in her shouting at me that she couldn't find anything after I'd been at her belongings. She knew where things were in the clutter. I fetch the nebuliser even though it's not quite the time for her to have it. She seizes on it greedily, sucking and drawing in the fluid contents. It too makes a bubbling sound. She begins to look drowsy.

'Mel can come back now,' she says 'we're sorting things out.' I can see a little pile of tidied papers on the desk.

'I'll get him,' I say 'he's talking to Joss.'

'Oh, that one,' says Marte dismissively.

Mel isn't talking to Joss, she is talking to him. He is looking at her in his focussed and neutral way.

'Okay?' he asks, moving his gaze to me.

'Yes.' There is a light and clear connection suddenly between us and I realise that we both love Marte in the same way. We both want her to have the best possible support – and to retain her independence and individuality if she can. We don't want her carted off into a home where she can't have her belongings and her own patch. I know we are aligned on all these things without ever having discussed them with Mel.

'I'll be off then,' he says 'see you again Joss.'

'Well, well,' she says as the door closes 'now there's a bit of excitement.'

'Where?'

'Oh, everywhere,' she says 'everything can be made exciting. Now I want you to have a love affair with this man, he's got nice arms, and then you can have dramas and we can have excitement – go and see my doctor – Now I have to go, I just came to see if you were still alive and you are, but only just if you ask my opinion. So I want to see improvement next time I come. Bye' she kisses me 'now phone me if you get fed-up again and have fun with you know who... we'll talk about Thailand later. Actually,' she turns and gives me a disarming, full look. Her voice changes and she becomes quieter, 'did you want to talk about the Italian – sorry I know I am being facetious and a bit aggressive but I don't feel good about him as I've told you before, and I know it's none of my business – I can stay a little longer.' I assure her I don't want to talk about anything. She leaves, flushing a little.

The distraction with Joss and the moments with Marte disrupt the downward plunge. I feel shaky but restored. Suddenly a reprieve: someone throws a rescuing rope into the hole, I am hauled up, and collapse my body onto the strong, warm presence of the earth. At this moment, I am grateful for small human interactions; to receive Joss; to see Marte. And Mel? There's a toughness in him. Not to be messed with. I feel distant but curious. I liked the momentary clean thread that swung between us earlier. Guido is a dark and distant shadow in my belly, in my heart.

The wild wind from Libya has dropped, the lunatic sleeps quietly in his cell, the hermit flies out of the arched window on a carpet of dreams in full colour and light.

CHAPTER 16

'Ellie, you in?' Mel – resident now for the past several weeks, dug in, and a fixture not only of the ground floor, but extending two floors upwards – has found out everyone's name, has introduced himself and spent doorstep time talking – is calling through the door. No one else has pronounced my name in this way, he puts an emphasis on the Ell. ELLie. He leans against the wall, carrying a mug of tea. 'Hey – you look bright – what naughty things have you been up to?'

Jinny races down the stairs carrying a large handbag 'Hello Ellie, hello Mel!'

'Hello sweetheart – how's the kids?'

'Fine Mel – we'll talk soon okay – I must fly.'

Mel comes in. 'Don't make tea, I've brought my own.' I make a cup for myself and he notices the candle burning. 'Ah – you've been doing that meditation thing.'

'Well no Mel, Tai Chi.'

'Well it does you good – what's it for?'

'Oh. It gives you balance.'

'I could do with that – I was out partying with the girls upstairs last night, hope you didn't hear me staggering in first thing…' His eyes look slightly shadowed. 'Yes ELLie I could do with the tie chee thing but I have no discipline. You are a disciplined one aren't you – ?' he makes several playful feints around the room, his mug of tea slopping just near the rim. 'Oops – Anyway, I've come to see you…'

'So I notice.' The thread is still there, barely visible but there.

'First of all will you read the newspaper to her – that's something I just won't do.' I groan. I like reading aloud and initially when Marte asks me I go happily through the paper looking for entertaining stories. 'No, no,' she anticipates sharply 'read me the financial page, the shares. You have to know what's going on in the world. Bet you don't have shares, bet you don't even have an accountant.'

'The financial pages, Mel?'

'Yep, you poor thing. Never mind, it makes her happy.' He sits down and his solid back moves against the chair to find the right comfort. 'Ell – let me put you in the picture a bit. My picture. I know you are in Marte's picture and I think it's great how you are with her but we need more.'

'More what?' I draw my feet up, and sit cross-legged. A thought wanders through my mind telling me that I will develop bow-legs if I keep doing this.

'Well – she hasn't got much time has she, we all know, so we all… need to give more help.'

'Who's all, Mel?'

'All of us in the house.'

'But have you spoken to everyone? To David?'

'I'm getting to know people.'

'But why should they all get more involved – they're kind of there anyway?'

'Come off it, Ell.' This is the first time I have felt a flash from him, a small gritty piece of irritation, even anger. 'We all live in this house don't we?'

'Yeah, but we aren't…'

'Look Ell, in my book it's not only Marte's life which is short, all our lives are short, and we can't do this prim English thing. One of the reasons I went to Israel. Okay, they're pushy over there – to the other extreme – but you wouldn't find this 'good morning' and then scuttle away to your mouse hole business that goes on here. Okay, we're not family but we're in the same house, doesn't that mean anything?'

'Well – no Mel – privacy – choice?'

'Oh bollocks – laziness and fear. Well enough of that. Look – let me tell you.' My stomach rumbles. I'm hungry.

'Toast, Mel?'

'No – too early, but you have.' I take out my favourite bread and hunt around for the thick fruity jam I'd bought earlier in the week.

'Keep talking, Mel...,' but of course I don't need to instruct him in this way. His face has assumed an intent rather inward look under the morning stubble and after-party eyes.

'I told you about my kid.'

'You mentioned him.'

'Well, his ma has another man – a good guy who's good to the kid, so he's quite settled you know. I am part of his life, oh there's no spiteful stuff like that but you know I can see he's settled so I have to weigh up me wanting to see him a lot with what's best for him. So, to be honest, I was having what you might call a breakdown just recently. Not really a breakdown, more a kind of stop. It was as if the birds had come home to roost, you know. After all the drama of separation, it was all quiet and then it hit me. The bird. Fucking great albatross. Round my neck. You have lost your son and your wife. I couldn't work, just couldn't go out there. Had to give up my job. Fortunately had a fair bit in the bank. You see after we separated I worked day and night driving people here there and everywhere – just to keep busy, to get exhausted, to get pissed and go to bed, wake up early, alarm clock and then again. Well, I needn't tell you I got wasted, so when I went to bed with that hit I couldn't get up. Couldn't read, couldn't watch telly – music drove me mad. Scary it was – and I lied to my friends. Pretended I had a new woman out of town. Then one day I was so desperate I thought I'd ring my old friend over there,' he gestures towards the door. I bite very quietly into the toast, noticing how delicious the jam feels, red and chunky. 'Hadn't spoken to her for a while. Not that I'm going to cry on her shoulder - you don't do you' he grins and I smile too, 'but her voice would give me strength I knew – ' He pauses, and rubs his hand around his unshaven chin in that gesture I am beginning to recognise. 'Well – I suddenly found the tables turned. She sounded so unlike herself, so weak, even though she was putting on the same tough Marte voice. 'I'm coming over,' I said 'I'll drop by London for a few days and come and see my old mate.'

'Little less of the old,' I say sarcastically.

'You got it,' he says. 'So I get here – as you know – probably frighten the living shit out of you – who's this bastard suddenly coming into our cosy situation?' I blush slightly and he notices. 'Well, I have decided – if she wants me to – I'm going to stay for the duration. Get my meaning. She hasn't got long, Ellie – I talked to the doctor and anyway you can see – can I say it bluntly? – the death's head is beginning to show through. I

worked a while as a hospital orderly here in London before I left – I've
seen it – and I think – she's a great lady – difficult old bird, nasty piece
of work sometimes, she did me good anyhow, I can't…' he hesitates
strangely, and then continues 'and we love her.' I don't question the
assumption. He's right. 'So that's it Ellie – let's give her a great exit, hey
– an outrageous going out. And we'll involve the others so she's spoilt
rotten.'

'She hates being fussed over Mel.'

'Yeah – but that I know – it's not fussing. We have to be artful about
this. We'll find a way. And don't worry. It's not time yet – I am getting
myself settled here. No hurry. Got other things on my mind too. So, we'll
just let the usual routine go on for a while. And then, when it's time,
show her out with style – she's a brave lady – I know her story as you
probably do.'

'What about Da… your boy?' I ask.

'I'll go back – it's not far – I'll go back regularly. And bring him things
from London. He'll love that. We talk a lot anyway. She's fine like that
his mother – no complaints really.' A film of tiredness crosses his face.
He gets up. 'Stocks and shares?'

'I'll be along in ten minutes.'

I want a little time to sit quietly after Mel has gone. I don't want to
be sucked into his slipstream just because it's there. Out of the Guido
frying pan into the Mel fire, even though the relationship is different.
And yet, there is a momentum about his approach – and I know without
too much thought that I'm in for the ride. I picture Marte sitting next
door, unable to see so that her telephone now has numbers the size of
plates – I like to watch her finger poking slowly at each number, and
listen to her swear if the person on the other end doesn't answer straight
away. I imagine us dressing her up in royal robes and carrying her on a
palanquin down Finchley Road. I imagine her bowing and waving to the
passers-by – and making snide comments at the same time. I imagine a
crown over her shapely head with its line of pink skin showing through
the white hair.

I've been happy to let the weeks continue, developing the new
order Mel has brought with him. Since Mel's arrival, I am no longer
as anxious about Marte. Mel is an unknown quantity and I am a little
wary about him, but essentially it feels as if he has come for something
himself, and there's an exchange, rather than an act of charity. He has
brought in a new energy, and it is like a finger of sunlight into a dusty
room. I realise again, with slight chagrin, that Marte and I had settled

into habit. The image of the palanquin and the bowing old figure has excited my imagination. I feel drawn into an unexpected diagonal line, slicing through the linear pattern we have become somewhat used to.

CHAPTER 17

We have done it, Guido and I, it is acknowledged as over. He emails me: Get on with it or basta. I email: basta, then feel graceless. And yet – this is what it is. Basta. Enough. We have nothing to sort out through lawyers, no property, children, work, finance in common. We shared time. Now we give it back to each other. I go through days (Doris – what would you have done in a similar situation?) writing him long letters, not sending them, reaching for the 'phone. Eventually I do send a letter, not an email. I tell him how much I love him, appreciate him. I talk about things we have done, places we have been. How sorry I am that we couldn't make it. The letter doesn't feel good, doesn't hit the spot, and yet I want some sort of closure. Tombstone more like. An epitaph letter. He doesn't answer. I wait for the reply which will tell me things I want to hear. I appreciate you, you are lovely. Blah blah. It doesn't come. I am deeply sad, frayed at the edges with loss, and wonderfully, unfairly angry with his silence.

Baubles and glitter appear in shops, punctuating the muffled darkness and cold of late November, and I remember the satisfying snobbery Gerry and I used to feel at this time, for we would escape to sunnier places. Guido and I did not spend a Christmas together. His family hive off into a singular unit at Christmas time. A bitchy thought without words arises and I let it drift off, like a bad smell. There is something in me that wants to make him into the villain, a target for feelings of sorrow or loss.

This Christmas, will the hermit abide in her cell, watching from the silence of the retreat the gathering of clans and the preparation of turkey and the mounting flurry of guest lists and presents? I feel excited at the thought of weathering my solitude and lack of distraction at this time of joy, of gathering and drawing together – and this time of the horrors of families magnetized back into scrapping unity amid the shower of discarded wrapping paper and leftover Christmas pudding. I also feel the shame of aloneness – even though chosen – at Christmas. I think about the glory of the 'we' at a time like this. Guido and I didn't spend enough time together to become an embedded 'we'. Gerry and I – a long-term known item – would discuss our we-plans with friends: 'We are thinking we might...' 'We're waiting for our tickets, aren't we?' 'We'll be back on the...' I think of the safety and warmth of the 'we', and also of the aloneness within the 'we', in those times when that joining can't reach fractured places, bruised inarticulate corners.

A significant early encounter with loneliness happens in the parental car, where, for some time, before baby car seats and seat belts, I am the child sitting in front, on my mother's lap. I remember the warmth and softness of this place, seeing my father's hand, grizzled and thoughtful, upon the gear lever, the murmuring talk between the parents as the car travels from one destination to another. My head is just under my mother's chin and I sit there like a minor royal figure, protected and enclosed. From one moment to the next – or so it seems, though I'm sure my mother will have prepared me in some way – I am removed from this place, to the back seat, where I join the dangerous Leonie. The seat is cold and slithery, my legs stick out straight before me. The parents are almost hidden by the upright ramparts of their seats. They seem very far away, cut off, in a different realm from which I am now banished. The marauding fingers of my sister could at any moment come and pinch me and then she will look innocently out of the car window if I protest. I hold onto the window-winder and emptiness rushes through me, as if sand were falling through a broken egg-timer, an experience of implosion and drainage, leaving what feels like a limp and useless body, clinging to the window-winder as if this plastic small object could save me. Something changes for me, I lose the textured symbiosis of my mother's lap, being turned inward to her soft breasts and accommodating arms.

The first fright of turning outward then slowly gives way to a shocked but wonderful embrace with the world that rolls by, unmitigated by my mother's body-zone. Roundness and sharpness, movement and colour fly into my vision and draw forth responses from all my senses. My skin seems to have a thousand eyes and ears to suck in and know what is unfolding around me. I look at picture books of the human body, stare at a large bloody red shape called The Liver and then find this shape again in the butcher's shop where my mother seeks out meat for the family table. My eyes track through the thick hides of sheep and cows when we travel in the countryside, seeing liver and kidneys and heart bouncing and pulsing inside the animal's body, connected by pipes and strings and tubes. I look at the way the indoor palm tree sheds its large leaves, and the marks left on the stem, a slashed pattern travelling upwards in meticulous asymmetry. I look into the brown eyes of the neighbour's dog, and into the eyes of passers-by to see what I can see. I watch my parents to see what it is that married people are, and see tension, boredom, humour and a real affection whose evidence has me turning away. My father puts his hand on my mother's hip and she brushes him off but with a look and a sound that I don't know about her. I turn away because I know this is a moment not for my looking. I begin to learn about privacy.

Sometimes the seeing of the world is so bright that I have to put my hands over my eyes to rest them. I see a dancing matrix that surrounds all, stones and vegetables and animals and people, nothing left out. I see a glistening web of life and connection whose beauty could hurt. I see the pressure rippling out from a harsh glance and how it travels like a bolt and hits onto other life; I see the rush of warmth carried on beyond a smile freely given, how it goes round corners like an echo growing fainter and fainter. I start to listen to music. And then my heart is like a bird in a cage too small, its wings beating with pleasure but not enough air or space for this movement really to happen; in my heart is a bird pushing against a bony container. Then the confinement bursts and the bird rides on the release, into massed voices, the deep tone of a cello, the sensual rigour of the piano. These are times of meeting, where aloneness melts, these times when the bird is out of the cage.

CHAPTER 18

Marte's husband, Harry, had a furniture shop which he ran with Sam and Cubby. I never met Sam and Cubby, I never met Harry. All dead now. But I can see their faces in my mind when Marte talks about them. She talks about them as if anyone listening should know exactly who they are. I see Cubby as plump, Sam as even plumper and Harry as a thick-set, benevolent-looking man. I see all three of them, solid, moving between their central furniture warehouse and the smaller outlets that sprang up here and there, and then wilted down just as easily. They opened shops all over London – and closed them when they didn't show profit. They sold heavy, dark furniture and seemed to make enough money to take their families to Majorca every year. Perhaps this is why Justine now lives in the Balearics.

Marte would help in the shop sometimes but this was not her interest. She developed a taste for antique furniture and objects, silver spoons, cups and saucers, mirrors. She went to classes and learned to upholster and repair old chairs, and to sand down and shine up battered-looking wood until it gleamed as new. She mentioned once in a bitter tone that this was how she'd buggered up her lungs – 'No one told us how to protect ourselves in those days...' In addition to this, she'd smoked excessively, always having a cigarette hanging from her bottom lip. This is told to me by Justine: 'And do you know how she used to tap the ash off?' asks Justine, looking at me with the expression of a mother talking about an errant child. 'She'd never take the bloody thing out of her mouth, and when the ash was nearly falling off it – you know, a half an inch of ash – she would stick an ashtray under the damn thing and just tap it straight off... or even no ashtray – she'd tap it onto the ground – still smoking – it never left her mouth.'

Marte's living room, which she hardly ever goes into, contains a chaise-longue in dusty pink, two concave mirrors, an oil painting of a solemn-looking man in a white cravat, several small elegant chairs with tapestry seats, and nests of tables, intricately carved. A glass-fronted cupboard is packed with porcelain figures and delicate cups, each object jostling the other for space. Then there are parasols, silver-backed hairbrushes and box after box of jewellery, some pieces tarnished and worn, others of beauty and possible value. There's a box of gloves, white, black, grey, some of silk and others of leather. Occasionally Marte says 'Let's go and sort out – maybe I should sell some of it' and we take a long time to move her into the living room where she sits, blanketed and enthroned on an embroidered chair, ordering me about and telling me to make piles for different things. Mostly we make piles, and then put the objects away again, usually in their original places. She asks me if I know the age of different objects, and where they are from and of what value. I have no idea and she takes great pleasure in informing me – in a lofty and pained way – that I am ill-educated and don't know about these things or about stocks and shares and what kind of education have I had and how on earth am I going to manage in the world? We end up scrapping about the aesthetic value of different things – and then she tries to get me to take one item or another. I resist, and this leads to further scrapping.

'I don't want any more stuff, I've got enough.'

'It's not stuff – it's valuable – and you should learn to appreciate these things.'

'I like to look at them here – not in my place.'

'You're peculiar Ellie – what kind of a girl are you? You don't collect anything.'

'Well… music.'

'Music – pah – heard one you've heard them all.' I know she's goading me – she has her own taste in music – so we play the game where I rise happily to the bait.

'Marte – you're a savage, a heathen… you can't tell Bach from Gilbert and Sullivan.'

'Well they're all Germans anyway…'

'Gilbert and Sullivan?'

'Of course – they just changed their names.'

The chest of drawers in lustrous walnut, just opposite the window, contains embroidered linen cloths. They smell of faded flowers, camphor and mothballs. Ironed into sharpness of folded paper, they lie there in quiet, stiff folds and are hardly ever used.

But the main eye-catching feature in Marte's flat, is the machinery of medicine: oxygen, inhalations, pills and brandy. Marte hoards half-bottles of prime brandy, keeping them in a box near her feet and complaining every now and then that there's no more left and someone must be helping themselves from her precious supply. The box of half-filled bottles is supposed to be her secret so those of us who care for her can't simply say, 'Marte there are four half bottles left…' when she exclaims that we have run out. We all know that her dependent life as it is lived is everyone's property who comes to look after her, and she has to have certain areas and elements which are hers alone and which no one else has their fingers in: her disorganised files and papers in the top drawer of her bureau, her antiques and her half-filled brandy bottles in the box. Her ideas and attitudes are also her own and her spirit and sharp mental faculties, which she keeps intact and exercised each day even as her body whittles itself down to the bone. Her memories and her regrets are her own and I know there are regrets about her relationship with Justine. She longs to like her daughter, knows that Justine finds her difficult and embarrassing. She is sharp with Justine, and then feels sorrowful after the door has closed and Justine has left for the airport. I can feel her sometimes chiselling and hacking away in her mind, thinking about the two of them. Sometimes I can feel her dusting and polishing her thoughts much more softly, and then a quiet and sad look comes over her face. I learned long ago not to advocate on Justine's behalf. Marte doesn't work well with diplomacy and intervention. She listens hard when talk goes on around her, and thinks seriously about what has been said, but she can't abide mutually trying to sort out feeling and behaviour. 'My mind is mine and yours is yours and let's face it they will never meet – it's like trying to unravel a knotted ball of string and you starting one end and me the other. Sooner or later somebody starts pulling because they think they have the right end and then where are you – it's worse knotted than before.' Marte's gruffness and seeming intransigence hides a courtroom mind – I have seen her do a complete u-turn about someone whom she has misjudged once she has collected enough evidence that her thinking had been incorrect. 'That's not fair' and 'that's fair' are two crisp ends of the scale of inner operation within Marte. She is swift to make amends when she has judged herself unfair. She is equally swift when someone else is – as she says – two-faced. 'Did you see those two-faces marching out of the door?' she'd asked me gleefully after she'd dismissed a nurse with proselytising aspirations who'd made the mistake of inquiring about the state of Marte's soul.

The brandy is consumed from an exquisite glass, and Marte takes on the demeanour of an expert as she slowly sniffs and sips the elixir. The glass – a large one – would be generously full and anyone else present would be invited to partake with her and given an equally beautiful glass to drink from. Her brandy bottles, like her nebuliser and her oxygen supply, have taken on atavistic qualities, and her rhythmic rites around all these aids, are done with an intense, greedy passion. She has become an ancient priestess presiding over daily rituals which keep life hovering, just so, on a needle of the bearable. These rituals consist of sucking and drawing in aids to survival, aids to breath and aids to soften pain: oxygen, nebulin, brandy, diazepam, nitrazipam, paracetamol, ventolin in her white handbag and becatide with volumizer in her brown one. Then there is the ritual of coughing up and coughing out yellow balls of mucus – the bigger the ball the more the triumph. One morning, after days of frustrating constipation, when she and I decide that a goat has been using her potty, she asks for a bottle of laxative. I read the instructions and carefully measure out a spoonful of liquid for her when her fingers reach out and snatch the bottle and, before I can protest, she gulps down several mouthfuls. After this act of devilment she shoots me a look and tells me to settle her on the potty and then get the hell out.

In Marte, the breathing, the sucking, the peeing, the farting, the bubbling and the belching are all simply happening to her. There are times when I want to run away and scream at the awfulness, and then I recall the desperate measures my mother had taken to hide her diminishing body from the world and how I would long for her to show us what she needed and ask for it. My mother had an innate and dogmatic sense of privacy and she fought for it until her last day. Only occasionally – and in spite of herself and usually when she was utterly exhausted – did she lose it. How I wanted then to gather her up like a baby and soothe her inflamed sense of dignity, but she would not allow this, pulling herself back into her citadel and restoring dignified order as soon as she could. I admired her for these acts of will, but at the same time I missed being with her in her distress and being able to help her not to have to bolster herself against disorder. These orderly efforts took enormous energy from her and distanced her from us into a grim place, but since it was her will, we had to comply. I wonder sometimes what path I am treading again with Marte – and what path she with me in the absence of Justine.

It is a full moon tonight, and I ruminate about Marte, and, sleepily, and at peace, waver and swim like a sea-creature in the moon's luminosity. Soft light enters the room and objects are touched. I feel tides in my belly, and float within my breath, within my belly and within the light. Every pore in my skin opens and breathes. I swim and I swim and the He and She, the two aspects of my Lord, enter me, She behind and He in front and then both to the side and then She in front and He behind, and I am penetrated and I am These and I am not These. The room is silent and yet there is the sound of water rushing in my ears and through my body as currents and waves – lighter than air – pull in and pull out. The sudden grumbling of a car outside trying to edge itself into a small space calls me back. I go to sleep, imagining rivers floating from me to cover the world in gentleness, embracing terror and shock and violence, streaming over mutilated bodies and bombed landscapes. I imagine the green emerald of the world held in my hands and then moved into my belly where I carry it safely. With my hands on my belly, I go to sleep, I in the world, and the world within me.

CHAPTER 19

A ngry with Guido for not writing to me and for moving on (can you beat the irrational cheek of this Doris?) I am walking out of the door when Mel emerges.

'Can I ask where you are going?'

'Thought I'd walk by the canal.'

'Going to jump in?'

'Not yet.' We are walking together now, towards Abbey Road.

'Marte told me you're getting over something?'

'Are you coming with me, Mel?'

'Looks like it.' His stride is easy. He is shorter than Guido, more stocky in build. I wait for him to ask whether it's OK that he comes with me. He doesn't. More cheek, Doris. 'What's he like this Guido? Don't think I met him. Did he cheat on you?'

'None of your goddamn business, Mel.'

'Hey!' He stops short, touches my arm. 'Sorry if I'm intruding. I get it wrong sometimes. Thought you wanted company; thought you wanted to talk.' As he says this I realise I do want company and I do want to talk.

'You're right Mel, I'd be glad of company.'

'And you want to tell me about this geezer?' We resume our pace. It is strange to be walking with a man and have a gap between us, arm-gap–arm.

We walk towards the canal, entering the narrow gate in Lisson Grove, walking past boats, shuffling through dead leaves, curled, and fast loosing their colour. A cold wind blows lightly. We pass mothers and babies, pairs of friends or lovers, and loners… I remember the notion, as I look surreptitiously at the two gentle lines which run from nose to upper lip on each person, the story of the angel pressing each of us with his finger, to see if we are done and ready to descend: the angelic remnant, that little conduit from nose to mouth, that distinctive hollow we each carry.

A bright ray of sun spins out unexpectedly from the white sky and illuminates the trees still carrying leafy remnants in gold and red, though many are now spilled. I still haven't answered Mel's question about the geezer but he doesn't seem to mind. We both are in our own thoughts, walking together along the slippery waterside path, arm-gap-arm. In the light I examine my thumbprint, its labyrinth, its whorl, my own marking, not available to anyone else. God's fingerprint coming through mine: this is your life, Ellie, your archaeology, your ground, your stars, your story. I imagine the thumbprint as an energy pattern, a field that I live in, which I have had no choice about. It is given, it is pressure, a crop circle hidden at the top of our thumb-field.

'Under pressure!' I recall the staccato, tap-tap beginning of Freddie Mercury's song with David Bowie.

'Do you like Freddie Mercury, Mel?'

'What's that? Oh, we're onto that are we – yeah, but not a favourite. What's he got to do with the geezer anyway?'

'Nothing. I'm just thinking about Freddie. I went with the geezer to a memorial concert in Hackney…' I think it too elaborate to say to Mel how I relish Freddie's slender, electric form, his large white teeth and beautiful lips which pull over them, his glorious, expressive voice which climbs and soars and stretches and pouts as his body does, while the instruments around him support him and help him fling his voice into the stars. And, at the end, showing us his pale face, looking at each of us who loved him, blowing a kiss from his exhausted body, and leaving.

'Freddie was under pressure from the inside, of the genius stamped upon him,' I say with peculiar formality, feeling foolish to bring some of my thoughts outward. Mel looks curiously at me.

'Well now, I wouldn't put it quite so… like him, but not one of my favourites. Don't quite know what you mean about pressure. He was camp, that's for sure.'

Watching the movements of the oily water in the canal, I feel myself increasingly vertical and receptive, a long antennae probing other realms and bringing back image and possibility. Mel is back within himself, looking at passers-by, pulling at stray willow branches which hang down before us. I am happy he is there, and that I can walk beside another human and privately be with my own thoughts.

I dare to imagine the whole of manifestation as a pregnant pressure inside God, and then the birth of humankind as co-creators, given the gift of naming the animals, a gift kept away from the angels who become single-minded, divine functionaries, of power and glory and of darkness, but without the pressure of free-will and imagination. Unable to name, and

yet cast in various roles around the unfolding of the whole phenomenal
mystery. I see our ancestors, the great yin-yang, Eve and Adam and the
hidden consort, Lilith with her claw, I see them descending to mirror
each other's opposite, and to play the joy and sorrow and tension of
these opposites. I see opposites and triangles, squares and pentagons, all
exploring the pressure of life, the pressure of unfoldment and expression,
the pressure of birth and death, sex and violence, appetite, desire and
elements. I see the gravity of earth, density pulling us deeper into the
weight of interaction, inner and outer. And I see – at the same time – the
breath of God, giving us lightness, refreshment, the upward, the space,
the wings, the expansion into refinement, soul and spirit. Music, writing,
painting, communion with others, the breath of God enlightening us,
blowing our minds, our limited concepts of ourselves, giving us – at the
same time – in relation to gravity, the push–pull of pressure and release,
contraction and expansion, matter and spirit, inextricably linked, each
one scrolling and playing with the other.

I lean for a moment against a tree as Mel walks on, and feel a shudder
of almost orgasmic love go through me. Who would know through
looking, what is happening to this small figure with its plain coat and
nose reddened from the cold? Who would know of this seismic, private,
hidden moment? This hidden intimate explosion feels like recognition,
as my spine finds purchase against the bark of the tree, of the co-creating
relationship we have with the Holy One. With That. The pressure to
know – know thyself, know God – and to communicate that knowing
back into Divinity by living it as consciously and willingly as we can;
to honour the gift of the imprint by surrendering to the pressure, to the
love-making with its naked mirroring, that we participate in with our
Creator. This is a Holy, wholly anonymous moment against the tree
along Regent's Canal, as Mel slows down, waiting for me, as rubbish
swirls around the bank of the canal and a solitary fisherman looks
gloomily at the dark water.

Later, after trailing our way to South Hampstead, we are waiting at
Hampstead Heath Station, peering down the line with others for the
sight of the green and yellow train chugging its way from Woolwich to
Richmond, so often late or vanished into a Bermuda triangle of non-
appearance. I talk to one of two cleaners who appear suddenly with
brooms and black bags and dustpans, to clear the station which is awash
with rubbish.

'Why aren't there any rubbish bins?'

Hollow, knowing laugh. 'They get thrown onto the tracks, dear.'

'So do you work just here at Hampstead?'

'Oh no, we go up and down to all the stations. They're all the same.'

They sweep up the mess, loading it all into their bags, and disappear up the stairs to the other side.

When we arrive at Finchley Road, a solitary cleaner is carefully picking up cigarette butts with a long, beaked instrument. One by one he picks them up and puts them carefully into a bag. Mel and I now talk a little about the geezer. I just give the bare bones of once upon a time. Mel comes up with a fairly blunt comment, as he pulls a woollen hat onto his shaven head.

'Well if you want me to go there and whack him with a packet of spaghetti, you just say.' This idea has nothing to do with anything, but it amuses me. It's continuing to be a temporary, meaningless satisfaction to cast Guido as the injuring party and me as the one needing protection. Mel goes in a different direction, on business of his own, and I go home.

CHAPTER 20

It is late morning, and I hear the front door open and I know it is Jinny, from the sound of her footsteps and her particular way of opening the door and then shoving herself and half a dozen plastic bags full of shopping through it. This time, unusually, there is no sound of heavy and loaded clambering. This time, there is a knock on my door.

'Jinny!'

'Am I disturbing you?'

'No – come on in – want tea?'

'I am gasping!' She arranges the bags in a semi-circle round her legs and then, a sturdy small figure in the midst of her shopping, she fixes me with steady blue eyes and trains a strand of brown-blonde hair behind her ear where it emerges a second afterwards to hang once more before her eye. Blinking, she grasps the cup. 'This Mel,' she says. I say nothing. 'Well, what do you think of him?'

'Seems to be a good man.'

'Yes but what does he want to stay with Marte for? What's in it for him?' Her tone is not bitchy or unkind, puzzled rather.

'He cares for her.'

'Yeah but...' she pauses, and then interrupts herself, 'hey – your place is so empty! Don't you have things like other people?'

'I do – but maybe not so many.' I watch her looking around, a kindly and somewhat flurried pretty little face, a few lines beginning to furrow the brow.

'Actually,' she says, looking straight at me, the stray hair like a winding distraction between us. 'I wanted to ask you something. No one else is home.' She looks embarrassed. 'Well as long as we've been here we've kind of been good neighbours, that is, I can call on you like that time you know... the hospital... but we also are careful of each others' privacy and that's fine I'm not complaining but there's, well... are you a Buddhist?'

'No – but I like what they say...'

'Well – it's nothing to do with you being a Buddhist or not... look, I'll just jump in Ellie, I've just had a weird experience and somehow as I came in I thought ' I'll go and talk to Ellie'... it's a bit of a cheek but...'

'Why don't you just say it?' I put to her, beginning to feel that the dancing frond of hair will somehow keep us away from the point, whatever that is.

'Look, you don't know me really but a bit, and as you can probably guess I'm quite a reasonable person, kind of middle of the road you might say, nothing much disturbs me – I don't get extremes – I suppose the only thing that disturbs me is that nothing really disturbs me –' she laughs 'well, that's not true Ellie, obviously things disturb me but not to a great degree.' There's a silence. I wonder if I should say anything, and decide not to. She twists her hair back behind her ear, it springs free, and she starts up again.

'I was in the supermarket. The guy behind the cash desk was unusually indifferent – he didn't say hello, checked the stuff in a half-dream, sulky, didn't make eye contact, took my money, gave change... as if I wasn't there. I took my stuff, thought of saying something sarcastic but didn't and when I walked away I felt the most peculiar...' She frowns and looks distressed 'I felt this anger, Ellie – I have never felt anything like this before. I felt so angry and hurt I thought for a minute I was going to go back and scream at him and scream at the whole shop, and hit him... believe me Ellie, I really almost had to shove myself out of the door, I nearly went faint for that moment, it just came over me, like a red-black cloud, I hardly could breathe... well I just managed to get out and I stood against the wall, nearly crying. I think people thought I was drunk ...I was so upset, and so scared! I just don't get it – what happened to me? I still feel shaky…' Two large pieces of water emerge from her eyes and slice down her face. I am distressed for her, don't know what to say. I give her a tissue and she wipes her eyes and then bigger pieces come down – they are long tears, like ribbons.

'Hey, Jinny,' I say awkwardly. I put a hand on her shoulder.

'I knew you'd understand,' she says, gulping. I don't understand, but say nothing. 'Does it ever happen to you?' she asks, looking at me hopefully, her eyes tied up in water-ribbons.

'Well, I'm not so reasonable as you, so middle of the road as you put it – so I get angry more often.'

'Ever like what just happened to me?'

'Not exactly, but sort of.'

'Do you think I am going mad? Should I go to a psychiatrist?'

'No Jinny – don't be crazy!' We both laugh at this.

'Maybe,' I say tentatively as if skating on very thin ice, 'he just caught you on the raw.'

'Well no, I was feeling pretty as usual. No – it was more the suddenness and unexpectedness of my reaction.' She looks at me hopefully.

'To be honest I'm not really very good at this stuff,' I say

'Well, I actually feel a lot calmer since talking to you,' says Jinny. I feel pleased.

'I've just realised something, that little bastard,' she giggles, 'oh, I did enjoy saying that… yes, that little bastard, come to think of it, reminds me of Henry Lemon.'

'What?' I ask, 'was someone really called Henry Lemon?'

'Yeah he was – he was the cleverest in the class – as mean as could be – big boy too so when he was teased about his name he bashed people. He had a way of just ignoring you and because I was sort of meek you know, middle of the road you know, he ignored me the most. As if I didn't exist… hey that made me mad but I never told anyone because what's the point and nothing would have come of it…' I watch her. Her eyes are clearer. She smiles and looks at me searchingly. 'You're an unusual person Ellie. You just don't have stuff,' She looks around again.

'I'm having a clear out,' I tell her, feeling excited that I am talking ambiguously. I could tell her what kind of clear out but I won't. I am enjoying Jinny being here. She gives a sudden look at her watch.

'Oh gawd,' she shrieks, 'I must go! Thanks Ellie – ' she pecks me on the cheek. 'And we must chat sometime about Mel and his plans for Marte. He's amazing but I don't get it really – anyway, see you soon.' She grabs the bags, and I hear her moving up to her door. This moment of unexpected action, my attention to it, the event of Jinny, her shopping bags and her anger, calling upon me, outlines in a very specific way, suddenly, my present out-of-usual-action state. Particularly I imagine now how it would feel if I were still been at work, inevitably and constantly engaged with work, colleagues, students, the institution, its politics and its rituals.

When I work, I am very absorbed. I love the challenge of new ideas, testing them, passing them onto people, seeing if they work. I become single-minded, hunting out radical theory, weighing it up against tried and tested methods and arguing, discussing and creating with colleagues. If something doesn't work, I am initially frustrated or upset, but then determination kicks in and I set to, looking around other corners, adjusting here, changing there. I am tenacious, dogged, and these qualities create a lovely substantial engine in me, ticking over and roaring off, requiring fuel and clocking up mileage. I have switched off this engine for four months now. I have not been near a textbook or dissertation. I have not wanted to – and also, I have put myself right out of this particular discipline and habit. It's a relief to be out – and a loss. I feel around inside myself, like a tongue probing a gap in the gum where a tooth used to be. I feel distinctly, paradoxically, the object that isn't there.

I am watching hard edges appear, jagged holes, the unease of loss of routine. And the beauty of the unknown and the shock of coming out of habit – for a moment. Canal path orgasm and rubbish, Mel, Jinny, and now, Marte. I look forward to seeing her. I like the different feeling now that Mel is in residence.

There's a cosy atmosphere in the flat next door. Mel, back from his business, is cooking sausages and mash, Marte is giving him instruction. The sausages are crackling and bursting in the pan, and Mel is beating a pile of cooked potato laced with butter and milk and mustard, salt and black pepper. I feel hungry.

'You look hungry,' says Mel without turning his eyes from the bowl and the wooden spoon.

'I wasn't before I came in. Now I am,' I say, kissing Marte. She shakes me off to look in my face.

'You don't eat enough – too thin – all that green stuff and no proper food, nothing substantial. No wonder…'

'No wonder what, Marte?'

'Oh you know… no wonder… now don't interrupt me, I was just telling that fox over there that he should watch his bushy tail.'

'Just because I have made the acquaintance of two innocent young sweeties upstairs …'

'Humph – Ellie, is that what you'd call acquaintance?'

'What's he done Marte, with his bushy tail?'

She crows with derision. 'Ask him! A grown man with responsibilities!'

'Marte!' I say in a mock-Southern belle accent, 'why Marte, I do believe you're jealous!'

'Humph! Of that fox over there? Him? Not now that he hasn't got…'

'… those lovely curls!' Mel and I both finish off. The sausages are done and Mel dishes Marte's onto one of her distinctive plates.

'You didn't have to cut it up – I'm not a baby,' says Marte, but clearly she is grateful that Mel has done this.

'Ketchup?' he asks, pouring red rivers onto his mash-mountain. There's a silence as we all eat. Mel and I ravenously, and Marte slowly and furiously, chasing a small lump of sausage around her mouth with her white and square false teeth. She eats very little and then, with a sigh, discards her teeth, dropping them back into the mug where they sit most of the time. She then pushes the sausage pieces to one side, and contentedly sucks in spoonfuls of soft mash. A small piece drops onto her green jersey. She seems unaware of it until Mel leans forward and lifts it deftly from the wool with a knife.

'Trying to stab me to death I suppose,' says Marte. 'Then you'll run off with all the silver.'

'This stuff?' says Mel with disbelief, 'these things… look missus, there's a dent here, and a scratch on this other one.'

'You don't know quality when you see it,' sniffs Marte 'now there's time for pudding, isn't there?'

'Too early isn't it?' says Mel with his eyebrow raised.

'Ellie darling,' Marte turns a face of transparent charm towards me 'fetch the brandy glasses darling – does anyone else want any?'

'No Marte,' I say, 'we'll have the usual jelly and custard.'

'Ooh,' she says, snickering, 'you know that fruit jelly you gave me some time ago, we had to throw it out – or he did, that fox, cleaning out the fridge.'

Marte settles herself around the glass of brandy, her fingers shaking a little as she holds the brown, rich liquid. She coughs and her chest bubbles. She closes her eyes and the life-giving effect of her sharp gimlet gaze and its momentarily greedy look disappears, leaving her face still and white and papery. The darkness of a late November afternoon sits around the window. December in two days' time. Mel takes the brandy glass from Marte's fingers; she has fallen asleep, and we both watch the pale stalk of her neck just about managing the heavy head as it droops forward onto her chest.

'I forgot to tell you on the walk, she drove me mad last night' says Mel wryly. 'She was very breathless and when she can't catch her breath back – as you well know – she gets panicky. We were up at two in the morning, reminiscing. That seeems to settle her. Tales from early times. Did you know that Marte's parents arrived here at the beginning of the nineteenth century? Settled of course in East London. He ran a grocery shop, an old-fashioned one that sold everything else too. She's old enough to be my grandma really – but she's so alive and...' his voice stops. We both look at her, her breath is scarcely visible. 'Yes,' he says after a while 'Our ancestors, the refugees. Refugees are never welcome don't you think... Of course there are people who make them welcome and there is an enforced attitude and altruism but refugees are uncomfortable. Like someone who's unhappy or sick or suffered a terrible loss... it's the dislike isn't it – a superstition – the dying remind us of our eventual death, the sick tell us of our... bodies.'

'Do you feel fragile being with her all the time, Mel?' I ask.

'Yes and no. Her body terrifies me – her spirit gives me strength.'

'Where are your parents?'

'He's dead and buried; she's in America,' he says flatly. A light goes on the window of the big house opposite. The figure of a young woman moves busily around the room. Mel notices. 'Ah,' he says brightly, 'the mad nymphomaniac bisexual tart is home again.'

'How do you know these things about her, Mel?'

'Where've you been doll? Look at the fluffy cardigan...' There's something unnerving in his distraction and the words he is using.

Marte grumbles, still asleep. A small drop of saliva drops from the corner of her mouth. 'I think I'll leave that,' says Mel 'she might wake from her boozy sleep.' We both know the brandy glass was untouched.

'I'm going to get you a fluffy cardigan Mel, and a pair of house-slippers to match.'

'Ooh – promises!' The light goes off in the room of the house opposite.

'I saw Jinny today – what are you organising with her?'

'Ah yes – this I wanted to talk about.'

'What are you saying about me?' mumbles Marte 'Don't think I'm deaf.'

'We're saying you're a nymphomanic in a green cardy,' says Mel.

'Ever since you lost your hair, all you think about is you-know-what ' says Marte, speculating. 'You know what they say about bald men.'

'Your husband was as bald as a coot,' replies Mel. Marte smirks. Her shoulders quiver. The doorbell rings.

Marte sighs, 'There's always visitors...' but she wakes up, looks interested.

'Must be Lulu,' says Mel.

'It's not bedtime,' says Marte 'Hey, pass me that glass.' I give it to her as Lulu comes in, tall, black, and bearing with her news from all the people in all the houses in the world she attends to. She walks and takes buses and trains to see her customers as she calls them. They are mostly old people, living alone, who can't fend for themselves. Lulu washes them, puts them to bed, deals with their evening medication, and, like a town-crier, brings stories from house to house. She is remarkably skilled in her practical work, knowing just how to lift a pained old body, where not to touch and what not to say. She has patience and strength and long fingers with curved fingernails, pink and unpolished. She tells stories that are funny, bizarre and touching – she tells stories of horror. I have noticed that she protects the characters in the stories, though. Never mentions names or places. The stories wind out of her like soft paper-chains, as she deftly carries out her tasks.

'Oh, it's Lulu,' says Marte with pleasure. 'Now girlie – what about that boy – did he phone you?'

Lulu assumes a bashful face 'I'm not telling you.'

'That means he didn't,' says Marte crossly. 'Stupid fool, doesn't know what he's missing. You're too good for him that's all I can say – don't know why you can't find a husband darling – perhaps you should learn to drive...'

'I didn't say if he did or didn't,' says Lulu, teasing Marte gently 'and what would I do with a car?'

'You wouldn't have to walk about at night... it's not right, they should provide you with a car.'

'Yes Lulu!' I pick up the thread, 'with a little blue light on top and a siren...'

'Whoopee!' she says. 'Now then … hey what's this?' She looks at the glass.

'I'm allowed,' says Marte 'it's medicine. Now then – what happened to that old chap – you know, whose son was taking things from under his nose while he lay there blind…'

'Ah!' says Lulu, as she prepares the washing water, soap and towel. 'His sister came.'

'Whose?' asks Marte impatiently 'the old man has a sister?'

'Yes – just as old as him.'

'Twins? You didn't say he had a twin.'

'No – can't be twins – so let's say she's nearly as old as him.'

'Now look sweetheart, be exact, careless talk costs lives – if she's not a twin, she can't be less than nine months younger, see what I mean.'

'Yes you are right,' says Lulu, taking an old, dry hand in her own beautiful warm hand, and washing with care and attention. 'So let's say she is at least nine months younger than him and maybe a little more…'

'Okay, okay – so what happened – did she catch that young bugger?'

'Well put it this way…'

'Now look darling there's only one way to put it and that's the right way, which is exactly what happened. So exactly what happened?' says Marte in a pained and instructing voice, constantly losing her breath and having to finish a word on a minus quantity of air. Lulu looks unperturbed as she continues her task.

'Okay, so put it just like it happened,' says Lulu peacefully, 'the old lady…'

'Mind your manners,' says Marte. 'Nothing wrong with being old.'

'Well, the sister, she catches the boy, he thought she couldn't see properly either so he was careless and he was going through a file of papers which he shouldn't have and she caught him by his ear – can you imagine – and said hey what's this? This isn't your property nor will it ever be.'

Marte settles back into her chair with a look of pleasure.

'Now that's the kind of person I like. Straight talk.' She begins to cough again, looses her breath, 'Give me that nebuliser, it's time,' she splutters painfully, wheezing and choking, a desperate baby now, urgent and ratty. 'Get it quick Ellie, you know how.' The hissing mouthpiece is given to her and she subsides, sucking and panting. The three of us busy ourselves with different tasks. I wash up, Mel sorts through papers with important telephone numbers and writes these down in very large print. Lulu separates clean clothes from those to be washed.

'She's right, gorgeous', says Mel 'you shouldn't be walking late at night – especially in winter.'

'Don't listen to him,' says Marte, hardly coherent through the uproar of her pipe, 'he's a fox with a big tail.' I notice again how Mel flirts and yet – seemingly – without personal intention. He throws a warm salutation to women, but if there's then a response from them to bridle and become coy and make more, he's not there. He's wherever he is next. And yet the warmth remains, reaches its target. Lulu is gorgeous at that moment, and should be cherished and protected. That's what he does. He transmits small, immediate transient packets of cherishing. I look at him with pleasure. He pulls a face.

Lulu puts the nebuliser back on its tray. Marte looks drowsy. Lulu places the used nebuliser upside down in a cup. The ritual has to be done with precision. The used nebuliser is washed and dried with a tissue each day. There are always full ones waiting, just as there is always spare medication on the black table underneath the tray. The lower shelf under the black table is a medical corner. This corner was recently re-organised by Mel in consultation with Lulu. Lulu now plucks out a nitrazipam, a diazipam and two philacontin. Marte is about to receive her night-time cocktail. Lulu puts strong arms around her, Marte leans on her and on her stick, and the time-consuming walk to her bed begins. Marte's back is bowed, her head droops, her jaw tightens as she prepares for this daily ordeal – being transported to her bed, where she will be propped up diagonally on large pillows, waiting with hooded eyes and a panting chest for sleep to come. Which it does, but fitfully.

I feel a tension inside me as I will her journey to be as easy as possible.

'Wait wait wait', says Marte at the door, 'I can't breathe.'

'OK' says Lulu, unperturbed, 'no rush dear.'

We three are quiet and attentive, a Pieta in the kitchen, Lulu standing beside her, motionless, me at the sink, dish in hand, not moving, Mel at the correspondence, pausing. This is a moment where we all want to be casual, yet we are all breathing for her, with her, as her battered lungs show the effect of doomed pathways, dried out lung-twigs rather than oxygen-carrying, sap-delivering avenues. 'We go on now,' says Marte after a very long moment.

Mel pours out two glasses of brandy.

'Are you going to top up that bottle with water, Mel?'

'You kidding!' We sip at the liquid thoughtfully. 'Ell, what about Christmas – will you be here.'

'Hadn't thought – but yes, suppose so.' Mel looks at me narrowly.

'Well, it's no big deal for me, nor channukah for that matter – but I'll go back over new year to see the boy. She won't like that, but you guys will be here I suppose – anyway let's talk about Christmas. I'm getting in real deep here,' he murmurs, almost to himself, 'but you know once you say yes you can't back out and I've said yes…'

'We've all kind of said yes – in our different ways,' I say, 'maybe without really knowing what we're saying yes to.'

'It's going the road with her, isn't it?' says Mel. 'That's how I see it. She drives me bloody mad sometimes – she can be so bloody selfish and rude – but then –'

'Yes – but then – it's also that which keeps her going and keeps her on her own ground and in charge as far as she can be… hey Mel, how would any of us be so helpless and sore and scared I suppose. I'd be scared if I couldn't breathe. Must be like drowning.'

'Well, I've spoken to the girls – they're going home, but after Christmas when it's cheaper – and I spoke to Jinny and they'll be here with family visiting – haven't checked out the others – so I thought we could do something for her…'

'She usually says she's Scrooge at Christmas time – no tree, no fuss…'

'Yeah – she says – but we can do something else for her. Call it not Christmas. Ellie – she's not going to be here for next Christmas do you know that?'

'You sure?'

'Yes. I think the Doctor's pretty sure too. Well, as much as they ever say.'

'How long Mel?'

'Can't say – but we're skirting around something very delicate at the moment – she's driving me mad with her will…'

'Yes, she and I had just started on that when you came.'

'And connected to that is – put in very roundabout terms – please Mel don't let me suffer. When the time comes, help me on my way – if it's unbearable.' Mel looks at me candidly 'and I know she means if it's unbearable for us too.'

'How?'

'Medication.' There's a silence. Each of us in our own thoughts.

'Mel – I'll think on it – Christmas.'

'Yes – and talk to the others. The one above you, and the mother and son combination…'

'I'll be surprised if they want to come.'

'Yes you'll probably be surprised.' We smile at each other and I go back across the corridor. I get my coat and gloves, and head out into the early night. The air is cold, crisp and tight.

CHAPTER 21

How does Marte manage her helplessness, knowing that it is ongoing, knowing that it won't ease, that she won't recover and get stronger? I resent her frailty. Is this what the old teach the young – or those of us coming up behind, but still distanced by autonomy and activity? Is this why, as Mel said, we can't bear the old and the sick and the injured sometimes? They hold within them the present, unarguable fact that death lies in wait for all of us, and we don't know how or when. Is this why we love old people who are still fierce and creative and who seem to have a deep inner core of courage, of peace and resilience? Is this why we love the gurus, the teachers, who tell us how to transcend fear and pain and death?

I am beginning to understand Mel's insistence that we give her a good send-off. It's the least we can do – not just for Marte, but for the whole damn circumstance of fading, bleaching, draining, reducing. How can I participate with her as the passageway she treads becomes narrower and darker, as she has to cope with the reduction of her strength and bodily capacity? How can we all manage the horror, the anguish of this slow and visible extinction?

And these acts of support are rituals to mark that contrapuntal reality infusing the fragile physical frame… I find a necessity to kneel, to agree, to acquiesce with that which unfolds time after time through each human form… the arriving, the departure, and in-between the glorious melting of flesh joined to flesh, the joyous pleasure of dance and song and the ecstatic energy of life moving through the flesh; the horror of illness and death, of physical limitation, violence, grime and ugliness. Kneeling, I move within flesh into soul and spirit, so that the physical heart beat is also the beat of that other reality, the melting point where the horizontal meets the vertical and the mysterious conjunction of spirit and flesh is made new and renewed time and time again... I have a painful and yet touching sense of Marte's body – our body – shedding its substance and its energy slowly, becoming a husk, a dried leaf, dust unto dust, birthing itself out as it birthed itself in. I remember Guido lying as if in death, after we had made love.

CHAPTER 22

There is a meeting tonight in my flat. Mel and I have organised it, and, to my astonishment, everyone is coming. Every tenant in the house – except for Marte who knows nothing about it, and who is being put to bed by Lulu – has said yes. I make sure there is enough tea and milk, and buy cake and biscuits. Mel arrives with wine and bread and salmon and fruit and an absurd bottle dispensing alcoholic coffee and cream from two separate spouts. He and I move around, each preoccupied with private thoughts, setting out plates and glasses. I haven't had a group of people in my kitchen for some time.

A social event is coming into the cave, into the rich patina that seems in the last few months to have coated the space, to have thickened the air, taking the shape of that Invisibility into which I am being initiated.

Through all this time of living the agreement, through all the changing tides of desire and fear and delight, I am coming to inhabit a quiet constancy that has developed in my hermit's cave. I rise, and spend time connecting with myself, peeling off tendrils and trails of thoughts and feelings from the night just left, stretching my body, and sitting up in bed to feel the in-breath of a new day after the out-breath of the night: another day opens which will reveal whatever it intends to reveal. Some days I awake quite empty, some days I awake with an ache, and some days I awake in happiness with an immediate sense of willingness to participate in whatever the hours might bring.

I am becoming more aware of the restful aspect of this retreat: the five senses are quietened. There is less of the delicious tension of activity and being in the world, the humming and fluttering and entangling of the senses as they race to meet the outside. I'm still living under tension and demand, but it comes from a different place. I have noticed for some time that the ridiculing voice that plagued me in the beginning, that told me I was mad, is not quite so loud and persistent. It is still there, but not quite in the front row.

The five senses having quietened, my actions and my mind are slower than usual. Sometimes I feel no longer an important, busy or interesting person, and as if my life has reduced downwards, has become a wizened little thing, a plum denuded of juice, a flower faded.

Sometimes, in the light of the privation, degradation and horror that some people have to manage, I feel this process as a decadent piece of indulgence.

Sometimes I feel wild, horny, impatient, greedy, unused. Guido comes to mind, or to body, with shocking speed. I bend, like a willow, to the cut that comes with the memory of him.

Mostly, I feel under discipline and without choice about the way in which my life is proceeding. I am compelled onto a narrow path in a deserted region. I can turn around if I want to, and then I see in the distance, that which I have left behind for now, a wide colourful road, furnished with sign-posts, side roads, traffic and all manner of barrows and shacks serving food, drink, entertainment. I see a variety of vivid people wandering about arm in arm, beguiling each other with stories. My narrow road has few markings, sparse vegetation dots the dry sand of the landscape around me. I am a sober and willing pilgrim, treading this quiet way, a way revealing diamond clarity in the air I breathe daily. This is a consequence of the journey that has surprised me.

A bright and unusual, unexpected flowering cactus in this landscape is Mel. He makes himself at home now in my kitchen, not asking direction if he can't find anything, but pursuing the logic of domestic placement as he opens a cupboard or a drawer in search of cutlery and crockery. He asks if he can put on the radio. A slow evening melody fills the kitchen and Mel hums and whistles. I wonder what his wife is like, and imagine her as a slim and dark Israeli woman, beautiful as a pomegranate. An unbidden picture of his firm arms wrapped around her slim dark form comes to me. My face warms a little. I try to imagine myself leading Mel off into my bed, but this picture won't form. Sexuality lies between us, but it's like a little lane off the beaten track and we just don't go there.

'What are you thinking about Ell?' he asks, opening a bottle of red wine and pouring two glasses. 'You said you like red?'

'Yes – what was I thinking about? Red will do.' There's a knock on the door. Jinny's face peers around.

'It's just me – Greg will stay with the boys, I know it's only upstairs,' she says apologetically, her curtain-hair swinging around her face 'but…'

Mel picks up a third glass and asks Jinny to join us.

'Um. Well…'

'Come on darling, you're not driving home.'

Mel pours a full glass for her. Jinny's eyes wander to the food.

'Oh heck, I didn't bring anything – shall I nip upstairs – we've always got crisps and things, you know with boys…'

'No,' I say 'There's plenty – take a chair Jinny.' I want to smack her, swear at her, and tie her curtain-hair with thick swatches of string. There's a second knock on the door. Just as I go to answer it, I notice Jinny looking in shy confusion at Mel, and then obliquely at me as if to see what liaison there might be between us. Her eyes retreat rapidly downwards after this quick glance. Washed and brushed, clutching a bottle of wine, David stands in the doorway.

'Come in David! Nice to see you.'

'Hey!' Mel greets David and touches him on the shoulder in a friendly way; David smiles a little, releasing the tension in his face. 'Red wine?' David takes a glass and sits opposite Jinny. My wish to punish her has dissolved and now I want to shake David. An impatient, bitch element in me, newly arrived for the occasion, parallels the sound of the welcome I extend as people enter my territory.

'You two know each other of course?' I ask.

'Sort of,' they both say, and laugh uneasily. Sara and Merry arrive in jeans and sweaters and boots and Mel puts his arms around both of them and I see for real this time the sexiness of his broad arms on small female figures. The girls jostle with him, and declare with candour that they are starving. They scrutinise the food and Mel in equal measure. I give them plates and they slice bread and peel off salmon slices. The bitch wants to ask them if they want to slice pieces off Mel's ass as well.

'Wait! Wait!' says Mel, 'don't bite yet!'

'Why,' asks Sara, 'have you poisoned it?'

'No,' says Mel, 'You must have lemon juice – Ellie do you have a lemon, I don't want to go back next door, I'll never come out again.' I find a lemon, the girls spray their salmon sandwiches and bite into them. Edie and Max are the last to arrive.

'Oh, my – a party', Edie throws up her hands as she enters.

'You look gorgeous!' says Mel. Edie has a smart dress on and shiny, old-fashioned shoes which look perfect on her feet. She has pinned a large brooch to her lapel and I am touched by her appearance.

'Max, you old devil!' Mel pats Max on the shoulder male to male, but with quite a different tone and weight from that given to David. Max shifts his broad frame and looks around.

'Red or white?' asks Mel.

'Just as it comes,' says Max, eyeing the girls swiftly. I fill glasses and encourage people to replenish plates. My bitch element – energetic and exciting and unpleasant – retires to a corner of the room where she picks at her nails. I remind myself that this is Mel's ballgame. And Mel – for reasons of his own – coaxes a disparate group of people, through gesture and tone, into a team that is now gathered together for a purpose other than practicalities to do with the house.

'So what's up with Marte?' Max's voice is rough, as he sits next to his elegant mother who is sipping wine in steady and absorbed appreciation.

'Precisely,' says Mel, 'thanks Max for starting things off. There's nothing up with Marte so to speak, except that she's getting weaker and going down – more down than up, Max, more down than up.'

'Is she… is she getting worse?' asks Edie tremulously.

'Ellie – that's not the word, is it?' Mel looks across at me.

'Well, yes and no – ' I respond, 'she's getting weaker as Mel says – crosser sometimes, more fragile really.' Max scowls and I realise it's a sympathetic look. David looks at his shoes, and the girls murmur.

'So what's that got to do with us meeting, Mel?' asks Jinny.

'OK yes – let's get to the point.' Mel stands up. He has his re-filled glass in one hand. 'As I've probably told most of you, I've known Marte for many years – she was a mentor for me – not so much a mum, though she took that role in a way – but a guiding force. Shrewd she was, shrewd as a whip – and I started off as an informal apprentice to her in the murky world of antiques and second-hand furniture. This is when I was here – I dropped all that when I went to Israel.'

'Oh,' says 'Edie – we know someone in Israel, now who is it Max?'

'Dunno mum,' mumbles Max.

'Well, I've probably ferried them to and from the airport,' says Mel with dexterity. 'Anyway – when I saw Marte, I thought I'll help out here – I can't tell you the number of people Marte helped one way and another, and you never knew about it because she was always like this, sharpish you know, but that woman was – is – a samaritan – an anonymous samaritan. She helped me – but never let me feel she helped me.'

'So where do we come in Mel?' asks Merry.

'You in a hurry girl?' asks Mel wagging his finger at her 'I know – fun calling – I won't keep you long… so this is where you all come in.' We look at him. Mel looks at us.

'I've already chatted to you all separately about this, and that's why I assume you're here – what I want to do is make her feel good, as much as I can. And what makes a person feel good? Warmth, hey? Appreciation. Fun. So I thought for an old Jewish lady on her way out – a Christmas party where all the good folks of the house attend – the community of this establishment, our city kibbutz – and she is the fairy on the tree. And nice for all of us too. It took me to go to Israel to learn how shy we all are here of each other. There of course it can be too much the other way – who do you know? What do you do? And they're already looking in your fridge the first time they've stepped into your house. But here we all are, living together virtually – so what that there are different front doors once we're inside. We all go up the same steps and in through the same door don't we? We're all sheltered by the same roof, aren't we? So. Down to the practical. Will all you guys be here, before Christmas?' All nod. 'Well then – how about a few days before – we do something –'

After exchanges about everyone's arrangements and commitment and shopping, we choose the twenty second of December.

'But what shall we do?' asks Jinny. 'Shall we come to her place – I suppose that's easiest.'

'Hey,' says Merry, 'let's go away and think – we can meet again – you can meet at our place next time' Sara pinches her and hisses 'It's a mess, you cow…'

'Well, I already have an idea,' growls Max unexpectedly. Edie smiles, proudly. 'A stretch,' says Max. We look at him again. 'You know,' he says, 'one of those long cars, limousine it's called – we can all fit in – they drive you around London – the windows are black – there's a fridge, champagne, a driver – everyone thinks you're a pop star and stares and waves – lots of room, she'll be comfortable – don't know about her oxygen and all that though,' he concludes, looking suddenly crestfallen. Mel moves over to Max.

'Wonderful!' he says, 'what a brilliant idea. Make her feel like a famous actress – she was a great dresser in her day, a real show-off, loved flash and going out, theatre and all that… never complains she can't do it anymore – would we all fit Max? Oh – and she has a portable nebuliser – battery operated. And I'm sure we could get a small supply of oxygen so we don't have to take that tank on a wagon behind us.'

'Ah, so there's no problem.' Max is relieved, his chest expands with happiness. 'So that's okay, and, sure, we'll all fit – and if we each put in twenty quid or so, that covers the cost see?'

'I know where you hire them from,' says Mel, 'shall I enquire?'

'Leave that to me, son.' Max is grand, his chest barrels out towards the girls.

'Can we dress up?' Merry shoots a provocative look at Mel.

'Compulsory.'

'I think I know one of the guys – trade you know – see if I can get a deal.' Max is unstoppable.

'Do you think,' asks Jinny, 'do you think the boys could come?'

'Of course darling,' Mel turns towards her. 'The house is going. It's a house treat, a house party. For all of us.'

'I've never been in one of those,' David looks up with a smaller version of his previous half smile.

'And you're going to be the champagne wallah.' Mel casts a suggestive eye at David who responds by looking down at his shoes.

We agree that, unless Max can't get a stretch, and at a price we can collectively afford, we will meet in a week's time to plan further, at my flat again so that Mel is near to Marte, and that others will bring food and drinks.

'Cheers!' says Mel 'Thanks guys – you're wonderful. Thanks Max. And thanks Ell for your kitchen…' The girls break the party and race upstairs, having promised to collect Mel on their way out, Jinny gives me a kiss, Edie and Max gather themselves reluctantly and leave, talking to David about his latest students as they all head for the stairs.

'Didn't I see some Japanese coming in the other day?' asks Edie in her bright voice.

'I have pupils from all nationalities,' replies David solemnly.

'Oh,' Edie's voice trails away, 'you must be ever so clever.'

'Well – that's great,' Mel fills our glasses, from the obscene bottle this time.

'Mel – we'll have to tell her something. She'll get agitated if we just say there's a surprise and she has no clue – '

'You're right. What shall we say?'

'Let's keep it as near to the truth as possible – we've arranged for her to go for a drive with some of the house friends – to see the Christmas lights – something like that. And talk practical – neb and cushions and hot water bottle and not out for long and all that…'

'Yes. And not too far in advance. She'll start to think too much about it...' Mel flops onto a chair, gives me a quizzical look. 'How was it having so many folks in your aesthetic abode?'

I look at him evenly.

'Bearable. But then you did most of the work.'

'Part of my trade,' he said. 'Used to be. I used to arrange parties – events, you know. Jack of all trades, that's me. I'm a sentimental old fart, Ell – I love it when people are happy. I'm better with groups than one to one. And it's so fucking easy to make people happy. Like I said – bit of fun, warmth, solidarity. Talking of which,' he eyes me narrowly but not without friendliness 'why don't you come with me and the girlies tonight – we're going in about two hours. Marte gets furious, but then she managed without me all these years, a boy has to have his night out...'

'Not my thing Mel. I love dancing – but not smoky, boozy, druggy clubs full of people half my age...'

'Okay okay – ' A creased, sour thing flares between us. We shrug it away in small gestures of irritation. 'Hey... I can't wait to see her in that big disgusting looking car, can you? We'll have to get her to dress up. Can't you just hear her Ellie – what a waste of money, whose silly idea was this, you won't get me into one of those stupid things, take me home...'

'Yes! And the whole house will already be sitting meekly inside, bullied by you, their little faces lost in the darkness, David snogging with Jinny, a grim-looking man in a dark suit at the wheel, and loads of food for Jinny's kids, and a bottle of brandy for Marte stashed away in the glove box...' I send my discomfort into hard words like bullied and grim. Mel continues in an even tone, but something usually connected has temporarily broken between us.

'I saw a limo the other day, and a bloke was mooning out of one of the dark windows.'

'There won't be enough windows for all of us!'

'We'll have to take turns.'

'You're a Mary Poppins, Mel.' The disconnection mends itself and we exchange a look of affection.

'Yes – and now I must iron my black trousers.' There's a soft tap on the door, it opens and Lulu's magnificent fingers stretch around the handle.

'Mel – she wants to ask you something.'

'Sure – is she in bed?'

'Lulu – have a drink, something to eat before you go,' I offer. She looks longingly at the cake. 'Maybe a quick taste – I can't stay too long.'

'Lulu,' Mel calls from the door. 'Ask Ellie to tell you what we're plotting – you've got to come too. Our guest.'

Much later, I've washed up, and I'm sitting at my altar, remembering the bitch-element that arrived at the party. She faded pretty soon after everyone had settled down. I think about the sour moment between Mel and me and hear the front door open, and the clatter of Mel and the girls leaving for town. A swift pang grabs at my heart, the bitch flips back and bites my throat. I think back to the earlier image of the carnival road behind me, see myself flouncing around in a tight dress and dancing shoes. I look fine and dandy. The dancing figure fills the room, I like her a lot. I feel her sexuality, her daring, her mean streak, her hunger for the sharp tastes of the world. Not tonight, Josephine! I kiss the bitch smack full on her mouth, and continue to walk the quiet road, the solitary road.

CHAPTER 23

Doris, you've had children. Some women have children. I have holidays. I can't remember ever wanting to have children. I have dolls and teddy bears when I am little. I also have an atlas, a globe and my father's cast-off National Geographic magazines. The dolls and teddy bears live in a corner of my room, the atlas is on my desk. I collect pictures of Alaska, Hawaii, Nepal, Ghana – along with all places large and small, known and unknown, which grab my fancy. When hormones kick in, I invent a companion, a handsome photographer. I write articles, he takes the photographs. We travel everywhere, go through danger and delight. We are a sexy, accomplished team. My first boyfriend has a camera and I drag him off on trains and buses so that he can photograph places – any places. He has no interest in becoming a world-class travel-photographer, he just wants to get his hand up my skirt, or more likely, down my jeans, and so he agrees to the missions I suggest. We are both fourteen. His hand doesn't quite know what to do once it has found its way in the upward or downward direction, but, worse than that, he has no talent as a photographer. We part company after an argument about lighting and angles. I have no gift for photography myself – the technology bores me, and I don't have the eye for balancing light and shade, subject and background. I can see wonderful images in my head, but these don't show through the viewfinder.

When I first fall passionately in love – I am seventeen and he is nineteen – it doesn't matter at all that he knows nothing of photography, for he is quite beautiful. Representations of the world fade into physical immediacy, and furtive and glorious sexual episodes inflame me into protestations of love-forever, and constant lust lights my womb into a longing which wants to draw him into me and replicate him and me and fill me with all that he is, duplicating his mannerisms and his smell and the way he walks, so that these can multiply and I can be full of him, bursting with his seed and his imprint. This can only be accomplished, I think, by making a baby, and for a while we dice with nature, for this merging fires him too, but nature chooses not to duplicate another of her creatures and when he discovers that he can't bear my silences, and I discover that I can't bear the way he becomes drowsy and repetitive when he smokes dope, we quarrel and kiss desperately, knowing that we are being separated by growing points of alienation... and then we part. He finds someone else, and I go on my first major travelling expedition.

My first baby, in a way, for the planning and the anxiety and the waiting is like I imagine pregnancy to be – and the birth – into Italy – is just that, something new arriving which I can hold and love, and which changes me. The comparison is foolish, of course, and yet not, for also – I give birth to a new and different Ellie each time I travel. And travels are sometimes a nightmare of sleeplessness and discomfort.

Gerry is a comfortable and secure travelling companion. He takes excellent photographs – but my adolescent National Geographic fantasy is far from the reality of me – impatient, and trying not to show it - and him, painstakingly and efficiently catching a flower or a sunset or a goat silhouetted on a rock. Somehow, his eye and my eye catch different moments in time... so his image and my narrative never quite meet. This is perhaps the sadness of Gerry and me. In spite of all our other intimacies, through long and friendly knowledge of each other, we miss the intimacy of a certain and subtle kind of mutual seeing. Mutual seeing is like an aphrodisiac, it arouses a soul-lust – a kind of primal narcissism – a vivid mirror in the face of the one opposite – reflecting your joy. I've seen that impenetrable look between mother and baby, the one aspect of having a baby I could easily have relished. Yes, and the tactile experience of such newness and beauty, mother and infant, united by each others' beauty and smell and proximity.

Weaving in and out of men, sex, holidays, a tease sometimes, but present in the twist, in the warp and weft, is the thread of THAT, and seeing from aloneness; the defined, crystalline seeing which comes from silence, from stillness, from the deepest longing of all – to see Oneself. One Self. In such a place do the bones shine like ivory, buffed and polished, naked and transparent. And the marrow sings, for in the revelation of its essence nothing is left hidden, no shadow or separation.

Marte is a baby I visit in a country I learn about these days. I cross the hallway, and I am in the kingdom of Marte.

The meeting and the prospect of the outing have generated a different atmosphere in the house. The change is subtle, you can't put your finger on it, but instead of remaining protectively furled as we come in and out of the house and into our own spaces, we open slightly and sniff towards each other.

Today Marte's domain smells faintly of pee, and strongly of wood-soap. Mel discovered wood-soap, and wipes floors and surfaces when he remembers, or feels like it. He has fixed rattling windows by jamming card between the window and the frame, and there's beer in the fridge.

'He's out again,' she says grumpily, bowed over a cup of tea, poured shakily, no doubt, out of her thermos.

I put the kettle on to make one for myself.

'Come on – there was a time when he wasn't here at all.'

'Suppose so – but you get used to a person don't you? And then they're not there.'

We both contemplate this piece of information. 'And what about you?' she continues with a sharp look as she appraises me. 'You're on your own too much – what happened to that nice man?'

'Which particular one?'

'Oh they come and go don't they... everyone comes and goes. It's only fools like us who stay.' This kind of talk – querulous and needy – is unusual. Marte is normally pleased but pragmatic about giving and getting. Mel's constant presence is creating a dependency. This is a different kind of Marte. She is a little like a child who has been left while a diligent mother has, for once, gone shopping on her own. Something that Marte had up till now been managing for herself, has been transferred to Mel. I don't believe he is in the dirty side of the dependency game, manipulating to achieve power, and then playing with the one caught and thrashing on the end of the line... I believe Mel is careful each day to give what he wants to give, and to give consistently and reliably, and to be sure that he doesn't disappear into the darker realms of Marte's hunger.

I have heard him snapping humorously at her 'You're driving me mad!' and I have observed him drawing the line at times, saying no, and standing up for his separate existence. Marte now has a live-in companion willing to give her decent time and attention, a luxury she thought, perhaps, was no longer likely. Regularly her stoical self talks to me about 'the end,' and declares that she will die in her bed or in her chair, but at any rate it will be in her house, even if she barricades the door and starves herself to death. 'I am not going into one of those old grey day rooms in a third-rate old-age home where you see all those old heads lining the windows and nodding and waiting for food and nappies and wondering who will be the next one to disappear...'

I decide not to enter the querulous space. If it is urgent for her to dwell on it, she will lead me back. I'll try a diversion first and see if that's what is needed.

'I've been thinking about holidays, Marte.'

'So where are you going now, you gadabout? I know you're not going to that Italian anymore.' She gives me a sharp, loving, non-interfering look.

'No – I'm not going anywhere, I'm thinking about holidays I've had. You and Harry used to go to Ibiza didn't you?'

'Yes – it was still a simple place when we went – but we also went on cruises, did I ever tell you? Harry was such a gentleman, he loved dressing up for dinner and the captain's uniform and all the fuss, you know.'

'Did you dress up too?'

'Bring me my photos – they're in the bedroom in that box under the shoes inside the cupboard.'

Marte's clothes: She has jerseys with slightly puffed sleeves, several in rainbow colours. They are all good quality wool or cashmere, and although years old, they are well kept. Tweed suits hang on the hangers, and trousers that used to be known as slacks – well-cut, tailored trousers in dark colours, usually hanging with matching jackets. Marte is clearly much thinner now than she used to be. She was never overweight, but the clothes exude a sense of a substantial, well-proportioned woman. Burrowing under boxed pairs of shoes, I find photo albums.

'Which one shall I bring Marte?' She doesn't hear. I bring the box; it is heavy.

'Why do you bring the whole thing? It's heavy.'

'Don't know which one you want.' She ignores my response, and tells me to select an album three from the top. It has a lavish cover, slightly soiled by damp, and one photograph slips out from its pages. I pick it up and see a robust, gimlet-eyed Marte, her imperious beak proudly to the front, a cigarette firmly between her fingers, and the other hand around a plump and anxiously smiling woman, clearly older than Marte and with a mess of grey hair falling out of a bun. The plump woman is wearing a shapeless garment. Marte has on a smart skirt and shoes.

'Who's this?' I ask.

Marte squints at the photograph until she remembers her glasses, hanging round her neck today on a blue ribbon. 'Oh!' a fleeting version of that sweet smile I love seeing. 'That's my sister Maisele. She died a long time ago.'

'Is that the one who couldn't cook?'

'Oh she was hopeless – I don't know what it was, my mother taught us all. In fact we had to learn – we all had to cook when she was busy.' Mother supplemented the income with dressmaking, and helped women try on various outfits; she had to be there with pins and tape measure, for she altered clothes that didn't quite fit. Marte remembers being terrifed, as a child, that her mother would one day swallow all the pins she kept in her mouth while she sewed in the evenings, and that the pins would go into her stomach and puncture it and they would all have to watch her expiring like a broken, farting balloon. When she'd timidly voiced this fear, her mother had laughed at her and said 'so then don't talk to me when I'm working and my mouth can stay closed.'

'Maisele had a house in Golder's Green with that softie husband and that softie boy of hers' (I know this story, but enjoy the re-telling of it, so listen like a child knowing the next word and waiting for its emergence.) 'It was always a mess, especially the kitchen. Every Sunday Maisele would bake, even though the softies didn't like cake – funny, because the two of them were big sponges, or meringues that hadn't quite baked… Oh I am naughty… Anyway on Sunday the kitchen was chaos. Flour, raisins, baking powder, eggs – she couldn't break eggs separately so she'd break them straight into the mixture and bits of shell would go in and she'd fish around with a wooden spoon and never find all of them

– and afterwards, you'd always see us all chewing really carefully – you know, expecting at any moment that horrible taste of eggshell… And do you know what?'

'No, what?'

'She had a small window next to the cooker, and underneath that window, in the yard outside there was a dustbin and on Sunday the lid was off and do you know why?'

'No, why?'

'Because,' says Marte triumphantly, 'any cake that was ruined went straight out of the window and into the bin.'

'Did that happen often?'

'All the time, darling, all the time. One ruined cake after the other!' Marte shakes with glee. We both do. She wipes her eyes. 'And the other thing about Maisele – you can't see it on the photo – she had a terrible wart on her chin – you know what happens when you get old, no you're too young yet… anyway they start sprouting whiskers – they fall out of your pubic area and fly up to your chin – Lulu helps me with mine – on the chin that is… and she had spiky whiskers out of her wart and Justine when she was little refused to kiss her and used to scream when I said she had to. I can't mummy – it stings she used to say. And in front of poor Maisele. Don't think she really got it – she would fuss around and say what's the matter with her, upset stomach? Oh we were not nice to her when we were little, my other sisters and my brother – but what can you do – she seemed to ask for it. She made herself helpless and stupid.'

Marte is caught for a moment in a private trail of feelings – about Maisele, I suppose. Expressions of regret, then soreness pass over her face, followed by a re-shaping of the lips into some kind of resolution. 'Well it all can't be helped. It's all gone now.' I notice again that Marte generally seems to be the last remnant of any sort of family. 'Anyway', she says briskly, retrieving the line as she always does 'we were going to look at pictures of cruises weren't we, and my Harry, bless him.'

I put the heavy old album onto a cushion on her lap and she silently and thoughtfully goes through it, the pages making a stiff, cracking sound as her dry fingers, with flesh loose over old bones, clip the top of each page and then, with her expression and bowed but stately head suggestive of an important ritual, the page is slowly turned, to reveal the contents of the next.

'Right,' she beckons me to stand next to her. 'Now here's Harry – just a year before he died. I was only sixty-one when he died you know. A young widow. It was cruel. Some people hate each other and live together forever.' Her finger points towards a photograph of her gallant and kindly husband. A shiny, round face beams at us. Harry, almost bald, is wearing a neat and immaculate jacket, with a handkerchief tucked artfully in the upper pocket. He is resting one arm on the deck railing of a large ship.

'That ship was so huge – the Princess Georgina it was called. My, Ellie, they knew how to do things those days. You should have seen the way they presented the food.' Marte's voice is beginning to fade. Her breath is starting to labour. She coughs unpleasantly, her small frame juddering. 'Neb,' she chokes, 'it's time...' and I hand her one, plug it in, and the spluttering, wheezing and sucking begins. Her pigeon chest dilates and pouts. I move to take the album from her lap, but she pats her hand fiercely onto Harry, shaking her head. 'No, no', she bubbles, through the mouthpiece.

After she has sucked herself quiet, I settle onto the other chair and pick up the morning newspaper Mel has taken to buying. I read but without taking anything in, and put it down. Marte's eyes are closed, she is snoring slightly. I watch her frail, extended chest rising and falling, fluttering. I close my eyes and breathe with her. As my belly softens and I welcome the rhythm of diaphragm rising and falling the kitchen fills with breathing. We accompany each other, and the ghosts of her siblings stretch languidly along with us, in ancient companionship, the belligerence she has often talked about momentarily stilled.

Marte naps for about twenty minutes, and then opens her eyes, looking lost and a little confused.

'What is it? Is it late?'

'You slept about twenty minutes.'

'He's late isn't he? Wonder what he's up to?'

'Do you want to play rummy?' I ask her, moving towards the game that she keeps on her bookshelf. The numbers are on plastic squares and each player has a stand for them.

'Oh all right then – humour an old baby, distract me with a baby rusk.' We spread the squares over the table next to her, moving first a pile of paper and glasses and mugs from it. When we play, Marte places her squares slowly and somewhat shakily on her stand, and then cups them with her hand, peering at me suspiciously as if I were trying to see what she's got. 'Start first.'

I pick up thirteen squares and arrange them in their four colours on my stand. Marte's fingers have trouble with hers but I wait until she's done. The game proceeds, and Marte sniggers when she is doing well and swears and looks at me with hatred when she is not.

'I know what's missing,' she says, giving me a straight, disarming smile. 'And it's in that bottle over there.'

We continue, with brandy. I win two games and Marte sips from her glass, muttering that I have cheated. She wins the third, and suggests, since it's best out of three, that we play another round.

'Are you keeping score, Marte?'

'What do you mean – writing it down? Don't be daft, it's in my head.'

'Lucky old you – it's not in mine.'

'Because you don't know how to think in straight lines.' There's the sound of a key in the lock – and cold, late afternoon December air comes through with Mel, dressed in a dark coat, and looking a little tired.

'Oh there he is,' she says, not looking at him.

'Where?' Mel trawls his eyes around the room. 'Who are we looking at? The naughty boy who went out.' He bends down and takes her hand. Her face softens. 'I won't interrupt you girls – see you in a minute.' He has several parcels, and goes into his room.

'Wonder what he's bought,' Marte turns her head a little, looking through the door where Mel has gone. 'Something for that boy I bet – he loves him – it's sad he can't be with him. Still, what can you do…'

'Do you want to finish the second set?'

'Yes of course.' She catches me out with a joker still on my rack. She wins two, and I win one.

'OK – we're square.' She's satisfied, the glass is empty and she holds it out to be re-filled.

Mel returns and takes a beer from the fridge.

'What did you buy?'

'I went to that toyshop in Regents Street' he tells us 'what a nightmare. It's not the people – it's the things. Hundreds of different things.' Mel is less buoyant today. It's not just the tiredness. Something hurts in me when I think about him and his boy who'll be growing without him.

'Does he tell you what he wants, Mel?' I ask. 'There are new crazes all the time aren't there?'

'You're right – Jinny helps me there.' There's a silence. It's as if we are all caught in a sadness that has fallen between us. Marte's shawl subsides from her shoulders and Mel re-arranges it. 'But I also went to do other shopping – ' He brings over one of the carrier bags and hauls out a small and rich-looking cheesecake.

'Oh my,' Marte's eyes are gleeful, 'the very best!'

'After supper!' Mel puts on a stern parental face, and I see him with Marte and I see him with his boy. Mel is a hunting kind of a man, going out to forage and bringing back spoils to the homestead.

'That goes well with brandy,' says Marte with authority. 'And we'll use our party plates.' Is this time to tell her about Christmas? I look at Mel and guess he's thinking about the same thing. I shake my head slightly. It's too soon. The moment passes, the day dips into darkness. Lulu arrives and Marte's evening ritual begins.

I want to get back to my hermitage and sit before the altar and let the day's events crystallise and take their place in my soul, bright jewels of interaction, memory and ghosts, and a mosaic of flinty, sharp feelings and thoughts colliding with others more rounded and soft. I have learned through many times of meditation that this sorting will not happen wilfully or through my mind, but like in those kaleidoscopes we had as children, where multicoloured shapes twirled and whirled and descended finally into a distinct pattern.

'Ellie.' It's Mel. I stop, on my way out. 'Could I come over for a short while.' I look at Mel, at his tired face and the crumpled look around his eyes. I hesitate.

'Mel – in about an hour?'

'Sure' Is it my imagination, or does he seem a little put out?

CHAPTER 24

I settle in front of the altar, moving this way and that to find comfort for my back and my legs, remembering my walk yesterday to the cemetery of my childhood. The statue of Martha had been reported stolen, and I wanted to check this for myself. Yes – a mess of small greenish stones on the ground, a gap where Martha had been, a shadow of her shape silhouetted against the large stone she'd stood against, the beautiful form disappeared. A violation of Martha. I feel upset and angry. Who came for her, and where would they take her? Subdued, I ignore the beckoning angels guarding other graves, and walk back to Finchley Road. On the way, out of the corner of my eye, I think I see you, Doris, or someone who looks like you, walking in a slow and measured fashion.

I light the candle, breathe, follow the breath in and out, notice anxiety

about Mel, follow the feeling, take it deeper, let it move downwards, let it
settle. It's an anxiety about the unknown – what might Mel be bringing?
Is something wrong with his boy? Is he planning to leave Marte? I see
the fruitlessness of my mind, trying to control the situation by offering up
possibilities. I shift the emphasis from up to down, letting the out-breath
carry each sensation back into bedrock. It takes time. I breathe into the
anxiety and sense that it's not a state especially attached to Mel, it's an
un-named restlessness, prickling within me. I breathe in, as if opening
the top of my head, and wait for the entry and then the descent of a cool,
calming energy, descending through my body, doing its work without
my intervention. Arising now, comes a moment like a small fig, rich
and luscious with seeds, unopened, but bursting nonetheless. This is a
tiny sensation, a miniature fruit that explodes to feed me, detonating its
nourishment into capillaries and nodules and unknown corners. I have
no idea what's going on, but just keep relinquishing one moment into the
next. All too soon, there's a knock on the door.

'Mel.'

'You look as if you've just eaten something nice.'

'Figs.'

He grasps my wrist, he has a strong hand. 'Come on, fish face... one
for me.'

'Where did you learn to say fish face? My ma used to say that – it's a
South Africanism.'

'I've learned many things from many people.'

We sashay around each other, but then I get a glimpse of his eyes and
they are sore and tired. 'Mel. Let's sit down.' He collapses immediately
on the sofa. I sit next to him, a small space between us. We are silent. I
am aware of his man-smell, and of his man-clothes, the plain shirt and
jeans.

'Has something happened, Mel?'

'Not exactly.' The silence falls again. 'There's something I carry with
me,' he continues after a while. 'It's heavy, and I can't talk about it.
I know that's absurd – can I talk about something I can't talk about.
What I mean is... what I need is... I just need you to know that I carry a
burden. And it catches up with me sometimes.'

'Is it...' I begin.

'No – it's not to do with Marte, but she knows about it.' His voice is
not severe, but it carries an injunction, a request. This is the end of this
particular conversation, I can tell. We talk for a while of other things and
as the conversation weaves around aimlessly, I look at him and look at

me looking at him, and I think of sex but don't feel sexual and I think of intimacy and feel intimate but in an impersonal way. I embrace this man with my listening and through my willingness not to intrude upon him. It is a new experience for me, to pay full attention and yet to leave someone alone. It is odd, and I feel partially that something is missing. Where is the hot part of me that wants to seduce? Where is the greedy part of me that wants to have and eat? Where is the push-pull and the to-ing and fro-ing of normal human interaction? In some ways I miss the excitement and tension of will he won't he/ can I can't I… in other ways I am enchanted by the peace of it all. At the end of this retreat I can go back to the heat and the play. If I want to.

I have become a little lost in my thoughts and miss Mel's words.

'What did you say Mel? I wasn't listening.'

'Ah, just that I'll be happy to see my boy after Christmas.'

'You always light up when you talk about him.'

'Is it that noticeable? I worry too about him being in Israel… the school-bus, the shopping centre… Ellie what pain is it that drives people to explode themselves and carry others into oblivion with them? I spoke to a Palestinian father once who told me that the land was more important than its children, and that he would be proud if his son was a terrorist. No, he didn't say terrorist – he said freedom fighter.'

Mel turns squarely towards me. 'Sometimes I think there is no solution – that things will escalate to a terrible point… loss, loss and more loss. Each family scarred and vengeful. I couldn't imagine sacrificing my son for land…' Mel has returned to this theme. I am uncomfortable on the ground we tread, suddenly. We are not talking abstractly. His son lives in Israel. We seem to be stepping around holes and hell-holes and carrion and hatred. And fear and shame. I touch into the collective and feel, in the pit of my stomach, Jewish identity. I think of my father's mild epithet 'Don't look for trouble' and yet there seems always to be trouble.

Mel turns towards me again. 'Do you feel identified as Jewish?'

I dig at him with my elbow. I want to tell him that I am experimenting at present with not having an identity, no affiliation but to silence, to THAT and to wherever the silent process wants to take me, to a place where there is no separation. I notice the veins in his forearm, the tight quality of his muscular leg stretched out in front of him. Stocky, muscular men look good in jeans. We sit in a silence that is packed full. The noise of the traffic comes and goes. Mel's breathing is slow and rhythmic. Wholly unexpected, a tear wanders down my cheek, and another.

'Hey,' says Mel, 'what's up? Did this talk upset you?'

'Yes – it's all right. I'm surprised.' I cry, and he puts his arm around my shoulder. 'Hey fish-face, Jewish folk aren't the only troubled ones… don't take it on, hey?'

'Mel, I haven't a clue why I'm crying.' I wipe my nose with my fingers.

'Here take my sleeve,' he offers, and then gets up, looking for a tissue. I blow my nose and snuffle a little, feeling like a child, a sweet feeling but also uneasy. I want him to go.

'I'm all right now Mel. Let's talk of something else. Shoes and ships and sealing wax, cabbages and…'

'Practical matters Ellie – the others are bringing food for the next meeting aren't they?'

'Yes –'

'You're a sweetheart,' Mel looks at me amiably and with an expression that shows he too has had enough and wants to go now. Whatever it was that happened in our initial brief, elliptical conversation seems to have quietened something in him. I can feel an excitable energy rushing off the front of me… tears and drama and need.

'Are you all right, Ell?'

'Yes – are you?'

'Yes. See you.' The door closes, I hear Marte's door opening. I think about being Jewish. Thorn in the flesh, thorn in the side. A valiant, nomadic, juicy, troubled, volatile people, of which I am one – tied by blood. Blood tie: a knot between me and my mother and father and their mothers and fathers. A coded double helix that seems to encode also character, attitude, history. Or – is that sequence of identification immediately conferred at birth and then reinforced within the living crucible of habits, ritual and conversation? If I had been left – a Jewish baby – to be brought up in a Palestinian refugee camp, not knowing as I grew, that I was Jewish, who then would I be? How do we manipulate blood-consciousness, and how is it unassailably itself? As these questions rise within, I feel like a rabbi with the Torah spread before me, debating this way and that. Thoughts flutter within me, like blind moths battering their soft bodies on the outside of a lighted window. I feel my heart in the place of light, in peace and acceptance; I feel my thought-moths swerving and colliding inside their own complex, miraculous and restrictive order; and outside and inside of this order, the light, the presence, illuminating everything.

I light a candle again, to continue the longing towards silence, which was interrupted by Mel with his mystery and our tribal talk. As I sit and yearn towards quietness, I continue to cry, and tears drop down slowly, taking me into a well of unknowing. I cannot rescue myself. The well is a watery place in which I repose, until the world pulls me to my feet once more with another knock on the door. Joss, looking very small and splinter-like, is standing there. As she comes in, she barely looks at me, and there is none of the usual ribald sniffing and poking which goes on when we meet.

'Tea or coffee, Joss?' A small sound comes from her. I go to her, we sit together and I put my arm around her.

'I've had enough,' she says eventually

'What's happened?'

'Nothing special – the usual – fun and games and fights and sex – nothing different. I'm worn out Ellie.'

'Are you ill?'

'No – I'm not ill, I'm sick – sick of myself, if you must know.' I don't know what to say. What can I say? I stroke her thin hand.

'What can I do for you Joss?'

'Nothing – ' A small sigh comes from her. It touches me and I want to wrap her in white cotton sheets, and a white cotton blanket, and lay her down on rush matting, and light a candle nearby and let her rest. 'Darling – when you were with Gerry, and with Guido, did it kill you that they weren't always what you wanted... you know...'

'Yes of course! Their bloody fault, hey!... and I hated it that I was probably just as disappointing at times for them. Yeah, it was sore. Both times.'

'Jack is gorgeous as you know. But – isn't it terrible how we always say BUT about someone, and they probably say BUT about us? Anyway – well, he's sharp-edged, you know, and that's sexy and alive but sometimes I'd just like something a bit more comfortable...'

'Aren't you comfortable sometimes with him?'

'Yeah – odd times – but not as a continuing thing, you know. Not as something I can rest in.' She sighs, and her skinny frame trembles. 'Fuck it, Ellie, I hate being unhappy. The gods have worked it out all wrong you know. We shouldn't have to struggle so much. It's not character making, it's character breaking.' I pick at a piece of loose thread on her sleeve. She's wearing a striped jersey in bright colours, and tight black trousers. Her dainty red boots, flung off as she came in, lie beside the door. 'Don't want to keep you from anything.' She looks at me for the first time since she's come in and her eyes narrow. 'Hey babe – have you been crying?'

'A little.'

'What's it?' she asks as she moves herself upwards and looks pointedly at me.

'Bit like you – kind of nothing and everything.'

'Was just going to say to you that you need a man... then I realised how absurd it would be under the circumstances to suggest that. Sorry darling, I just arrived here and dumped on you...'

'It's okay, Joss – just more of the same.' She settles back down again.

'Oh well, in that case where were we?' I lay my head against hers and feel the strong, coiled springs of her black hair pushing against my cheek.

'The weak holding up the weak.'

'Fuck it,' says Joss again, and we slump together until it's uncomfortable, and then Joss moves away and starts to roam around looking for alcohol.

'There's a little bit of that chocolate and cream stuff.'

'God Ellie – your taste is descending to the lowest of low. But I might just swallow my pride and have some.' She pours two glasses and we sip together. 'Yuk!' she snorts through a creamy moustache. 'I might even have some more just to punish myself.' My eyes are beginning to close. Joss decides to stay, and we sort out the spare bed. I wrap her in sheets and cover, and then fall into my own bed. I am tired, tired but sleep won't come. In the morning, Joss, renewed, is standing over me with a sweet expression on her face and a cup of tea in her hand.

'You look like a baby when you sleep.'

'You're up early.'

'Have to go – working today.' Joss looks after a small art gallery for the owner when he is away. She moves towards the door and then comes back. 'By the way – talking of men, what about you and that dish next door.'

'What about me and that dish...'

'Have you...?'

'No.'

'Don't you want to?'

'Joss – darling – it's not that simple.'

'It's always that simple,' she says nimbly as she closes the door.

Evening, and the dish is laying out dishes for the second house meeting. Mel says nothing about our conversation of the night before. He'd be a plain, square dish, I decide, with a surprising swirl of a signature in delft blue on the other side. Jinny brings a plate of sandwiches, the Australian girls bring beer and wine, Edie carries in two cakes, Max adds to the beer supply and David presents cherry liqueur chocolates, the sort with the stem still attached through the paper. There's more ease this time, quite a babble as I pour tea and find glasses for the beer.

Max can't wait to tell us that he has hired the car and that he bargained a special price. Mel tells us that Marte's has a battery-operated nebuliser, and that he will get hold of a smaller bottle of oxygen so that we don't have to disturb the heavy canister. David has already bought two bottles of champagne – and should he buy brandy for Marte? I offer to get her favourite items; the inevitable cheesecake, and smoked salmon sandwiches, and the girls will organise plates and napkins. Jinny wonders what she might do…

'OK,' says Mel, 'I think we have enough food and drink but why don't you be responsible for making a gorgeous comfortable seat for Marte. We'll bring her down in the wheelchair and somehow get her in – and you could have cushions and a rug.'

'Oh yes!' Jinny is delighted. 'Yes I know just what to do.'

'I…' says Edie slowly and loudly, 'will bring crackers and paper hats.' There's a silence after this announcement and then we all applaud. Edie, dressed smartly, in a different outfit from the one she wore at the first meeting, nods her head to each one of us.

Jinny is thoughtful. 'Well, the boys will be there. Would anyone else might want orange juice or coke…?' She looks around enquiringly and we all nod agreement. It feels almost too agreeable until a small sound of dissent creeps in. David is airing a grievance about the dustbins and how people put small pieces of rubbish into them not properly secured in rubbish bags, so that there's always sodden detritus swimming around the bottom and he's the one to fish them out and…

'I do my fair share of fishing,' says Edie loudly. 'And I throw in that dustbin cleaning powder sometimes for good luck.'

'She's a camp old trout,' I hear one of the Australian girls whisper to the other.

'I heard that!' says Edie loudly, 'I wasn't fishing for trout – but for rubbish – small bits like David said – which some people… just drop in.'

'Could be people walking by – not us,' says Max anxiously, peering at his mother

'They'd have to have long arms to reach around the hedge,' snorts Edie. Jinny rolls her eyes.

'Jinny, I'd love to cover you in glitter and put a pineapple on your head.' Mel (the dish) throws in a distraction.

'Why are you talking about pineapples?' asks Edie

'Do you remember Carmen Miranda?' Mel rolls his hips and clicks his fingers. 'Have you got a pineapple Ell?'

'No – how about a lemon?'

'Won't do – anyway, David's right – why don't we just put in a large bin-liner… each week. Any of us can be responsible for putting them in the bins.' David and Edie look slightly disappointed at this resolution. The dissenting fun is over. I wonder why Mel needed to resolve this small flutter… he doesn't strike me as being afraid of conflict. And although he is willing to take the lead, I don't see him as controlling.

Mel and I decide to tell Marte a week before the event – and we all agree to meet at the door at 7 on the night. Marte will be brought out after we have all taken our positions in the car.

'Now remember – dress for the occasion,' says Edie as she departs, with Max. 'Our generation likes an occasion…'

The girls invite us all to come upstairs and watch their new DVD system. They have hired a horror film about ancient Egypt. David declines, Jinny heads back to her family, I too decline the offer and Mel takes the remaining beers and wine and goes upstairs with them, promising that he'll spend an hour with Marte first and that they're to start anyway if he's late.

CHAPTER 25

These days towards Christmas roll by fast in damp dark hours, and I am free of shopping and cards and arrangements. I walk, after my early morning practice, observe the happenings in myself and spend time with Marte. Mel seems to be on an extended bender – he is red-eyed and either very wide-awake or very sleepy. He seems at the same time to be managing the usual routine with Marte, and he and I are making wider circles around each other. It feels as if the intimacy that opened up through talking was too much for both of us, and we are stepping back a little. The upstairs girls have extended their party calendar to Mel, and the front door opens and closes at odd hours as the three come in and out.

Christmas, and I feel the paradox: I am excluded but of my own volition, and I can feel left out and I feel not at all left out for I am so inward into a deep current.

I have been meditating upon the phrase: 'Be still, and know that I am God.' It's not 'Be still and know God.' 'That I am' creates the necessary distance and humility and unknowing. We cannot move any nearer.

These winter days I cannot deal with the idea of God, I don't have the vessel to carry that kind of fire, that atomic blast, even of the word, or the idea. When I look at a photograph of the Indian saint, Ramana Maharshi, he of the radiant eyes, I imagine that to have been in his presence would have been to experience extraordinary beauty and love, and also to experience being burnt, exposed so that all places where there was lack of integrity, lack of integration, would crack and burst. To know God, I imagine in my little brain, my seeking consciousness, my hungry soul – would be to be consumed, to be annihilated, to be blasted out of any identity, to be no more anything but God... the Unknowable. And I know my use of the word THAT is not a synonym for God, but a description of the reflection, the refraction, the Light within a prism, within a diamond, the Light beside a shadow, the light of the moon from the sun... We know of God through manifestation, and feed from the light of God through the mighty beings who reside amongst us, through unseen angels, and those who have passed on and those who are alongside us seen...those who vibrate to a different order of music, who shine and radiate love and wisdom, who carry mercy towards us that we might learn of mercy, emissaries of the Holy One so that we might remember we are accompanied through this journey, this dwelling and living on a pinhead, on a narrow bridge like a hairpin across an unknown chasm. I am grateful for a shaft of light across the bedroom wall in the morning, for a passing pair of eyes, clear and light, for music, for a joke well told, for a baby, for the hieroglyph seen when an apple is split in half... When I use the word God, when I have used the word God, it is more to describe the sense of that which is allowed to us, that which has descended, or the echo of that which can be present.

Be still and know That: the myriad and countless dots of light implicit in the whole creation; the holes and the darkness and the terror, the winding and re-winding of chronological time through timelessness.

What is it that is handed to us, or carried within us, at the time of birth? What is our entitlement?

When I pray, and am able at times to use the word Lord, or God,

these words move through the veils and shimmering stuff of the hidden.
These words carry longing and love and faith, and ride for me into the
unknown; children looking for a hand in the darkness, running through
the rooms, the corridors.

My long evening walks past windows lit with Christmas trees carry
these meditations, as do times of sitting. The inner current takes so much
juice, it is hard to be present on the outside. I am careful about holding
this current to one side when I am with Marte. She is ultra-sensitive at
the moment, struggling with demons of helplessness and jealousy.

Marte is not happy with Mel's comings and goings. She is sharp about
his bedraggled face, and then has a sorry look and after that a stubborn
look. She wants to make him responsible for her unease, but she knows
well enough this is a fruitless path. I watch her dragging bad feeling back
into herself. We talk a little about it. It is quite clear to her that she is not
abandoned, that he has not withdrawn care. She is however, not the only
focus, these days of pre-Christmas frenzy. The greedy and scared parts
of her are furious and agonised at his betrayal. I see those parts in myself
too, when Mel fastens his energies to the party-girls, and romps out with
them. Most times, when this fear arises in me, I have to face a belittling
identity I want to give myself – that of an aging, boring woman. I watch
myself choosing to let this be true, and then I watch horror settling upon
me. Alternatively, when I consciously choose a different attunement, I
watch myself gentling the child who feels left out, and then I see – if the
touch has been true – a settling and an agreement that, underneath the
hollow and fear-inducing description, all is quietly well, and that I have
chosen to be quiet and that I will support myself in this choice.

'Christmas time,' Mel says to Marte firmly, holding her hand, 'I am
going to party like everyone else – except our nun over here,' pointing
at me. 'I'm still here for you darling – so, no long face hey?'

'What's with Christmas? You're not Christian.'

Mel doesn't pick up the bait. 'If I could take you clubbing I would
– and if you weren't so cross I'd tell you the funny things I've been
seeing.'

'Don't want to know – and those two are young enough to be your
… sisters.' I half-expect Mel to over-compensate for Marte's distress, by
bringing back extra goodies or making other concessions, but he doesn't.
It is quite hard to be together with the two of them at the moment. Don't
know what to do anyhow, except maintain my own rhythm with Marte.
Mel looks depleted but also satisfied, in a smoky private world of his

own. He hums and closes his eyes, and drops little items of information my way about extravagant moments with strangers, men and women, music to die for, and the fun of hours of dancing his tits off, as he puts it. I feel disconnected from him, we are in different worlds, but the deeper empathy is not broken. In his own way, he is re-charging his batteries by exhausting himself. He is running on his own current.

The days are drawing in, getting colder. There are times when I feel as if the whole world is shopping, phoning home and planning menus, and I am as small as an ant. Sometimes I weep with loneliness - other times I am still, and wanting for nothing; the restrictive carapace of my habitual identity incrementally loosening its tight hold, the breath of life moving in and out more freely. During moments of freedom that come upon me in their own time – everything that I see is vivid and full of its essence: a cat on a roof, water running down a road, an old woman sitting on a bus. When I am in this place of no preference, there is no argument, it is as it is, and I am grateful for it to the edge of every cell in my skin.

When I grew up as a Jewish girl in a loose-knit Jewish community, we didn't say Christ – this word, this god made flesh, was not in our idiom. Our messiah was yet to come.

When I am young, I feel guilty… and confused, because I am – by birth identity – implicated in my ancestors' actions. 'And anyway', my school friends say 'Jesus was a Jew.' I am never sure how that resolves anything. It is often the last phrase of an uncomfortable and belligerent argument about the role of Jews in history and in the present, the ancient nature of anti-semitism, and general distress and paranoia about who did what to whom and why.

Sustaining me, somewhat, during these times, is King David. I fall in love with him because he is alive and demanding and vigorous and lusts after Bathsheba and then has a difficult time with God…

Psalm 22: 'My God, my God, why hast thou forsaken me? why art thou so far from helping me, and from the words of my roaring?… I am poured out like water, and all my bones are out of joint; my heart is like wax; it is melted in the midst of my bowels.'

David threw words like molten stones at his God. His psalms are love letters, arguments, reproaches and desperate pleas for help. As a young girl, I pretend that I know him, and I sit, quietly next to a warm, wild rock while he writes and curses and sings and cries. I know the beginnings of a sexual love for David. My David has dark brown skin, thick dark brown curly hair, and a wiry torso. The Hebrew words, running out on the resonance of his voice, amplify further on the strings of his harp. Among quietly grazing sheep I sit, baking on the hot ground, not moving a muscle; he knows I am there and looks at me, but we never touch or speak.

These days, after the times of seeking, and now in the time of pilgrimage, Jesus is the one I reach back to through the decades and centuries. Jesus, also, is sinewy and dark. In my imagination he has a beard, whereas David is clean-shaven. Both men have courage and fire but Jesus is softer, reaching more out of himself to the world. Inside the noise and babble of Christmas, is a story of regeneration.

Marte's Justine is coming for some days to see her mother and visit other friends. Marte, sour and miserable, begs me to be with them on Christmas day – they are going to a restaurant, already booked. Marte is anxious about being out, though the restaurant is known to her, and around the corner. I know the anxiety is also about being with her daughter.

CHAPTER 26

Doris, the stretched white car is at the door. It is too long to fit into even the largest parking space, is spotlessly clean, and has dark windows. The driver, taciturn and block-faced, stands to attention in a neat suit. Neighbours peer and wonder. Mel brings Marte out in her chair. She is protesting, and continues to spit and splutter until she is installed in the car, on the throne which Jinny has prepared for her. Inside the car, arranged around the fridge and upon the long white seats, peering out shyly through the gloom, are the inhabitants of our house. I repress a terrible, explosive giggle that wants to erupt – partly embarrassment and nervousness as well as pure delight at the sight of all of us encased in this monster. Mel catches sight of the slight tremor of my shoulders and shoots me a look that suggests that he too is nervous and about to explode. Marte has no restrictions about what she might say or do.

'What are all these balloons for?' she barks. 'This isn't a children's party...' Edie tightens her red lips just a fraction.

'Edie brought them, Marte,' says Mel, closing the door. 'This is your treat – this is for you, Marte. I know you're not sure about it yet – give us the benefit of the doubt.' He strokes her agitated arm gently, his eyes soft. 'It's an outing and we are all here to travel with you.'

'Where the hell are we going? Why doesn't anyone tell me anything these days?' The driver, having already been instructed to take us on a classic tourist route through London, has slipped into his seat, and, like a dark mountain, sealed off in the front section, starts the car, which rumbles and vibrates.

'We're just staying in the car,' says Jinny, leaning forward, and at the same time shushing the boys who want to investigate all the facilities of this remarkable limousine, whose fitments look at first glance grand, but at second glance, is seen to be meanly furnished with pseudo-leather white seats, cheap red carpet and only a small set of loudspeakers.

'We're going on a tour,' says Edie loudly, her lips forced apart by the will to speak. 'We won't be long and we have everything in the car you need.'

'How do you know what I need? I need to be at home, that's what I need, what about...'

'Marte,' says Mel softly, 'like I promised you, we have your travelling neb, we have oxygen', he holds up the two slim plastic tubes and inserts them gently beneath Marte's nostrils. 'We also,' he continues 'have champagne and brandy... only the best, for you.'

Max is sitting like a stone next to Edie, Sara and Merry float within a cloud of perfume, Greg – not usually present – has the boys pinned down, one under each arm, Jinny's hair has closed around her face, David is setting out glasses on the small table next to the fridge. I am impressed by his imperturbable air in the middle of this rather awful beginning, and start to unpack the food. I see the anxiety behind the fuss in Marte's eyes. Her little flat, her chair, her bed are safety – all else is risk of panic and discomfort. In a moment of regret, I feel we have kidnapped her and are forcing her into a good time that isn't at all a good time.

Mel is setting the neb in order next to her, he has arranged her favourite blanket and her two essential handbags and her box of tissues. Whenever she's out in the wheelchair she always takes two handbags. Each has a five-pound note tucked into its small pocket. One contains house-keys and a neatly ironed linen handkerchief, and the other contains sucking sweets and paracetamol. I have never been able to fathom why Marte needs to take two handbags on every outing, but any discussion to rationalise the system provokes such anger and distress that it is clearly best to leave things as she wants. Regrettably Lulu is not with us for I think her presence would have been another stabilising factor. Tentative movement starts in all corners of the car, as everyone reaches for the food. And then Edie presents crackers as if they are gold-plated. At the same time, a sepulchral, accented voice issues from the ceiling.

'Do you vant music?'

Mel leans forward and speaks through a microphone in the sheet of glass between us and the driving mountain. 'Got any trad jazz?'

'Glen Miller?'

'Let's have it.' A muffled sound of trumpet and sax introduces a strange, tinny sense of jollity into the vehicle.

The girls are moving their shoulders and shrieking that people are staring at us and that everyone thinks we're famous and isn't it absolutely gorgeous. David snaps open a bottle of champagne and it bubbles and streams onto the carpet. Jinny leaps up from behind her curtain, and grabs glasses to catch the overflow. I steal a look at Marte. She is holding Mel's hand, and there is an expression of softness and embarrassment in her eyes.

'Did you really arrange this for me?'

'Yes.'

'I don't understand why.'

'Because we love you,' says Mel simply. By now we all have champagne, the children have coke, the car is rolling down the Edgeware road, past cafes and ornate furniture shops, and we drink a toast to Marte.

'But why...' she starts. And then takes a sip of champagne. One of Edie's balloons, a bright yellow one shaped like a phallus, pops. Marte shrieks, then looks out of the window and says, 'My God Marble Arch! I haven't been here for years... look how many people there are!'

'What about the Christmas lights, dear,' says Edie smugly as though she has invented them

'What a waste of electricity,' says Marte sharply. 'Could have hung up something just as nice without all this fuss.' However, her eyes are glistening, and we all sit back in our seats, except the boys who have discovered that the roof opens slightly, and they have stuck their heads into the cold night air, whooping and calling until Jinny pulls them down. Greg is quiet. Jinny feeds the boys as if they were fledglings, dropping titbits straight into their open beaks. Sara and Merry chew one nut to every glass of champagne and David, in a dark suit with a striped tie, is becoming more and more affable as the bottle empties. Max is puce-faced and beaming, Edie, in an elaborate two-piece outfit with a velvet collar and a small corsage of artificial roses, sips slowly and chews a crumb at a time from her sandwich. I'm thinking back to times in childhood when adults forced children to have a good time on their terms.

'This is the life!" Max is expansive and benevolent in all directions.

'Next thing we'll be on a cruise,' says Edie happily. Max contracts slightly.

'Now cruises!' says Marte. 'I can tell you about cruises.'

'Hey!' Mel peers through the window. 'Embankment.'

'Now I've always loved the river,' Marte has a full glance of champagne next to her, and a half glass of brandy. She is wearing a red woollen suit that took ages to choose. Her white hair is standing up in little spikes, and her breathing is rapid and shallow and hurtful to hear and I want to put my hand into her bubbly chest, like a healer from the Philipines, and draw out all the phlegm and rotten tubes. 'Look at the ship,' Marte commands. 'Now that I never saw before.'

'It's a restaurant,' Mel informs her.

'How do you know?' One of those sharp looks in his direction. 'When were you there, gadding about?'

I withdraw my attention from Marte, to gaze out of the window of the gently cruising car, and to see the delight of London spread out before us. Illuminated bridges span the river, and many people, dressed in coats and scarves and hats, move around the metropolis, on this dark and cold night. The atmosphere in the car is warm and friendly; we are on our third bottle of champagne and bubbles and fizz have united us all in bonhomie and chat. The girls have taken to unwinding the window every now and then and blowing kisses to passing men. The small boys are shouting at people who don't take any notice of the grand car. Empty paper plates and crushed serviettes pile up on the little table and Marte has ordered that we unfold the crackers quietly rather than pull them. Lopsided paper hats sit on David and Greg's heads. Marte wears a green crown for a while and then – while she nods off for a couple of minute – it floats from her white head and lands on a damp corner of the carpet.

The driver brings us to Leicester Square, and Merry and Sara wake up from a dreamy state and demand that we stop outside Planet Hollywood. 'Photo!' demands Sara, and brings out her camera. We stop, the driver comes to our door and opens it as if inviting precious cargo to dismount. Edie comes out, closely followed by a blushing Max. People have gathered to stare, and some are looking puzzled, frowning intensely at Edie as though she ought to be recognised. The girls climb out, and their long, naked legs and short skirts cause one or two comments from the audience, now beginning to look more interested. Jinny comes out with the boys and Greg, interest flags, David emerges, unwillingly, pushed by Mel, and then Mel and I support Marte so that she can lean from the car-door. The driver offers to take the photograph and we all hang around the door, to the cheers and boos of a desultory small crowd, as several flashlights go off in our faces. The girls, looking somewhat shamefaced, declare that their ride is over, and they will stay in town. Kisses all round as they depart and we watch them disappear. Marte is brought back to her throne, and we continue our ride.

Marte's bony nose is beginning to jut more strongly from her face, usually a sign of tiredness. She is laughing about being a celebrity at last when the coughing begins and she cannot catch her breath. I rub her back, her shoulders have shot up like two door knobs under the woollen jacket. The stress is intense and we can't release her from it. The others become silent and then falsely talk to each other again.

'Mel,' Marte whispers hoarsely. 'Neb.' She is beginning to look strained, and I wonder whether we shouldn't cut the trip short and head home. She fastens onto the nebuliser and sucks, head down, and withdrawing from the rest of us. We look away and out of the windows to give her privacy, and Greg and Jimmy curl around their mother and for a mad moment I think she's going to start breast-feeding them, urged on by the suckling noises coming from Marte. Greg has his arm around Jinny, Max and Edie sit side by side with a gap between them, looking out of different windows, David is beginning to tidy up, putting paper plates into a plastic bag.

'Should we take a slow ride home now?' I suggest. All agree. Marte nods over her neb, her eyes are closing, her jaunty red suit looks brave, like a flag after battle. Her chest wheezes and rolls, accompanied by sounds from a different tape chosen by the driver, undistinguished muzak that actually feels appropriate. We pass through the hectic streets of central London and head off to the north-west via Regent's Park.

'Regent's Park, Marte,' I tell her, but she is asleep.

At the door to the house, Mel gets out first and fetches the wheelchair. Marte wakes up slightly like a child in the backseat when the holiday car has arrived home in the middle of the night. She looks tousled and a little bewildered. Somehow, she collects herself and, in a soft voice, thanks us all. She holds my hand and Mel's hand, and squeezes our fingers. Her mouth is trembling. We wait, thinking she might want to say something more, but she shakes her head, looking downwards.

Tears collect under her eyelids and roll down into her smart, white blouse. Mel gives her a kiss and together we lift her into the chair and wheel her into the house. Max sorts out the driver, and David brings in two unopened champagne bottles and gives the brandy bottle to Marte. It sits on her lap next to the two handbags and the box of tissues and the special blanket. The little boys make tired, whiny noises as they stumble upstairs. Jinny and Greg hold hands and say goodnight to Marte. Mel and I manage to get Marte into her nightgown and bed-jacket. We plump up her cushions and sit her almost upright for her night's sleep. Mel finds the medication, adjusts her back to the regular oxygen supply, and we say good night.

I give Mel a hug at the door. Back in my own flat, I light a candle and smile at the wonderful, strained ridiculousness of the evening, and I soften for my aged friend, sleeping now, or maybe still awake, upright in her bed, hooded eyes open like a night-bird watching the dark sky, full of her own thoughts, whatever they may be.

And in the morning, Mel leaves for a short holiday of undisclosed duration with his boy, and Marte is a brave figure at the kitchen table, gruffly waving him off and warning him not to go anywhere unsafe.

'See you when I see you, darling,' he calls as he leaves. 'Probably early new year. Can't give an exact date – have to see what's happening.' I walk with him to the station and, as he'd left a little early, we have time for coffee before he goes off to Heathrow. We stir the cappuccino with its thick layer of foam and chocolate swirl.

'Do you know, Mel,' I say, 'before you came we just did things – there was no overseer, as it were, with Marte. Now that you're here, there seems to be a routine. I'm aware of most of it. But I think there are things you do that I need to know while you're away.'

'Well yes – it's only just beginning to happen.' Mel spoons off the foam and chocolate and pulls his bag closer under the table as other customers come in after us. 'And by the way, it's rootin', as Lulu calls it, not routine.'

'Before you came, I'd take her in the wheelchair sometimes, and the young man Terry from the community centre would come – but it was kind of sporadic. You take her out often, it seems.'

'Most days, unless it's really cold or raining – or unless her breathing is bad. And sometimes we just go around the block, but it gives her a sense of an outing.' Mel looks at his watch.

'Is it time?'

'Sorry to be rude, no we've still got time.' He signals for a second coffee. I refuse, I'm already beginning to twitch from the caffeine.

'Well, briefly.' He stirs the second coffee, looking again at his watch, patting his pocket. I know that feeling from travelling: money, passport, ticket, time. 'In the morning, after Lulu's been, we have a breakfast – well, she bites a piece of toast or a poached egg... then we deal with the business of the day, as she calls it. The silver box has been coming out lately – you know, the will, the money business and all that... and then when the box is out I have to double lock the front door. We have to talk about anything from the will, to what shall we do today. There are piles of documents on the table – which get put away hurriedly when we're done, or if anyone rattles at the door. Ah, before that, she's had her potty. Then there's the incredibly long process of getting her from her chair to the wheelchair. This you know about.'

'Mmm – the halfway stop down the hallway, the anxiety and the panic.'

'Just that. So, after the outing, it's meals on wheels, and then maybe when sunny, she's parked outside with a neb. And there's the two-bell system we got from the hardware shop – she can ring me and I can ring her back to indicate I've heard her. It's become a damn nuisance.' Mel calls for the bill, pays, and starts to collect his two bags. 'Just quickly then Ell... a nap, and then tea and cake – or something savoury, she loves that. Visitors very occasionally – and, apart from one or two like yourself – she hates visitors after seven. Lulu comes at 6 to put her in her nightie, – we do the night-time medication – and then there's the night-time conversation when I'm there, which could last anything from one hour to three.'

We are walking to the station now. 'Of course I give her diazepam and temazipam for sleeping – but she always insists that what I'm giving her is paracetamol – doesn't want to acknowledge that she needs sleeping pills.' Mel gets his ticket.

'Have a lovely time,' I say, 'hope all goes well for you.'

In a moment he has disappeared down the stairs, and I feel a sense of loss, as well as a feeling akin to guilt – but that's too strong. Regret more likely, that Marte was maybe feeling at sixes and sevens before Mel came, and that those of us around her couldn't quite give her what she needed, that sense of order and firmness.

CHAPTER 27

Back at the flat she has her ruffled beaky look, and she knows it and she's trying to cover it. We studiously don't mention Mel, and begin organising for the arrival of Justine.

'We don't have to change the sheets – or maybe we could anyway for… for later. She's not staying you know.'

'Yes. She's staying with Martin and Jo – her friends in Highgate?'

'Yeah. Posh they are. Come and see me sometimes because I think Justine asks them to. Then they phone her and tell her how I am. Do you think my hair is OK?' I get a comb and smooth down the spiky points. I like her hair when it is spiky but I know she wants to look smooth for her daughter. Well, she does and she doesn't. Marte is nervous, and asks in quite a docile tone for an extra neb. I can tell she is inwardly preoccupied by what seems to be a too-quick turnover from Mel to Justine. I too, am preoccupied by the short exchange Mel and I had about the rootin'. I can't see myself taking Marte out daily in the old and heavy wheelchair she has. She refuses to buy another, saying that there isn't time, and this remark could be interpreted in more than one way. We have been out before the arrival of Mel with me pushing the wheelchair, and I find its wayward wheels almost spiteful, and I am always afraid that when we go off the pavement, that Marte, without a belt to hold her in, is going to be tipped out, handbags, blankets and all. The days are cold and murky, and not the best for outings. I am aware that I am feeling a weight of responsibility that I hadn't felt before Mel turned up.

Marte listened a lot to radio 4 and sometimes to radio 3 and I realise the radio hasn't been on so much recently. Through Mel's presence, and the dialogue that has developed, her life has become more visible to me. I had an overview before, but not in terms of hours through the day. I assumed she passed the time with books, friends, radio and sleep. Now that I think about it, she's hardly read for quite a while, though there are many books on the shelves, including big print books from the library where young Terry would push her. He has not come very often since Mel arrived although when he does come, Marte is happy, and he seems pleased to see her.

'What about my clothes?' A gloomy voice emerges from Marte.

'You look OK. Do you want to wear something different?'

'Is this cardigan too bright?' It's one of her striped cardigans and it makes her look like a parrot.

'Well I like it… but you choose.'

'No', grumpily, 'you choose.' I bring a selection of cardigans from the wardrobe. Together we find something a little more sober in colour. 'Shall I wear a scarf? No they annoy me.' Marte is fretting and pecking away at herself. This is the Justine syndrome. I recognise it each year. Marte is, and has been, a strange mixture of conservative and socialist. She likes tradition, order, the old order, courtesy, and hierarchy when it takes responsibility and behaves with humility. She also fiercely champions the dispossessed, minority groups and those who are too weak to speak up for themselves. Justine is interested in the good life, and can't understand anyone who isn't fighting for their share of the goodies. She has a way of scrutinising people from top to toe with one quick, smooth glance, and then it's as if a register is clicking its way rapidly in her head, coming up with caste, class, financial status, appearance-status. I know that I failed the test ever since we first met, many years back. I have to watch my step, or I move into some of the pain about my sister. And who knows – I reflect once more – what pain there is for Justine in witnessing my affectionate relationship with her mother?

Marte and I wile away the time with cups of tea that stand untouched and get cold, and she increasingly pats herself here and there to tuck in the scarf and groom her hair. I feel a bit gloomy and know that if I tried to cheer Marte up it would sound false, and she'd bite my head off.

When Justine arrives the room is hectic with scarves and perfume and smooth cheek kissing and me biting my lip for the tightness of it and the intrusion of a cold sophisticated winter wind that cuts into the warm atmosphere that has become our routine and our habitat. I watch how I avoid sight of my own bitch, in contrast to seeing Justine's bitch so clearly. It suits me well to create Justine as a cold wind so that I can be the pleasant tropical breeze. I tell myself that this is another sentient being, and that my task is to love her, as I love flies, rats and dengue-carrying mosquitoes. I am not sure if she is aware of the Buddhist dialogue that is going on within the figure that stands before her. She has inventoried my pale face and lack of lipstick, she has seen and discarded my green cotton trousers and favourite green sweater. Her eyes have swept the acreage of my bare wrist, unadorned, and my bare neck, decorated only by its newly developing motif of age. 'Fuck you,' I think, without compassion. The bitch is out, and then feel myself caught, like a wasp buzzing in the narrow neck of a bottle, aiming for sweet remnants at the bottom and then stuck halfway down. At this point, it's not so much the spiritual ethics that bother me, as the horrible feeling in my eyes and my throat and my stomach. And then I give in and decide I might as well be really nasty and stop arguing with it – and a voluptuous surge of dislike radiates through me, discharging colour into my face.

'You look well,' says Justine

'Yes I'm very well – and you?'

'Marvellous, darling.' Marte is sitting in a sweet and sour mist, her eyes moving from one of us to the other. 'I understand that Melvyn has been here.'

'Melvyn? Oh Mel.' I can't see him as a Melvyn. 'He's been very kind.'

'What's he after?' Justine turns to Marte, and then disguises the sharpness of the question with a light laugh. 'No one does anything for nothing.'

'Well,' I say innocently, feeling my strength surge back 'They have a lot to talk about.' Marte picks up on this little current and hoists her sails. She looks suddenly more like herself. 'Yes! We talk all night sometimes.'

'You always liked him,' says Justine sharply. 'Especially after…'

'Enough!' shouts Marte in a way that is suddenly shocking, 'Don't you!' but anything further is left unsaid and Justine moves to the window and stares out.

A curtain opens on a distant stage, and I receive an abrupt scenario of Marte and Harry with the son they never had, and a small girl, flouncing and sore next to them. The scene dissolves, but just before it does, I see the features of this child imposed upon Justine's immaculate face. I am relieved to be able to busy myself with soup and rolls. Mother and daughter do their best to pick up on each other's lives. Dropped stitches lie all over the floor as they each knit, plain and purl, trying to keep the garment intact.

'No bread for me,' says Justine though her eye light upon the warm roll, as I spread butter on it for Marte. I feel her hunger, and her pride. We talk about different people, about Marte's medication and the sparse and irregular visits to the Breathe Easy clinic, about the awfulness of the meal on wheels that is cooling on the work surface next to the sink. We had forgotten to cancel it for today. Justine tells us of difficult clients and of big deals she has snatched from other agents. I admire her independence and her business skill; at the same time, I imagine she must be a ferocious enemy.

'Your father should have been as tough as you,' says Marte. 'We'd have had a lot more money!'

'Yes – but he wouldn't have been so nice,' says Justine unexpectedly. There is a silence.

'I was showing Ellie the other day, photographs from the cruises. He always looked ever so smart, liked his blazer and his pocket-handkerchief. Always had to make sure there was one ironed.' Marte asks Justine to fetch the albums. I decide to leave.

It's a choice between going across the landing to warmth or out again into the cold and damp of the outside world. I walk, after fetching scarf and boots and coat and the grey beret I acquired from a mail order catalogue after seeing it on a friend, who wore it with aplomb and dash, its small leather ribbon at the back giving the finishing touch. I am happy in this beret.

Fragmented pieces of the jigsaw of the life of mother and daughter cross through my mind and float out again... and more dominantly in the forefront, I recall the effect of practice from the morning, where I felt sucked onto the earth and pinned there through the soles of my feet, sticking there through the force of gravity. I think of astronauts floating on the moon, of the lunar cold dead rock without the same quality of magnetic heat that lies at the centre of our planetary home. This morning when I begin the practice, I express the effort of simply lifting a hand, a finger, defying gravity and inertia and the horizontal. I feel the thrust under my arms, the will to rise, like a balloon full and thick, pushing from beneath me, and I feel the weight and the pressure of gravity on the upper edges of my arms, pushing downwards. Gravity and lightness mingled, upward forces pulling me up and downward forces pulling me down; the image of having a pendulum or weight pulling down at the base of the spine, and having a thread lightly pulling the head up I experience not as image, but as bodily reality.

I go through a slow Tai Chi form: hips, belly and legs moving the base triangle, the driving engine beneath the empty upper body and its complementary triangle of back, shoulders and arms. There is distinction between hips and waist, both moving smoothly like well-oiled cogs. Sometimes I ache with effort of practice, or feel that I have done time without good effect. This time, the practice is sweet and easy.

Walking now through cold and wintry streets, past people carrying parcels, I still feel remnants of the morning joy, downward and upward spirals recognisably pulse through me, I feel as if I am wearing a pair of expensive bouncy sports shoes. In spite of being told not to, I decide to buy Marte and Justine a small Christmas present each. Marte is easy – a box of classy cherry liqueur chocolates; for Justine I eventually find a notebook, a slim leather-bound book into which I can imagine her writing details about villas and apartments. I will have the delight later of rummaging through my wardrobe and spending a long time arranging my features for the world, something I haven't done with this degree of commitment since September, really, when the retreat began.

On a whim I buy myself a pair of black knickers, beautifully shapely for my nice bum – the one physical item I have which is prettier than Leonie's! It is small but very feminine – rides high and tight. I don't know where it came from – no one else in the family has this kind of arse. Certainly didn't come from auntie Bessie! In the past, if I was especially interested in a man, I would wear tight stretch black trousers, and high heel shoes, and tuck in a crisp white shirt. I'd make sure to turn my back on him at least twice, and if I was strongly keen, I would drop something and bend over.

Back home, I raid the wardrobe, choosing a short black dress from my working days, with pert black high heel shoes for dinner with Marte and Justine. The dress is close-fitting enough to show off my rear, and I will turn my back on Justine as often as possible to show it to her. I am enjoying the arrival of this competitive instinct, it's a sharp taste to compensate me for all the tastes I am not having at the moment, and then I spend careful time exploring the two jewellery boxes I have put away in the spare room.

CHAPTER 28

I apply a new face with care and extravagance. I cream and tone and blend and paint. The products sit on my face, warm and heavy. An image stares back at me from the mirror. I tease out its curly hair and walk around the flat in black suede shoes. I have wrapped the presents in tissue paper and now I put on my coat, lock the door and pause in the hall before going in to Marte's. I feel quivers of dread and anxiety. Like a child I say to myself, 'I don't want to go.' This feels like one of those times when I just don't have enough skins to be in the world. My heart is a transparent, roaring jelly, my lungs peer out from beneath the ribcage like spongy trees, breath springs from them in irregular bursts. I want to be wrapped around by a huge family – to give me back my skin which is peeling off in delicate strips as I stand, transfixed, before Marte's door. I want to be at the head of a big family table, ladling out soup, delegating responsibility for the turkey, noticing everything, noticed by everybody.

An emergency siren starts to roar within me and in the next moment I gather my will and focus. Slowly self-pity retires to the corner, and my discarded skin – like a reversed film – ups itself from the floor, and winds itself back around my body.

'Oi! Look at her!' Marte herself is wearing black, with three black artificial roses pinned to the lapel of the jacket. I think she looks smart and tell her so. 'And look at you,' she repeats, 'Now if you dressed like this…'

'All the time…' I chorus with her.

'Yes all the time,' she says severely. 'Now don't mock my words – you could find a man like the best of them.'

'Who's finding a man?' Justine appears, in dark blue cashmere.

'You two girls, maybe,' Marte sniffs. 'If you play your cards right. I should give you lessons. Elegance, that's the word.'

'Aren't I elegant enough for you?' Justine retorts. Marte appraises her for a quick second.

'Darling – you are sometimes too elegant – you understand what I am saying? But not today,' she adds hastily, noticing the flush appearing on Justine's cheeks. 'Today you are just right.' As if to test this statement, Justine pulls heavy gold jewellery from her handbag and fixes a broad chain around her neck, and another one on her wrist. Marte looks as if she is going to speak, then doesn't.

'You look nice,' says Justine to me. It is a candid comment, without any extra spin. I smile at her, and the taxi arrives.

'This will cost a fortune,' grumbles Marte. 'Christmas fares.'

'We're only going around the corner,' says Justine pulling on a pair of leather gloves. We bring the portable nebuliser, and just one handbag for Marte. In it, there's a spray, two valium and a crisply ironed handkerchief, along with her wallet and a comb. Marte struggles to get out of her chair and I see how weak she looks and how the smart black suit appears more substantial than she is. I can see her making an effort, and I know she would rather not go out. Christmas means nothing to her, she told me previously. Christmas has come to mean something to me since I came face to face with Jesus of Nazareth, brother of David.

The restaurant, Italian and lively, is full. Marte is supported by Justine and me and the taxi driver – a soft-hearted fellow - as she stumbles up to the door like an old beetle manoeuvering its way across an intricate branch. The manager greets us, and with a special welcome for Marte. It's a wonderful performance, and Marte rises to it. Her body remains as brittle and bowed as ever, but her spirit rises, and this gives a momentary impression that she is suddenly taller and stronger. We are given a table near to the door, and it takes a long time for Marte to settle, with her essential belongings nearby her. She is deathly white underneath the two round spots of rouge on her cheeks but her bright eyes glitter as they take in the scene around her.

Justine and I choose fish, Marte wants turkey 'with all the trimmings.' The waiters are attentive and all around is a buzz of talk and the clatter of cutlery. The room is warm and attractive, and I sink into the joy of being brought food, tasty food, by a deft waitress. There are white and green decorations around the windows.

'Well,' says Marte as the wine glasses are filled 'Do we wish each other merry Christmas, or what? I want you to know it means nothing to me.'

'So what should we say that has meaning for you?' A question from Justine. Marte coughs and bubbles slightly, wipes her lips with the heavy linen napkin.

'Going back to Harry,' she says gruffly. There's an odd silence.

'Do you mean,' Justine speaks warily, 'remembering…'

'I mean until death do us part and then afterwards we are not anymore parted. That's exactly what I mean.' We three are silent, each in our own way. Soup arrives for Justine and me, Marte breaks a roll with shaky fingers, but doesn't eat anything. She pursues the roll further until there is a pile of crumbs on her small plate. Justine gives a sharp look that Marte fortunately doesn't catch. 'Harry would have liked it here – though it's expensive, and he would have said so. He would have had turkey too with the trimmings. He would have asked for the leg, too.'

Marte is looking into the middle distance, her eyes are suddenly less bright, they are moist and reflective. Justine eats her soup slowly, keeping a wary eye on her mother.

'What was Harry like as a dad?' I ask.

'Well actually,' after a pause, 'he was quite strict with me.'

'Strict but fair,' says Marte, brought back from her reverie.

'Yes – that's true. What was your dad like Ellie?' Justine clearly wants to skate away from the focus on her family.

'Well – what can I say? – mildly strict – you know, we always knew there was a strict element somewhere but it was very hidden.'

'No good if you're not strict,' says Marte firmly. 'Children don't know where they are.'

'I knew where I was,' mutters Justine.

'Yes, usually in your room, dreaming and drawing.'

'What did you draw?' I finish the soup – and instantly can't remember what flavour it was.

'She was good at drawing – then stopped suddenly.'

'I drew houses funnily enough.'

'We thought she might want to be an architect.' There is a sudden burst of laughter from another table, followed by a slapping of backs and a calling for more wine.

'It's not that funny,' says Justine, looking across with mock indignation.

'No, it wasn't funny when you threw it all in – you were a clever girl, you could have…'

'Ma, I'm just not going down this road.' Our second course arrives and I am relieved at the interruption. Justine looks flushed and slightly upset. Marte starts grumbling into her chin and no one can hear what she's saying. I feel a sudden sympathy for Justine and I know this could be me sitting with my parents. I feel disappointment and love and sadness between Marte and her daughter and watch as they distract and busy themselves with cutting up Marte's turkey. She can't do it herself, and she hates us doing it for her. She is though trying to be appreciative of Justine's efforts and I think she knows her remark was an irritant.

'Fish is good,' I say. Marte looks at me with a piece of turkey speared onto her fork. 'Would you like a taste Marte?' She angles her face towards me, screws up her eyes and opens her mouth. I put a small piece of fish into it, and Marte chews carefully.

'Nice. Nicely done. Do you want some turkey?' I turn my face towards her and open my mouth. Her hand is shaking a little so I take her wrist and guide the turkey morsel between my teeth. 'Darling – you have some.' She turns towards Justine.

'Just a little.' This communal feeding procedure softens us all, and we carry on in silence, Marte eating little amounts very slowly. Her plate hardly seems to empty when she puts the fork down and closes her eyes. Justine looks at me – I shake my head as if to say leave it, it's all right.

Marte is in familiar communion with discomfort and not enough air. Her chest heaves and flutters, her attention seems riveted internally. I get the nebuliser ready and put it near her hand. Without opening her eyes she somehow senses it is there, and takes the spout into her mouth. Desperate sucking turns to dreamy sucking and a slightly dazed-looking Marte regards her full plate of food with disbelief and worry and then closes her eyes again. The elderly couple at the next table regard Marte with uneasy concern. Justine and I smile reassuringly at them and start talking about property in Ibiza, and the possibilities of second homes, all the time keeping Marte's state well in focus. I know she prefers to be left to re-constitute herself at times like these. The waitress comes and takes away our empty plates.

'Marte, shall we have dessert or would you rather go?'

'Stay girls – I know you're having a nice time.' Her voice is quiet as is her demeanour. We put a shawl around her legs and the waiter brings a cushion, softening further the back of her chair. Marte settles into a temporary nest, crumpling up somewhat, and receding from the world of food and chat, neglecting even her glass of wine, hardly touched. Her neck sinks into the collar of her black suit so that her nose seems to jut out from her lapel. She looks as though she is sniffing the artificial black roses pinned onto her jacket but it sounds as if she is breathing through sandpaper. Justine and I look wordlessly at each other and I see a curious, tired, sad look in her eyes.

'Dessert?' She offers me the menu and I choose plum tart and cream. Justine goes for fruit salad and refills our glasses with wine. She moves her chair a little closer to me. 'Mel,' she says cautiously, 'do you trust him?'

'Well yes – I think I do.'

'Do you know – oh never mind – sorry. Sometimes a young, well, youngish man wants to hang around with an old woman, and a crotchety old woman at that. And anyway, there's…' Her voice trails away in an unsatisfactory way. We both look at Marte who is snoring faintly, her breath coming in and out in little bubbles. Again I am conscious of a narrative coming towards me, and then veering away rapidly.

'Yes, well – she's grumpy that's true, but she sort of has an endearing quality. Maybe it's different if she's your mum.' Our desserts have arrived. Justine orders coffee.

'Espresso please – very strong.' She looks at me quizzically 'Endearing is never the word I would use. But then, nor would she use that word with me.' The tired, sad look I saw before has retired behind an expression of cool, business-like inquiry. 'I tell you Ellie, she taught him a lot when he was young – all about antiques and restoration. He hung around us a lot – things weren't too good at home for him.'

'What are you talking about? What time is it?' Marte is awake, looking confused.

'We're going to get the bill, mother,' says Justine crisply. 'It's about three o 'clock now.'

'Three o'clock in the afternoon,' says Marte. Justine is about to reply and checks herself. She calls to the waiter and insists on treating me. I collect our coats and ring for the minicab. The same driver returns, and we create a slow procession out of the restaurant. Getting Marte out of the taxi at the other is a lengthy operation. Her limbs feel like pieces of burnt wood and she groans and protests as we three move her into what seems to be the best position. The conversation with Justine about Mel is still in my ears, and I wish he were here for he has a way of managing this kind of practical situation – seeming to know how Marte's limbs work. I can't communicate Mel's wish to give her the best time until she dies… I know I will fumble for words that simply won't work. As we arrive home, I remember I still have the Christmas presents in my bag. When we are back in Marte's flat and she has had her medication and is beginning to be safely comatose, I give them each a prettily wrapped parcel. I can tell that Justine wants to continue our conversation, but I don't. I am feeling suddenly very tired. I am full of food and wine and I don't want to talk. Justine looks disappointed and a little angry as I leave. Marte is fathoms deep into her afternoon sleep.

In my room, on my bed, in the late afternoon of Christmas day, I dive deeply and powerfully. I remember the moment of naked skinlessness outside Marte's door before we left. Now it feels that my heart is beating and bouncing outside of me. I know that place in my heart when I am caught up in my own sorrow - in this moment it is empty and calm. What's happening now is the rising of an impersonal grief; tears gush like small fountains, the sensation is almost pleasurable. I burrow under the duvet, mopping the flow with wads of tissue. This is the kind of crying that comes if I watch someone running as fast as they can to get to the winning line, or when footballers embrace the one who just scored the goal, or listening to great choral passages, or while watching certain films. I am awash with unknown feelings, riding a tide. Outside of me spins the world and all its happenings; between me and the world is the ocean I am riding. And deep inside me, dry and small, is a small world, a seed, a kernel, quiet and at rest and without thought, only full of seeing and knowledge. Mopping my face, hooded under the covers, images from the day whipping to and fro before me. I slide like a lucky child in the playground, down into this tiny place. The seed, the ocean, the world.

Many years ago, when Gerry and I were together, we looked after a small baby for a day. She was three months old perhaps, and her parents, good friends of ours, were desperate for a day off and so we volunteered to baby-sit. For a few hours all was bliss as small Molly slept. Then at four, two hours before the parents were due, all hell broke loose. She started to cry, and no amount of jiggling on the hip, distracting with colourful, noisy toys, tickling of the corner of the mouth with the bottle-teat helped. There seemed to be no reason for the outburst. And it increased in volume as our efforts to placate her failed. Gerry tried; I heated a bottle. The bottle was rejected, Gerry pulled faces and shook rattles. Looking at each other in utter dismay over the red, desperate face of the infant, its mouth pursed in rage, its voice surely audible to the parents, seated in an auditorium in Leicester Square, we decided to put it into the smart baby buggy, ignoring screams as we buckled her in. We trailed around the block several times until the screams subsided and an exhausted baby fell asleep. I was sure that when her parents returned, they would find a ragged scrap, with sticky eyes and blanched face. However, when Molly awoke, a short while before their return, a gleaming rosy-faced being met us, plump and content. We left her in the chair, being afraid to disrupt this miraculous recovery, pushing her up and down the passage, smiling like idiots. When the parents returned, their gurgling infant was there to meet them, its eyes like polished blue marbles. I'm not sure if they noticed how haggard Gerry and I looked.

Gerry and I had a strange evening after that experience. It wasn't the tiredness; that soon passed. It was something else. We had talked about having children and there were times of sexual passion when the presence of a child seemed to hover around us, fruit of love, completion of partnership. We went to the edge, and never crossed over.

There was something about Molly's weeping. It had a primal savagery that somehow shook us both, and talking didn't resolve the unease that we subsequently experienced.

I know that sense of primal savagery in me. I am sure it exists too in Gerry. We never experienced it between us, we were constantly equable and agreeable with each other, rows flared up and flared down. We teased and sometimes didn't speak, but there was always

resolution. We had never experienced between us, this degree of
naked rage, of primary need so nakedly expressed. Had he been with
me this evening, post Marte and Justine, he would have put his kindly
arms around me, said soothing things, and his very kindness would
have made somehow an indecency of the intensity of the weeping. If
I had needed to continue, I would have had to go to the other room,
and then he would have come in, worried and puzzled, to protect me
from my ghosts and demons. These wild creatures simply had to lie
down and give in before Gerry's immense and consistent kindness.
'What the hell are you complaining about?' friends would ask,
puzzled, when I wailed that Gerry was too nice. And then they would
take up space talking about their drunken, adulterous, aggressive
men. No, I didn't want Gerry to be drunken, adulterous or vicious.
But where was his edge? I knew him always in the middle, or just off
the middle, reasonable, decent. What the hell was the matter with me,
I used to wonder. I'm partnered by a saint, what more could I want?
'You always look for trouble,' my mother used to say as I crept off
to the graveyard. What is an edge anyway; what is the middle? All I
know is that the more Gerry stayed in the middle, the more I crept off
to the edge. It was nothing that I did rationally, through decision; it
was more an unconscious response and then suddenly I'd find myself
in a situation where we were located in different places and couldn't
reach each other. Gerry was a little like my father, reasonable, staying
out of trouble. Everyone used to say – your dad is so nice. Everyone
used to say – Gerry is so nice. And I used to see myself as full of dark
dissatisfaction, an unwholesome child, full of strange imaginings, a
Molly-mouth, brutal with primal screaming. The mouth I have on
me tonight, deep under the covers, is a heart-mouth, registering the
flub-a-dub sounds of this perpetually pumping organ, this tender
drum and its blood-beating source. 'What's the matter with her?' my
mother would say 'Leave her alone, she's all right,' my father would
say mildly. I knew in response to both of them, my decent parents,
that there was nothing the matter with me; and, at the same time,
I knew that many of the elements of programmed, received reality
were not all right, and caused me to live off an engine of tension and
release of tension.

I knew that to find deep space, the luminous essence in my core,
I needed to go to the edge of not all right, and in it and through it,
eyes wide open, and jump off the world and into black space, to find
the empty pregnancy, the inexplicable empty fullness. This I always

knew, and until now, this time of the hermitage, had always been too surrounded by life and its actions to find the space to jump, or dive.

The night is gathering around me. I don't know whether to get up or stay in bed. I wonder if Justine is still next door; I wonder how Mel is. I think briefly of Guido, and then stop myself. I think about New Year's Eve. This will be the first time that I can remember having no plans for celebration. I think – unless I am surprised by anything unexpected turning up – I am going to sit in my ruined shepherd's hut, near the wondrous ghosts of David and Jesus, under the cold night stars, wrapped in a fleecy jacket, an old jacket still smelling of sheep. The landscape will be empty of people. An occasional tree will stub the horizon, and the sound of quiet wind will move through my ears.

CHAPTER 29

I am aware these days of the archetypal Lords, Chronos and Chairos, who guard the passage of Time. Chronos, Lord of the horizontal – the clock, linear measurement, days, months, years, date of birth, date of death. Chairos, vertical, Lord of that which happens in its own time, by its own rules, through its own mysterious measurement and requirement.

In Chronos-time, days have passed, and I am in my routine, and then with Marte and sometimes with Marte and Justine. In Chairos-time, I am in a slow and measured state, paying attention to what I do, washing up without haste, watching steam rise off the plates as I set them on the rack, getting ready for bed, saying a short prayer as I close the blinds, noticing the feeling in my body after changing from standing up to lying down. Every now and then I have caught myself rushing, or doing two things at once, or allowing my mind to scatter, and I have breathed out, and re-assumed snail's pace. The way of Chairos takes me deep into my spine, settling that reactive force in the front of the body which makes me want to leap up and shoot my energy outwards. I am not finding it an easy discipline, but the rewards are multiple. I am moved into long periods of sitting in a restful and yet alert state. When I lose this through impatience, boredom or anxiety, I feel disrupted and at odds, and this loss of quality signals the imperative which pulls me back in.

This day, as dusk is falling, I return to the house from a long and ruminative walk and find a a scrawled note, almost illegible, stuck to my door. 'Please come up to Edie's, Jinny,' I go upstairs immediately, and find Edie, a small and bewildered ghost, sitting in a deep chair in the living room, her legs invisible underneath a blanket, a glass of water at her side. Present is Jinny, two elderly women and a professional-looking woman who introduces herself as Edie's doctor.

'You're another neighbour? We have bad news.' I shoot a look at Edie. Has she had a stroke? She looks at me, and doesn't speak, staring at me as though I am a stranger.

'What's happened?'

'Can you come next door?'

I follow the doctor out of the room, into the narrow passageway. 'How well do you know Mrs. Trammler?'

'Not so well – she and Max...' The doctor interrupts me, looking at me soberly.

'Max... Max died just a few hours ago.' A silence, filled with chalk, moves the length and breadth of the walls and ceiling.

'What happened?'

'A heart attack. Here, in the kitchen. Edie called to him to make tea, and there was a crash. She came in and found him on the floor.' The chalk is now in my mouth, and I can't speak for its white, dusty taste. Through a muddled tongue, I manage somehow to make words.

'Is he... is he still... did they take him away?'

'He's in his room,' says the doctor gently. I realise I don't know her name. She must be in her late forties, has a plain, pleasant, tired face, and is wearing a grey skirt and jacket.

'So sorry – I don't know your name.'

'Dr. Oldham. Do you want to see him?'

'Well,' I say, and realise that, strangely, I am struggling for etiquette. How well do you have to know someone if you're going to look at their dead body? 'Well, I didn't know him really...' Then I remember Max happily providing the stretch limousine for Marte and his pride at having a part to play in the whole enterprise. I imagine Mel being here with me and not hesitating for a moment. 'Yes, yes of course I'd like to see him...' I grab at my dusty tongue just in time before it says 'If he doesn't mind'. We go into Max's small bedroom. It is like the room of an adolescent boy. On the painted white walls are posters of rock stars and beautiful women. The room is very tidy. On a small, single bed lies Max, wearing a blue paisley dressing gown. 'Max,' I say quietly 'I am so sorry...'

Dr. Oldham is standing at the door, with her back to me. I whisper 'Max, I hope you were not afraid, and I pray that the guardians of your being are with you now.' I touch his hand and it is cold and clammy. I want to study his face. The usual sense of curiosity rises like a vivid snake from a basket. I can really look at him now without reservation, but then I feel shame, and withdraw my eyes from the slight stubble on his chin, the odd baby-droop of his mouth. Again, I remember my parents' bodies after death, and I am struck by how absent he is. This is matter quite without animation, yet it is Max. It is all we have left, the rest has gone to its destination. Or is Max still present, hovering in puzzlement around his discarded form? I move towards Dr. Oldham, and she turns around.

'Did he know he was ill?'

'Well, he wasn't ill exactly – very overweight, drank a lot and ate the wrong food for his condition. He had some warning episodes – but he chose not to take them seriously although we requested he attend the clinic and alter some of his habits… What can you do?' A tight expression crosses her face. 'What can you? You can't force people. We did tell him that though he wasn't ill, he did need to take action.'

'What about Edie?'

'She's totally shocked. A sister is coming to take her up north to a family home. Shall we go back?'

I go to Edie and take her hand. Jinny is making tea, and her eyes are swollen. When she brings the tray in, she and I exchange glances.

'Edie, I am so sorry.'

'Yes dear.'

'If there's anything I can do…' Edie is stroking my hand as if consoling me. There is a distant look in her eyes, she's staring ahead as if she can see something far away which the rest of us can't see.

'Do you know dear, when I asked him to make tea, he asked if I wanted sugar. He knew I never took sugar. He never asked me before if I took sugar. Why did he ask me that?' She stops stroking my hand and looks at me. From the movement around the room, I know that she has been asking this question of all the others.

'I don't know Edie – perhaps…'

'He knew all my life I didn't take sugar.'

There's a knock on the door. Dr. Oldham greets two men whom I guess have come to take the body.

'Edie, dear,' she says to the small figure under the blanket. 'These men have come to take Max's body. Do you want to see him before they take him?'

'No dear, I know about Max. I have seen him. I saw him on the floor. It doesn't make any difference now if I see him. He wouldn't listen to me you know. He took too much sugar, and too much beer and I always told him...' Her voice trails off and tears of bitterness and shock filter into her eyes but don't have the weight or strength to fall down her cheek. Jinny is crying behind her handkerchief. I wonder if Marte knows. I wonder about the young woman Gerry and I saw with Max and whether she knows, whether indeed they are still together. My mind is prowling around into all sorts of corners as the two men, discreet and quiet, disappear into Max's room with an awful-looking bag. I don't want to see Max going out of the door like this.

'Shall I close the living room door?' As I do so, Edie lets out a thin, narrow piteous wail. I feel a flash of useless resentment. Why on earth did a stalwart son depart this earth before his fragile and aging mother? This is not in the order of things. I feel angry with Max. The doctor is sitting next to Edie and the dust of helplessness settles all over the room, its neat and clean furniture, its evidence of two lives going on together: habits of conversation, the placing of furniture, habits of eating, habits of lying, habits of care and of indifference.

The two elderly women turn out to be rummy-playing friends of Edie's. They have a practical, firm, kindly way about them that I begin to admire. I imagine they have had to attend to death and its consequences before, I imagine them as the valiant remnants of a large group of rummy players, who know how to play a canny game. One by one they have had to bury each other. The older of the two women is now on the 'phone to the sister from Sheffield. She has a note-pad by her side, and is writing slowly, repeating what she has written. Another knock on the door, and a slim, dark-eyed man comes in, moving straight to Edie and taking both her hands in both of his. 'It's Edie's vicar,' whispers the second rummy-player. 'A brilliant man.' Jinny gets up to make tea for the vicar, and I go to kitchen with her.

'Jinny, does Marte know?'

'Don't think so.'

'Perhaps I'll go down and tell her – come and get me if anything needs doing.'

'Okay Ellie – ' Jinny turns from the kettle, and looks at me with swimming eyes. 'It's so horrible – poor Edie, what's going to happen to her?'

I shake my head and leave the awful room. I don't want to tell Marte – but she might hear abruptly in another way, so perhaps it's better coming from me. I stop halfway down the stairs and tell myself to wait a moment, take a breath, and think about what I am doing.

Marte is dozing. A cup of tea sits on the table next to her. The two oxygen tubes press against her nose and her head falls at a slight angle to the cushion behind it. The blanket over her knee has slipped to the ground and the radio is on very softly. I sit opposite her and she moves and opens her eyes.

'What's all the fuss about? Lots of people tramping up and down. What's going on?'

'Marte, it's Max.'

'What's the silly man gone and done?' She looks at me sharply and then says in a different tone 'I've made a bad remark, haven't I? Something's not right – Max is ill, isn't he, it's something bad.'

'It's bad Marte.' We look at each other. 'It's more than… Max is worse than… he…'

'Did he have an accident, is he all right?'

'Heart attack, Marte.'

'And… did the ambulance take him away?'

'Marte – he died.' Marte looks at me with an expression of shock and desolation. There is a long silence between us devoid of the usual responses of wanting to know how, where, why, how long …

'Edie?' Marte asks.

'There are people taking care of her.'

'Edie,' says Marte again 'Poor, poor girl.'

The Australian girls are away, back home for an extended New Year; David – without having mentioned anything to anybody – is away, and Jinny's family, Marte and I are the ones left in the house to mark Max's going. Jean, the sister from Sheffield, arrives by taxi, and proves to be quiet, practical and plump where Edie is slim. She, the rummy-ladies and the vicar begin to organise the funeral, and Jinny and I offer to arrange food and drink at Edie's flat for afterwards. The two sisters have long and difficult discussions about Edie's future and come to the conclusion that the flat is best eventually sold and Edie moved up north. Edie seems to be participating in these arrangements, but each time I look at her it is as if she has already vacated the premises. Edie for a while has been firmly living in a past decade of her choice. I think of her coming to the meetings to organise Marte's outing, elegant in her old-fashioned suit, and of her sitting in the limousine, graciously pointing out sights, as if electricity had just been invented, and the twenty-first century didn't exist. This style, this etching of Edie, is no more. Instead, we meet a wraith, bewildered, and without any energy of personality to inhabit the physical form.

The next day, a small trace of the old Edie comes back when she goes downstairs to see Marte. Marte asked Justine and me to help her up the stairs, but after a struggle which conquered only three steps, a message is sent, Edie agrees to come down, and I go off to find the best cakes and Justine is made busy preparing the tea-table. Jean takes the opportunity to visit a lawyer, and an estate agent, and Justine and I, having welcomed Edie, decide to leave the two women together. Edie comes down in her smart black skirt and jacket, touchingly elaborate for a visit to a neighbour, and yet somehow fitting. Marte, too, had made a fuss about her clothes, and receives Edie in her best cream blouse, with a large brooch too heavily hanging from its top button-hole. A deep, misery-laden silence falls between the two women as they pick up delicate old teacups, and bring them slowly to their lips.

'I'd like to be a fly on the wall,' Justine is on her way to her hired car. I don't answer. I am thinking about Mel. There has been no word from him since he left. I am surprised and not surprised he hasn't contacted Marte. She has his number in Israel but I don't think she has phoned him. She talks about him not at all. In an odd way, it fits my experience of Mel. When he is there, he is very present; when he is not there, he is very absent. I miss him. I miss him as himself and I miss him with Marte.

I walk the hilly streets of Hampstead up to the Heath. A hole has opened up in the world and swallowed Max, and we, in our mortal bodies, are left, just this side of it.

When the burying day comes, it wheels its way in, pulling us with it. In church, a traditional red-brick building off West End Lane, there are flowers abundant on Max's coffin, and a surprising number of people. Edie is a sepulchral figure, supported by women. Marte sits, hooded and bleak in her wheelchair, nebuliser and oxygen handy, Justine, in black, next to her. There is quite a tribe of Trammlers, it seems, and a contingent of friends and acquaintances from the van-hire business that Max was involved in. The hole in the world is still with me. I feel sad and uncomfortable and tired. The vicar moves through the service with practised conviction, his words strike a solemn bell in the heart, and the singing is slightly off-key, but touching. I imagine Max's weighty body lying, cold and dead, in the coffin at the front of the church. After maybe forty minutes into the service, Marte hisses at us that she has to go immediately. I am relieved that I have a reason to leave the church, although I am also sorry to miss personal tributes, and we take her out, and prepare to push her back home. I won't witness the sight of the polished black car taking Max away to the cemetery. I will go and help Jinny, who elected to stay behind and prepare food.

'All this God stuff I can't stand it,' grumbles Marte sharply as we wheel her along 'I don't like funerals and I don't like this pavement it's too bumpy.' It is wonderful to hear the vigour and ferocity of Marte's voice. She is all present and correct in her ailing body, and Justine and I smile at each other as we walk. Justine stays with Marte, who drops into a fretful sleep, and I go upstairs.

In Edie's flat Jinny has arranged the food: sandwiches, varieties of quiche, biscuits, small cakes and large cakes. Someone has brought an indecent pile of chicken drumsticks, and someone else donated dozens of sausage rolls. Alcohol there is a-plenty, and the efficient rummy ladies have made sure there are enough glasses, serviettes and plates. Marte complains about not being able to come, but I sense she is grateful that she won't make it up the stairs. Max's absence is heavy and painful. I catch myself thinking about times I met him on the stairs or just outside the front door, and I wonder whether I was friendly enough each time... and what does friendly enough mean, and should we treat people all the time as if they were about to die? I think about private thoughts I'd had in the stretch limousine, seeing Max as somehow childish and under Edie's thumb. I seem to be weighing and measuring my interactions with Max, spoken and unspoken.

Edie is almost carried up the stairs by stalwart men who seem to have been Max's friends and workmates. As the booze flows and the pile of food diminishes, I notice that Edie seems to be enjoying the enormous amount of attention she is receiving. A sour Trammler female at my side comments 'All very well now – you get all the fuss – it happened to me. But wait a few days hence. Everyone forgets, you know, and then you realise what loneliness is.' Her lips set in a firm line, and her fingers take two sausage rolls and a sandwich onto her paper plate. 'We had two hundred in when my Terry died. Some of them kept up, but some of them...' she chews vigorously and little crumbs and specks of sausage meat fly onto her sweater. '... some of them you'd think you'd died yourself.' I pick up a plate of sandwiches and tell her I am forgetting my duties. A plump young woman with red-rimmed eyes takes a sandwich and I notice she stands alone.

'Are you a friend or relative?' I ask

'Friend.'

'Did you know Max through work?'

'No.'

'Would you like something to drink?'

'Whiskey, please.' She's too young to be the woman Gerry and I noticed all those years ago, but somehow she has the same look about her. I bring her a whiskey and she fastens onto it, the sandwich half eaten on her plate.

'My name's Ellie.'

'Oh.'

'I live in the house.'

'Oh.'

'Would you like another drink?' The glass is empty. 'Same please.' She downs the second.

'Did you know Max for long?'

'Yes.'

'It's very sad.' She picks up her sandwich and examines it closely, saying nothing. I sense a heavy sweat coming from her. As I move on with the plate of sandwiches, I pick up an intense scrutiny from her. Antennae move from her dank region, and cruise around me, snuffling and wavering. I put a knot of people between her and me. They are talking about Max, and behind the knot and around Edie there is a solicitous scrum. Laughter comes from the window, and it feels incongruous and blasphemous. It is also a relief and I want to know what the joke is. I go nearby with my passport of glass plate with ham sandwiches, and connect with a group of burly men who are telling stories about Max.

'Do you remember when he shot off in that little white van, and he thought he was in first gear but actually he'd slammed it into reverse, and he went sharpish backwards into that other van...'

'Oh typical – wasn't that just typical of Max?'

'Well I remember something even more typical – he'd hired the same van to two different people at the same time on the same day – and just as they both came into the office, he realised... and do you know what he did?' The circle of faces obliges with a collective, interrogative eyebrow. 'Well, I'll tell you what he did because muggins was there and muggins was left to carry the proverbial can – yes, he scarpered and I had to deal with two very angry people!'

The circle chuckles with affection and the word 'typical' rises and falls as if, through it, the bluff gentlemen are raising their glasses to Max. Homage to the departed, and scraps of memory and anecdote pinned to his ghost. Absently, two of the men pick ham sandwiches from the glass plate 'thank you darling,' with a kindly and blank look in my direction. I am awash with thoughts and sensations that seem to have everything and nothing to do with the present moment. I have a strong sexual urge, plainly, explicitly in the genitals, nothing to do with the men around me, nothing to do with anybody, just simply there. Sex confronting death? I don't know. People die – and they die before their three score and ten. Max is dead, Edie is alive, as is Marte. Gerry and Guido – where are they? Not dead, but no longer in my life. A nauseous feeling of loss washes through me, the fire in my belly trembles. Even with deep meditation, hermitage, and everything that this silent focus provides, I am not free. I am pursued by loss. And I know I am not alone. Is there anyone who is not afflicted in this way? Is this not what we carry as soon as we're born? There is nowhere to go away from our experience of loss: separation from our unearthly origin, from mother, then from known places, people, possessions, ideas, notions about ourselves, all this sliced through by our longing for satisfaction, for peace, for enlightenment.

Nudging at the edge of me, is something I momentarily, acutely, know – an invincible law, printed in its invisible perfection. Now, quietly holding a plate of ham sandwiches, I become a hologram of awareness: the hermitage has been haunted by an agenda... that I would 'find' something through giving up my normal life, and then I would find something which would mean – maybe – I am no longer suffering loss, or which would bring me compensation or another way of bearing it. This obstructing bargain of which I was previously unaware, caught in the light, dissolves, shifts, moving away like a dog with its tail between its legs. This is the kind of blessed seeing which I know holds up the structure of the hermitage. I stand, emptied, clear, loosely attached to the circle of reminiscence, still holding the glass plate with its diminishing pile of white triangles, pink tongues of meat poking oddly between slices.

'You all right darling?'

'Yes, thank you.'

'Terrible about Max. Lovely man.'

'Yes. Terrible.'

The scrum around Edie has thinned out to reveal two persistent

Trammler cousins who have found a photograph album. Edie, a bereft, ghostly child, is being prompted to remember.

'Oh look Edie darling, isn't this a gorgeous one of Max. Do you remember he had those cute big eyes as a baby? He was such a plump little thing wasn't he?'

Death of plump, cute Max. When an unknown photographer held the camera, this was the capture of Max. Max was there, present, caught. And then – instantly – gone. We experience, and each experience lines our being with layer upon layer of imprint, but we don't possess. In moments of acute sexual joy, we gaze at the face of the beloved who has 'given' us such pleasure and experience the sated body in its bliss before the sadness comes that we are two again after being one.

Omnes animales triste est. And I see us now, like elephants fondling the corpse of a calf with their delicate trunks... I see us all now in Edie's immaculate living room, fondling the memory of the departed one, each of us dealing with loss, all of us in our incarnate bodies, Any moment each of us can be – and are – devastated by something, someone, absolutely taken away.

That night, I keen and mourn at my altar, and give in to a river of sorrow which floods through me. I watch in utmost softness as an incoherent howling shakes my innards, and pieces of memory move oddly together down the current, disturbing pictures that have no name. I go to the gate of something unspeakable in me, the knowledge of my own physical death, already written in some way that I cannot grasp, the knowledge of the death and loss of others who will go before me, the knowledge of pain and illness which might strike, of random accident or elemental disaster which might happen. At the same time, in a way to which I have now become accustomed, I experience something different. By agreeing to give time to whatever is happening, without censorship, without alteration, I seem to land on the riverbed, I seem to inhabit the deepest corner, now more willing and transparent after the revelation and dissolution of 'the deal' at this afternoon's wake. This is the way it is; this is what we are given.

The last tear trickles down my cheek. My body shakes and shudders, and at the same time it is quiet all around, and, within, a deeper quiet is growing. It is as if I have agreed to something and am now to be left in peace. I fetch a pillow and a blanket and remain, lying on the floor, succoured, gentled, loved and attended to in a manner free of language.

CHAPTER 30

Out of the house goes Edie. Into the house comes a bright postcard from Australia, from the girls, and addressed to Everyone.

Edie's immediate belongings have been packed into old-fashioned suitcases, and they are taken downstairs for her by burly Trammlers. Her sister is solicitous and smaller nieces and nephews flock around her. I don't remember seeing Edie with her family before. She and Max usually went north for family meetings. 'There are more of them than us, dear,' Edie used to say repeatedly as they went off, she with neat luggage, Max with a bulging sports bag. The flat is to be let in the meantime, with precious furniture stored and basic furniture left for tenants. The rummy players helped with sorting and organising, and the precious furniture is in a safe lock-up at King's Cross until further decisions are made. An efficient and apparently necessarily ruthless organisation went on, based on the rationale that the sooner Edie was taken away from what began to feel like the scene of the crime, the better. I don't know that I agree. I put my arms around this prematurely discarded mother, and smell cologne. She has tied a pink scarf around her neck and it looks incongruous. The farewell between Edie and Marte is painful to watch. Neither of them makes noises like 'come down and visit' or 'keep in touch.' Rather like the time when they took tea together after Max's death, there is a violated and sad silence between them, the light meeting of two papery cheeks, powder drifting from Edie as Marte kisses her. When she steps into the big car awaiting her, she is like a small fish disappearing into the belly of a whale. I wave until the car has gone around the corner, and come back into a very quiet house. The air in the communal hallway is somehow changed. Marte wants to be left alone, grumbling and snuffling into a large, man-sized tissue. 'Mel didn't even say goodbye to her', she says ferociously.

'Are you missing him, Marte?'

'What for? What good would he be at a time like this?' I don't answer. Lately I have been aware of mixed feelings towards Mel. I'm pissed off that he's away and that we don't know when he will be back.

Two days later, I am starting an early morning walk after a night of dreaming in which I seemed to be part of a bad science fiction movie. I walk down the steps and see a tall, thin figure, minutes away from the house, loping thoughtfully along the pavement, chin pressed downwards, a bag on wheels trailing noisily behind him. I stop for a moment to check. Yes, it is David. A block away, walking vigorously and whistling, is Mel, his rucksack solidly on his back. I greet David, and we both turn to wait for Mel, murmuring about the coincidence of their arrival. Mel relieves himself of his luggage, and takes me in a friendly embrace.

'You look awful, Ellie,' he says as David blushes at this candour and prepares to climb upstairs. I call David back and tell them both what has happened. 'Didn't know you were so fond of him', continues Mel, irritating me with his comment, which feels witless. I want to hit him. For leaving, for coming back, for saying stupid things. David is asking about practicalities. They both want to go and see Edie, but I tell them she has gone.

'I'll go up,' says David nervously. 'See that everything's okay in the flat.' He edges past me, with a weak smile on his face. Mel is silent until the door closes upstairs.

'Give me a cup of coffee Ellie, and brandy if you haven't had it all.'

'I was going for a walk.' I sound like a grumpy child

'Well, surely you can go ten or fifteen minutes later.'

'Yes, of course I can,' We both laugh, more with nervousness than with humour. Mel tiptoes into my flat with false care.

'Marte better not hear me – she'll be furious I don't go straight to her. Is Justine there?'

'Due later today.'

'Has she been… Ellie – let's start at the beginning. And I'll provide coffee.'

He fishes into his bag and brings out a small parcel. 'Here – straight from the winding streets of Jerusalem.' He digs deeper 'And because you don't have proper equipment, here's one of those little coffee pots. Two heaped spoons of this delicious stuff – then let it rise to the boil and simmer down three times. Then you have coffee, not this brown water you usually make.'

'I won't sleep tonight.'

'So don't sleep.' He gives an expressive shrug of his shoulders.

Over the coffee and a mouthful of brandy, I tell him what's been happening. I am glad he is here. I absorb his masculinity, his attention and his response to my words. I am also irritated. There's a certainty to Mel but when I ask him eventually about his time away, he becomes less certain, more diffuse and evasive.

'Fine, fine, all well, good weather.' I give the comment about weather the look it deserves. Mel stretches and prepares to go across the landing to Marte.

'Nice to see you Ell. Enjoy your walk.'

'Nice to see you too.' As I take my crumpled face for a walk, my sore eyes, the delicate skin beneath them creased and vulnerable-looking, I feel the lurch towards Mel, his arms, his shoulder. Make it all right, Mel, make this all go away. I am a little girl and you are my daddy. My dad could make nasty things go away – but he couldn't prevent them coming back. The respite never lasted. And I couldn't bear to tell this sweet, tired, vulnerable father that his comfort wasn't working.

When I return from the misty streets, in the damp and muffled dusk, I call by at Marte's. Justine and Mel are cooking and I am invited to join them. Marte looks as if she's really pleased, but committed not to show it. There are interesting bottles and jars on her table and I see that Mel the hunter has brought back culinary trophies from the Middle East. I am watchful of the grumpy girl Ellie who demands, 'why the hell should he just come and go.' I answer her gently, 'why should he not come and go? That's his business. And after all, we all knew he'd be back before Justine left.' I see the desperately hungry younger of two siblings, aching for it all, not just half, wanting ladles and buckets and bowls of it all. My parents were good at watching out for fairness and unfairness – but there was something false about always turning to the other – and compensating for whatever the first had been given. I remember winning a competition at school and bursting through the door with a prize. I was received with congratulation, and almost instantly some reference was made to Leonie's skill. If it had happened the other way round, I would have been compensated. They tried so hard to be fair – and it never felt fair. I know there's a very young Marte in the room, but that she is now mollified.

'You look very peaky,' says Marte sharply, staring at me. 'This has all been too much.' I don't contradict her. 'Give her lots of meat,' she instructs Mel and I see my plate being heaped with steaming slices of chicken. 'I know you don't eat meat, you're one of those vegetable eaters, but you eat meat, darling. Protein.' Marte's face looks furrowed and collapsed, and then I realise she doesn't have her teeth in. 'Pass me the fangs, Mel.' Justine flinches. Mel discreetly cuts her small portion of food into very small pieces. There is a warm feeling around the table. I begin to allow the link to Marte and Mel and Justine. We take food together, we watch out for each other, passing salt, commenting on taste, all of us aware of the bubbling, rasping noises of uncomfortable breath coming from Marte.

'Just turned up, hasn't he, no news of a where or when or what time. There you have it.'

'Do you remember Errol, mother?'

'Yes. What's that? I'm not talking about Errol am I? An accountant wasn't he? Is that the one you mean? I was talking about this one here, wasn't I?' she glares at Mel, with love.

'Yes, still is.' Justine and Marte now pull at this scrap of material from their shared ragbag. What are they going to do with Errol?

'Skinny bastard,' Mel's mouth is full, he is relishing the food.

'Not anymore. Goes to the gym, works out now.'

'Works out, hey? Does anyone want that last potato?'

'Thought we might have it tomorrow.' Marte's eyes are shining with mischief. 'Did you see that Errol then? How come?'

'Funny coincidence. His brother is in property now – we talked over a deal – he reminded me about Errol, suggested we met. His brother was in the class below, remember?'

'Fat bastard.' Mel reaches for the unclaimed second drumstick.

'Errol married that fancy girl from Hampstead didn't he?'

'Was married to.' Justine looks as if she has a delicious taste in her mouth.

'Oi – is that over too? People can't stick together these days – Look at all three of you.' Marte's eyes wander accusingly around the table, across the plates of discarded bones and demolished potatoes and beans.

'Not everyone's marriage was made in heaven like yours, mother.'

'Heaven? I wouldn't say heaven, but we stuck together because we thought we had to. It's what you did in those days. And we made it work.' Marte's head sinks down into her chest; she looks like a bright fowl today. An odd, soft clucking noise emerges from her throat.

'What are you up to my girl?'

'What do you mean?'

'I know you. You look as though you're not flirting, but you are.' Justine is not sure whether to be offended or pleased. She clearly decides to be pleased, though it is obvious that the remark from her mother could begin to rankle in her.

'Mother – what you call flirting is just people having eye contact.'

'Eye contact shmy contact. Never had those things before and we all got on fine.'

'Guess what I brought for pudding.' Mel unveils a chocolate cake.

'You didn't have that all the way from Tel Aviv in your rucksack?'

'No Marte – the baker around the corner.'

'The ones that cheat?'

'No, the ones that don't cheat.' We clear away the debris of the first course and share out the cake. Justine, with a determined look, and a spoonful of desert hovering near her mouth speaks again.

'Well, I had lunch with him.'

'Who?' Marte is dribbling with joy at the taste of the crumbly base and rich filling of the cake.

'Oh gawd – am I sitting with imbeciles or what?'

'Come on darling, get on with it, tell us what happened.' Marte fixes her daughter with a flicker of affection in her eye.

'He's a nice guy.'

'Justine,' I pat her arm, 'you're preening.'

'Why not?'

'Are you going to be an item?' Mel leans back and looks at her.

'Don't be silly – all I'm saying is we had lunch and it was nice –'

'What about that fancy wife and his children?' Marte looks at her too.

'I'm not going to be asking millions of questions if I'm just having lunch am I?'

'You ask, darling, you ask. Ask, and you find out and then you know whether to do this eye contact business. The trouble is…'

'You never ask…' we all chorus. Oh, the sweetness of this game, and cake and friendly ribald laughter and Marte contented and Mel back and Justine not so prickly and I contented. The fact of connection just as it is… and then dissolving like a cloud in the late afternoon sky, pink with rays from the departed sun.

The sun has been missing for so long now, it seems an age ago when we had hot days and light clothes and green grass and people loafing outside at café tables. We've passed the winter solstice, so the days should be getting longer, but it doesn't feel like it. Trees are bare, the nights are long, the days are short and there's memory only of the palest version of the sun we remember from summertime. People wear dark colours, doors are closed against the chill and damp, there's hot soup on the menu, hot chocolate, scones, warm apple pie and cream. It's a time for turning in, burrowing, like plants, beneath the soil for rest and replenishment, dark undertakings, unseen and only guessed at.

'And what about you, young man, the prodigal son, returned all of a sudden?'

'Yes, and what about me?'

'Here today, gone tomorrow, back again today.'

Mel pokes a fork towards Marte. 'Well, as long as I'm back. Could be here today, gone tomorrow, gone the next day.' Unseen and only guessed at is the dark rooting of this man, the dark roots of each of us. Justine is nibbling on a chicken bone, eating more slowly than the rest of us who are now on chocolate cake. There's a far-away look in her eyes and I wonder if she's thinking about Errol. And who of the three might guess that I want to be back in my solitary cell, tracking the thread of solace and loss? On the outside, I feel bedraggled and quiet; on the inside I feel like a scientist, an archaeologist, a bone-doctor privately following the DNA of an ancient piece of sun-dried matter.

Mel is clicking his fingers before my face. 'Wake up, dreamy.'

'I'm going home, guys, I need twelve hours sleep.'

Justine promises me she will look in tomorrow before she leaves.

'Did you order the taxi?' Marte is replete and benevolent.

'No – actually Errol will drive me to the airport.' I leave as a potent silence envelopes Justine. I am sure she will deal with it.

I wash myself, I wash my hair. I dry it and massage rose-oil onto my skin. I put on a silky dressing gown. I remember the days of preening like Justine is doing now at the thought of Errol. I remember the wonderful joy of being desired and being excited and in preparation for meeting. After Gerry and I finally parted, I had a short love affair with a man eighteen years younger than me. I met him at a dance and our eyes locked together and erotic power was fed from there. He was tall and thin and pliant and when he pressed himself against me and fitted the palm of his shapely hand into the small of my back I wanted to lie on the floor and have him fall onto me. He came to see me once after that but it felt awkward and nothing happened. Then he phoned me a year later – and he returned and we smiled at each other, sitting on the floor of my living room where I am now, and then began a kiss where we breathed into each other and each sucked out a kingdom of breath from the other and – although I didn't fall in love with him – I fell in love with the way his dark hair met the top of his ears and the way he kept his eyes open when he lay on me and he watched me and let me watch him as he entered me and our hands moved and our mouths stayed in rapture together. In each others' eyes we saw the nakedness of desire and ecstasy. We would lie in the bath, I leaning against him, and he would soap me and sponge me slowly, washing my face as if I were a child. I would cover his back with soap and then squeeze the sponge. The water would run off his skin. We were intensely together for a couple of months and then he went away to play music in Spain. Our meetings grew less frequent. We are no longer in touch. As I think about him, now, I hold my breath and close my eyes. I don't remember his name; he was an angel.

I feel as if I'm to meet a lover now. I feel the pleasure of my body, it is at ease, flexible, experienced, shapely, tiredness making me sensual and lazy in my movements. I take a long time oiling my legs, each toe, round the knee. I feel quite beautiful, and the candlelight softens the sparse, quiet appearance of the room, holding the distinction of the altar within it, like a bed or like the stone where sacrifice is placed. A contrary script, playing itself out, seems to spool off-centre, sidelong, around my consciousness, a script in which I am sexual and partnered, and there is a he and a me. Guido is that he; the angel in the bath is that he. A faint wistful longing slides around my periphery. These are lost thoughts, wandering in a vague hinterland and the faces of other men, remembered, come and go.

I soften myself back into centre. I am rooted there, in a place of richness, soft power and movement. My body is infinite, and dark sweet birds slowly wheel in its upper reaches. I am in sojourn with myself, with the unknown mystery of myself.

Different versions of other lives I lived in the world, touch the edge of awareness as I sit before the altar, arranging myself carefully so that my back feels right. This turning away from the world feels so extreme, that I hardly read newspapers or watch television. I listen to the radio sometimes, to the news programs.

One of the touch-stones, one of the primary understandings arising from this hermit-time, tells me that there has always been war and pain and aggression and survival issues and predators and victims; there have always been those who are willing and able to turn with care towards others, and those blessed beings who carry deeper knowledge and the courage to live from that knowledge. Through decades and centuries, millennia, we experience our own version, our own form of the primitive level of survival. This time, our time, we have weapons of mass destruction, instead of bows and arrows. The impulse behind their use might be more sophisticated technologically, but the deep impulse is the same.

In my early years of teaching, I was a front line political fighter, out on marches, working late in community groups against the exploitation by the powerful of the weak: the aggression of the status quo towards women, ethnic minorities, the third world, persecuted minorities, the environment. This effort felt strong and meaningful, and it still does. People of will and integrity and energy and conscience still take on the world's problems and bring energy and strength and commitment to them, without becoming guilt-provoking zealots and adding to the ranks of left-wing and right-wing fundamentalism. I was part of sisterhood and brotherhood in those days of alternative political activism. We really did make things happen: shelters for battered women, increased provision of child care and protection for endangered children, action to alleviate the loneliness and desperation of political refugees and of the members of our community who were facing racism. There was a radical, pioneering spirit working down all these avenues in the seventies, a spirit birthed in the sixties. This was a raw and sound apprenticeship for us. We also made naïve mistakes, we were confused at times, personal agendas acting as the political, and some of us were addicted to the heady ride of anarchy and subversion. Now there are younger apprentices as well as the greying remainders of us: older ones still committed to the activist spirit, dedicated for the rest of the lives, these days perhaps focussing more on global and ecological issues.

My second touch-stone in this hermit-time tells me that pain and war and terror and fundamentalism are also in me, and that to study my own nature is to discover the nature of the world. I think of the small child who was grumpy that Mel had gone and then come back within some arbitrary time-plan. I imagine the child that I might have been, if I had been one suffering from deprivation or abuse from an early age. I imagine the rage and terror and monstrous reaction there would be, if I were that child, each time I experienced abandonment. And what if this child grew up by chance with the skill and destiny to become powerful and in charge of other people? Under the smart clothes, the smiling mouth, would lurk the bared teeth of self-protection. Through tinted glasses I would look at the world through primal eyes of survival and retribution at all costs. Equally, that child might have responded by collapsing inside, imploding rather than exploding, and being forever a victim of aggression.

The livid eyes of third world children stare at us from posters, and dare us to look further in. The eyes of children in our street stare at us, and we don't know what goes on at home.

In my time as a political activist, I – like many of my comrades - am troubled by shame and guilt, a haunted feeling that I am somehow implicated, and should make amends. This still feels true – though in a different way. I am implicated because I am here, planted with this crop of human life on our green and plentiful and terrifying home. Making it a better place is implied in the effort towards right action suggested by the Buddhists; simply wanting to be kind seems like a pretty good recipe for making sense of it all. Another gainful procedure is in exploring how things work, and developing that which works for the common good.

And then there is simply seeking; the inner imperative. Carthusian monks shut themselves into their small rooms and are bent into prayer most of the time. Their faces are luminous with silence and inward turning.

> *Whether one moves slowly or with speed*
> *The one who is a seeker will be a finder*
> *Always seek with your whole self,*
> *For the search is an excellent guide on the way.*
> *Though you are lame and limping,*
> *Though your figure is bent and clumsy,*
> *Always creep towards the One. Make that One your quest.*
> *By speech and by silence and by fragrance,*
> *Catch the scent of the King everywhere.*

(Rumi III 978-981)

And with me, the scent of the beautiful men I have known; the beautiful imprint of their bodies upon mine. And with me, the bent and clumsy figure, just that, ready for the scent of the King.

CHAPTER 31

Errol arrives in an urban jeep and Justine's luggage is loaded into the back. After the initial growl of the vicious bitch between us when she first arrived, I have come to appreciate Justine. The moment, early on in her visit, where I sensed her struggle as a young one with Marte, helped me to go behind the paint and the aggression. I am still wary of her, and am particularly cautious when she is in hunting mode, as in this situation now. Her nails are blood-red and a proprietary musk surrounds her. Errol is handsome, dark, with excellent manners and a quality of being present without really being present. He is charming to Marte and to me, slightly less charming to Mel, who responds by being laconic and friendly. They shake hands, there is time for tea before departure and we sit around Marte's chair exchanging opinions about property and aches and pains. Marte runs out of words, becomes watchful, and I cannot tell what she might be feeling about her daughter's departure. Mel makes himself scarce, and Justine goes to seek him out and speak to him privately. When she returns, an enigmatic expression on her face, I say my farewell to her and we hold glances for a moment in a non-committal, questioning way. I go to the car with her and promise to let her know if Marte's health deteriorates.

'Thank you for what you do. You are in my place, in a way. Yet you are less of a daughter than Mel is a son… Feel better about it though. I don't think he's a bastard – he's never been a bastard, it's more…' she hesitates. 'I could be proved wrong – don't bet on it, just a feeling.' She pauses. 'You're a strange one Ellie, I don't quite know what's going on with you right now – if I may say so – you seem to have a secret, but I'm not sure what. You're different from other times I've been here. Mel clams up when I ask him… you two aren't…?' she surveys me intently and then shakes her head, '… no I don't think so, somehow.'

'Well, not much I can add to that, Justine,' I say.

'You're not offended?' she responds quickly

'No offence taken.'

'What is it? Do you mind telling me – ?'

'Nothing to tell. I'm having time off. Kind of sabbatical.'

'I see…'

Errol comes round. 'Let's go – better to be early.' There's a strong, animal charge about the two of them together, yet I get the sense that they don't especially like each other. Errol brushes Justine's hip with his hand and she climbs up into the high passenger seat. I wave until they have rounded the corner.

'One back, one gone, at least you're neither coming nor going,' Marte greets me, growling from her chair.

'Don't be so sure.'

'What do you think of him then? He's up to no good, but then neither is she. Good luck to them I'd say. At least she didn't have to pay a fortune for a taxi.'

The house creaks down into its foundations like an animal with cold bones digging in the ground for winter. The Australian girls are back, healthy looking, and busy attaching themselves again to the supply teaching system. The term has already started, so they have some tramping around to do, as they put it. They are dismayed and shocked at the news of Max's death and have decided to go and put flowers on his grave. They meet at the top of the stairs with the rummy ladies who are helping with the letting of the flat, and the four of them go to the girls' top flat for tea, and to talk through the whole event. Before they go up, we find ourselves, the Aussie girls and I, in an sweet embrace, heads together.

'Shit, Ellie, can't help thinking of the limo outing, hey? He was a sweetie, wasn't he? The ladies are so lovely aren't they? They want to give us some pots pans and things. Doesn't seem quite right to take it, what do you think?'

'Take it,' I encourage Sara, who has spoken.

'There's a new tenant I think,' says Merry, 'rides a classy motorbike. Big guy, didn't smile when I smiled at him; small girlfriend.'

I had heard people going upstairs to Edie's flat, but hadn't realised anyone had moved in. I go into Marte's to see Lulu who is back on duty after a break. I am glad to see her as she moves around the kitchen getting Marte's night-time medication ready. We chat idly as she gets on with it. Lulu went to the USA to see an auntie over Christmas and New Year, but although she is willing to pass on anonymous news, she is clearly unwilling to say too much about herself. Mel is pre-occupied with a phone call, and comes in and out, and he and Lulu talk about Marte's rootin', and whether anything needs to be adapted or changed. I'm half attending to their conversation and half absent when I hear a strange noise, like the yowling of a cat.

It's the new people, on their way upstairs to Edie's flat. We listen intently, and then hear Marte calling from her bed.

'Who the hell brought in a baby? There's a baby above my head.' We troop in and stand around the bed, a complex affair with an electric motor so that the back can be raised for her night's upright sleep. All is quiet but for the sound from the oxygen container, and Marte's breathing. Then we all hear it. The sound of a baby, crying in long bursts, the sound becoming weaker and eventually disappearing with the distant sound of Edie's door closing. 'That's all I bloody need. This is going to be a dead loss, I can tell you. Edie was quiet, no trouble.' We look at each other. We know it's not about a baby. Jinny's family make enough noise above Marte's head and also there have been agreements – largely kept – about quiet hours. This is about change, and strangers and the loss of Edie and Max.

'That's all I need,' Marte continues to grumble into her chin and Lulu stays with her. Mel and I wander back to the kitchen and I want to ask him about his time with his son. Then I decide not to. Mel looks pre-occupied.

'There's always something, Ells', he says with uncharacteristic bitterness. 'The guy dies, the old lady goes and now there's a fucking baby.' I put my hand on his arm. He doesn't shake it off, but he doesn't respond. I take my hand away but remain next to him. 'I want to talk but I don't want to talk, Ell. So I won't, hey. I think I'll go and get smashed, and I'll see you tomorrow.' He calls out to Marte that he's going for a drink, and gets a grunt in return. I cross back to my flat, and cold air comes in as Mel swings open the big front door, and lets it shut heavily behind him.

I feel an ache in my heart, and it's taking the shape of Guido. I haven't thought about him for a while. He was responsive and I could stroke his thick dark hair and thin face. Even now, thinking of Guido brings him to centre stage. I feel breathless, visceral sorrow, as my body copes with the notion that it will no longer lie with him and experience the contact with his skin, and the smell of his body and its weight on me, or its weight underneath me. I reach for the phone. 'And then what, Ellie?' And there is no answer to that question. And the silence following the no answer, is clean and truthful. There is not to be a then-what for us. I know that.

The agitation in my body is Ellie, a fretful child. She can't have what she wants, and her fury travels into my blood, and sends a loaded charge through the nervous system. My first impulse is to get rid of her, send her packing through the front door, suitcase in hand. But how can I do that? She lives with me till death do us part. I retrieve her from the doorstep. She wants to blame Guido for making her unhappy, she can't understand why she shouldn't have what she wants, why she shouldn't be held and rocked and stroked until all the demons go away.

I feel the roaring life-engine in me, with its fears and desires. I stretch out my arms. Yes, I say, yes to the whole damn thing. My yes thunders out, smashing the roof of the house. It comes back in a radiant firework show, wild gigantic fiery blossoms roaring at me, popping and exploding and spreading colour into the dark sky, and spreading trails of smoke through every room. We watch, the child and I. Slowly, as the last petal fades, as the smoke dissipates, I, the child, am calmed.

One day after another, dark afternoons. I don't know what day it is, or what time it is. I have left my watch in the bathroom. The low sky, the cold and damp weather create a pressure, an inward-going pressure. I follow a pattern of small actions, sometimes private firework displays, sometimes the planting of quiet seeds. I spend regular time with Marte. Mel is meticulous in his attention to her, but quite absent in his manner otherwise. He has resumed his late night jaunts, either with the upstairs girls or on his own. Jinny and family are back into post-Christmas routine, and David has burrowed into his corner of the house, receiving the occasional student and making the occasional expedition outside. The house settles into its own slumber, hibernating within central heating and curtains drawn.

Normally I would be busy with the necessities of the new term, arranging curriculum and lectures and tutorials, sitting in warmly illuminated pubs or restaurants with colleagues, creating light and energy to push against the downward pressing climate. It is strange not to be in that mode.

My secret love affair continues in the half-light.

Returning one day with shopping for Marte, I come in to find a woman holding a baby standing with a helpless and agitated air near the front door.

'Hello,' I say.

'Hello – do you live on the ground floor?'

'Yes – I've been meaning to come up and say hello – sorry I haven't.' She extends a pale, small hand.

'It's okay.'

'My name is Ellie.'

'It's a nice name,' she murmurs abstractly, shifting the weight of the baby in her arms. It makes a small, hiccupping sound. I am not – as I have said – familiar with babies so I have no idea how old it is. There doesn't seem to be much substance within the bundle of lacy white blanket and woolly pink hat.

'What's your name?'

'Oh, yes, sorry – Zandra, With a Zed. And she's called Lennie. With an I, E.' Zandra looks around her again with agitation. I wonder at this recitation of letters, ZED, EYE, EE that maybe accompanies all introduction.

'Is everything OK?'

'Well yes, I mean no – Mike's at work, that's my partner, and the babyminder was supposed to come – I'm going to college your see ...' a small, proud smile opens and then closes. Zandra has a pretty face. She's maybe in her late twenties – I can't really tell. Her body is thin and small.

'What are you studying?'

'Computing – because then I can get a good job, see Mike has good work at the moment but we don't know how long it will last – he's a motorbike salesman and now it's winter... We'll have to get rid of the bike now anyway because of her...' She shrugs, then looks as though she's going to cry. She glances at her watch. 'I have to be there at four and I've never missed... it's only a two hour class but I must be there..' Zandra looks at me and a different expression comes over her face. I know what she's going to say and I can't stop her. 'Would you mind her? She's so easy – just sleeps, and if she doesn't I've got bottles ready and nappies.' I don't see any reason why I should say no, although I do not want to say yes.

'Just let me know what to do if she...'

'Oh, that's so wonderful – look let's go up and I'll give you everything – and my mobile number just in case.'

I leave the shopping bag outside my door and find myself reluctantly climbing the stairs and into Edie's flat. Everything looks more or less the same, but with an overlay of different clutter and another smell. Zandra brings two bottles from the fridge, and a packet of disposable nappies. 'It's breast milk,' she looks at me quickly. 'I express it. You just need to put it standing in a small jug of hot water for a few minutes before she drinks it. Test the temperature on your wrist.' I am aghast but try not to show it. 'She's only little, perhaps we'll bring the moses basket, she could sleep in there, she's used to it.' Now there is a baby, two bottles, a packet of nappies and an elaborately frilled basket with a white sheet and a white blanket in it. We are walking downstairs, Zandra writes down her mobile number and with anxious peek at the baby, asks me, as she opens the front door, to please put a note on her door for her Mike in case he gets home before she does. 'I'll be back at 6.30.' The door closes and I am left with a baby in a basket, and Marte's shopping. I cross the landing.

'Marte, here's your stuff.'

'Good thank you darling.' Marte looks ruminative today and is wearing a pink cardigan with large embroidered pink rosebuds on its pockets. 'What the hell have you got there?' she coughs.

'It was given to me with the shopping.'

'It's that baby from upstairs isn't it? Why have you got it? You're not a baby-sitter.' I tell her the story.

'Humph – wait until I tell Mel. You know what he'll say.'

'Haven't a clue what he'll say, Marte.'

'Same as me – give 'em an inch and they'll take a mile. Before you know where you are you'll be minding it night and day.'

The baby moves a little and makes a sound.

'Do you know anything about them?'

'No. And until I do they're them.' A waxen look comes over her face. 'Doctor's coming tomorrow.'

'Check up or something special?'

'Medication check up.' A look of pain clouds Marte's face. 'And I've got pain in my back.'

'Shall I do anything for you?'

'No.' Rude gesture. 'You take that thing away before it wakes up.' She gives me a soft look. 'Thanks.'

Back in my flat, I investigate what I have in front of me, before writing the note for Mike. Gingerly I move the side of the pink cap. The baby's face is very small and non-descript. Thin features, like her mother, that seem to be without any special definition. I write the note and then race upstairs, leaving the baby alone, to attach the small yellow piece of paper to Edie's door. When I come back nothing has moved. I boil water and put out a jug in readiness. I decide to put a bottle in it, just in case. I put the basket on my sofa, near the heater, and I sit and watch. Removing the little pink cap from her head, for the room is warm, I can see her more clearly. There is a light dusting of hair on her, and her eyelashes look a little sticky. I lean over into the basket and smell the downy, milky, strange new smell that she has. I don't want her to wake up. There's a very light tap on the door. Mel. He tiptoes in and whispers, 'Marte told me to come and check you out. She thinks you've gone soft.' He goes over to the basket and looks in. I watch him. 'Poor little bastard,' he says lightly.

'It's a girl, Mel. Lennie. EYE, EE,'

'It's all the same at this age – one lot wee upwards and the other downwards as far as I can tell.'

'Mel – why's the doctor coming tomorrow?'

'Pain in her back – '

'You worried?'

'Sort of – just waiting – could be nothing, could be something.'

'Apart from that, she seems in reasonable good spirits.'

'Yeah…'

'Mel?'

'I'll check out with you one of these days. I didn't have the best time back home – and it's not anything I can really talk about because there's not anything I can really do – I'm not avoiding you, it's not about you. And the girls – they're just a springboard out. Uncle Mel knows what he is doing.' There's a murmur from the basket. Mel puts his arm around me and we sit quietly for a moment, watching movements under the white blanket. I wonder why he is reassuring me about the girls. I feel strangely pleased that they're 'just' something, rather than significant. It's a pleasure to have his arm around me, it has weight but rests lightly, and I am in agreement. 'Let me know if you want anything. I know how to change a nappy. I've done plenty of those,' says Mel and takes his arm away gently.

After he goes, I pull a disposable nappy from the packet. It looks easy enough. Sticky bits for fastening, no more terry towelling and pins and nappy liners. I realise, from the response in me to Mel's few words, and his arm, that the distance between us since his return has been hurting quite a bit and that I had put a stoical curtain around it all, since it didn't feel right to ask him about it.

The movements in the basket are becoming more pronounced and whimpering sounds emerge from the small, undistinguished, pale face. Her mouth opens and turns into a toothless hole, and suddenly there is a loud wail. 'Okay, okay.' I dive into the basket and pick up the bundle, 'SShhh, it's all right, don't be sad.' I manoeuvre the baby so that her head settles into the crook of my arm and I put my other hand under her back. The crying doesn't stop so I jiggle her up and down, at the same time walking towards the bottle of milk. With difficulty, I test the temperature on my wrist, pick up the bottle and it feels just warm enough, so I take it and we go back to the sofa, and I tilt the horrible-looking teat towards her face, not quite understanding how she can bear the size and taste of this rubber nipple. After some adjustment, Lennie hooks on and the crying stops and her little mouth works intensely. As I watch her, her utter dependency and vulnerability grab me by the throat and by the heart. I remember that brief interlude with Molly, Gerry and me. Lennie finishes the bottle, and I pack her onto my shoulder and pat her back. She gives a loud burp. I decide to hold her for a while, and walk up and down. The small package in my arms becomes heavier, and is very warm. How odd – and ruthless – this new life in Edie's flat.

CHAPTER 32

Zandra is back when she says and Mike arrives with her, a shy man rather than an unfriendly one, with a bullet-head and washed-out eyes. They are young, grateful, and tell me that Zandra's mother lives on the other side of town in Croydon, frustrated at the distance that lies between them. The babysitter has bowed out altogether and I agree to look after Lennie for two hours a week until the course is over in another five weeks. This creature has entered the hermitage and the pilgrim in search of stillness is not going to refuse her.

Dr. Marcus visits Marte. He prescribes pain-killers and says to Mel afterwards that a visit to the hospital for investigation might be necessary sooner or later. He doesn't want to subject her to unnecessary stress, and adds, just as he is leaving 'interpret that as you will.' I don't like the sound of this parting shot. Neither does Mel, but, helpless, I want to leave it in Dr. Marcus' hands. Mel agrees, absently. A dark mist seeps around us and through the rooms.

After two weeks' caustic pronouncement on my babysitting, Marte says to me indifferently that she wouldn't mind helping by holding the baby next time it is around at my place. Soon after Zandra leaves it for the third time, with its paraphernalia of moses basket, nappies and bottles, I go across the landing, bottle and jug in hand. I am now becoming proficient at this game.

Next to Marte, on her table, is the usual tray with glasses, each holding a nebuliser, upside down so that we know which are full and which empty, and Marte is sucking hard at a half-full neb when I come in. She gestures to the chair, and looks at the baby.

'He's gone shopping,' she burbles, with her mouth full. Lennie is wakeful this late afternoon, regarding the world. Her hands are furled tightly. I pull a chair close to Marte and take hold of her free hand.

'Try this.' I put her finger into the small pink fist. Lennie's fingers uncurl and then curl back again, grasping the bony finger hard. We remain in this configuration until the neb comes to an end. 'Do you want to feed her?'

'What do I want to do that for?' but she turns towards the baby, and I put Lennie into Marte's arms.

'Put a bloody cushion under her, I can't hold her like this.' Half on a cushion, half in Marte's arms, Lennie blinks and begins to fret softly. 'Take her away now...'

'Just a minute, Marte – she's probably hungry.' Swiftly, I put the teat into Lennie's mouth and the bottle into Marte's hand. There's a moment of awkward adjustment and then the baby settles and sucks and Marte watches her and I watch Marte's finely carved, bony, white face, and how the hairs of her eyebrows are stiff like toothbrush bristles; I see the myriad lines carved into her papery countenance, and I see an expression of sorrow and tenderness gathering in her eyes like a faint sheen over darkness. Marte curves around the dowager's hump of her back, and yet part of the shoulder revealed as her cardigan pulls away a little, is pink and smooth. Lennie comes to the end of the bottle, and I arrange her on Marte's shoulder, supporting her weight by placing my hand under her bottom.

'Do you remember this bit?'

'Of course – what do you think – you have to wind them, don't you.' Her hand circulates round the infant's back, and Lennie obliges with a loud belch.

'Pardon! Where's your manners?' Marte looks pleased with herself, and keeps her hand rotating, patting Lennie's back every now and then. 'Take her now darling. It's enough.' I take the baby. 'We have to do some practical things, Ellie darling.'

'Right now Marte? Wait until Zandra comes back.'

'Zandra – such a name. Never heard of Zandra did you – should be Sandra. What's the point?'

'What do you want me to do, Marte?'

'Oh it's not for now – I was telling Mel. You know that box in my bedroom, the silver one...'

'Oh yes – '

'Well, we have to take it out and get on with the will. It's got to be sorted. It's not quite all tied up – and I want you and Mel have to get it sorted for me.'

'OK. When he's back we'll arrange...' It's now Marte who's looking at me.

'Suits you, with that baby I mean. Didn't you ever...'

'No Marte – it's not something I...'

'Was it low sperm count with that man of yours – the one who went to the seaside? Oh I'm sorry that's rude – isn't it, but it's usually the man and then they say it's the woman and now it's all that stuff in the water from the pill. In the old days...'

'Men were men!' I say, sticking a tongue out at her. The baby goes red and farts.

'Take her away darling – go and do all that nappy stuff in your house.' Not long after I leave I hear the front door open and slam shut and then the sound of Marte's door opening. Mel and the shopping are back.

I put Lennie on the floor onto a changing mat, and undo her babysuit. I clean her with cotton wool and warm water, pat her dry. From a small jar I take cream to stroke onto the new skin. Her limbs are soft, her vulva out of proportion large to the rest of her body. She kicks a little and we look at each other. A warm, astonished feeling arises in my heart and I tell her that I love her. I pack her neatly back into her new nappy, dress her again and wrap her in a blanket. We walk up and down my room, and I sing to her and sway with her against my body, until I put her down into her basket and sit quietly next to her. Images of Marte's pink shoulder come into my mind. What does she want us to take out of the silver box? I know that box – it sits in her bedroom and she has the key hidden in one of the drawers, under her long, elasticated knickers. I look again at Lennie and wonder at her leaving the treasure house of souls to come down and enter the body of a being entrusted to Zandra and Mike. What complex and mysterious threads of intention have been at work to let this particular destiny come to pass? My mind circles with the question and comes back, fruitless, like a boomerang obediently returning on its own ellipse, while another part of my knowing, wordless and patient, sits with me like a monument of sublime weight and amplitude, decorated with soft calligraphy, only just glimpsed through the veil that flutters between this world and the next.

The young parents, arriving to collect their baby, dive with their eyes and their hands straight to the basket, then apologise for not saying hello to me.

'Same next week?' Zandra confirms. 'Was she good?'

'Very good.' I intend to follow them out into the hall towards the silver box, but something holds me back. Something is arising in the hermit, and I am interested to see what it is. I sit before the altar, light a candle, breathe and wait. There it is – a slight but perceptible flicker in the heart. A movement arises from the flicker, like a wave coming suddenly out of a placid sea. I rise with the wave and it gives me a sense of the beauty of this time of solitude and enforced minimalism where I meet myself as often as I can, naked and unadorned by distraction. And what is this nakedness? It is the heart daring to open, even in the face of pain and exposure. My heart yields to Lennie, to her parents, to Marte, to my own turbulence. No cover-up or distraction, no cool exterior – I look in the mirror. This is a second-rate mirror, though, inferior in reflective quality to my heart, or the eyes of another. I see only the silvered rendition in the mirror above my fireplace, of a version of a woman looking at herself.

Keep walking, though there's no place to get to.
Don't try to see through the distances.
That's not for human beings. Move within,
But don't move the way fear makes you move.

I make Rumi's words mine, shape them to my story. By giving up the search outside, and searching the world inside, I am full of unspoken poetry. Rumi speaks to my heart. My eyes fall on the bright card on the mantelpiece, sent by Joss from Thailand. She and Jack have been there since early January, wiling away the winter hours 'having fun, bought you a sarong.' Next week we will enter March, with its promise of wind, rain and the barely perceptible smell of spring, and Joss will be back. I imagine her body brown and sharp as a hunting knife. I blow out the candle on my altar, and go across the landing.

Lulu is busy with Marte's medication when I come in. Mel is hunched over the kitchen table, reading the newspaper.

'I heard about the baby,' says Lulu archly, cutting a paracetamol in half. The baby is becoming known as Ellie's baby, and Mel, without looking up, tells me I'm a natural-born mother.

'I'll clip your ear, Mel,' I say and rattle his newspaper. 'Look at you with your with page three babies!'

'A man's got to do what a man's got to do. If they put these pictures in the paper, we have to look at them, don't we?'

'I'm not going to bed yet,' says Marte crisply. 'I have business to do.'

'Can't it wait till tomorrow?' Lulu isn't interrupted in her task. 'I'm not leaving you in the kitchen for the night.'

'Well then, they'll have to come into my bedroom.' Lulu takes Marte by the arm and the long trek to the bedroom begins. Mel folds up his paper.

'It's silver box time, she wants to sort some things out.'

'What's the urgency, Mel?'

'Don't think there is any – but since I've been back – you know she's started these long night-time chats. She goes to bed and then the bell rings – that one I brought for her from Jerusalem – and I go in and there's either 'I'm dying' or 'It's time to talk.' And so we talk. Long-ago reminiscences – stories about Harry…'

'Did Marte have brothers or sisters? You never hear about them.'

'She was by far the youngest – the others were quite grown-up when she was born – they're all dead now.'

'Do you have brothers or sisters Mel?'

For reasons that I don't understand, an icy silence arrives between us – an encompassing cold darkness gathers in from nowhere. Mel looks unlike himself, then seems to draw back, make an effort, draw forward again. 'I have a sister,' I say 'Leonie – I never see her, she's in the States – I don't remember Marte talking about brothers and sisters – Cubby was more like family wasn't he…' I am aware I am babbling. Mel stands up and puts the kettle on.

'No. No siblings.' Slowly, painfully, the darkness partly disperses itself. Threads of it, like torn pieces of cloth caught on a barbed wire fence, still hang in the room. My heart is racing, I don't know why, and I feel relief when Lulu comes back.

'Okay guys, she wants you two now.'

'I'll just make coffee Ell – do you want any?'

'No Mel – I'll see you there.'

'Ellie…' Lulu calls after me. 'Just in case she forgets, she wants you to invite Hilde and Madeleine for tea.' Marte is sitting like an imperious gargoyle against her raised headboard. Her teeth are out and her lips are pressed back in a death's-head grimace. She is coughing, and the gurgling sound of phlegm in her chest is disagreeable to hear. I want to clear my own throat, I want to turn her upside down and shake her so the mounds of stuff can come out, all at once.

'When do you want Hilde and Madeleine to come to tea?'

'Saturday.' She makes a guttural, unpleasant sound and seems to be gasping for air.

Mel comes in with coffee, followed shortly afterwards by Lulu. The watery upheaval in Marte's lungs starts to settle.

'We'll talk about the menu later... for Saturday,' I say

'Saturday?' Mel sits on the edge of the bed. 'Vicar's tea-party?'

'It's not so funny,' says Marte around the mouthpiece of a neb, 'Actually I want the rabbi to come...' We look at her.

'You haven't set foot in a synagogue for years, Marte,' says Mel, amicably.

'Not Saturday,' she says. 'Not the rabbi on Saturday – the girls on Saturday. The rabbi during the week. When he can. He's a busy man.' Lulu goes back to the kitchen, and we hear her calling out that she's going. The door closes and Marte lies quietly, the nebuliser slightly falling out of her mouth, spraying a drizzle of chemicals onto the sheet. I take it, switch it off, and put it down on the bedside table. Mel is looking at Marte in a serious way. She looks at him through half-closed eyes.

'The girls on Saturday for tea; the rabbi during the week, and Ell and I to help you sort out the silver box tomorrow maybe?' Marte seems to sink further back into her pillow, relieved that a program has been spelled out. There is order and procedure, in the way that she wants. 'Shall we leave you to sleep?'

She looks at Mel craftily through her half-closed eyes. 'Perhaps just a tiny brandy – and one for you two if you want to stay a little.'

We are now in attendance to three small brandies on a silver tray and we sip slowly and silently. I am still disturbed by the blackness that descended between Mel and me. On the surface all seems well and as usual, but underneath is fragility and a secret and I don't know what soreness I trod on, unwittingly.

'How well do you know the rabbi?' asks Mel.

'You don't have to know him well. I am a member of the congregation – that's how Harry got buried properly.'

'Is that why you want him? Thinking of being buried one of these days?'

Marte looks at Mel with affection and amusement. 'You can't provoke me, my boy, we all know what's going on, and things have to be organised.'

There's a bond between Marte and Mel which I can't quite fathom.

There's a quality of shared understanding between them, and that's about as far as I can get. Meantime, the brandy is going down slowly and smoothly and I feel a warm and trusting sensation in my breast. I slip into a light and peaceful feeling, as if all is well in world. The quantity of brandy I have sipped is scarcely responsible for this state. It has arisen of itself and for no reason. This is something I have come to notice – that the states that come and go are not necessarily affixed to an obvious event. I don't want to ask why this is happening, it would be like treading on a dream with heavy boots. I am beguiled though by an immediate experience of Ellie less provoked by her needs and fears and clamorous thoughts. What is left is an abiding state in the belly, and a quieter mind, and I have acute attention for what is around me – the rictus of Marte's mouth, and Mel's expressive eyebrows.

Marte is falling asleep, and breath rattles through the dark cavern of her face. Mel is far way in his thoughts. I get up and take the three empty glasses.

'Ell, I…'

'No, I…' I stand at the door of Marte's bedroom. She stirs and sighs uncomfortably in her chest. Into emptiness I receive Mel and whatever it is he wants to say and can't say.

'Goodnight Ellie – we'll do the silver box tomorrow.'

'Good night Mel.'

CHAPTER 33

'Well of course there's Justine.' The silver box is open and an assortment of documents, folders, envelopes and scraps of paper fill it to capacity. Mel and I nod. Of course, there's Justine.

'Now she's a woman who has made her own money and I'm proud of her for that.' Marte's forefinger pokes emphasis at both of us. 'So she's getting… but not everything. You have to be fair.' This process of approaching fairness has given Marte an energy, a temperature which lights up her face.

We are in the kitchen, she is sitting on her adjustable chair. On her lap is her favourite small rug, a hot water bottle and a handbag and a nebuliser is ready and waiting next to her. She wears a navy cardigan. The silver box is on the table, its key, on its tarnished ring, sits in the lock. 'Mel – do you have paper and pen – you can't remember all this.' Mel demonstrates, like a good – but droll – schoolboy, that he has a notebook and pencil. 'Write on the front – Will,' says Marte firmly. Mel hesitates for a moment, and then does that. 'Let me see.' Marte peers through her glasses. 'That's good. Now we know what's what and we don't have to scrabble around looking for things when we need them.'

Marte sits back in her chair, taking a difficult breath that wavers through her damaged lung, a breath which can't find purchase on the collapsed surface of the alveoli, a breath which has no space to land. Her chest and shoulders puff out in an attempt to help, the navy woollen shoulders ride up in tandem. I find myself holding my own breath, then as I breathe out, Marte finds some sort of narrow purchase in herself, and the violent moment is over. The tiny bubbles of healthy alveoli normally create extended area for oxygen exchange. Marte's bubbles have burst – and the breathing-ground is diminished, and diminishing.

'I know spring is coming,' she says breathlessly, 'I am just going to be able to see the buds open and turn into leaves and flowers.' Mel and I are silent, attentive. 'Lulu,' Marte says firmly. 'I know I pay her, but that's different. She's an angel. Write Lulu, Mel. Then there's Hilde and Madeleine. You don't forget your friends. We've had our fights but that's friendship.' Hilde and Madeleine, brave souls, still tottering around where Marte is unable to, golden-curled and rouged, fragile, brittle and defiant, maintaining artificial trappings of summer, while, beneath this catalogue of colour, autumn and winter suck out colour and sap, disturbing the skeletal structure and the flesh still clinging to it. Regularly, the taxi brings them to Marte's door, and they eat smoked delicacies and maybe drink a little gin and tonic after tea. They play cards, but mostly they talk, trying to remember what they have forgotten from the immediate past, but remembering in full detail, stories from long ago. 'Hilde was a transport-kind, you know,' murmurs Marte. We know. 'She has really been a survivor. Lucky though, she landed with good people. Many didn't. Madeleine, she and I were more from the Russian end – Hilde had German ancestors. Isn't it strange – lots of German-Jews really liked being German. They were happy there before... before all that. Being German suited them.' Marte glances at us. 'You two came after all that. But it is still part of you. Only – you have to work it out for yourselves what that part is. We all have to work it out for ourselves. That's why I don't like religion – they think they have to work it out for you. That you are too stupid or too scared to work it out for yourselves...' Marte pauses, looking clammy and exhausted. She closes her eyes. Mel and I wait, saying nothing. I wonder whether Marte is making good because time is running out, or whether she is simply organising because she wants to. It's hard to tell. Marte's eyes open. Again she looks at us. 'And you two', she says, 'write down Melvyn and Elena. Now don't be shy – you have been good to me and I don't really know why, I'm an old crab. But still... I want you two to...' Mel puts down the pencil.

'Marte, if you're doing a will, and we're included, I don't think we can be doing this...'

'Yes, yes of course, I'm not a grandmother sucking eggs,' she cuts in impatiently. 'This is the first step. I'm not saying amounts – that's none of your business. I know that – so let's just leave your names, eh? And now – there are various people you don't know about...'

Over the next hour, Marte reveals a cluster of names and circumstances, people in this country and in other countries, old people and young people, whom she has been helping over the years. Standing orders, personal donations... When she mentions a Palestinian family living in the Gaza strip, and shows us an old photograph, there's a silence in the room of attention and respect. As we go on, deepening our attention, the more business-like is Marte. She is avoiding our eyes now, somewhat exhausted, but clearly determined to reach a certain point before the box can be closed and locked again. Pale and shrivelled, finally, her energy having completed its task, she lies back. The next step, after clarifying amounts and addresses, is to contact her lawyer and make formal this informal preparation. I have been given this task, and told chop-chop, he who hesitates is lost.

When Lulu comes in, she rounds on us in mock critique, asking us why we have let Marte become so exhausted.

'They kept me up all afternoon', says Marte, glinting with mischief. 'Now I am going to bed and I'm going to bed in this chair.'

'No, you're not,' says Lulu. 'Bed is bed.'

'Bed is wherever you are lying,' says Marte sharply, 'and I want to stay here tonight.' Lulu looks at us. 'No good making eyes with them. It's nothing to do with them. It's me. It's what I want.' There is something childish and wilful in Marte, but this is not all. Something else is driving her wish.

'One night, Lulu. We can make a bed here – organise a footrest. And she has the alarm buzzer around her neck, and the bell for Mel,' I suggest.

'The bell for Mel, ding dong bell,' says Marte gleefully. Lulu is a little ruffled. She enjoys doing things professionally, and this clearly feels messy. After grumbling, she capitulates, and Marte is arranged, in her nightwear, and she and Lulu go through all bedtime procedures in the kitchen. Mel and I go across the landing into my flat to give Lulu time to make her usual advance on Marte with warm water, soap and towel.

'Ellie – ' Mel and I sit together on the sofa. 'I will see her through – we will – I will repay her for…'

'For what Mel?'

'For the way she saw me through.' I assume Mel means the divorce – he has tears in his eyes and his voice is uneven. I stroke his hand. The phone rings. I wonder whether to move, but Mel breaks our contact by getting up and going into the kitchen.

'I'm back,' says Joss.

'Good time?'

'Depends what you mean. I'm coming over.' Joss-language: not can I come over, but I am coming over. The receiver has been replaced, and I can almost hear her front door closing.

When Joss arrives, sun-browned after weeks of Indonesian sun, a knife-edge presents itself, a knife-edge carrying a small satchel, her eyes glowing brightly within the narrow confines of her face.

'Ellie, you look so pale, let's look at you properly, are you all right?' We survey each other under the lamp-light. She looks magnificent, but there are dark rings under her eyes. 'How's everything, the old lady and the gorgeous semitic Mel Poppins..?' She doesn't wait for an answer, but ruffles about in her satchel and produces a silky, colourful stretch of material. 'It's for you – it's got the greens and blues you like.' I stretch out my arms to my friend and her lean shape comes right in to the proffered curve and her head is on my shoulder and we both somehow wrap ourselves into the beautiful piece of material, and into the blue and green silk sarong she cries. I have no idea what it is about and I think – I have just sat here with Mel and I have no idea what was going on for him, nor what was going on for Marte earlier. Now here's Joss whose unexplained short, sharp shower is soon over, leaving her dry and musky again.

'Ellie,' she is holding my hand, we are still connected shoulder and hip. 'It's so gorgeous there – well, you remember – and kind of decadent. You know, long showers and massage and lying on deckchairs and we met this couple and played scrabble with them. Jack was flirty-flirty with the woman – his type you know, bottle-blonde and tits ready to explode…' She gets up and cavorts obscenely in front of me.

'Okay Joss, I want to know – how did she play scrabble…?' Joss licks her lips and leans over the table so that her breasts show.

'Mmmm – now what can I do with a zed and a queue?'

'How do you fight back Joss, when you haven't got big knockers really?'

'With difficulty,' she admits ruefully, peering down into her compact cleavage. 'But I do eyes very well as you know,' she says, looking deeply into my own eyes. 'What about 'quiz,' darling, all you need is a 'you' and an 'I…!'

I roar with laughter. Joss has a prime sense of comedy, using her expressive face and voice, and we roll about, repeating words and mannerisms, rioting as we call it. I can hear my grandmother's voice 'This will end in tears children.' But it doesn't. It began in tears and it ends in helpless laughter, laughing at nothing really, nothing that could be explained. It is as light as can be, and my head and belly feel sweet.

'Where's Jack?'

'Off to see his ghastly mother – back tomorrow – I refused to go. Now tell me about you – what's been happening and have you and Poppins been at it like rabbits?'

'No, we don't do rabbits – '

'More's the shame, you're a monument to celibacy, and you're in your prime, well…'

'Joss – if my hormones started jumping I'd jump with them.'

'Do you think he's gay?'

'Who?'

'Who? Father Christmas? Poppins of course.'

'No.' Joss' energy pulls and tugs at me like multi-coloured, effervescent, streamers. I begin to circulate around my own may-pole, flying with my own ribbons as we talk.

Joss and I discard the subject of Mel's sexuality and reinvestigate and embroider stories from the past. We eat and drink, prepare a bed for her, examine each other's faces for blemish and aging under a cruel light in the bathroom, and after application of a rose cream from Thailand, we end the day.

I'm awakened by the sound of doorbells, and doors opening and closing, and immediately think it must be Joss, deciding suddenly to go home, although it is still dark. Mad woman, I think, but since it's Joss, let it be, I'll hear in the morning. Then Joss is in my room, in a white tee-shirt, asking me anxiously whether I think we're being raided.

'Oh God, it must be Marte' I say, flinging on a dressing gown. Joss puts a big winter coat over her tee-shirt and we go out onto the landing. Marte's door is open, a sleepy-looking Mel, his clothes seemingly put on backwards, is talking to a man in a uniform. Another man is there, and I hear Marte barking in the background. Eventually we discover that Marte, initially upright and sleeping on the kitchen easy-chair, began, without waking, to move down its slippery surface. As she landed gently onto the floor, she leaned without knowing on the alarm button that hangs around her neck at night, and social services were there rapidly. They have a key to the house and to Marte's flat, let themselves in and discovered her.

'There's no problem,' she had said from the ground, seemingly unperturbed by the commotion or by any thoughts of guilt. 'I am warm and wrapped up, and the only person who is going to lift me up is asleep in the room next door.' Astonishingly, Mel hadn't heard anything of all of this, until aroused by a man in uniform suggesting that it would be best if he came and put his relative to bed. As the men departed, they left behind them an unsaid sentence, heavily painted onto their facial expressions and body language. We all felt as though we were monsters who had been mistreating an innocent old woman by leaving her in the kitchen all night because it was too much trouble to put her to bed.

At four in the morning, Mel, Joss and I are drinking tea and eating biscuits, and Marte is telling us stories from the days of auctions and going around to markets in the countryside. The adventure seems to have given her life. By five o'clock we three are exhausted, and have no fight left when Marte again refuses to go to her bed. Eventually – and what would the two rescuers say to this? – at her instruction, we tie her into the chair, by binding soft scarves around her waist and under the chair seat. I am quite horrified by this procedure, imagining that she will slide down again and ring for help, but this time when they come, she will have been strangled. Mel seems to be in a sleep-deprived, malleable frame of mind, and ends up placing small cushions under the scarves to soften the tightness of captivity. Joss and I creep back to my flat and to our beds.

CHAPTER 34

'Am I disturbing you?' Joss asks, much later in the morning. 'No – it's nice to have you back.'

'Then I'll stay a while.' We lounge on the sofa, sprawl on my bed, sit at the kitchen table, talk gently. Joss rummages in her bag and brings out further bottles acquired in Thailand from a woman who gave her exclusive facial treatment, spraying her face with oxygen-laden vitamins and minerals.

'Tincture of papaya, exfoliant.'

'How does it work?'

'Oh, let's not get technical – it feels wonderful. Let's try it on you.' We examine my skin in the magnifying mirror. I see soil erosion and empty water holes.

'This is a lousy mirror, Joss.' She's busy with pads of cotton wool, murmuring over my lunar surface as she dabs and pats.

'You've got good skin but it's a bit neglected. Now I'm going to deep cleanse, London's pollution is a horror.' I lie back and Joss' face, a concentrated brown triangle, comes close to mine as she opens and closes creams, jells, lotions and oils. I allow her to play. In matters like this, Joss is the queen of arcane knowledge. She finds remedies, and unusual ingredients, checks carefully for a possibly insincere sales pitch. I feel like a baby monkey being groomed by its mother, and submit happily to her. We know each other's bodies well. Things we have revealed to each other have probably not been revealed so nakedly to lovers: moles and marks, orange peel and subsidence. We know each other's sexual joy-spots, as Joss calls them – second-hand – for sexuality has been discussed and turned upside-down though it generates no personal spark between us. It's a relief to have all that agitation and tension located elsewhere, leaving us to tend to each other and investigate in peace.

Finally, the process is complete. We rest for a while and then, under careful instruction, I do the same for Joss.

'Now do it well, sweetheart, I'm much more fussy than you,' she insists.

'In this respect, yes –'

'Yes – this may be the only respect – my skin is delicate. I know I'm fussy about my skin whereas you lie back and let me get on with it. You seem to be easy-going Ell, but it's deceptive. There's a moment when you – you don't even say it – there's a red light.'

'How can you tell?'

'Your nostrils and your upper lip!' I smooth the skin under Joss' eyes. 'Your nostrils flare slightly and your upper lip tightens. It's very subtle. But I notice it. Then I know you're going to be fussy.'

'Funny – that's how I see Leonie…'

'Oh no!' Joss would shake her head if she could but she has to remain still under my busy fingers. 'I've seen Leonie – it's not fussy, it's in a tantrum – and she's more like a horse! You know – you can see her snorting a mile off – and no, her upper lip doesn't tighten, it simply juts out.' I remember Leonie's tantrums from childhood, she would make a big noise and there'd be a scurrying and a placating around it. We all knew what she wanted, and very often she would get it. My nature I suppose was basically different, but maybe I realised that the noisy, temperamental corner was occupied and I chose a different position.

'Yes Joss, I'm more of the slow burner… cooking away inside and then suddenly steaming.'

'So how did you get what you wanted?'

'I suppose I just worked away around things – asking carried too high a premium. They were exhausted from Leonie's way of asking. I suppose also, the things I wanted were quite interior things – atmosphere, a certain kind of attention, a certain way of being.'

'A little more attention on the neck – and not too much cream,' murmurs Joss with her eyes closed. I watch my fingers, moving over her face. I know I have skilful fingers, Joss has told me this. And men have told me this too. I remember one time slapping Leonie with those fingers and then being slapped by my mother. I am about eight, and Leonie is teasing me. It is a hot day in August, we are both irritable, and I am the only target in sight.

'You're not interesting,' she says to me firmly and with conviction. 'You don't say anything interesting, and you don't look interesting.' This hits a very sore spot. Leonie's volatile temperament and luscious looks mean that she always catches the eye before her little sister does. How does she know that this is how I torment myself when I feel sore and invisible? How does her pincer-mind find this place? I am enraged at this exposure, and before I can stop myself, my right hand lifts itself and lands with a hard clout on Leonie's cheek. For a second, the two of us, horrified, gaze at each other. Leonie's cheek reddens and she lets out a mighty howling. Mother runs in and I receive a smack on the backside and, crying, rush into my room. At the same time, I am redeemed and triumphant. Most of all, I become visible and interesting to myself.

Joss' treatment has come to an end, and we turn on the TV, lounging against each other on the sofa.

'How long's Mel going to stay?'

'Don't know. For the duration, I think.'

'It would be devastating for her if he left, wouldn't it? Hasn't she become rather dependent?'

'Yes – but on the whole contented. I can't help feeling he's good for her… they have a deep bond. And don't keep giving me that sharp look. I like him, and we have a strange, unspoken closeness – and that's it.'

'But he's dishy, and if you don't mind my saying so I prefer him to that Italian.'

'So what?'

'What do you mean so what? Dishy means on a plate, in front of you…'

'So what…' I poke her slender ribs. 'Doesn't mean I have to eat it.'

'Yes, but if you don't use it, it will grow over, you know – use it or lose it – hey, aren't you frustrated?'

'Sometimes. Anyway it's not that long since the Italian as you call him, was here.'

'I can't stand it when you get into your nun persona.'

'Bless you my sister.'

'Oh piss off.'

Joss goes to explore the fridge and the grocery cupboard, and brings back a plate of cheese and biscuits and chocolate. We eat and then Joss starts to worry at me again.

'But what's up Ell?'

'What's up where?'

'Well, nothing's up your pussy that's for sure. No, you're different these days. Can't say how.'

'Am I different towards you?'

'No I can't say that.' She chews on a piece of cheese. 'It's not obvious.' She gives me a hard look. 'You're not dying of some filthy disease without telling me are you?'

I put my arms around her.

'No, I'm fine, just taking time off – I've been working real hard.'

'Aren't you bored?'

'Sometimes.'

'Ellie – stop it with this sometimes, hey. It's annoying me.'

'Joss, sometimes I am bored and sometimes frustrated and sometimes peaceful. It's just going on…' She is mollified, for the moment, and turns back to the TV screen.

Why didn't I tell her? Wouldn't it be so easy? Isn't it unfair not to? We are so close; she knows of my quest, she knows of that longing in me. She has her own version of helplessness before her daily hungers, and a place of quietness where she rests. She has a capacity for acute, insightful observation. I am so near to telling and imagine the relief of doing so.

'Ellie,' Joss disconnects from the screen. 'I was watching myself, you know, my behaviour, while I was on holiday.' She looks at me, her face caramel-brown beneath the pearly sheen of lotion and cream. 'I feel terribly sheepish now and then.' She frowns. 'I know I'm a sharp, fierce bitch, I'm a dog-face with a sheep underneath!' I look at my friend.

'I don't see you as a sheep.'

'Yes – sheepish, woolly. Sometimes I don't know what I want and then I just follow the herd. No – maybe I'm a chameleon. I adapt to the environment – the people environment.'

'Yes, chameleon, I see you more as an actress – a mimic.'

'Yes – all very well – but you know how some people make demands on the environment – lay down their colour, so to speak – well I soak up colour from everyone all around me. And then I don't know what colour I am.'

'Give me a for instance.'

'What shall we do today, what shall we eat? I don't seem to mind. We'll go this way or that way, I'll eat this or that.'

'Maybe you really don't mind.'

Joss puts her hands on my shoulders and shakes me.

'I do mind – if I didn't, I would just go on soaking and agreeing, but I don't know why I mind, and what I mind. That's why I love Jack. He knows exactly what he wants, and he thinks he knows what I want. And that's why I hate him, too.' I want to laugh but Joss looks so sad that I put my arms around her. She sighs. 'I want, I don't want. I like, I don't like. It drives me mad.'

'What do you want Joss?'

'To know what I want, of course! Or not to want at all. But that's not how we're constructed. What a sadistic game this is … Given a set of wants, and then tormented by them' Joss wanders off to check her phone for messages. I think about what she's said. Ever since I can remember

I've known what I want. A memory arises of walking along the Thai beach – Guido is not with me, I take a late afternoon walk after we make love. He lies asleep on the sheets, his arms languid by his side. I walk through throngs of people, Thai families, tourists, fishermen, until I come to a quieter section of the beach. I stand and watch the waves rising and falling, and the rising and falling starts to happen inside of me, in my chest, in my throat. I am not big enough to contain that which is happening and it becomes like an inner shout of I want, and what I want is all of this, I want to be big enough to encompass the rising and the falling, and the more my skin stretches and my chest expands, the more the waves crash into the still-constraining edges. The wanting is of and beyond Guido, of and beyond the sexual delight we just experienced, the wanting is for my energy simply to receive the magnificence of nature around me, for my energy to rise up without question and meet this expression as all of nature rises and falls, as Guido and I had risen to each other and fallen to each other. As I stand there, I become a colossus, straddling the ocean with naked body – and the foam arising and entering my body through the fissure between my legs, and my hair working into the clouds, my hands clutching the crowns of perpetual trees, pulling at vines and startling the birds lying under thick, green leaves. That's what I wanted then... and now I want to become tiny and to enter, like a benevolent micro-organism, the consciousness of my friend, for a fraction of a second, to experience first hand, under the skin, her nature.

Joss moves around in the kitchen again, opening cupboards and closing them and something opens and closes in me. A movement in my chest, like a plunger which bores into the earth to seek for oil, is on its way slowly downwards. The sensation is excellent and heavy and grave and I am pulled into the geo-strata of my belly and there I sit.

'I'm going to make us tea,' says Joss 'and then I'm going to go home and see what kind of mood that man is in after seeing his mother.' We drink tea, and I am, for no apparent reason, replete, now drawing up rich oil from my innards, sending barrels along the arteries, streamlined tankers along the veins.

The plunging moves downwards as I have known it move other times before, and felt before; bringing up with the oil, also shards and slivers of artefact, the shapes and purposes of spiritual teaching, of travels through myth, through the stories we create and re-create to underwrite our existence, to stabilise a bed-rock of meaning. I used to think that if I dug down hard enough I'd find my Emerald Tablet, my stone of stones, the story of stories. And, digging, I sought truth too in the faces and words of those who seemed to carry facets of knowledge within their demeanour, the vitality of their eyes, the resonance of their voices. I handled beautiful, mysterious fragments with passion and delight. When I found the sephirot, the spheres of the Kabbalistic Tree, humming and vibrating, I lay on holy ground, embracing the molecular shape of this map, struck through my body by its mathematics, its physics and poetry.

Joss looks at me. 'I don't know where you are. You've just left the premises.'

'You're dear to me,' I say.

'And you to me, and now I'll go.' She puts on her big coat, slips her bag swiftly over her shoulder and I catch a sweet line of bergamot oil hovering even after she has gone, and the door has closed behind her. Immediately, I miss her. I miss the intimacy, the petting, the scrutiny, the grooming. I miss the odour of her presence. I enjoy it when I am a creature with other creatures, nuzzling skin to skin. This musing drifts away into cloud as the dowsing in my innards resumes, drawing my attention back and downwards. 'Seek the greater pleasure', is the phrase I seem to hear. So, again, I am present, sacrificed in the sacred crucible, the present, my body writhing and complaining for the loss of its transient delights; the brilliant pin-head of light, in the dowsing and outside of it, steadfast and burning... this unseen, speechless intangible greater pleasure, that which is also pleasure free. So much masquerade has to be given up, burnt, consumed.

Mel taps on the door and enters. 'What a night! And you know, she wants to stay in the kitchen.' He does a little jig, as if caught in Joss' slipstream. The echo of her, the fine filaments of her presence now wrap around the savoury sense that Mel brings with him. I ask Mel what he thinks the reason might be.

'You know her – I want to because I want to, and that's that.'

'We can't be tying her to her chair night after night!' Mel sits down and pulls out a rotten-looking mint from his pocket.

'Ell, do you ever think what you might be like when you're old?'

'Don't like the idea of it, Mel. Everything hanging, drying, hurting.'

'Shrinking... you left that out.' He looks at me speculatively. 'We'll end up like little shrunken gnomes, do you realise.'

'It stinks, Mel.'

'Yeah – I suppose, watching her – it's like we have no choice. Except suicide. Well, no choice but how to manage it, and our own attitude.' We sit side by side, two depressed ancients, frowning over the Talmud.

'Look here Mel.' I pinch the skin on the top of my hand. 'See – it's supposed to go down real fast. Mine subsides in its own time…'

'What's that supposed to mean?'

'Losing elastic.' Mel pinches my cheek.

'That subsided pretty quick. Now I'm going to pinch your ass.' I look into his dark, bright eyes. 'Don't think I didn't notice it's your prize possession.' I get up and wiggle my backside in his direction. 'You're a wicked cow, tormenting this poor man.'

'The girlie next door torments you more … and the sexy girlies upstairs,' I add.

'You jealous?'

'Madly.' We look at each other. A mild frisson sits between us, contemplating whether to play or to slope off. The deep well, the archaeology, goes quiet, I am rising rapidly to the surface.

'I was really jealous of my wife,' says Mel, breaking the silence. 'If she just spoke to another bloke I'd think the worst. I'd do awful things like go and stand between them. It caused reactions as you can imagine. I tried to control myself. Got better after she had the kid. But then I was jealous of him sometimes!'

'Was she – is she – a flirt?'

'No – I can't say that – not especially. She was, or is, just naturally sexy.' The mild frisson between us kicks up its heels and leaves. My behind is now just a plump device for sitting on. Mel and I cruise towards and away from each other. He stands up. 'I'm going shopping for her. Want anything?' There is ease to his movement, and at the same time it's abrupt, as though he's moving swiftly away from something in himself.

'No – thanks Mel.'

As the door closes, I return to the fire, the pleasure, the pinpoint of light. In that awareness, I stretch and bend in preparation for Tai Chi practice. I stand, feet shoulder-width apart, relaxing, melting tension, feeling the texture of the floor meeting the soles of my feet. I direct attention to my belly, breathing into it qualities of depth and fullness. I stretch my arms and feel spaciousness through my chest, the spaciousness of quiet landscape, over which hangs the bell-dome of the sky. I direct intention towards my head, imagining softness and whiteness moving through my skull, leaving a cool and empty sensation. As I stand, allowing all these imaginative processes to work their alchemy, a rush of joy runs through me. Certainly, yes certainly, it's as if a strong timeless male form is standing behind me. My familiar – I know him – is back, standing without any gap between his body and mine. In visage, he is like the Hairakhan Babaji, a figure of androgyny, and yet with maleness gently potent. This is one of the archetypal soul-forms from my inner library; this is not the formless fire of impersonal spirit.

Joy amplifies, swelling and intoxicating, and yet I am steady, rooted and quiet, returned now to the place of dowsing. This being, this radiant aspect of myself gently cups my elbows with his hands, the air has thickened around me, to take on this soulful form; a loving, sensual, sensing presence guides me. My arms feel quite differently weighty, and, with the softening, slow guidance from behind, they take a long time to rise into the opening movements of the form. Hip to hip we fit, he and I, and from the distilled elixir of authority and excellence, my waist moves with fluidity, my belly turns like a warm ball, my arms lift without effort. When he draws me down, enabling my weight to sink, and as I prepare to turn, bringing the right hand forward and the left hand back, I am moved without haste, within unified expression.

My arms curve through the thickening dimension of space, and the cherishing essence behind me moves my right arm forward again until it comes to rest, on a cushion of air, in the optimum place, where all is in balance, and yet dancing with movement. We continue to move, through all the postures, and I don't remember when I have completed a form quite so blessed with knowledge and beauty. I light candles and burn fragrant oil, and sit he/she/I, I and That, lovers meeting in the afternoon.

CHAPTER 35

It is my fifth baby-sitting day with Lennie. One more, and Zandra will have finished her course and our arrangement will be over. Spring is in the air, a promise of colour and freshness and warmth, and so I suggest that I might take her for a walk. Zandra brings the pushchair downstairs, showing me how to use the brakes and how to arrange the various positions of the seat. She moves quickly down the road, and, as I bump the chair slowly down the front steps, thankful that she can't see how I fumble with it all, a brisk middle-aged man in a dark suit, wearing a neatly trimmed beard, glasses and a hat, steps purposefully towards me.

'Is this where Marte Hirsch lives?' He has a rich voice.

'Yes.'

'Thank you kindly.' He gives a courteous small bow, and I am quite sure he must be the rabbi. He has a measured, reassuring presence, and I want to take him by the lapels and tell him what I am doing, and ask what his God might think about this eclectic Jewish pilgrim. I miss the moment, and continue manoeuvering Lennie down the steps as he ascends. Mel answers the door and I cautiously mime a question – is this the rabbi? – behind the broad dark-suited back. I do this by clasping my hands, rocking my body backwards and forwards, and raising my eyebrows interrogatively. Mel has a hard time looking solemn and respectful to the figure before him at the same time as mutely answering my question, in the affirmative. For a second he flicks his eyes away from the rabbinical figure, and in that moment nods slightly in my direction. I move away with the small figure of Lennie, a wizened queen in her chariot, her pale features surrounded by a pink, woolly hat with two strange animal ears knitted onto it. My heart turns over when I look at her, and at the same time I am remembering the rabbi who officiated at the funerals of my parents. He looked very much like the substantial person I've just encountered, and I recall the power and solemnity of his words as he intoned 'ashes unto ashes; dust unto dust.' There are no flowers, there are no decorations in the Jewish funerals I have known. There is the body, the hole, the digging and the covering up, and words of terror and splendour. Is this what Marte is going to discuss? These particular details the three of us did not talk about during the ritual of the silver box. Contemplating these things in the abstract is all very well, but how might it be to discuss them when your body is beginning to give up its substance, to relinquish its sense of solidity and capacity?

Lennie's pale eyes look newly at the world. She knows nothing of death or coffins or cremation. She is an innocent in her garden of Eden, living in ignorance of the testing snake and the tree of knowledge, of good and evil. She is only beginning to know of comfort and discomfort, of tastes, hunger and fullness, feelings of well-being or unease in relationship to the large creatures around her. How might she perceive the world today as I perambulate her along avenues of my choice, up the hills to Hampstead Heath? How could she ever guess that as I wheel her along between the newly budding trees, I am looking for you, Doris, hoping for a glimpse of your small figure and beautiful face. Joss has tickets for an event in the West End in April, where you, Doris, will be reading extracts from your writing, along with other writers who are not English, who have found themselves in London after a childhood spent in some far distant land. Doris, Marte, the rabbi, the baby... and I. I have put these people together in my particular focus today – I am the point of origin of these spinning thoughts, recollections, curiosities, longings. I am the initiator of movement, one foot in front of the other, the one who experiences the pleasure of mobility, the luxury of good health. What might be the way of my body when it starts to lose its substance and function? Is it already encoded, the way of my departure? I don't like the trail these thoughts are taking, I feel cold in the spring sunlight, my body uneasy and fragile.

There is no sign of you, Doris, though the more stalwart of café society, still in winter coats, have already begun to gather around the tables, drinking cups of coffee and eating. Lennie is starting to cry, in a muffled way, and I lift her out of the bindings which fasten under her armpits and are complicated to undo when the infant in question is in a suit quite clearly manufactured for a small Eskimo. I hold this child, parcelled in goose-down, and kiss her smooth, pale cheek and we look at each other. Her murmuring subsides and I take her to the duck pond, holding her and wheeling the pushchair at the same time.

We watch the ducks, or, rather, I do, for I don't know what she is looking at, all I can see is the curved line of the Eskimo hood, her face hidden within. Doors are flying open in my heart, for Lennie, for Marte, for all the people I can see around me, for all of us stationed on this bright and precision-tumbling ball, held in its space between guardian sun and moon. My heart in its micro-galaxy now is like a green tunnel, lined with foliage, tracking deep. I remember a verse from the Tao te Ching and recite quietly to Lennie, whispering into her ear, past the fronds of hair, wispy and new:

> *Heaven and Earth are not kind:*
> *The ten thousand things are straw dogs to them.*
>
> *Sages are not kind:*
> *People are straw dogs to them.*
>
> *Yet heaven and Earth*
> *And all the space between*
> *Are like bellows:*

Empty but inexhaustible,
Always producing more.

Longwinded speech is exhausting.
Better to stay centered.

Lennie, an apparently blank slate – though I don't believe that she is – gives me her attention. I pack her back into the fastenings, and return her to her mother. Zandra, somewhat shy, has brought me a bunch of bright yellow tulips. I am touched, and put them in a round-lipped, slate blue vase. The green way through my heart is still open, and this territory has a different quality from the place of downward dowsing. This track goes not downwards, but inwards: into bowers of multiplied green, fragrant and shadowy, each leaf nonetheless radiant. I am penetrated by a green spiralling energy.

I hear doors closing across the landing and wonder if it is the rabbi departing. I now remember his name – Schlomo Landsmann. Rabbi Landsmann and Marte Hirsch. The man of the land meets the stag.

It is still light outside for the days are lengthening. Unexpectedly, an idea for a piece of educational training comes into my head. This is unusual so I make a note, but it has the look of a scribbled fragment from a dream. Back at work, I probably won't remember what it was about.

When I go over to Marte, in the early evening, there is a veiled reference to the Rabbi. 'You get what you pay for,' Marte announces, and I have no idea whether this refers specifically to synagogue dues, or to a more metaphysical sense of giving to life and receiving from it. From the emphatic slam of her lips after this statement, I realise no more is to be said – for now – on the subject. Lulu is busying herself, and Mel is reading the newspaper. Marte asks me to rub her shoulders, and I perch on a chair next to her. She is quiet, the room is quiet and the four of us in it are quiet, each of us distinct and separate, and yet bound together, the old figure in the corner pulling us into mutuality. The usual congealed, cast-off remains of the meals-on-wheels offering sits on the corner of the sink, the core of a pear decorating leftover mashed potato.

I don't want Marte to die. I feel a shadow today, and it's not just witnessing the arrival of the rabbi. Something feels even less substantial in the wings of her shoulder-blades; her fragile neck, barely holding up her drooping head, looks as if it could snap.

We don't stay chatting much, and I soon go back across the landing. Sitting before my altar, preparing for sleep, I go back to the sensation of Marte's body beneath my fingers. Unbidden, an image cuts through of galaxies, millions of them, and their relationship to the tiny speck of our blue rotating paradise, our dot in this cosmic ocean. An unquiet mixture of wonder and fear lurches through me. No wonder we need to cleave unto each other, and work the livelong day and jive the livelong night. Movement, and huddling and warmth at all costs, to stave off the surrounding immeasurable depths. My body, this transient measurement of experience, shudders to its pit as I sit without defence and without knowing.

Somehow, the poignant numbness around Marte the night before, continues into the next day, and we all seem affected, despite the bright, sweet days of spring coming.

Mel takes on the odour of quarry being hunted down as Marte reacts to him from a suddenly needy, demanding persona. Her eyes are hollow and greedy, they follow Mel around without disguise of separation or independence. Her proud, bossy energy just simply isn't in evidence at the moment, it's as if she has sloughed it off as an unwanted carapace, a skin too tight to hold the inevitability of the downward slide. He goes out and she wants to know when he will be back, calling after him as he moves towards the door, 'Are you sure?' He tells me this one evening as he smokes a roll-up on the front doorsteps, staring into the fading light.

'She's testing me all the time, to see if I am going to stay.'

'What do you say?'

'Whatever I say doesn't help – she rings the bell day and night, and when I am next to her she grabs my arm.'

'This is not Marte...'

'Yes and no.'

Lulu puts her head out of the door. 'She's calling for you, Mel.' He gives me a despairing look and goes in. I want to blame courteous, dark-suited Schlomo Landsmann, but I know it isn't him. I feel knowledge moving through me, and it is that I can't hold onto Marte, and she can't hold onto Mel. None of us can hold on to each other, and, her claw-hands grabbing, Marte knows this more nakedly than we do, and naked she is in her will to survive, grabbing at the warmth and strength of her friend, resenting him for it, resenting her need of him, struggling these bright days with inchoate, confusing emotions of love, despair and resentment. This is no dear old lady going gently into that good night. This is a savage creature, fighting without mercy.

Over the days and nights, Mel looks more and more drawn. I go across more frequently though Marte wants me more softly and easily than she wants Mel. She scolds him whether he is there or not: 'I know he wants to go out; I know he can't bear me at the moment.' Mel ripostes: 'You're damn right I can't bear you at the moment – you're driving me nuts. At this rate I'll be in the ground before you.' I hold my breath when I hear exchanges like this, but then, when I look at Marte, she looks like a toddler who has come up against a restricting parental arm.

We are given many tasks to do. One is to cut her nails, fingers and toes. Her toenails are quite impossible. I try – after soaking her feet in warm water. The nails are like the rhinocerous horns and the sharp blades of the nail scissors skew around without getting a grip. Marte regards her toenails with bleak satisfaction.

'See – they'll be around after I'm gone.'

'Pity the poor bastard who trips over them,' Mel says gloomily. Marte lets out a shriek of laughter, and then coughs until her eyes weep.

'Now my fingernails,' she says to me, displaying her hands with the withering arrogance of a lady before a foolish underling. She flaps them in my face. 'Go on then, girl, the best colours… No, no more colours – just file them nicely and get the cuticles down.' I cannot get the cuticles down. She grimaces and jerks her hand away. The skin, rising onto the nails, is like petrified leather, and will not be moved. However, I do a passing good job of the nails themselves, and though Marte sniffs disparagingly, she is pleased, and then asks for cream, lavender-scented cream, to be rubbed onto her skin and between the fingers. I enjoy doing this.

'What about that baby?' she barks

'What about it Marte?'

'How much longer are you going to be free nursemaid? It's a liberty, I think.'

'One more time. Don't mind doing it sometimes.'

'Young baby upstairs; old baby downstairs. Don't think I don't know. It will be nappies soon. Then you can shoot me.'

The other task is to sell some of the household treasures: porcelain ornaments, an old sewing box, elegant elbow-length silk gloves, two paintings, linen tablecloths beautifully embroidered. She first asks us what we want – and then whatever is discarded is carefully packed into boxes, and Mel and I take them to the owner of an antique shop off Finchley Road. She doesn't say why she wants to do this, and when we ask we receive grunts of impatience. The money that comes in from these sales she tries to press into our pockets. When we demur, she produces extravagant shopping lists, and we buy salmon and mangoes and the best grapes and olives, and cheeses from the delicatessen in West End lane. The silver box business is now complete. Her lawyer has been to the house – or, rather, a younger member of the firm arrived, for her original lawyer has long passed on. The young man had to undergo a rigorous test before the box was restored to its usual hiding place. I have been asked to go through the chests of linen, and to find several rather faded handkerchiefs of nonetheless excellent quality. These have been washed and ironed and stacked next to the box of tissues. The mobile hairdresser has paid a visit and I am charmed by the emergence of Marte's small, shapely elegant ears, as the more woolly fronds of hair which have distorted the neat oval of her head are shorn off. And all the time that we prepare, and fetch and organise, her eyes follow us, and particularly follow Mel.

Late one night, as I am preparing for sleep, Mel knocks on my door.

'Ell, I've got to get out. I'm going uptown. Would you go next door – I know it's late. You could sleep in my room if you want – I'll be out until morning.' I don't really want to, but then I see the expression on Mel's face. 'I don't have to tell you, Ell, I feel like a prisoner. I'll scream at her if I stay in much longer.'

'Okay. Does she know?'

'She's asleep. I feel guilty sneaking out. But I have to.'

He goes rapidly out of the door into the darkness. My heart lurches uncomfortably. I don't want to sleep in Mel's room but I go quietly across the landing. Marte is snoring slightly, propped up, looking like a predatory bird, in the frilly incongruous plumage of her bedjacket. I haven't been into the spare room since it became Mel's. It smells masculine and smoky, there are clothes on the chair, a stereo-player and a clock and a lamp on a small table, scattered newspapers and a hurriedly made bed. A wheezing, snuffly noise comes from a small box on the bedside table. I am puzzled, and then realise it's a baby-alarm, and the other end of it is in Marte's room. How does Mel mange to sleep with Marte breathing into his ear all night? I am tired, switch off the light, and climb into the bed. It feels strange, but the mattress is softer than mine and I roll into it and feel drowsiness descending over me.

I am woken by a sharp voice 'Come now, come now, quickly!' I roll out of bed, wondering where I am, remember, switch on the light and see that it's two o'clock in the morning. Marte stares as I enter.

'Where is he? What's wrong?'

'Marte – he's out tonight, asked me to stay.'

'You don't have to – he can't stand it anymore can he… you can go, it's all right…' She coughs and gurgles, her shoulders rise in agitation and I get a neb. 'No, no, no – I'm dying that's what's happening. Get me a brandy. I can't stand this anymore.' I don't know whether it's all right to get her a brandy, but I do. I pour out a small one and she aggressively pushes my hand so that more slops into the glass. 'I can't stand it anymore Ellie darling I can't stand it – and he can't stand it, has he gone back to Tel Aviv?'

'No – just out for the night.'

'He'll get into trouble, he's not careful enough, he'll get…' She hawks and spits and coughs and her chest trembles. 'I can't shit anymore that's the trouble, I'm all bunged up, get me that bottle…' She points to the jammed medicine cabinet. I get it, begin to pour out a generous spoonful, but she grabs the bottle, and swigs it rapidly.

'Marte – you'll be running all night.'

'Don't care. How would you like it? It's like having stones up your arse. I can't stand it any more Ellie, I want to go now. I want to see my Harry. He's waiting for me, he told me.' I take a sip of brandy. Marte slides me a look, and then sips her brandy too. After a silence, she continues, but in a different tone of voice. 'Ellie, I know I'm being horrible but I truly can't help it.' We look at each other. 'No truly – it's like I you know you're going to wet your pants – and no matter how hard you clench', she pulls a graphic face, 'you know it's going to come out. Well it's like that with what I say to Mel. I know it's not fair. But it slips out.' We sit, each of us digesting this information in our own way. Her voice changes tone again. 'You see Ellie, I know this about me. My mother – bless her soul – was very busy and I was the last so there wasn't much, you know, affection. More like a clip around the ear if I got under her feet. And I was scared because of all those pins in her mouth.' She pauses, panting a little from the effort of speaking. Her breaths are very short and high in her chest. Then she's back on the trail. 'My darling husband, now he was a cuddly man. Always cuddling me. He was a better mother than my mother, bless her, shouldn't say these things but it's true.' She looks at me searchingly. 'And then,' she sniffs and dabs at her nose, 'he dies. And I'm back in that place. Believe me Ellie, at sixty it's just the same, I'm not talking about bed, you know, all that… but touching. You need it.' She touches my hand. 'I don't mean you darling and Lulu and the others. You are all so kind.' She coughs, and I become alarmed, as she seems to have lost her breath, and makes little whooping sounds in the back of her throat. I put my hand on her sternum, which is heaving rapidly up and down, and rummage with the other hand round the bedside table until I find a medicated cough sweet which I edge into her mouth. After a time, the spluttering ceases. She looks exhausted. I feel drained. 'So then Mel comes – he's not Harry of course – but he's like family and he's here all the time and he knows me very well and we have a story – I'm not saying you don't darling, don't take offence, but he and I go back, you know – .' Her head and chin subside into her chest. There's a pained silence. Lightly I stroke her hand. She absently strokes mine. There is a feral quality of pain in the room, and curled into the shadows is a fox like the old fox of my female ancestors which I saw when I did my initiating ritual into the hermitage. It's Marte's old fox, her creature-pain, her bedraggled animal. It is curled up at our feet. The quality of peace that came in before, comes back again. We sit with it, breathing fitfully together. Now there's a slight snore from Marte's open mouth. If I get up and go I might wake her. And actually, I don't want to get up and go. I am sitting with my own sore creature. My mother did pet us and give us affection, but these gestures nearly always carried a ripple of anxiety and absent-mindedness with them. From inside my skin, in memory now of its childhood hungers, I look at Marte's old skin, enclosing its memories still intact and ready to speak.

PART 3

COMPLETION

*The Wandering Circle
Is Never Broken*

*We cannot Tell
The Tail from the Mouth*

*We cannot Tell
The Story from the Storyteller*

We cannot Tell …

CHAPTER 36

Lennie, on her final visit, is warmer than usual and sleeps for a long time on my shoulder. She's flushed and dazed when Zandra picks her up, and we both think she is brewing an illness. Whatever lurked in her system penetrates my immunity. I too become ill. Lennie goes under for four days, I am now on day seven of debilitating misery: running nose and eyes, sore throat and chest and a painful cough. Mel puts his head around the door, as do Jinny and Zandra and they bring supplies although I am not eating. I have not been to see Marte, and we send each other messages via Mel. It is a wet and windy April evening, blossoms falling from their trees and early daffodils bending on long stalks. Night is coming in, and the light of day slowly edges away.

I have long hours of fitful sleep, day and night. My sanctuary is contracted into the space of bed and bathroom and occasionally kitchen. Can't read and not much interested in listening to music. Now and then I switch to Radio 4 and lose myself in the cultivated voices of storytellers. The pull of the outer world is ghostly and without substance, stronger are the several realities I am living all at the same time inside the dwelling place of myself: a droopy child, sorry for herself and weak; a nurse, observing the patient and deciding what's best for her; an adolescent girl feeling desolate and alone, and an unassailable kernel of being, watchful and benevolent, holding me in quietude. Around this centre, but not of it, are currents and ripples, interlinking, drifting together, drifting apart. Obedient to watery movement. I am floating on a raft, I am tethered to wooden logs, damp and salty, as the ocean laps under me and the sky turns above.

I have not closed the blind on my bedroom window and watch night falling, veil upon veil to cover this part of the earth. I float on the bed, I float in a watery prism. Marooned upon my primitive craft, I am pulled from pole to pole, from fear to love, riding the ocean between. Tides of longing – for that which did not happen, might not happen – pull me. Misty scenes of imagined great personal success and triumph, of passionate and eternal love, of utter peace and enlightenment, rise and fall. And sluicing through this hallucinatory theatre, the waters of despond come and go, the waters of stillness and calm, the waters of rage and loss, the waters of union and peace with That which is. I see Guido's face and, in a scene which provides me with the utmost satisfaction for all of the few seconds it lasts, I see him hammering on my door, shouting to be let in, bearing buckets of deep red roses, bearing diamonds and rubies, robes and garments of silk and chiffon. He kisses my feet, covers them with salty tears. Behind him, a group of musicians waits to play for us. The scene is overlaid by an unexpected fragment from a dream that leaves me rigid and then shivering in bed. I dream I've killed someone. Or, more accurately, when I awake I know without any doubt that I've killed someone. I know too that I am going to be found, and I am terrified.

The taste in my mouth is sour, metallic. The water seems full of whispering: the whispering of countless beings, now gone, consigned to the deep. I'd like to sit up, but I have no energy for it. I want my mother. I want to be back with Guido and I want us to be on holiday, riding through the dark night, smelling the scent of tropical flowers. What did I know about my mother? She collected money as a young woman in South Africa to buy trees for Israel. One thing we do together – Leonie doesn't participate – is to press flowers. We pick small wild flowers and press them into books, between tissue paper. 'I don't want to make squashed flowers', Leonie says coldly, and then goes in search of more interesting games. My mother and I find heavy books, and pile them onto the flower-pressing book. I feel sad. I feel a dumb hatred for my sister and her claims upon my parents.I am terrified at the ferocity of the thoughts aimed at my sister. I am also in love with her, with her beauty and courage and independence. I am proud of her. When she is kind to me, sunlight floods the world. At the times when we are both in trouble with our parents, we form a tight alliance, swearing love and honour to each other. When she is in puberty, I see her as a luscious hibiscus flower, sodden with pollen and perfume, heavy with the weight of its own beauty, surrounded without effort by swarms of bees... boys from her class who would fly ellipses around her, cavorting and competing for attention. Leonie ignores them, and goes for successful older boys. I envy her beauty, her power. I feel excitement and worry when she clashes with my parents, stalking out into the night to a waiting man, usually poised for getaway in the sort of car which provokes mother and father into further fury. I am astonished – we are in our twenties – when she tells me she envies me. 'I'm going to lose what I've got,' she says. 'You've got something you can't lose.' I want to speak to her. I want to speak to my sister and start a closer contact between us.

It is quite dark now. I have no idea what the time is. The hermit in her damp cave turns and twists and the world shifts around her. Dust unto dust. Each day, we carry with us, the knowledge in our bones that we will die. Carcasses hanging from the hooks in a butcher's shop, dead wild animals left on country roadsides, decorous messages in newspapers, framed in black, laid to rest, passed on, in the arms of angels, all reminders, gravity and grave, woven thick and dark into the upward thrust of action and creation. Horrifying it is to look upon the face of my mother after is has been rendered back into clay, without spirit. 'She looks so peaceful,' says the attendant nurse. She doesn't look peaceful. She is present without animation, she looks like an empty glove dropped after a struggle. And it had been a struggle. My father had gone out like a light. There, and then gone, without much pre-warning. My mother breathes and rattles, birthing her weary soul out of finite time, hour after hour, contracting her body to expel that which is not of clay and dust. It is the most intimate thing she ever gives me, the possibility to be present beside her as she leaves.

I am looking into the gap that lay between my mother and me; in life that is, even before the unbridgeable gap that opened up when she died. She went, and none of us could follow.

I fall without resistance into the dark ocean; I am at the same time the interior of a cathedral, and I am the choir, full and pitched, packed into the forefront, voices uplifted, garments of one colour, lines of white billowing sleeves and full throat arising from rounded seams. A glorious Te Deum soars into the high reaches, into the vaults and the rich-painted ceilings and the light from an hundred candles flickers and then burns strong. Such a procession of excellence is offered to the Creator and all the pews packed full of witness and participation. The raised hand of the choirmaster keeps the note focussed and deliberate, and the voices open in obedience and ecstasy. This, too, am I. This bed my cathedral, my heart singing its hymn of devotion, the five senses turned away from the world. The ocean brings shreds of flotsam and jetsam, and underneath... underneath is That. And That am I in my darkness. This is a moment, unexpected, a gift, so weighty, and peaceful, that I feel I have touched the ground beneath the swelling waters. I lie, a small piece of seaweed, partly hidden under a rock, cherished by my Beloved, cherished by That simply because I am. And I am That. Angels and cherubim gather round my bed, fanning the crumpled and sweaty sheets with their wings.

I have been born, I inhabit this finite life. The rest, I create as I go along. I create misery, glory, cathedrals and images of myself refracted through the eyes and thoughts of others. When these images are beautiful I am delighted; when they are dismal, I am in despair. Millions, billions of refracted images of me beckon and smile out there in the world. I can be tossed up, and thrown down. Slivers and scraps of Ellie in the world beam back at me. This beguiling stimulating seductive playground beckons and calls and I go...

So quiet here under the rock, so rich here in the cathedral. The hermit, coughing softly in her hermitage feels her eyelids full and lustrous, closed like shutters. Breath comes and goes; comes and goes.

In the morning, I am weak, but not as poorly as I have been. I get up slowly, unfamiliar with being vertical, and walk carefully to the bathroom. I have the energy to pull the frowsy sheets from my bed, and to choose clean, new ones. I empty the bedroom of glasses and cups and take them, cautious as a sleepwalker, to the kitchen. The kitchen is like a foreign country, and light comes through the window, resting on the pot of parsley in its place on the windowsill. I cherish the feeling of weight in my hands, and the soft run of warm water as I wash up the cups. I make tea with lemon and wash my face and hands.

Back in bed, I breathe in the comfort of fresh linen. I hear a key turning softly in the lock. Mel's face peers around the bedroom door at me.

'Still alive?'

'Yes.'

'Feeling better?' He flicks a white handkerchief around his nose. 'I don't want to catch it. Nothing personal.'

'I'm getting better.'

'Need anything?'

'Not right now.' He scrutinises me further.

'You look beautiful.' My insides churn. The space between us stays taut and new, but nothing else happens. In the usual way we have, we step back. I wonder what it is he sees; I haven't looked at myself in days.

'How's Marte?'

'Missing you. Fretting about how you are.'

'I'll see her soon.'

The door seems a long way distant. Mel, now posed within its frame, looks dark and unshaven. I notice the cut of his shirt, the shape of his hand around the white handkerchief; I feel breath rising and falling within my chest and lay my two hands upon the slight mound of my belly beneath the sheet. At the same time, we two seem caught in a mutual breath that isn't ours. It's as if the room heaves a sigh and us with it. In this small shudder, an ant turns in its nest in Equador, and a woman, washing her clothes in a river in Rajasthan, moves her head as if to hear someone who has spoken. A discarnate scribe, hovering over the records of what is, was and shall be, pauses, and I feel the presence of Marte next door, caught in a moment of significance that none of us could really know or tell.

The next day, pale and shaky, I traverse the passage toward Marte. Dr. Marcus is there, Mel leans against the far wall, and a sturdy woman and stocky young man, uniformed ambulance attendants, are also present. They have their arms around Marte, and are lowering her onto a stretcher. Her face is alight with expression and dictation. She is telling everyone exactly what to do and exactly what she wants, and tells me that all is well – that she is going for a check-up and how she'll be back in a few days. She is going to the local Queen Victoria hospital, and I mustn't come and see her until I am properly well.

I notice irrelevant things like the colour of the small suitcase Mel has at his feet, the prominent jaw of the stocky young man, and that a half-eaten scone lies on Marte's chair-side table.

'Nothing wrong,' Mel mutters as he walks past me. 'Just what she says… check-up.' Dr. Marcus leaves after comment upon my wan state, and Mel organises the nebuliser as he is to accompany Marte in the ambulance.

'Why didn't you tell me?' I hiss furiously at him.

'Nothing bad to tell. Talk to you later – it's not as bad as it looks. Promise.' Marte complains about a bumpy ride as the two attendants lift her and bear her towards the door. In a few minutes they have all gone, and I am left in the empty flat. I have never been there when Marte was not present, and I feel like a thief. Can I trust them nothing's wrong? I sit at the kitchen table on a hard chair and wait. I get cold and tired and my limbs ache so I go back to bed.

'Ell… don't get a fright.' Struggling out of sleep. I switch on the bedside lamp, and Mel is there, sitting on the edge of the bed. 'Do you want a cup of tea?' We two sit without speaking, stirring the hot liquid unnecessarily – neither of us takes sugar. 'She has been complaining recently of pains in her chest and lower back. So Dr. Marcus decided to take her in and check out a few things...' As if reading my thoughts he tells me she is in a small ward in the geriatric unit and he is going back in the morning.

'I wish you'd told me... and what about Justine?'

'It was only in the last couple of days – she made me promise not to tell you or Justine. She was anxious about you and didn't want...' Mel takes the cup of tea from me and holds my hand. He covers my hand with his two hands and I put my head on his shoulder. 'She loves you, you know...'

'Mel are we getting to the...'

'I don't know...' A dark bird covers the sky with its wings, and my body feels sick with the unavoidable presentiment that the dice has been thrown, that events are proceeding in the way that they have been written. 'Don't jump to conclusions.' Mel's voice is soft. 'You go back to sleep and tomorrow you can come and see her for yourself if you're well enough, OK?' After he goes I turn the light off and turn my face into the pillow.

Though it's not far, I take a taxi to the Queen Victoria. Weak and nervous, I inquire at the Information Desk about Marte's whereabouts and am directed to the fourth floor. The lift is full: anxious visitors, exhausted-looking hospital staff, and a patient in green pyjamas and yellow hospital dressing gown. I find Marte, looking like a grasshopper in a cottonfield, buried in her white hospital bed.

'You shouldn't be here. You're ill.'

'Well then, I should be here.' I give her flowers, several bunches of yellow sweet-smelling freesias, and find a hospital vase on the window-sill. I draw a green plastic chair up to her bedside. Marte looks tired and a little disorientated. The hospital oxygen supply follows the well-worn trail to her nostrils and her chest rises and falls rapidly. She beckons my ear near to her mouth and gives a rapid, hoarse description of the other two patients in the room and of the drama the night before when the fourth occupant was taken badly ill and removed. The fourth bed is empty, stripped of sheets.

'I think she died last night,' whispers Marte. I look into her eyes, wondering how this might have been for her, but see in them only the light of interest. She tells me that tests have begun, that the hospital is severely short-staffed and that Mel was running around for her like an orderly until he left in the early hours of the morning. A rotund woman enters, pushing a trolley of tea and biscuits and Marte places an order as if she were in the finest restaurant. 'And one for my friend..' The tea-lady demurs, but Marte gives her a wink and I'm permitted a cup of weak tea and a utilitarian biscuit. The ward is air-conditioned and the artificial movement and temperature of the air sits around us like medication. It has a depressing, compressing effect and I feel my eyes wanting to close. Marte's bed has protective rails on either side and now she looks like an old baby in a cot, her body occupying scarcely half the length of it. She is wearing a pink bed-jacket from home, and her hair has been neatly brushed. Mel comes in, looking tired, and Marte subtly changes her demeanour. Her voice becomes weaker and her face shrinks. She tells us that she wants to pee and she wants us to help her as the nurses don't come and anyway they will be too rough. Mel, in the way that he has, is already integrating himself into the hospital system. He finds a bedpan and a nurse who draws the curtains around the bed and – after a pointed query as to our capability – we are left in purdah with Marte and a shiny bucket. She stretches out her arms in a vulnerable gesture and we both manage to manoeuvre her onto the cold rim. Her nightgown rides up and her legs dangle oddly over the bedside. The spectacle is awkward and distressing as she clutches at us, waiting for the naked, tinkling sound. After she has wiped herself with a wad of tissues I take the bowl and its sodden paper to the patient toilet in the corner of the room. Marte looks exhausted and strained, so we leave the curtains closed. We sit, Mel and I at either side of the bed. Marte closes her eyes and falls into a broken sleep. I feel disturbed, but at the same time want to ride with Marte through this time, doing whatever needs to be done.

We watch the world darken through the large window at the end of the ward, and Marte goes through wakefulness and dozing, pausing to eat a few morsels from an unappetising plate.

'Ellie,' Mel points to a large, shabby easy chair outside the ward. 'I'm sleeping there tonight.'

'Are you crazy? They won't let you.'

'There aren't enough nurses – so I've been making myself useful – with other patients too. They'll close an eye.'

'Aren't they looking after her properly?'

'They try – no criticism – they're stretched – and she's scared, I can tell. The pain in her back, something's there… they won't operate… it's a matter of management.' My head swims with unpleasant thoughts, I feel stifled in the medicated air, and I don't want to listen to Mel anymore.

'Mel, I'll go home now. Phone me if there's anything you want me to do. What about Justine?'

'Let's see what they say tomorrow.' I kiss Marte on the cheek and feel the prominent, familiar cheekbone under my lips. Mel walks with me to the glass swing-doors and I watch him walk back, talking to a nurse.

It is dark and cold and I feel ill, but I walk home slowly. If this is the end, it's come too suddenly. But who says it's the end?

CHAPTER 37

In the early afternoon, I go back to the Queen Victoria. Marte is looking slightly demented, hair tufted every which way, and eyes a little vacant. Mel looks similarly undone.

'Can't talk now,' he says quietly 'been a helluva night. And today she's agreed that the priest and the rabbi come and see her.'

'At the same time?'

'No – one in the afternoon, the other this evening.'

I take Marte's hand and she pushes me off.

'I've had enough of it all – you'd better bring that daughter of mine here, and those two friends ... everything's sorted, you see – and I told you I'd go when the blossoms came out.' Through the dirty window, through the dirty, dull April sky, I see a weak ray of sun moving downwards. 'In fact what you could do is get one of those wheelchairs and take me out for some air. A person could die in here from lack of air.'

I go to obtain permission to take Marte out. A thin-faced nurse is on duty.

'Are you family?'

'No – close friend. Neighbour.'

Referring to Mel – 'we can't have him staying, you know. Someone complained.' Another nurse comes by and catches the end of our conversation.

'Come on Emma, he was damn useful last night.'

'And I'm saying,' continues the first nurse 'it is not allowed. We are not a hotel – can't have everyone's relatives sleeping over...' and she indicates a wheelchair in the corner.

'Only just outside the hospital – ' and walks swiftly away, her rubber-soled shoes making a squealing sound on the floor. As she goes, she drops a page and I feel a nasty sense of glee. It is as nasty as the taste

I have had in my mouth since eating a long snake of liquorice on the walk up to the hospital. I wasn't hungry, but I felt a gnawing ache in my stomach. I push the empty chair towards Marte's room. She is dozing and Mel walks to meet me. We stand outside the room, keeping her in vision.

'It was good I stayed, Ell, she became really frightened and confused. There was a fuss about me but I didn't entertain it – just got on with looking after her as if we were at home. Potty, you know, and neb, and checking the medication, and stories and assuring her the Will and everything is sorted. The only missing element was the brandy...'

I feel the quality of mercy from That which moves and shapes the web of it all so that in this night of fear Marte had Mel beside her. I remember that I have in my bag a sandwich and a drink for him. Chicken and salad, well seasoned. He takes it with gratitude and eats it almost without pause for breath.

'You look exhausted, Ell.'

'I'm not quite well yet – and I feel scared and horrible about Marte.' Mel puts an arm around me.

'She's okay. Well... at least I know that if I'm here she's as okay as she'll be, given what's going on.'

'What about the tests, Mel?' He gives me a long, level look as if he's weighing and measuring thoughts and words.

'Well, you could look at this in different ways. And I think this is where Dr. Marcus is coming from. I think it's about regulating the present procedure and making sure it's all as easy as can be.' I gaze past Mel at the child-like shape of Marte under the hospital bedcover. 'Ellie – there's something between us, you know, and we have made a pact. It's about the end and it's very clear. She will let me know.'

'But you can't... we can't...'

'Not suicide Ellie – not even euthanasia. Just knowing about the time ... and what to do. Does this sound mad – I really trust her with this. And I kind of know she'll tell me what to do.'

We hear a rich, deep voice behind us, and there, in dark suit and sober tie, is Rabbi Landsmann. Mel introduces us formally, and I shake a warm hand, feeling the texture of strong black hairs on the back of it.

'I had a message to come and see her. How is she?' We all look towards the figure in the bed.

'As ever,' says Mel.

'Is it – does the doctor say...'

'It's a getting things clarified time – if that makes sense.' We three are present, the rabbi, Mel and I, the friend – perched on the bedpost, and drawing fingers through Marte's white hair.

Marte opens her eyes.

'Oh, here he is. I can't offer you a cup of tea.' The rabbi moves forward. He is easy with her, he sits on the green plastic chair and takes her hand. Marte obediently lets her hand rest in his. Mel and I go down to the hospital café. As we talk, discussing the doctor's opinion and the merits of being in hospital and the merits of being at home, a picture emerges, a graphic picture of Marte's body, host now to another visitor, not just the slow, tidal process eating at her lungs and moving towards drowning her in her own fluid, but another one lurking... announcing its presence through the dark pain in her lower back.

'She thinks it's cancer,' says Mel 'And if it's moving fast, there's no point going through intrusive investigation and chemo-therapy. We all know that. So it's careful medication and management.' We drink strong tea from plain white cups as do many others, patients and visitors. The tables are strewn with left-over sandwich wrappings and empty cups.

The rest of the day, and into the evening, Mel and I move between the sandy, utilitarian garden in the front of the hospital, the café and the ward. Constant activity causes currents and swells along the passages, rising and falling via the lifts. Nurses, doctors move fast; visitors move in rapid or slow streams as they filter off into various wards. Patients lie marooned in bed, jovial, desperate, frightened, hopeful. Some of them sit outside in their hospital pyjamas, adding butt ends to a pile already there. It's an exciting, horrible place to be in. There's a sense of death and of ailment. Nurses paddle around with trays of medication, and in Marte's ward a doleful-looking woman dispenses tea.

Marte begins to shrink as darkness falls. The electric lights in the ward create an unpleasant effect, exposing the dark edges of faces lying against pillows shrouded in hospital linen. There are hardly any visitors left, and, looking at Mel's pallid face, I decide to stay, not necessarily overnight, but as long as needed. The nurses tut-tut a little as they pass us, but this seems to be a token gesture. Mel has become useful to the three other women in the ward too. He particularly has taken to Salma, a Russian woman with the kind of face found on a mediaeval woodcarving, long and still and ageless. As much as Marte is grumpy and demanding in her anxiety, Salma demands little and has no visitors. Mel, watching her grope ineffectually towards the plate on her tray, goes to help her and discovers she can hardly see. Her English is minimal, and she has chosen to try and manage the situation without comment. He sits next to her, cuts the food, and helps her spear each piece with her fork. It is a slow process. Marte watches them with resentment.

'What's he up to?' she hisses loudly at me. Her face contorts in a painful attempt to hide childish jealousy. My heart aches for her as she tries to ignore Mel engaging with someone else. I see the still, inward Russian woman opening up to him, hear her confess that her extraordinarily youthful skin – and she is eighty years old – is because she never had sex. She tells this to an attentive Mel with a sweet and guileless smile. Mel asks her how she acquired her apparent equanimity.

'It is my Lord Jesus,' she says. 'Nothing that happens to me will be as bad as the things that happened to Him… this gives me strength.' Marte, the jealous struggle now quiet, lies in exhausted quietude. The night shift comes on, and with them, a site manager, a small and distracted-looking man.

'We can't have this. This is a women's ward,' he says to Mel.

'I see your point,' says Mel, 'but there are male nurses.'

'But you're not a nurse – you're a visitor.'

'He's my nurse,' says Marte, in a strong voice, shooting an ambiguous look at Salma.

'He's your visitor,' says the site manager mildly, turning towards her.

'Let's talk outside,' suggests Mel.

'What's so secret?' demands Marte. 'I can tell you what you know – there aren't enough staff here. If it wasn't for him bells would be ringing in this ward all night. Your people are rushed off their feet.' The site manager scrutinises Marte, her papery skin, the tubes attached to her nostrils.

'Don't worry – we'll sort something out,' he says to her, his mouth working awkwardly, as though invisible hands are pulling at it, and stretching the lips left and right. Marte observes his struggle without mercy. 'If we open this procedure to you we have to open it to others.'

'What do you mean?' Marte scoffs. 'Most people can't wait to get out of here – never mind patients, I mean visitors. Come with their old carnations that no one likes and can't wait to get out. Unless you don't have a visitor,' she looks at Salma, in a manner different from the hostile child of before, 'and then Mel goes around and sees to people who haven't… he's just like that. I've known him since a boy… he's not going to cause you any trouble.'

'Let's go out,' interjects the site manager hastily. The main nurse of the ward goes with them and later, through the doorway, I see that a man in a priest's collar has joined them too. Mel looks very tired, and I see him talking without attempting to convince, in a tired way, using few words. Something seems to give way in the group. The tension seems to dissipate, so perhaps an agreement has been reached.

'Well,' says Marte looking combative when he comes back. 'Where is he then? Gone off?'

'He's a busy man,' says Mel. 'And it's okay to stay for tonight.'

Mel and I go into a familiar rootin' with Marte, and we do small things for the other three women as well. Night staff generally ignore us though one or two give us small signals of support. I am exhausted and yet awake like a strange night fish in the eerie atmosphere and light, swimming slowly between Marte and the chair, Marte and another patient – the uncomplaining quiet Salma, garrulous Elsie and grim Mary. This is a geriatric ward, and though Elsie and Mary are plump where Marte and Zalma are thin, they too have an ethereal quality to them, as though their flesh has begun to give up its rude blood. They are given food, liquid and medication, examinations and attention but there isn't the same sense of energy feeding upon energy as in a body with time still on its calendar. I imagine each with a finite number of breaths still left… as women have a finite package of eggs given to their bodies. At menopause, nothing but artificial re-arrangement will produce another possibility of pregnancy. A finite stock of eggs; a finite stock of breath.

This ward is a place where the clinical is still presiding over old age. It is not a hospice, with softer furnishings, carpets, curtains and careful plants. The clinical trolley has been round with its gifts from Morpheus. Old bodies settle, and sounds of laboured sleep arise from watery depths. We too, Mel and I, watch our baby as she too sleeps, an upright bony fish, beloved of us for all her sharp fins and razor-blade scales. Mel arranges himself on a battered armchair and I prepare to go home.

'I'll be back tomorrow, Mel.'

'I don't think there's any danger at the moment – but if it has to be, I'll phone you.'

'What about Justine?'

'She knows her mother's in hospital – she's on standby.'

Mel and I embrace each other. I feel the hard line of his collarbone against my forehead, and the sound of his heart is in my ear. He suggests I get a taxi, but I want to walk.

An exquisite tiredness propels me, dreamlike, back home and then I am jolted awake. There are lights on in Marte's flat. Without thought for possible danger I open the door with my key.

'Who's it?' a sharp voice calls out, and Justine comes towards me from the kitchen. In relief, we embrace each other. 'She called me – said come tomorrow but I came straight away. I'm worried. Well, not worried – oh, I don't know. How is she? You look dreadful.' I haven't known the cool Justine so flurried in appearance.

'She's okay. Same as ever. I don't think she's…'

'Well, knowing her, she'll probably just go… if you know what I mean. Tea?'

'Actually, I'm starving – why don't you come to me and I'll make some food?'

'Don't be ridiculous, I brought enough for an army.' She brings scones and dark brown bread with olives and avocado pears, just ripe, and she and I eat without much talk, in an interlude of unexpected intimacy. It is odd to be in Marte's home without her being there. And yet she is most certainly present – in the atmosphere, the artefacts, the objects, the smell, and the arrangements of all in their crablike patterns, idiosyncratic spirals in the sand of her outwardly expressed habitation.

CHAPTER 38

I walk to the hospital in the early afternoon, Justine shouting across the hall that she will come later by taxi. It's a cold day, sporadic sunshine touching its ragged fingers on the few daffodils struggling for life in pocket-sized gardens. On the way I buy flowers for Marte and food for Mel, watching my thoughts as they cruise around – nothing special, a rigmarole of curiosity, opinion, repetition, memories of the evening with Justine, and of a slight headache lodged in the left side of my head. I brew a mixture of adrenalin and heartache as Marte comes into mind. What's she up to now? What's going on in the secretive tunnels of her will, where none of us can penetrate? I think about a charming small figure she has of a Japanese woman in geisha costume, and wonder if I can have it after she dies. My face reddens and I feel ashamed, imagining Justine knowing that I have thought this. A counter argument arises:

it is just a small object, and after all she would like you to have it. I breathe slowly, watching the breath rise and fall with each step. Into my awareness, crossing the carousel of titillation and reaction, comes a small sensation of completeness. It is quiet and has nothing to do with anything, simply there, under whirling colours and shapes.

The hospital, as I walk through its plate glass automatic doors, past the small flower shop and large reception desk, is now a familiar place. In a crowded lift I see my face, and the faces of others, grotesquely illuminated in the mirrors at the back and sides of the lift. A small boy is almost buried between adult bodies, and clutches the hand of an old woman. He looks afraid. I tuck another note between the crowded stones of my wailing wall. A man presses against me – he smells sour – and I move away from the contact. I get out at the geriatric ward.

'Oh, here she is,' says Marte in a loud, gruff tone. She is sitting against a large white pillow and her hair is neatly brushed. My first impression is that she is in duchess mode, expecting flunkeys and visitors and I am the first, too early, but she is prepared to overlook that. Her wheeled bedside table is tidy, flowers neatly arranged next to a bowl of fruit and a jug of water.

'How are you?'

'As you see me, dear, as you see me. All in the eye of the beholder.'

'Mel?'

'Stealing a shower. Poor man – looked very unsavoury this morning.' Her voice becomes more sibilant, her face blanches. I look automatically for the nebuliser. 'Don't worry. I just had, they're strict here.' She gives me a look, a quite naked look of tenderness. 'How are you my dear Ellie? You have been very good to me.' We both remain silent in the aftermath of this statement. The woman in the bed opposite stares at me through rheumy, pale blue eyes. I look at Salma. She is asleep, her face long and quiet in repose as it is in wakefulness. The fourth bed is concealed by pink floral curtains, and intimate rustling noises and murmurs come through this make-shift wall. I return my gaze to Marte. Her eyes have closed, and her chest rises and falls rapidly and lightly. I watch her without really knowing what I am looking at.

'Dreaming?' Mel stands behind me. He is damp around his ears, carries a towel and a bar of soap. 'Five star hotel this,' he says drily.

'What's the news?'

'We've had a busy morning,' he says in an undertone. 'Last night was tricky again. She was uncomfortable and in pain. Had to get extra medication.' Mel touches my shoulder. 'She's quite frail Ell, though she looks bold this morning… it's the business you see. Always wakes her up.'

'What business?'

'She's summonsed everybody. The two ancients – Hilde and whatsername – Lulu, the house, Justine of course.'

'For what?'

'Your guess is as good as mine,' he says lightly. 'She's asked Justine to get biscuits and fruit … as if she's having a party.'

'Maybe,' I say lamely 'she's feeling a little better.'

'Yes, maybe.'

Doris, I wish you were here to see the party we are having with Marte, the duchess. We sit on the uncomfortable green plastic chairs, Justine, Hilde, Madeleine, Jinny, David, Lulu, Mel and I. We are eating grapes and good quality chocolate biscuits brought by Justine. A ritual has developed and I don't know who suggested it and how it started. Two people at a time are holding Marte's hands, left and right – now it is Lulu with Jinny on the other side. Lulu's long brown hand encloses Marte's little claw as it has done so many times. Marte's head inclines towards Lulu as a child leaning into a trusted relative. Her eyes are half-closed and her breath shallow and uncomfortable. Lulu focuses her eyes in a fixed way out of the dirty window and I feel her unshed tears. Mel is slumped into his chair and I think he might be asleep. When Jinny and Lulu slowly move away Hilde and Madeleine sidle up to grasp Marte's hands, flanking her like two worn-out gladiators, bright in their ancient plumage and breast-plates, their faces ghastly with the effort to remain still, and to keep whatever thoughts or feelings locked in place until afterwards. I start to fret about my turn and when I should go and that I would rather Mel was on the other side than David when the hospital chaplain arrives.

Garrulous Elsie is directly opposite Marte and sits in bed still holding newspapers and cards brought by her husband, who sits awkwardly bundled into the chair next to her. The two of them are turned towards the regal tableau as if they are watching a film. Elsie's mouth hangs silently open, while her husband's mouth is pressed shut, and his eyes follow the scene with unblinking attention. The two of them feed off the event before them as if they are trying to learn something that they will re-produce later, intact and juicy.

Unobtrusively the priest enters our midst. 'She sent for me?' he says to the assembled party. Justine rises to the occasion.

'Let's leave mum with the chaplain for a minute,' she suggests brightly. We all rise, disentangle ourselves, and assemble outside the ward. I look back and see Marte regarding the chaplain with a pleasant and intent look. Mel is the only one of the throng still on the green chair. He is oblivious, eyes closed. The chaplain unexpectedly touches Marte's forehead, and Marte takes his other hand in hers. They murmur to each other. Hilde and Madeleine are hissing like agitated geese, and they round on Justine, whispering indignantly into her ear.

'Please,' she says, 'what does it matter? And, yes, she has seen the rabbi – '

Marte, I love you, the unexpectedness of you, the cheek. Is this a party, a piece of drama – or do you really feel you are leaving us? I have no idea. Do you know, Marte?

The chaplain leaves. We return and Mel wakes up. Marte pats the bed and asks Justine to sit with her. 'And you the other side,' she says to Mel. I feel a terrible sense of heartbreak and abandonment. 'And you darling,' she says to me, 'come here too. I don't have three hands but you sit with Mel. We'll manage.' My eyes swell with tears I don't want to shed. Mel and I touch her left hand, Justine her right. She looks at each of us. 'Don't worry,' she says firmly. 'There is nothing to worry about. Everything is happening as it should.' Justine looks grim and I feel for her. Mel is grey with exhaustion. The others alternate between looking at us, and looking away.

A woman arrives with the tea trolley and makes a cup of tea for Marte, ignoring all of us in the process. With eyes only for the patients, she moves on to the next bed, the thick white cups clattering as she goes.

'Have your tea mum,' suggests Justine.

'No, darling. It's for cats.'

'Cats don't drink tea,' says Justine firmly

'Exactly what I mean,' says Marte just as firmly. The inevitable process of communication between mother and daughter. Hilde and Madeleine make a show of standing up, brushing their skirts and loading their handbags. 'Go and get them a taxi,' says Marte, looking at me. 'Please darling.'

I chaperone the two venerable women to the basement where we phone for a taxi, listening carefully to their concerns – especially about the chaplain. When the taxi comes they climb into the back seat and my heart turns over as the driver moves off. When I return, Jinny and David are holding Marte's hands. David, having said little the whole afternoon, is addressing Marte, a formal speech of appreciation, for some reason including predictions about the weather for the following week. Marte looks at him carefully as he then announces that he has to go, and Jinny says hastily that she will walk back with him. Lulu informs Marte she will be back as usual, when Marte returns from hospital. Marte smiles at her.

'I know darling, I know you will be there.' Lulu kisses her cheek and follows Jinny and David. Justine, Mel and I are left. 'Mel,' says Marte firmly, 'I am staying here one more night to get things sorted. So you go home now with Ellie. Justine can stay.'

'No – I'm staying,' says Mel. Marte calls to the nurse, beckoning with a crooked finger.

'Tell this man he's a danger to himself and to others.' The nurse smiles.

'I'll be back in a minute,' says Mel. He goes to the main desk and I see him talking to the sister in charge. She is nodding vigorously, even as she busies her hands with a file full of notes. 'I'm going home now for a sleep, but I'll be back later.'

'No you won't,' says Marte. Their gazes lock. Mel turns away.

'Come on Ellie,' he says, 'let's go dancing.' Mel slowly gathers up a few belongings. He looks at mother and daughter. 'Okay then girls. Have a good time together.' Justine smiles at him, a small collision of her mouth within her face. As we leave Marte's face is unreadable.

Mel refuses a taxi. 'I've got to walk, I'm as stiff as a board, and I need to eat some proper food – let's stop at the curry house.' He hardly speaks, concentrates wholly on chicken korma and rice. I don't eat. I am bolted, transfixed, next to a question mark. What is happening? I know only that time is moving fast. When we get back to the house, Mel tumbles towards his room and I to my chair and then, restless, to my bed, and then, restless, to the kitchen. I can't sit, can't be still.

At about nine Justine returns and comes to my door asking for alcohol. I open a bottle of wine and we sit together. She bursts into tears and then dabs her eyes vigorously. 'Oh how silly. We don't even know if she's… if she's… I don't know what this is about. She's such a tease – always has been.'

'She's an amazing woman Justine – though I'm sure it's not always easy for you.'

'Damn right.' She sniffs. 'Oh what's the point. It all goes down in the wash.'

'You sounded just like her when you said that!'

'Yes!' She laughs. 'She has these sayings that sound wise, but then they don't make sense.' She puts her hand on mine. 'I know we're different sorts really – don't really get you, to be honest, but so what? I appreciate what you've done.'

'Justine, I don't want you to talk as if it's past tense – we don't know, do we?'

'Oh – change the subject then, tell me about the men in your life.'

'Have to be past tense then. Nothing happening at the moment.'

'Not Mel?'

'Not Mel.' A silence sits between us. I imagine Mel next door, sleeping as dead as a dodo. 'What happened with that guy – Errol wasn't it?'

'Obviously made an impression on you?'

'What about on you?'

'Now you're being a naughty girl Ellie. You're older than me, aren't you? Have you given up on sex? Does the urge go away when you're older?' I move to answer, but Justine isn't listening. A sharp look sits on her face for a quick second. 'Yes he made an impression all right if you mean what I think you mean. But I think he was after a free holiday in Ibiza. He was good in bed as you can imagine – nice-looking wasn't he? – but it's not enough is it? I'm not just a holiday home in all senses of the word.' She pours a full glass of wine. I cover my glass. I've had enough.

I hear a knock on my door and then hear it being unlocked. Justine is startled, and when she sees Mel she says, 'Oh, have a key do you?' Mel ignores her. He looks rested, but only a little.

'I'm going for a drink – want to come? I'll go back to the hospital later.'

'Mel it's late – ' I don't say anymore. There's a strange set to his jaw and he doesn't meet my eye.

'Who's measuring?' he says. 'Look, the sister said she'd ring if anything was wrong. And she hasn't.'

'You're not her fucking son,' Justine snaps unexpectedly. There's a dangerous silence suddenly around all of us. Justine looks as if she regrets her words, and then immediately looks defiant.

'I know. But I am her fucking friend,' says Mel in a menacing way.

'Yes, she made sure of that, didn't she,' Justine's voice is bitter and painful.

'Let's not go to the past,' says Mel, suddenly more placatory. And then – with menace again. 'And you mention any of the past to Ellie and things will be forever finished between us. It is my story to tell.' His body, in front of Justine, is not aggressive, but it is frightening in its conviction. Something very heavy is in the room, the return of the animal wounded and desperate. Justine suddenly slumps.

'I don't give a shit about your story. My mother's dying and I'm not part of it whatever she does. And when she was alive I wasn't part of it.'

'That's not my fault.' Mel's voice is calmer now, his body less frightening. 'What went on between the two of you was nothing to do with me and I didn't make it any worse. You were jealous of me and that was that. I never tried to take your mother away from you.'

'You didn't have to try,' says Justine. I don't know what to do, caught in the crossfire between them. The animal in the room smells rank and without law and order. I move to the side, and put the kettle on. The domestic sound distracts them and they both look at me.

'Sorry Ellie,' says Mel, wearily. 'Sorry Justine. It's not a good time, is it? Look, let's put it down to the stress of the situation.'

'What's said cannot be unsaid,' Justine snaps sharply. I reach to her and put my hand on her arm. She shrugs it off. 'I'm going to bed.' Her face is unbearable when she goes. I put my hand out again but she ignores me.

'Ell.' Mel puts his hand on my shoulder. 'This should never have happened. But it did. I'm going out now – I'm sorry – I just can't talk about anything right now.' He closes the door with a bang. I hear the main door open and close.

My room reverberates with pain and anger. I light a candle and am finally able to sit down quietly. I am exhausted and distressed but no relieving tears come. Dry-eyed, I look into the flame.

CHAPTER 39

There's no sign of Mel in the morning so I assume he's at the hospital. I remember the storm between him and Justine and am cautious as I knock on Marte's door. Justine opens it, looking drawn and tight.

'Any news?' I ask.

'Like what?' she says belligerently, and then softens. 'I feel awful, and angry and it's not your problem, but you're friendly with him and I can see he's won you over so there's no point in talking.' She blocks the doorway with her body, a dressing gown, silky and full-length, wrapped loosely around her.

'What do you want to do Justine? Do you want to go to the hospital – or shall we phone?'

'Look Ellie, just get on with what you want to do. I'll look after myself.'

I've had enough although I feel for her in her misery. The walk to the hospital happens in an odd and empty time zone, and I arrive again in what seems to be early afternoon.

The duchess is no longer present. Marte is small and tired and very quiet. 'I'm going home today, Ellie dear.'

'That's good, Marte. We'll be glad to have you back.'

'Mel's organised transport – not an ambulance or a car – something between the two.'

'You should be comfortable in that.'

She sighs. 'Yes – I expect so.' Her voice is soft, without the usual gritty strain, the barking quality that the emphysema has given her. I find her very beautiful, her elegant head and transparent skin, the great hooded eyes and beaked nose. The love I feel for her fills my heart and reaches my fingertips. I stroke her face gently. She pretends not to notice, but I can feel her skin absorbing the touch. The nurse arrives with Mel. He is friendly to me but distant. He seems intent on the strong almost visceral chord that plays between him and Marte. Not much is said between them, but a hidden communication vibrates back and forth, back and forth.

A strong and humorous orderly arrives with a wheelchair and Marte is carefully moved into it. The nurse has packed her few belongings, and so we go towards the lift. Our faces stare blankly into the three-sided mirrors. We move silently through noisy throngs down to the basement and out through automatic doors to find a car waiting for us. Marte is lifted carefully into the back seat, Mel goes beside her and I go in front. The driver and I talk, but there is only a taut, unbroken silence, from the back. We pull up to the house, and Justine comes to the door. She brings the wheelchair and has clearly ordered herself to be pleasant. She and Mel lift Marte from the backseat, and bring her back into her home. There are spring flowers in the kitchen, but Marte, for once, asks to go to her bed, so we take the flowers into the bedroom. Justine, has also bought a new bottle of brandy, and the sight of this provokes a weak snigger from Marte.

'We'll get blotto tonight,' she whispers.

I am dispatched, with a hospital prescription, to Dr. Marcus, and then to the pharmacy to pick up Marte's diamorphine. The greengrocer is just closing and I quickly buy a bag of lychees. I don't especially want to eat them, but their spiky texture attracts me as they lie in a nest of green paper outside the shop. When I get back, Lulu is there, preparing for the evening ritual. It is a perfunctory version, Marte has no energy for being tidied up or cleaned. She is already in her nightgown so there is no necessity to change her clothes. She drinks juice from a glass with a straw, and closes her eyes.

'You haven't had your evening paracetamol,' says Lulu.

'I'll have a little rest before I sleep,' says Marte. 'Mel will give me my evening paracetamol, darling, you go now, you must be tired.'

Justine, Mel and I gather in the kitchen to make toast and cheese and tea. Conversation is sporadic. Justine and Mel avoid each other's eyes, but each is making an effort to be gentle. The wounded animal is present, lying hidden in long grass, licking itself and resting a little.

The nurse from Marte's ward phones. We have left Marte's bag of medication behind. Justine volunteers to go. 'I need a walk, for once. See you in a while.'

'Come back soon darling,' Marte calls from her bedroom as Justine opens the front door.

'I will mum,' she says softly. I hear the door close and Mel and I sit quietly, each with our own thoughts.

'Mel,' Marte calls. He goes to her. When he comes back, his face is stiff and white.

'She wants a little drink,' he says. I go for the brandy. 'No.' He opens the diamorphine, fetches a spoon and goes back to Marte. I experience vertigo, darkness and depth that is accompanied by a sense of immobility. If I wanted to get up at this point, I couldn't. I feel pinned to the chair. Mel is with Marte for what seems like a long time. When he comes out there is an expression on his face that I cannot stop looking at. He takes my hand and pulls me up. I imagine that I am heavy to lift.

'Come, let's sit with her.'

The atmosphere in Marte's room is of stillness, and in the silence, we hear her breathing, strangely light and irregular. Mel and I sit side by side on two wooden chairs, and we watch our friend. Her mouth falls open and Mel takes a sponge, dips it in water, hesitates and then puts it down again. Marte seems held within an invisible, highly-charged, oval presence, not to be disturbed. The sound of her breathing changes. There is guttural turning in the back of her throat and her head twists. Together, Mel and I reach out and touch her hand. We hear a small, choking, wheezing sound, her chin works, then we hear a dry, rasping sigh. With this sigh, Marte leaves us.

There is no more breath, no more movement in her chest. Mel brings his ear to her mouth, her nose, bends to her chest, listens, but I know without question that a life is departing, that it is being picked up exquisitely, and that it has been willingly and tenderly yielded. This giving up the ghost is quite unlike the hard struggle I witnessed when my mother died.

Left behind is a dear, Marte-shaped cast-off husk, a little shell, and around us and in the room and pervading everything, every speck of dust, every molecule of oxygen, is an atmosphere of focussed love and fruition such as I have never experienced before. Mel and I do nothing, say nothing. Then I hear a wretched coughing sound, a sound of grief and pain, and it comes from Mel. His tight face has broken and he is weeping, his head in his hands. I hold him. Another sound adds to his, and it comes from me, and I too am engulfed in grief for the loss of Marte. She has absolutely gone, leaving behind this remnant of matter, and us with it.

'Oh God', says Mel, and reaches out and tenderly closes her eyes. 'Oh God, and Justine isn't here.' I force myself to my feet and ring the hospital. I ask them to tell Justine and to find her a taxi so that she can come home as soon as possible. I go back to the room, and kiss Marte's face. I kiss her hand. We two sit, looking at our friend, propped upright, becoming colder to the touch.

'I wonder what she's thinking,' says Mel. 'She looks as if she's thinking. I suppose we have to do things'.

'Not yet, we mustn't disturb this'. Somehow I know we mustn't intrude, for the oval is still present, but dissolving its force-field now. We remain sitting, silently still and attentive, until Justine gets back. She comes quickly into the room, dishevelled and awry.

'Here's her medicine,' she says. And then stops.

'Mum…' she cries. Mel and I leave the room and the sound of sobbing comes to us as we sit in the kitchen. After a time she calls me and I go in. She lifts up her face and I wipe her tears away with a large man-size tissue, and hold her in my arms. We rock together, and she whispers into my neck. I can't hear what she's saying. She lifts her head. 'Ellie, it's better she didn't suffer too long. It was beginning to be bad wasn't it?'

'Yes – I think it was more tough than she let on, sometimes.' Mel has made tea and brings cups into the bedroom. 'Let's sit with her,' says Justine.

'Yes, she'd like that,' says Mel.

'Hey Mel,' Justine looks momentarily younger, washed out and miserable, and her voice is higher than usual, 'do you remember when my dog died and she dug a hole in the garden...' I listen to stories from their childhood, I get a picture of an indomitable, bossy, life-giving woman. Justine and Mel seem to want to amalgamate at this time.

'Justine,' says Mel 'let's do what she would want. She would want us to be friends...' He goes over to her and embraces her. They hold onto each other in an awkward way. 'Sorry I was a bastard.'

'Sorry I was a bitch.'

Through the night we drink tea, and drink brandy. We inform Dr. Marcus and, solemn-faced and with some personal sorrow it seems to me, he conducts the official procedure. We ring the rabbi, and ask if the undertakers can wait a few hours before arriving. Through all of this, the still, cold figure of Marte presides over us all, a slight smile – or is it? – on her mouth. We phone Lulu, and she comes. Jinny arrives. We phone Hilde and Madeleine but they don't want to see their old friend in this way. They ask in tired voices to be informed of the funeral. Slowly, after about five hours, the deep quietness moves on. I have a sense that Marte has left, that the transition is over. The transparent darkness that began the ending has lifted. Sorrow is in the room, and shock, but it is a component of this world, not the other.

The undertakers come at midnight with a bag, and I remember Max. I leave the room. 'I can't bear this,' I murmur. Justine remains. Mel stays with me in the kitchen.

Marte has gone. We stay and we talk and we drink until the early hours. As soon as I decently can, I phone Joss. I am lucky to find her, she has been away in Rome, on a project with the director of the art gallery. She comes to me as fast as she can. She lies next to me on my bed and holds me as I cry, her thin body mother enough to a bereft and exhausted child.

CHAPTER 40

The rabbi comes to inform us how to proceed. Marte requested a simple, Jewish funeral, and to be buried next to Harry. I didn't realise that Harry was buried in Enfield; somehow when we talked of him, Marte and I, we talked of him in his life, not about him being in a box somewhere. It looks as if we'll make do with the limited family resources available, to have a reduced form of ritual since there aren't seven relatives to observe the seven day mourning period.

Mel disappears, leaving the house with a hunted look, desperation around him like the ragged sail on a ghost ship heading for unknown horizons. The funeral, according to Jewish custom, is to be the next day. We inform Hilde and Madeleine, Lulu and the occupants of the house. I have seen very little of Zandra and Lennie since my babysitting stint ended and am surprised when their two faces appear at my door. Lennie has grown a little, and manages a smile.

'I'm so sorry about the old lady. She was so sweet,' says Zandra. 'We've been away at my mum's for a bit – and we just heard.' I let Zandra's character assessment of Marte remain intact. 'Can we send some flowers?'

'Well actually – it's a Jewish funeral so there won't be flowers.'

'Oh.' Zandra regards me doubtfully as though she's seeing a different person. 'Well, tell her family anyway … heartfelt sympathy.' I am touched by the old-fashioned phrase from Zandra.

She pats Lennie's head protectively 'Well, see you then.'

'See you Zandra, thank you.' Joss is still with me, and raises her eyebrows.

'Well now, what's that?'

'As you see, it's a mother and baby.'

'Ellie, what's happening to Marte now?'

'Well, clever old thing, she organised it all when she called for the rabbi. The synagogue alerts the burial society, and they take care of the body, and the coffin.'

'Thank God I don't have to come with you to the funeral. I can't stand them. But I'll come over when you get back if you want me to.' Joss leaves. I watch her click-click down the road in her high-heeled boots. Which one of us will have to bury the other? What a horrible thought.

Time moves again, and brings with it, the next day, two funereal black cars. One for Marte and one for us. We travel through London, up to Enfield, people looking up momentarily as the hearse drives slowly before us. Marte, do you remember the white car, the tacky stretch limo at Christmas? I remember you, surrounded by all of us.

Mel sits beside me. He is hidden within himself, unreachable. Justine is heavy with grief, sniffing and blowing her nose. The journey is a tedious one, traffic congested.

The funeral is simple and short. It is a postscript, a ritual, necessary and practical. We'd said goodbye as we sat with her, her essence hovering in the ethers as her cast-off body became colder, showing the absence of colour, as life and temperature drained out.

Rabbi Landsmann delivers apt eulogy to Marte, capturing her character with truth, affection and wit. He talks of her honesty, her generosity and, also, of her sharp tongue. The small plain casket sits in the plain ante-room and I am again the exalted child at the cemetery, at the heart of the place where the vertical crosses the horizontal. Marte, dearest Marte, go well, winging away from us. Thank you for your love and your strength. I love you. I will miss you. You taught me much and you gave me joy.

I am unaware of the others around me, though I hear Mel crying. So many have gone before us, so many of us will follow. There is a radiance in the core of my being, even as my face contracts and hurts. It is a pain and a radiance of submission to something incomprehensible. Nothing to do but submit, and to love the mystery, and watch the distinct way in which each of us pilots our way through it.

> *Baruch ata Adonai Elohainu melech ha'olam dayan ha'emet*
> *Blessed are You, Lord our God, Ruler of the universe,*
> *the true Judge.*

We walk across the stones and the ground and the grass, following Marte in her coffin. The rabbi speaks. We hear the words of Psalm 91:

> *He that dwelleth in the secret place of my most High shall abide*
> *under the shadow of the Almighty...*

> *He shall give his angels charge over thee to keep thee in all thy ways.*
> *They shall bear thee up in their hands, lest thou dash thy foot*
> *against a stone...*

Marte goes down into hollowed out emptiness and earth is thrown in handfuls upon her. I remember Marte how you said to me that we end up covered in earth. Tears well into my eyes and run down my cheeks. There is something dreadful about the hole, and the hideous, uncompromising box and the earth raining down upon it. Next to this hole is a gravestone upon which is carved 'In memory of Harry Hirsch, beloved husband of Marte and father of Justine.' Marte you said you wanted to go back to your Harry. Side by side your bones will lie now, in this dark place. Ashes unto ashes; dust unto dust. The absence of flowers, the gash in the ground, carry unarguable, speechless severity. For the first time I look around at the others, at valiant derelict Hilde and Madeleine (how many funerals have they attended?), at Lulu, stabbing her eyes with a small handkerchief, at Justine, white-faced and frozen, at the Rabbi, solemn and quiet, at Mel, weeping aloud, his face wretched and swollen. My heart is caving in, as if it cannot hold this sodden, absolute moment. Loss throws me a vicious damp, punch to the belly. Loss again, of something precious and dear; unrepeatable and personal. Hole upon hole opens up inside me as I think of my parents, of the child in Hampstead cemetery looking at the lopsided gravestones, at trumpeting angels.

Before we leave the cemetery, we wash our hands at the taps outside the building. This is a strangely comforting act. We all shake hands with the Rabbi and I look into deep, brown eyes, shielded by thick eyebrows. I see goodness in his eyes, tiredness and familiarity.

'She loved you,' he says, holding my hand in his hairy hand.

'I know. I loved her too.'

Joss is back at home when we arrive. She has helped Jinny prepare a small meal. We sit in Marte's kitchen, which is already looking bare, as Justine has packed away all evidence of medication. We drink tea, a forlorn band of people, added to now by Jinny, David, the Australian girls, and Justine's friend, Jo. We sit around and tell stories but they are limp and meaningless. I know that we will often recall with glee, Marte's wicked, crackling energy and force, but now we are sore and emptied out. I notice a bunch of lilies, white and waxen, on the table. Joss brings me the card. 'With sympathy, Edie Trammler.' Zandra must have told her mother, and her mother must have told the rummy ladies, and they must have passed the message on to Edie. I want very much to leave and to go across the landing to my flat, but I stay to the end and help wash up. Joss offers her company but I embrace her and tell her I want to be on my own.

'I'll be ringing you darling. This is big deal for you I know.'

'I'm so sorry Ellie,' Jinny is holding my hand, with a tight, strained smile on her face, and my tears come again. 'Oh dear I didn't mean to upset you...'

'No you didn't...' I give up on explaining, it is all too much. I give Jinny a kiss, Mel has vanished, and Justine looks as if she wants to busy herself until she drops.

'Justine do you want me to help you?'

'No Ellie – I have some help. You look done in, go and rest.'

Finally, I am back in my solitude.

I stay a long while in the bath, adding hot water every time the temperature drops. I light candles in every room, and add rose oil to the burner. Wrapped in a large towel, I lie down in front of the altar and let go of sorrow without restraint. The room darkens, the day turns on its axis and I continue. As long as it takes; as long as it takes. The sobbing turns to prayer as I speak the business of my heart to That which knows me better than I know myself. Small tokens of tenderness post themselves into me as if my watching angel now reverses the wailing wall procedure, and asks me to receive an ethereal abundance of strokes from the angelic pen. This elemental calligraphy winds itself into my being and I am im-pressed with words I feel, but cannot understand.

In the night, Marte appears to me. No, it is not a dream, but she comes to me in dream form. She tells me that she is moving to another country. My heart opens and a wave of love moves from me to her. On the crest of this wave, she leaves.

CHAPTER 41

I don't want to go into Marte's flat, and I can see that Mel is no longer comfortable there, though Justine is perfectly civil to him and he to her. Bags and boxes are piling up as they did in my front room eight months ago. Justine tells me that Marte wanted me to choose whatever I liked from her furniture, clothes, linen and ornaments. I take the Japanese figure, blushing slightly as I do so, and watch Mel look around the room, wondering what he will select. Mel and I have been left £20,000 each. I don't know how to think about this figure and what it might buy for me. Inscriptions on paper have a flat feeling, but this amount also has the quality of a warm blanket, a cushion, a protection from Marte against lean months. Mel's eyes move over the tables and shelves.

'I will take her handkerchiefs,' he says abruptly, looking at no one. 'The pile we washed and ironed the other week...' Justine looks at him in astonishment.

'Mel, there are some quite nice antique things – valuable you know – the clock for instance she thought you'd like.'

'Justine – I don't want things. I'm not in a proper home at the moment. Those handkerchiefs I will use – I will wash them and iron them. I know it's funny for a bloke, but they remind me of her – they have her initials. She loved them – made her feel like a lady.' He pauses and smiles at each of us. 'And listen, girls, I am leaving in two days. I booked my ticket. No more reason to be here – with respect – I belong back there now. Have to get back to pick up the threads. And anyway I don't like it in the flat without her.' Mel looks steadily at me. I look at him. No, this is not how it is. Sorrow and shock pass through me, stopping in my belly, in my chest. I feel as if I can't breathe. It is too soon, Mel, too soon for me. I also have an exposed feeling, as if I were fourteen or fifteen, and I have been left standing outside a cinema on Saturday night. Someone I thought would meet me and buy tickets, and walk into the cinema with me, is simply not turning up. Justine throws us a look, from him to me, and back, and I don't see whether it is sharp or soft. Anyway, her response is quite irrelevant at this point. I need to get out of the room and find air and calm myself. Mel follows me out.

'Ellie – sorry to be so abrupt. It's going to be hard to leave you. I don't quite know what you mean to me – can we spend the day together tomorrow?'

'Sure Mel.'

'It's strange about the handkerchiefs – I was surprised myself to hear what I said.'

'No stranger than anything else, Mel – it's all going too fast. Ever since she died. Before she died, there was the rootin', and that seemed fixed in time – and now you're going.'

'I have to Ell, but we need time before I do.'

'I know you have to – and it's okay. Just a shock upon the other shocks.'

'Shall I come over to your place and stay with you a little while?'

'No Mel – I'll see you tomorrow. Let's go to Hampstead Heath shall we? Might be a nice day and we can walk – get some coffee?'

'Yes.' Mel takes me in his arms and we hold each other quietly on the landing. This embrace is comforting but I step out of it after a while, and he goes back to the objects and possessions, and I go to my ark, my hermitage, my altar, to meet the girl outside the cinema.

There we are, sitting with That which Is, and that which is. I feel exhausted and heavy. I acquiesce with the downward, following into the dark place with all my heart, wordless, sorrowful. At the same time, oddly, rising is an experience of opening and emptying. What will be present here now – or absent – after this death and this departure?

There's a soft rattle at the door.

'Mel?'

'No, it's me – and you've forgotten, but I can't blame you, given everything – it's that reading at the ICA.'

'Oh Joss – give me a minute, are we late? I'm so bedraggled, I'm not sure I can manage.'

'We've got plenty time, and anyway, maybe this is just what you need.'

Doris, it's the event I've known about for a while. You are reading with other immigrants and exiles who have found their way to London. I am full of Marte's death and its aftermath, but yes, Joss is right – here you are in the middle of it all.

We head towards Trafalgar Square. I hang onto Joss' arm and there's kindness in her as she walks with me across the road and into the foyer of the venue. Ahead, I see someone solicitously and respectfully walking with you, Doris.

Doris, Marte is dead, and Mel is going. How would you have framed these two events? You write in your first autobiography, 'Doors have been shutting behind me all my life.' This doesn't feel like a door shutting. It's more a like a door opening into an unknown place without Marte and Mel. Marte, Mel and I have shared a room for a while, linked in love. Now this particular room is empty but for me. I sit there in the shadows.

'Let's go in…' Joss and I negotiate a platform of steeply ascending steps. The theatre is full, and you, Doris are on first. Behind you, there is a sequence of enlarged photographs, and you turn your head to see, and speak from the images of yourself in London in the late forties. I am so in the shadows of loss, I can hardly hear or follow what you are saying, but I absorb, once more, your particular intensity. I feel the cadence of your voice and expression. Thank you for being one of my significant companions. When I was a child I had an invented friend. His name was Louie and he looked like an elf. He was full of kindness and mischief and I would speak to him when the alienation within my family became difficult to manage. It is not alienation that bonds me to you, Doris. You are a fellow pilgrim along with others who accompany me, hooded and calm as we walk the unknown road.

There are several writers who speak after you, and I go in and out of attention to them: an African; a tall and handsome writer from China who speaks his poetry in Chinese and is translated by a woman in red; a writer from the Middle East. The whole tableau passes by me like whorls and curls of transparent smoke. I am sitting on the steep diagonal, in an uncomfortable seat, Joss' arm at my side. I feel safe and connected, and watch with wonder the way adults are and what pleases them. Doris, you know this phrase 'to be full of oneself.' It has a negative connotation usually, but I am full of my self now, sitting here, full of the experiences of death and departure which pull upon me, teasing my nervous system, informing my bones and imprinting the marrow within them.

When we get back home, I notice that my eyes slide painfully away from the left, from the familiar door to Marte's flat.

'Joss – let's have tea, and then I'm going to bed.'

'Aha! You're finally going to make it with that poppins next door – but then he'll take you to Israel and I'll never see you again. Can't have that.' The ribald thrust has no substance. Joss looks small and sad. The words drop into nowhere.

'You haven't talked about your poppins for a while…'

'Oh – Jack – it's nice. Quieter. We're kind of getting on okay.'

Joss and I sit together, drink tea and lean against each other. We are like two absent-minded apes, aware that night is falling and that our leafy bed-branches are darkening. Joss calls a taxi, and disappears into the darkness.

I remain, picking over sore places gently, now that my fellow-ape has departed. I snuffle around, patting and soothing. It's as if I've been in an accident – I feel bruised and dislocated. I go to the altar to meditate, but can't stay still. I am restless and decide to let it be so. Pacing up and down, making more tea, not drinking it, I spend the time until I am exhausted. A fractious time, in pieces.

In the morning, Mel and I walk to Hampstead Heath. We talk amiably, like old friends, walking easily together in the clear spring day. We are waiting, I think, to make camp, to sit down somewhere, and then we will speak of more substantial things. The pain of the night before has settled, and the clear beauty of the day soaks into my skin and quiets my eyes.

It's cold to sit outside, but we find a table at the Golder's Hill Café, and buy coffee and cakes. I wrap my warm scarf around me.

'Ellie,' Mel stirs his coffee absently, 'do you remember very long ago I said I wanted to tell you something? And you heard me tell Justine that it was not for her to say – that it's my story.'

'I do.'

'Now's the time. But I find it difficult. This is a thing I don't speak about and it is from a long time back. So just bear with me.' I look around at the freshly planted hanging baskets and at the figures walking beyond us on the grass. Two boys play with a football, and an old woman is supported in her slow walking by a sulky-looking younger woman. I feel as if the whole scene before me is a light transparency that could be peeled away to reveal a different substance beneath, vibrating at a different frequency, an imperative of cause and effect beneath the manifest consequence.

In this moment, Mel's arm couldn't be a different shape, the old woman has to walk on that particular stretch of grass, the warmth and noise from the café have a distinct quality which lives in this moment and then will die, never to be heard again. If I fight Mel's leaving I will suffer. I look at myself wanting something from Mel, wanting him to fall in love with me, to make me happy ever after. Then I open my heart to the mystery of this man in front of me, the beauty of his eyes. I see the outline of his broad chest, sense the muscularity of his legs. The shape of his mouth causes my mouth to soften. this is hankering, wanting, devising, planning. That unfolds according to its nature, no more and no less. Mel is looking at me and I look at him. His eyes become moist, and I see desire and love and then something so naked and raw that I have to take my eyes away.

'I love you Ellie.'

'I love you, Mel.' We sit in silence. We have given each other something; gifts have been exchanged. Mel arches his shoulders. I wrap my scarf more tightly around me.

'Ellie – yes – I'm, going to tell you the story. I also want to say again how much I love you. Yes, you are an unusual person. I don't sense any bitch in you though you're not a soft option either. I feel anchored when I am with you – there's a kind of deep thing in you I don't really get.'

He puts a hand on mine. 'I have a usual reaction to women. With you it's unusual. We could…'

'Yes.'

I look at Mel and enjoy the symmetrical structure of his face, the strong nose and straightforward expression. I taste his warmth and his liking of me. I taste the love and the grief we both have for Marte, and I know my eyes too are unveiled, and that Mel can read love in them. In a quick parallel ricochet, comes an imagined scenario of Mel and I in the action of love-affair. Sex, me going to Israel, meeting his ex-wife and son, drama and joy, upsets and negotiations, Mel coming back to London, the excitement of meeting, growing intimacy, finding out things about each others' habits, being satisfied, being dissatisfied, the smell of him, the look on his face after love-making.

'Ellie. It's time.' The light of the day deepens and we are linked by that which will now unfold. Mel's face tightens and he looks away from me. His voice is low and carries tension. 'It happened when I was young. I was about ten. Family life was a bit of a misery, to put it mildly. My folks didn't really get on. Marte and Harry were friends – not close, but enough for me to know her, and I really liked her. She was really good fun. I think she wanted a boy really. So it was awkward with Justine because they've always been like they are now.' Mel pauses and gets out his cigarette-making equipment and begins to roll. The action is so pleasant to watch that I want to roll a cigarette too, to have the satisfaction of creating a white paper tube neatly packed with tobacco.

'Can I roll one Mel? Not for smoking… just for…'

'Sure.' He pushes the green and gold tin towards me. My fingers find satisfaction, though the end result isn't as plump and resolved as the cigarette Mel is smoking now. 'So I hang out with Marte sometimes, going with her to auctions and junk shops, looking for antiques, and learning about wood and decoration and prices…' Mel pauses and smokes and looks away over the grass and into the trees, searching to bring something into his inner focus. 'One day – I am on the roof of our little ramshackle garage next to the house. When things were particularly bad in the house, I would climb onto the roof by holding onto the gutter and digging my feet into broken places in the brick wall. It wasn't really dangerous – my mother shouted about it, but then sort of gave in, because I just went on doing it. I would sit on that roof, sometimes with comics or something to eat. It gave me separation. I could breathe.' Mel draws the final smoke from his cigarette, and puts it out in the ashtray. His face is pinched. I feel anxious, a hurt feeling catches at my throat. 'Well, you see – I had,' he falters, 'a little brother. He was six. Anyway, I was on the roof and I looked up from my comic and I saw the top of his head. He'd never done this before, but he had climbed up.' A miserable pinched feeling comes to settle between us. Mel's face is white, his eyes close and he swallows in a dry way. 'The gutter collapsed and he… couldn't hang on… lost his, lost his … I couldn't get there, see? And he fell from the roof and – and I saw him – They always say it's slow motion, and it was slow motion I can tell you and then at the end of the slow motion there was this noise… a dull crack sort of…' Mel stops and hides his face behind his hands. The air quickens and sucks us both in. I am falling with Mel into a terrible place. 'He died. Broke his back. They took him to hospital but it wasn't... he was...'

I raise my hand as if it might find its way to Mel, but it's not going to, I know, and he doesn't want it, I know. I put my hand down and wait, sitting by my friend, the unbearable taking its place with us.

After a long time I speak. 'Mel, what happened then?' He looks at me.

'Everyone kept telling me 'It's not your fault; it's not your fault.' But they said it in a way I didn't believe. I thought it was my fault. My parents were kind to me but in a strange untruthful way – it was as though they were being kind to a leper. And the whole thing eventually set them apart. Later they divorced. What I really wanted to tell you was that I went to hell. And no one could reach me. Except...' Mel looks at me again and then takes my hand. This is a great relief. His hand is warm and I hold it tightly. 'Marte. She came by one day. She used to drive one of those old Morris Minor cars – a green one. She came steaming up the road, came into the house and called: 'Melvyn come with me.' I went. We drove to Highgate Woods and walked without saying anything – but I didn't feel from her that I was a leper. We sat down on a bench away from other people, and she said: 'You feel it is your fault and you might always feel that in some way. It will get softer, but it is a terrible thing that happened and it was terrible for you. It was not your fault, but no one can tell you that. It was life doing what it does. He took a chance – and it killed him.' That's more or less what she said, and it was the way she did it – looking at me with such kindness and concern and then she just took me in her arms. And I cried and cried. And she saved my life.'

We look at each other. Tears come to my eyes and I understand now the intensity of meaning and connection I often felt between Marte and Mel. 'From then on I was at her house more than at mine. I couldn't bear my house. Anyway, it was sold and my father went to the States. My mother – no, I don't want to talk about her. Marte didn't become my mother, she became my old friend. Hard for Justine, I know, but... she saved my life, Ellie. She always kept me busy, we went to auctions, sales, junk shops. She taught me more about polishing and repairing.'

'Mel, what a burden for you.' I put my arms around him and he buries his head in my shoulder. He breathes in a muffled way. I hold this man and – in this moment – would hold him for the rest of my life if he asked me, if that would make gentle the memory of what happened.